DON'T TURN AROUND

MICHELLE GAGNON

HARPER

An Imprint of HarperCollinsPublishers

Don't Turn Around

Library of Congress Cataloging-in-Publication Data
Gagnon, Michelle.
Don't turn around / by Michelle Gagnon. — 1st ed.
    p. cm.
Summary: After waking up on an operating table with no
memory of how she got there, Noa must team up with
computer hacker Peter to stop a corrupt corporation with a
deadly secret.
ISBN 978-0-06-210291-1 (pbk.)
[1. Computer hackers—Fiction. 2. Experiments—Fiction.
3. Foster home care—Fiction. 4. Abandoned children—
Fiction.] I. Title. II. Title: Don't turn around.
PZ7.G1247Do 2012   2012009691
                                                              CIP
                                                              AC

Typography by Tom Daly
14 15 16 17   LP/RRDC   10 9 8 7 6 5 4
❖
First paperback edition, 2013

For Taegan

One narcissus among the ordinary beautiful
flowers, one unlike all the others! She pulled,
stooped to pull harder—
when, sprung out of the earth
on his glittering terrible
carriage, he claimed his due.
It is finished. No one heard her.
No one! She had strayed from the herd.

(Remember: go straight to school.
This is important, stop fooling around!
Don't answer to strangers. Stick
with your playmates. Keep your eyes down.)
This is how easily the pit
opens. This is how one foot sinks into the ground.

—Rita Dove, "Persephone, Falling"

CHAPTER ONE

When Noa Torson woke up, the first thing she noticed was that her feet were cold. Odd, since she always wore socks to bed. She opened her eyes and immediately winced against the glare. She hated sleeping in a bright room, had even installed blackout curtains over her apartment's sole window so that morning light never penetrated the gloom. Noa tried to make sense of her surroundings as her eyes adjusted. Her head felt like it had been inflated a few sizes and stuffed with felt. She had no idea how she'd ended up here, wherever here was.

Was she back in juvie? Probably not; it was too quiet. Juvie always sounded like a carnival midway: the constant din of guards' boots pounding against metal staircases, high-pitched posturing chatter, the squeak of cots and clanking of metal doors. Noa had spent enough time there to identify it with her eyes closed. She could usually even tell which cell-block she'd been dumped in by echoes alone.

Voices intruded on the perimeter of her consciousness—two people from the sound of it, speaking quietly. She tried to sit up, and that was when the pain hit. Noa winced and fell back on the bed. It felt like her chest had been split in half. Her hand ached, too. Slowly, she turned her head.

An IV drip was taped to her right wrist. The line led to a bag hanging from a metal stand. And the bed she was lying on was cold metal—an operating table, a spotlight suspended above it. So was she in a hospital? There wasn't that hospital smell, though—blood and sweat and vomit battling against the stench of ammonia.

Noa lifted her left hand: Her jade bracelet, the one she never took off, was gone. That realization snatched the final cobwebs from her mind.

Cautiously, Noa raised up on her elbows, then frowned. This wasn't like any hospital she'd ever seen. She was in the center of a glass chamber, a twelve-by-twelve-foot box, the windows frosted so she couldn't see out. The floor was bare concrete. Aside from the operating table and the IV stand, rolling trays of medical implements and machines were scattered about. In the corner stood a red trash bin, MEDICAL WASTE blaring from the lid.

Looking down, Noa discovered that she was wearing a cloth gown, but there was no hospital name stamped on it. She tried to get her bearings. Not juvie, and not an official hospital. She got the feeling that whatever this place was, bad things happened here.

The voices grew louder; someone was coming. Noa had spent the past ten years fending for herself. She'd learned better than to trust authority figures, whether they were cops, doctors, or social workers. And she wasn't about to start trusting anyone now, not in a situation like this. Slowly, she eased her feet off the table and slid to the floor. She wrapped her arms around herself, repressing a shiver. The cement was freezing, like stepping barefoot onto a glacier.

The voices stopped just outside the chamber. Noa strained her ears to listen, catching a few fragments: *"Success . . . call him . . . what do we . . . can't believe we finally . . ."*

The last bit came through crystal clear. A man's voice, sounding resigned as he said, "They'll handle it. She's not our problem now."

Fighting to keep her teeth from chattering, Noa desperately scanned the room. A few feet away, a metal tray held a variety of medical instruments. She'd nearly reached it when the door at the far end of the room opened.

Two men dressed in scrubs crossed the threshold. The first was a thin white guy, a few strands of blond hair pasted across his forehead beneath a surgical cap. The other doctor was Latino, younger and stockier with a straggly mustache marring his upper lip. Seeing her, they froze. Noa seized the opportunity to edge closer to the tray.

"Where am I?" she asked. Her voice came out weaker than usual, like she hadn't spoken in a while.

The doctors recovered from their surprise and exchanged a look. The blond one jerked his head, and the Latino rushed from the room.

"Where's he going?" Noa asked. She was two feet from the tray now, and he was three feet past it.

The doctor held up his hands placatingly. "You were in a terrible accident, Noa," he said soothingly. "You're in the hospital."

"Oh, yeah?" Her eyes narrowed. "Which hospital?"

"You're going to be fine. Some disorientation is to be expected." The doctor glanced back over his shoulder.

"What kind of accident?"

The doctor paused, his eyes shifting as he searched for a response, and Noa knew he was lying. The last thing she remembered was leaving her apartment and walking toward Newton Centre station to catch the train into Boston. She'd been heading downtown to pick up a new video card for her MacBook Pro. Noa had turned right on Oxford Road, passing Weeks Field on her way to the T stop. The last heat of an Indian summer day was soft on her skin, daylight sifting through trees already shedding their leaves in a riot of fiery oranges and reds. She'd been happy, she remembered. Happier than she'd been in a long time, maybe ever.

And then, nothing. It was all a big blank.

"A car accident," he explained, a small note of triumph in his voice.

"I don't own a car. I don't even take taxis," Noa said warily.

"A car hit you, I mean." The doctor looked back again, increasingly impatient. Clearly the other guy had gone for help. Which meant she was running out of time.

Noa suddenly fell forward, as if the wooziness had overwhelmed her. The doctor lunged to catch her. In one smooth motion, Noa scooped a scalpel off the tray and pressed it against the side of his neck.

His mouth opened wide in a surprised O.

"You're going to get me out of here," she said firmly, "or I'll slit your throat. Don't make a sound."

"Please." The doctor's voice was hoarse. "You don't understand. You can't leave, it's for your own—"

A rush of footsteps pounding toward them.

"Shut up!" Noa shoved him in front of her, keeping the blade pressed against his neck as they went through the door. She paused outside: not a hospital at all, but a giant warehouse the size of an airplane hangar. Makeshift aisles composed of cardboard boxes and long lines of metal filing cabinets surrounded the glass chamber.

"Which way out?" she hissed, keeping her mouth close to his ear. They were nearly the same height, five-ten, which made it easier.

The doctor hesitated, then pointed right. "There's an exit, but it's alarmed."

Following his finger, Noa spotted the narrow hallway leading off to the right. She propelled him toward it. Someone was shouting orders. As they entered the hallway, she heard the chamber door being flung open behind her. More yelling as they realized she was gone. It sounded like at least half a dozen people were after her.

The hallway was long and narrow and lined with more boxes stacked to shoulder height on both sides. One of the fluorescent tubes overhead flickered, casting them in a pulsing strobe. Noa fought to ignore the stabbing pain in her chest, and the ball of panic right alongside it.

Ten feet farther and the hallway turned right. They rounded the bend and came face-to-face with a large metal door. It was chained shut.

"That's not an alarm," Noa said flatly.

"There's no point hurting me," he pleaded. "You can't leave. He'd never let you go."

Beside her, the top box on the stack gaped open. Noa dug her free hand inside, then risked a glance: metal bedpans, nothing she could use to break a padlock. She was trapped. Noa fought the urge to scream in frustration. Out in the expanse of the warehouse floor, she'd stood a chance of escaping. Now, she was a rat at the end of a maze. At most, she had a few minutes before they found her.

"Take off your clothes," she ordered.

"What? But—" he sputtered.

"Now!" She pressed the scalpel deeper into his neck.

A minute later, the doctor shuddered in his underwear as she stepped into his crocs and pulled the mask up over her face. Good thing he'd decided to stay—the Latino's scrubs would never have fit her.

"It won't work," he said.

Noa frowned and responded with a double-fisted upper-cut: a trick she'd learned the hard way, by being on the receiving end once. It connected with the doctor's jaw and his head jerked back. He dropped hard, knocking over boxes on the way down. He didn't get back up. "I hate negativity," she muttered.

The Latino doctor suddenly darted out of the hallway, skidding to a stop in front of them. Noa reached into the box beside her.

"Jim?" he said, eyes widening as Noa raced toward him. As she ran she drew her arm back, then swung the metal bedpan as hard as she could. He shied away, drawing his arms up to protect his face. The bedpan made a loud, hollow sound when it connected with his temple. His eyes rolled back in his head, and he dropped to the floor beside the other doctor.

Noa dashed back down the hallway, pausing at the end. She was still clutching the scalpel in her left hand, but chances were the people she was up against had knives, maybe even guns. The warehouse was dimly lit, which worked in her favor. It was enormous, too, so the people searching for her would have to split up. The scrubs might fool them at a distance, but that trick wouldn't work for long; they were sure to find the doctors any minute now. She had to find a way out.

Noa edged along, keeping to the shadows. Ten feet down the adjoining wall she spotted a gap: another hallway, about thirty feet away. It was a risk—she might get to the end only to discover that the door was bolted like the other one. But spending too much time on the warehouse floor was suicide.

She moved as quickly as possible toward the opening, hoping that at a distance she'd be mistaken for the blond doctor. The crocs weren't exactly ideal: They squeaked against the raw concrete, and there was no way she'd be able to run in them. Better than being barefoot, though. At least her feet were finally warming up.

She'd nearly reached the corridor when someone shouted, "Hey!"

Noa slowly pivoted.

The guy facing her was large and lumpy; he looked like a kid had stuffed clay into an oversized security uniform, dabbing on a stubby nose and ears as an afterthought. There was a gun in his right hand.

"I already checked down there," the security guard said, indicating the space behind her with the gun barrel. "Don't waste your time."

Noa nodded her thanks, hoping he wouldn't find it strange that she wasn't answering. He sauntered off toward the next hallway, the one where the doctors were stashed.

She was about to slip down the corridor when someone across the room hollered, "Stop her!"

Turning, Noa spotted the blond doctor standing at the

edge of the opposite hallway. In the darkness, his bare skin practically glowed. His arm was extended, finger pointing at her accusingly.

The security guard swiveled back toward her with a frown. Their eyes met, then Noa spun and broke into a run.

Peter Gregory was bored. He spent most weekends at Tufts University with his girlfriend. But Amanda was swamped with a huge paper, and she'd told him in no uncertain terms to not even consider showing up to distract her. His parents were away in Vermont celebrating their thirtieth wedding anniversary at the type of pseudo-bed-and-breakfast they loved, an alarming amount of chintz the only thing that differentiated it from a regular hotel.

At first, Peter had been kind of psyched—a whole weekend to himself, no one to put up a front for. He could spend it online, monitoring the projects birthed by his brainchild, /ALLIANCE/. Yesterday, a Croatian member announced he was on the verge of tracking down the kid who posted a video of setting a cat on fire. That had been a particularly gruesome attempt to garner fifteen minutes of fame, but sadly not an unusual one. Peter had been checking all day, though, and there were no new posts. Hardly anyone on /ALLIANCE/ at all. Maybe everyone was busy logging rest bubbles on World of Warcraft, he thought with a grin.

Peter liked to think of these vigilante hackers as his minions. Since he'd founded the underground website a year earlier, it had snowballed. It turned out he wasn't the only one ticked off by all the hypocrisy out there. They'd become a loosely knit community of hackers with a mission: to target Internet bullies, animal abusers, sexual predators, and everyone else who took advantage of the weak. Peter's only rule was no violence. He saw /ALLIANCE/ as a way to wreak justice by pranking the bad guys, and so far, that hadn't been an issue: After all, the people who counted themselves as /ALLIANCE/ questers could wipe out someone's credit history or destroy their privacy with a few keystrokes. In the end, that was a lot more effective than beating someone up.

Peter had already made the circuit of the house a few times, absently flicking lights on and off. It was big, a four-thousand-square-foot McMansion, so that consumed some time. He ended up in his dad's office. He plopped down in the Aeron chair and spun a few times, then propped his feet on the desk as he tilted back. Through the picture window beside him their lawn stretched away from the house like a rolling black tide, stopping at the street where it lapped at towering elm trees.

Saturday night, and he was home alone. There was a party at his buddy Blake's house, but he wasn't really in the mood. After going to college parties with Amanda, the high-school equivalent struck him as a lame waste of time. Still, there was nothing to stop him from having some fun. His dad kept a bottle of twenty-year-old bourbon in his lower right-hand desk drawer. He wouldn't miss a few pulls.

Peter punched in a code and the bottom drawer popped open. Ridiculous of his father to think that a three-digit lock would keep anyone out. Peter shook his head as he uncorked the bottle. It was insulting, really.

He took a swig and leaned back. Someone had inscribed a note on the label: *For Bob Gregory, with sincere appreciation.* The signature was illegible; probably another jerk his dad had thrown money at to achieve some awful end.

His father was the reason Peter had initially started

/ALLIANCE/. A self-described "do-gooder investment banker," his dad was the kind of guy who insisted on driving a Prius with all the bells and whistles, but couldn't be bothered to drop his Pellegrino bottle in the recycling bin. He'd make a show of tucking a five-dollar bill in a homeless guy's cup if people were around, then go home and donate the maximum amount allowed to a campaign geared toward keeping that guy on the streets. And Peter's mother was no better. As a high-priced defense attorney, she spent her time ensuring that Boston's most lethal lowlifes never saw the inside of a prison cell. The two of them were perfect for each other, Peter thought with a snort. No wonder they'd made it thirty years.

It had been a while since he'd checked out what Bob was up to, Peter mused, scratching his chin with the mouth of the bottle. Couldn't hurt to take a look.

A stack of papers and files filled the rest of the drawer. Peter dug them out and splayed them across the desk, then started flipping through. Mostly dull stuff: stock reports, investor statements, prospectuses from a variety of hedge funds. One file was thicker than the others. He recognized his father's careful writing along the tab, *AMRF* in block letters. Peter frowned. He went through the drawer fairly regularly. This was a new addition.

He perused the papers inside the file: more quarterly reports, meeting minutes in some incomprehensible short-hand. His father was listed on the letterhead as both a board member and financial adviser. No surprise there—Bob always jumped at the chance to join a board roster, and "financial advisers" surely got some sort of kickback.

Peter took another tug from the bottle of bourbon, then eyed it. If he drank much more, Bob would be able to tell. Reluctantly, he replaced the cork.

He was about to tuck the various papers and files back in the drawer, rearranging the bottle on top of them, when his eyes alit on the line item "Project Persephone."

That was pretty exotic for a financial company; they tended to have a penchant for testosterone-driven names like "Maximus" and "Primidius." Peter scanned the page, but all he could tell was that whatever Project Persephone was, it consumed a hefty chunk of AMRF's significant annual budget. As in, almost all of it.

Something about the name, though, struck him as familiar. Peter keyed up Bob's laptop, typing in the password when the box appeared on-screen: his mother's birthday, of course. He did a quick web search for *Persephone*, and realized where he'd seen the name before: When they studied Greek myths back in middle school. Persephone was the girl who got kidnapped and dragged down to Hades, but her mom cut some deal where half the year, she returned to live back on Earth.

Peter sat back in the chair, puzzled. His eyes fell on the clock across the room: nearly seven thirty, *SportsCenter* would be on soon. The Bruins had played a game earlier, and he wanted to see the highlights. He debated closing the drawer and going on with his evening, but something nagged at him. Peter sighed and ran his fingers back over the keyboard, instituting a basic search on AMRF.

A long list of organizations went by that acronym, including the Algalita Marine Research Foundation and Americans Mad for Rad Foosball. Skimming the list, none of them jumped out as the kind of company Bob would invest in. Peter hesitated, then decided to dig further. He shut down Bob's computer and went to retrieve his laptop.

Twenty minutes later, he was pretty sure he'd found the

right site. From the look of things, it was some sort of medical research company, although whatever they were researching was buried under a string of code names. He dug around some more, but the majority of the company's files were locked behind firewalls that resisted his first attempts to throw a ladder over. Peter knew that given enough time, he could surmount them—in the past, just for fun he'd hacked unnoticed into the Pentagon, FBI, and Scotland Yard databases. The question was, could anything Bob was involved with possibly be worth the time commitment?

Probably not, Peter decided. With a yawn, he powered down the laptop.

A minute later, his front door was kicked in.

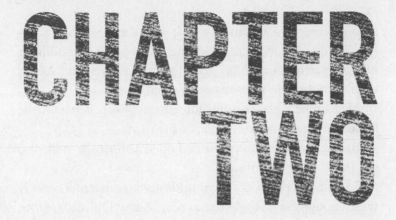

CHAPTER TWO

Noa found herself in a corridor identical to the one where she'd left the doctors. She raced down it, the guard's footsteps pounding behind her, joined by the sound of others giving chase. The crocs flapped against her feet, slowing her down. She finally gave up, kicking out of them as she hit the corner. No point keeping her feet warm if it meant getting caught.

She glanced back—the guard had just rounded the corner, huffing hard, his face beet red. Just ahead of her, another set of double doors. No padlock, but one of those red signs that warned of an emergency alarm hung above the exit.

Noa ignored it and pushed through. The alarm sprang to life, blaring in her wake.

Outside, it was dusk. Freezing cold air hit her immediately, penetrating her thin cotton scrubs. Noa quickly scanned the surrounding area: It was some sort of warehouse complex, battered-looking, dust-colored buildings lining a narrow road. The pavement was uneven and scored with potholes. No cars or people in sight.

Noa broke right, aiming for a narrow gap between the buildings on the opposite side of the road.

Behind her the door slammed open against the wall, and she heard the guard shout.

The space between the buildings was narrow, barely wide enough for a single car to pass. A few Dumpsters, but otherwise no signs of life. Noa tore by a set of doors identical to the ones she'd escaped through. Too dangerous to go back inside a building, though—she had a better shot out in the open.

The part of her brain that was geared solely toward survival was screaming at her to *go go go* . . . it was a familiar voice, and listening to it had gotten her through bad situations before. Noa shut down the rest of her mind and let it take over, pushing aside the other distracting thoughts flitting through. Like the possibility that there might be more kids like her in each of these buildings, laid out on cold steel tables with bandaged chests.

A sudden sharp pain in her right foot nearly sent her sprawling. Noa staggered to the nearest building. Leaning against it, she lifted her foot and dug out a jagged piece of glass embedded in her heel. She bit her lip as blood flowed freely from the wound. She could hear them getting closer. Ignoring the throb in her foot and the matching one in her chest, she pushed off the building and started running again. The alley crossed another road before continuing on between an identical pair of warehouses. Everything looked abandoned; there wasn't a vehicle or person in sight. Where was she?

Noa chanced a look back over her shoulder. The original guard had fallen back, but five others in the same uniform and much better shape were gaining ground. At the sight of them, Noa started to despair. She didn't even know if she was still in Boston. And there didn't seem to be any end to this warehouse complex.

Noa shoved those thoughts away. She wasn't the type to give up, not even when it was probably the smarter choice. She ignored the pain in her chest and foot and the shouting voices behind her. Warehouses streamed past, punctuated by more narrow alleys. She abruptly broke free of them and nearly stopped dead.

She was facing an enormous parking lot, the blacktop so shiny it looked like a pond that had iced over. The air was thick with salt and oil, the wind tugging at her now that there were no buildings to catch it. As far as she could see, there were rows of boats perched on trailers.

Noa realized where she was: a marine shipyard, dry-dock storage for boats. Off in the distance she was relieved to recognize the Boston skyline, a cluster of dark brown buildings aspiring to be skyscrapers but falling short, tapering off as they slouched west.

As if on cue, a plane roared past a few hundred feet above her head, making a final approach. Her heart leaped: South Boston, then; somewhere near Logan Airport. An area she knew relatively well, thanks to six months spent in a City Point foster home.

The realization spurred her onward. Noa darted between the boats. They were parked close together in narrow slots. Some were battered workboats, with barnacles and algae smearing their hulls. As she progressed, they increased in scale until she was threading between daysailers and trawlers, cabin cruisers and sloops. Glancing back again, she realized with relief that, at least for the moment, she'd managed to lose them.

The voices sounded like they were spreading out—the search would slow them down. And it was unlikely they'd be able to check every boat for her.

There was also no way she could keep running. As her adrenaline reserves dissipated, her muscles started to protest. She felt weak, exhausted. The pain in her chest had escalated until it felt like someone was punching each breath into her, and her foot killed. She finally slowed to check it: bleeding, but not too badly. Despite the core heat she'd built up running, she was shivering. She needed to find real clothes, and some shoes. And if she kept going, she risked charging straight into one of her pursuers.

Noa scanned the boats, looking for one that would suit her purposes. A hundred feet away towered a miniyacht, with a sleek cherry hull and a dive platform hanging low over the back of the trailer.

She raced toward it.

Without breaking stride, Noa grabbed the rung of the ladder leading to the dive platform. She slung herself up and over the gunwales and dropped to the deck. She lay there, keeping very still as she tried to control her breathing.

Footsteps approaching. They suddenly slowed. Noa stopped breathing entirely as they paused. The deck of the boat was ten feet off the ground; she could hear someone panting just below her.

"Where the hell did she go?" a guy gasped.

"Damned if I know." The second voice was deep and guttural, the accent more Rhode Island than Boston. "Wicked fast for a little girl. How'd she get out?"

"Jim was supposed to be watching her."

A snort in response. "Figures."

"Cole is gonna go ballistic when he finds out."

At that, they fell silent. Out of the corner of her eye, Noa saw a smear of blood on the gunwale where she'd stepped on it. She must have left other traces on the blacktop and ladder. She silently prayed that they wouldn't notice.

A radio crackled.

"I'll get it," Rhode Island muttered. After an electronic chirp, he said, "Yeah?"

"We're meeting in the far east quadrant to regroup." The voice coming through the radio was authoritative and deadly serious. *Cole,* Noa guessed. He didn't sound like someone you'd mess with.

"Roger that," Rhode Island replied. Another chirp, and he laughed. "You believe this guy? 'Far east quadrant,' like we're back in Haji-land."

"No kidding. Man, I hope this doesn't take long. I wanted to catch the end of the game," the other guy said.

The voices started to move away. Noa waited a few moments, then released her held breath. She was ten feet from the door to the main cabin. She crawled forward quickly on her belly, then reached up to turn the handle. The door was locked. She fell back against the deck and gritted her teeth. Finding it open would have been too much to hope for.

Noa scanned the deck for something to pick the lock. She knew from past experience that boat locks were designed more to stymie problem teenagers than experienced burglars. Luckily, she just happened to be both.

The deck was clear except for a small tackle box tucked beneath one of the benches lining the railings. As quietly as possible, Noa eased over and got it open. Scrounging around inside, she found a small fishhook: not ideal, but it would have to do.

It took five minutes to pick the lock. It would have been quicker, but the throbbing in her chest and foot was distracting. Plus she was forced to work at an odd angle, reaching up with her arm. Twice she had to yank it down as more guards passed the boat.

Noa waited another minute, straining to detect anyone nearby, then slowly opened the cabin door and slid inside, shutting it behind her.

Blinds were drawn over the tinted windows, shadowing the interior. She could just make out a plush living room set, leather captains' chairs, and a solid table. Everything was bolted to the floor, but otherwise could have been straight out of any upscale furniture catalog.

Noa got to her feet and went down a few steps to the lower deck. She was in a narrow hallway, four doors off either side and one at the end. The first door on her left accordioned open to reveal a tiny bathroom. She went in and unhooked the latch for the medicine cabinet. She was in luck: It was fully stocked; apparently the owners didn't bother clearing the boat out for winter storage. She sat on the toilet seat and examined her foot. A gouge ran along the heel of her right foot: It was long but didn't look deep. She awkwardly held her foot over the sink, biting her lip as she poured antiseptic over it. After the wound stopped fizzing, she dabbed it with Neosporin and bandaged it with gauze.

She took a deep breath, which sent another spasm of pain through her chest. Reluctantly, she eased up her shirt.

Noa had seen the bandage when she changed into the scrubs, but there hadn't been time to check under it. Plus, part of her was terrified to look. The oversized bandage was large, rectangular, a few shades darker than her skin. She forced herself to peel back a corner of it.

What she saw made her gasp. There was a three-inch-long incision running down the center of her chest. Small red marks on either side where sutures had been tugged out—she'd had stitches before; she recognized the aftermath. The cut had already scabbed over, but the skin around it was swollen and red.

Slowly, Noa pressed the bandage back into place and lowered her shirt. She frowned at her reflection in the mirror. In the light of the tiny fluorescent bulb above the sink, she looked much paler than usual. Dark blue circles under her eyes, hollow cheeks, lips cracked and peeling. She ran a hand through her jet-black hair and it came away greasy, as if she hadn't showered for days.

Had the doctor been telling the truth? Had she really been in some sort of car accident? Noa shook her head—that didn't make any sense. Otherwise she would have woken up in a regular hospital, and there wouldn't be guards after her. No, this was something else.

Not that she had time to figure out what, exactly. She still had to get out of this shipyard somehow. Which wouldn't be easy—she had no idea where the exit was, and wandering around looking for it was a bad idea.

Noa splashed some cold water on her face and dabbed it dry with a corner of the shirt. Feeling slightly better, she limped across the hall to a tiny bedroom with taupe curtains drawn over the portholes. The queen-sized bed against the bulkhead was stripped down to the mattress. Noa slid open the drawers built into the wall, but they were all empty.

She got lucky in the next bedroom. It was similarly

barren, but on the closet floor she found a ratty, faded Wesleyan sweatshirt, baggy black sweatpants, and a pair of rubber fishing boots. Based on the smell, this must be the owner's designated fishing outfit. Digging through the drawers produced a pair of mismatched sweat socks and a black knit cap.

It wouldn't really be enough to combat the cold, but it was better than what she had on. Noa changed quickly, then sat on the edge of the bed to puzzle out her next move.

If she stayed on the boat, there was a good chance they'd find her. The shouting had diminished, but that didn't mean anything. For all she knew, they'd called another hundred guys and were planning on searching every boat.

Why they were devoting so much energy to looking for her was the larger question. Her fingers went to the bandage on her chest. What had they done to her? Noa had heard stories, kind of the foster-kid version of the bogeyman: street kids getting drugged by a stranger and waking up without a kidney, that sort of thing. She'd never put much stock in it—even if the stories were true, she considered herself too smart and experienced to have to worry about it.

But she was wrong. Someone had taken her, and she couldn't even remember how or when. Besides, the cut was on her chest, not her back. It wasn't like they could have taken her heart, right? What else was in there?

She might not make it through the next few hours anyway, Noa reminded herself. So worrying about that now was probably a waste of time.

She'd gotten lucky once, though. Maybe it would happen again. Motivated, she got up and went back into the hallway. Next was another empty room, this one with bunk beds. The final door at the end of the hall opened onto the ship's bridge. It was stocked with an elaborate array of marine equipment and controls. Unfortunately, no sign of a phone or computer.

Then her eyes alit on the ship-to-shore radio. Noa turned the dial, and the receiver lit up. A smile slowly spread across her face.

Peter was choking on a mouthful of carpet. One of the men who'd stormed into his house was driving his knee into Peter's back while simultaneously pressing his face into the rug. The cloying sweetness of rug shampoo was making him gag, which helped allay some of the shock.

"What do you want?" he asked, trying not to sound as scared as he felt. "There's no money here."

No one answered. He started to struggle. The guy on top of him increased the pressure until it felt like he was being driven into the floor like a nail, and his head might actually go through the rug and pop out the other side. Peter went limp. He was terrified. He'd heard about home invasions before. His friend's dad worked at a bank, and when they were younger two guys held the whole family at gunpoint overnight, then forced the dad to help them rob the bank in the morning. Was this something like that? They seemed official, highly trained. Or maybe it was a kidnapping? His parents were rich; he'd heard about stuff like that happening, too.

The scary thing was that he wasn't so sure his parents would pay a ransom for him.

It was hard to see, but Peter was pretty sure there were three guys in the room, all dressed identically in black. When they'd first stormed in they had guns drawn, but from what he could tell they'd tucked them away. At least he hadn't been shot yet, which was probably a good sign. There were others with them; he could hear them moving from room to room, muttering to one another in low voices. They seemed to be waiting for something. Or someone.

"Get off me!" he managed, the words muffled by piling.

A set of loafers entered his line of sight. Black leather buffed to a shine, black suit pants, cuffs broken in a sharp line at the heel: the mark of a pricey tailoring job. Peter followed them up. A tall guy loomed over him, dressed in a full three-piece suit with a red tie. A lawyer, if Peter had to guess; everyone at his mom's firm looked and dressed like that. That provided a measure of relief. A lawyer wouldn't let them hurt him. And the guy seemed to be in charge; the mood in the room had shifted when he came in.

Still, he looked peeved, like Peter was an annoyance he'd prefer not to deal with, a piece of gum he'd just discovered stuck to his heel. He was probably in his thirties, dark hair cropped short, cold gray eyes. "Let him up," the guy said.

Peter felt the pressure release. He got to his feet, trying to hide the shakiness. His back ached where the knee had pushed on it. He tried to sound confident when he said, "Get the hell out of my house, or I'll call the cops."

The man in the suit eyed him. After a beat, he said, "You're the son."

His voice creeped Peter out; it was completely flat and toneless. Disinterested.

"I'm going to say it one more time. Get out." Peter went to the phone on the desk and picked up the receiver. Held his breath the whole time, waiting for them to stop him.

The suit appeared amused. "There won't be a dial tone. We cut the line."

Peter pressed the on button to double-check. He was

right; there was no dial tone. He went for his cell phone, which was tucked in his pocket—hopefully it hadn't been damaged when they threw him to the ground.

But the suit held up a hand to stop him. "That signal is being jammed, too."

Jamming a cell signal was no mean feat—as far as he knew, it required the kind of military equipment only governments could afford. Peter left his phone in his pocket. "Who are you?"

"Is anyone else in the house?" the suit asked.

Peter opened his mouth to answer, but paused. Lying seemed like a bad idea. Besides, they were searching the rest of the house so they probably already knew. "No, I'm alone."

"And this is your computer?" As the suit approached the desk, Peter eased to the other side, keeping it between them. The guy didn't seem to notice. He flipped it open, and glanced up when it came out of hibernation. "Password?" he asked, looking at Peter.

Peter drew himself up and tried to sound defiant as he said, "No way I'm telling you that."

The guy shrugged. He unplugged the power cable and started to leave the room, the computer tucked under his arm.

"Hey, wait!" Peter said. "You can't take that!"

"I just did," the guy said without turning back.

Peter went after him. The others just watched as he passed them and followed the guy into the hall. The suit was walking briskly, like he had somewhere to be. "That's mine. You steal it, I'll call the cops."

The suit stopped walking. He turned to face Peter, his expression grave. "You won't do that."

"Why not?"

The suit's eyes narrowed. "Because if you do, we'll come

back. And next time we'll take you," he said, a note of menace in his voice.

Peter paused at that. It was just a computer, and it was automatically backed up to an external server. Still, the way the guy was acting bothered the hell out of him; like he had the right to do this, and Peter was the one in the wrong. "My folks are going to go nuts when they hear about this," he said.

The suit smiled. "Give Bob and Priscilla my best. And tell your father to call me at his earliest convenience."

It took Peter a second to recover from the fact that this guy seemed to know his parents, and well, from the sound of it. "Who are you?"

"My name is Mason," he said. "Someone will be by shortly to repair the front door."

Without breaking stride, he marched out the door and into the night.

"I told you, this is a private facility."

"Yes, sir, I heard you. But we got a call about a fire here, and we're not leaving without checking it out."

Crouched beneath a boat trailer fifty feet away, Noa watched two men argue loudly at the entrance to the boatyard. A fire truck was parked in front of the open gate. The sirens had been turned off but the lights still spun, carving a steady red swath through the scene. The rest of the firefighters stood back, watching their chief argue with a security guard.

"Who called it in?"

"The harbormaster."

"Well, he was wrong."

"All due respect, we don't need clearance." The chief's

eyes narrowed. "We're the Boston Fire Department. That gives us the right."

"I'm under strict orders here." The guard tugged at his shirt collar, as if it were slowly choking him. "I can't let anyone in."

"When we get called somewhere, we go. It's a boatyard, not a nuclear power plant. So what's the problem?"

"Do you even see a fire?" The security guard gestured behind himself.

The fire chief looked past his shoulder, then snorted. "Yeah, actually, I do."

The guard pivoted. Halfway through the boatyard an oily plume of dark smoke was rising.

Noa exhaled hard, relieved. If the truck had driven away without coming inside, any hope of escape would have gone with it. She'd waited for the truck to arrive before lighting an improvised fuse: a couple of strung-together candlewicks that led to a stack of oily rags. It was the best she could manage with the limited supplies on the boat.

As soon as the fuse started smoking, the remaining guards went nuts, practically tripping over one another in their haste to track down the source. They tore past the boat a few aisles away, where she'd taken shelter. Noa waited until it sounded like most of them were gone, then ran as quickly as possible toward the red lights. And now it looked like her plan had worked—the first part of it, at least.

The guard turned back to find the chief grinning at him. "So you guys got this handled, or you want us in there? 'Cause I'm looking at about a billion dollars' worth of boats that are about to become kindling. Then it'll jump to those warehouses, and you're gonna want to break out the marshmallows."

At the mention of the warehouses, the guard blanched white. He stalked a few feet away and jabbered into a radio. A minute later he came back and waved the fire truck in.

The chief issued a cheery wave to the guard as the truck drove past. The guard closed the gate, then watched the truck turn down the main aisle. Hands on his hips, shoulders tensed, he muttered to himself. Then he ducked back inside the small hut at the entrance.

Noa stayed low, bent double as she followed the truck from a few aisles over. She'd spotted cameras on either side of the gate, four of them aimed to cover the entrance on both sides. So just strolling past was out of the question, even if she managed to distract the guard. And someone had to be watching the gate; it wouldn't take a genius to figure out this was her escape plan.

On the other side of the gate, she'd seen a long strip of pavement stretching off into the distance. The road was lined by parking lots ensconced in high fences. After about a half mile, the pavement jigged right.

That was a lot of ground to cover. And she wouldn't be able to make it without being seen: It was wide open, with nothing to hide behind.

Luckily, the cameras were pointed down. Bearing that in mind, she'd developed a backup plan.

Night had fallen, and the dark sweatshirt and sweatpants made it easier for her to move freely. Noa zigzagged through the boats, keeping her eyes and ears peeled for pursuers. Most seemed to have slunk back to the warehouses when the fire department responded. Having a few dozen security guards for a boatyard would probably have raised some eyebrows, she thought with a snort.

The truck stopped. Peering beneath the nearest boat, Noa watched the firefighters scramble toward the burning yacht. The fire had developed nicely—she could feel the heat of it from here, and bits of black ash swept past on the wind. A long white hose unraveled, bouncing off the blacktop as the firefighters dragged it forward at a trot.

One stayed with the truck. His focus was directed toward where the rest of his battalion had disappeared. They must have signaled him, because he suddenly deftly spun a wheel, turning the water on. The long white hose went taut.

Noa watched him, her anxiety growing. She'd hoped the firefighters would leave the truck unattended; it hadn't occurred to her that one might stay close by. To execute her plan, she needed to get past him.

She'd already considered approaching the firefighters directly to ask for help. But that would open the door to a whole host of other problems she wasn't ready to deal with. They'd call in Children's Services, and Noa would be stuck dealing with social workers, judges, and cops again. No matter what had happened to her, she refused to get sucked back into the system after devoting so much effort to escaping it.

Of course, if she couldn't manage to get out of this boatyard . . .

There had to be a way. Noa frowned, thinking. She still had the rest of the matches, tucked in the front pouch of her sweatshirt. Maybe another fire?

As she was digging for them, there was a sudden call from the yacht.

The firefighter's head jerked up. "I'll be right there!" he called out. He flipped open one of the panels set in the side of the truck, extracted something, and trotted off toward his companions.

Noa hesitated, but just for a second. No knowing how long he'd be gone, and the fire would surely be extinguished soon. She edged out from the shelter of the boat she'd been hiding behind and made her way toward the main aisle.

It seemed clear. She peered in both directions, but couldn't make out anything except the shadows of firefighters cloaked in a wreath of dwindling smoke about a hundred feet away. *Now or never,* she told herself, drawing a deep breath.

Staying on the ball of her injured foot, she raced for the side of the truck. Awkwardly, she scrambled up the ladder mounted on the side and landed hard on top. She pressed herself flat against the roof. Panting, she strained her ears, listening for any indication that she'd been spotted.

A minute passed, then another. Nothing.

It felt like an eternity, but probably only fifteen minutes went by before she heard the chief say, "Wrap it up, folks."

Noa lay still as they packed up their truck, chattering the whole time about what a jerk-off the guard had been. She prayed they wouldn't have to put anything on top. Minutes passed. Finally the engine roared to life, gears whining as the truck jerked back toward the gate, going in reverse down the main aisle.

A metal beam ran the length of the roof on either side of her. Noa braced her hands and feet against it, holding on tight. Her right foot throbbed in protest where she'd cut it, but she gritted her teeth against the pain. If they accelerated sharply or went too fast, she'd be sent flying.

At last the truck cleared the gate, concertina wire retreating in the distance. Hopefully the cameras had been directed too low to catch a shot of her as they lurched past.

After a slow three-point turn, the truck faced down the

road. They were driving at a leisurely pace, clearly not in any hurry now that they were headed back. As they hit the right turn, the truck slowed. Noa seized the opportunity to roll off the back. Her foot protested, sending a shock of pain all the way up her calf. The sensation knocked her off her feet, and for a second she lay in the middle of the road, curled in a ball.

The truck slowly eased out of sight. Summoning her last reserve of strength, Noa forced herself to get up and break into a trot, following it. A couple hundred yards away, the truck stopped at an intersection. The light turned green and it hooked right, joining the sweep of cars driving back to the city. Noa ran as fast as she could until she reached the road, listening the whole time for a car coming up behind her. Once there, she turned right and jogged a few more blocks before stopping. Looking up, she got her bearings. She knew this intersection; there was a T stop about a mile away.

She pulled the hood up, shading her face, and tucked her hands into the sweatshirt pouch. Shoulders hunched against the cold, Noa crossed the street and started limping toward the station.

Peter paced across his father's office: five steps forward to the shelves filled with decorative leather-bound books, then five back to the desk where his computer had sat ten minutes earlier. He didn't know what to do.

The rest of the guys in black had left with Mason. No one seemed particularly concerned about him once they took his computer, and he'd discovered why pretty quickly. The landline into the house had been sliced, and so had the cable, incapacitating the network. Not a huge deal—he had a satellite hookup. But after getting that set up on his father's computer, Peter realized he didn't even know who to contact.

He'd dug out his cell phone; there was a signal again, so they must have stopped jamming it. More than anything he wanted to talk to his parents. The familiarity with which Mason had said their names freaked him out, and Peter was suddenly convinced that something terrible must have happened to them. He'd already called three times, but neither of them was picking up, which was a really bad sign. Priscilla and Bob were never without their phones. Peter always joked that they'd be taking calls during the apocalypse. They walked around all day with Bluetooth devices jutting out of their ears. Half the time Peter would think they were talking to him, only to realize after a few sentences that they were actually engaged in a work conversation. It was one of the things he really hated about them.

And now, the one time he was desperate for them to answer, they weren't picking up.

He redialed. Again, it went straight to voice mail. "Yeah, Dad? Peter again. Listen, something kind of . . . bad happened, and I really need to talk to you. It's important. Call me back."

He hung up, frustrated. Peter was tempted to call Amanda and see what she thought he should do. But he could predict how that conversation would go. She'd immediately start criticizing him for not calling the cops, and would probably insist that he hang up and dial 911.

Which he'd been tempted to do, but something stopped him. He got the feeling that calling this in would make things even worse. And would they even believe him? It sounded crazy—that a bunch of armed guys had broken into his house but only took his computer, leaving behind the more expensive one sitting beside it. The only sign that the guys had been there at all was the damaged front door—and Mason had said someone would come by to fix it. That was what was stopping him, he realized; what kind of thief offered that? What was really going on here?

Peter went behind the desk and collapsed back in his dad's chair. He opened the drawer again and took a big pull off the whiskey bottle, not caring anymore whether or not Bob noticed.

His cell phone rang.

Peter sprang to answer it, nearly sending it flying in his eagerness. "Hello?"

"Peter? What's going on?" his dad demanded.

Peter fell back into the chair, overcome by a profound wave of relief. "Dad, I'm so—"

"What's he saying?" Priscilla's voice in the background.

"He's not saying anything yet; give me a chance to talk to him." As always, Bob sounded annoyed. He was one of those people who firmly believed that the world was engaged in an overarching and continuous plot to get under his skin and make life difficult. Peter could never figure out why. As far as he could tell, Bob's life couldn't be going much more smoothly. "Peter, you're only supposed to call in an emergency. I thought we made that clear. We're celebrating here, and don't want to be disturbed."

"This is an emergency," Peter said defensively. "A bunch of guys broke into the house."

"What? When?"

"Tonight. They just left."

"Did you call the police?"

"Not yet," Peter said, thinking, *Nice of you to be concerned.* Not *Are you okay, Peter?* or *Did they hurt you?* But then, nothing unusual about that.

"Well, why the hell not? What did they take?"

"Just my computer." Peter paused. "Dad, he said his name was Mason. He seemed to know you and Mom."

Silence on the line.

"Dad?" Peter finally said.

"We're on our way home now. Just sit tight until we get there," Bob said. There was an undercurrent of concern in his voice, and maybe even a little fear as he forcefully added, "Do not call the cops. I mean it, Peter—don't tell anyone about this."

"But Dad—"

"We'll see you in a few hours. Remember, Peter—not a word."

Peter heard his mother protesting in the background, then silence. Bob had hung up.

He started to lift the whiskey bottle back to his mouth, then changed his mind—he needed to be able to think. Peter put the bottle back in the drawer. As he was closing it, his eyes fell on the AMRF folder again. Twenty minutes after he started snooping around that firewall, a bunch of private security lackeys busted into his house. The chances of that being pure coincidence was slim.

What was AMRF, really? And what were they trying to hide?

The only way to find out was to make an active assault on their firewall—this time, covering his tracks. There was only one problem: They'd taken his laptop. And clearly, he couldn't use Bob's computer to hack in. Mason's threat had been clear enough, and Peter didn't want to think about what would happen if they caught him sniffing around again.

Peter tapped a finger against the desktop, his mind whirring. He wasn't about to leave this alone, though. He needed help with this, from someone who couldn't be directly linked to him. Someone that even those guys would have a tough time finding.

And he knew the perfect person.

He signed in to /ALLIANCE/ again—it was his website; even if they were somehow monitoring Bob's computer, they couldn't expect him not to manage it. Someone had posted a new video since his last log-in, but he didn't have time to look at it. Peter tapped a series of keys to gain access to past posts.

He'd deliberately built anonymity into the framework of /ALLIANCE/. Similar groups had faced lawsuits in recent years, with governments from the United States to Sweden trying to track down hackers and penalize them. Plus there was always the danger that some of the more anarchically minded members might do something that wasn't in line with his mission statement. So Peter made a point of loosely tracking regular posters, making sure they weren't either government flunkies trying to co-opt the site, or people just trying to enact retribution on someone for personal reasons.

So while there were no real names used, Peter could get in touch with anyone who posted if he needed to.

He composed the email to Rain@me.com. Subject heading: *Research for paper*—keeping it innocuous in case the computer was being monitored. In the body of the email, he wrote, *Wanted to talk more about our term paper. Meet @ the quad later to discuss.*

Before hitting send, Peter hesitated. Getting someone else involved might put them in danger. Based on past postings, Rain sounded pretty tough, but still—it was a risk.

Then he remembered the feel of the knee in his back, and the arrogant expression on Mason's face as he walked out the door with Peter's computer. He clicked the mouse, sending the email out into the ether. Then he sat back to wait.

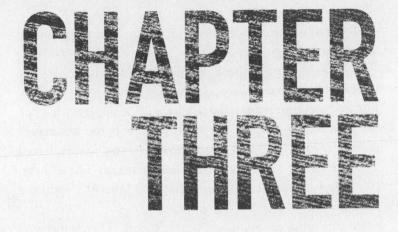

CHAPTER THREE

Noa rushed up the stairs. She'd gotten off the T at Copley Station, the closest stop to the Apple Store on Boylston Street. But the store would be closing in fifteen minutes.

She'd kept her head down on the train, but no one seemed to notice her. It was always almost too easy to sneak a ride on the T. Noa made a point of paying when she could, honoring their honor system. Still, it was times like this that the lax security came in handy. The train had brought her past the stop nearest her apartment. When the doors slid open, she'd been tempted to jump out and head to her place. Maybe it was just a fluke that she'd been grabbed while walking away from it; maybe whoever took her didn't know where she lived. She could take a shower, put on her own clothes. Crawl into bed, even though she didn't feel tired despite everything that had happened.

Too risky, she decided. Not until she found out more about what was going on.

When she stepped through the doors into the cool white interior of the store, she was enveloped by a wave of calm. Funny how just seeing the giant logo of an apple with a bite out of it did that to her. For most people, home was represented by four walls and a roof. Not for Noa. She preferred a motherboard to a mother, a keyboard to house keys. Nothing was more comforting than the hum of a spinning hard drive.

At this hour, the store was nearly empty. The greeter was a geeky-looking guy in his midtwenties with a pocked face and spiky hair stiff with gel. His smile was strained as he said in a single breath, "Welcome to the Apple store can I help you with something we're closing in five minutes."

"Fifteen," Noa corrected him.

"What?"

"Fifteen. You close at nine."

He opened his mouth as if to argue, but she'd already moved past him, headed to the laptops bolted to a table at the far end of the room. There were a few other people checking out iPads nearby. No one paid any attention as she started tapping a rapid sequence into the keyboard of a floor model.

A minute later, she logged off and went to the register. A bored-looking clerk handed a bag to the customer ahead of her, then waved her up to the counter.

"My dad ordered me a computer. I'm here to pick it up," Noa said.

"Name?"

"Latham. Nora Latham." The Lathams were the fictional foster family she'd invented to fool social services. After a series of less-than-stellar experiences with the foster-care system, Noa had come to the conclusion that she was better off on her own. So she'd established a bank account in their name and filled it with cash earned by her fictional foster father. As far as her clients knew, she was Ted Latham, a brilliant yet reclusive IT consultant. He worked freelance, primarily for a West-Coast-based company named Rocket Science. They were perfect in that they held Ted's skill set in such high regard that they threw a lot of business his way and didn't question eccentricities like his refusal to make on-site visits. Ted had a social security number, a PO Box, and a stellar credit rating. And he was extremely generous with his foster daughter, transferring nearly his entire income into her personal account every month. Plus he and his wife, Nell, were big believers in homeschooling: so good-bye, high school. They were easily the best parents she'd ever had.

The clerk tapped some keys, then said, "Yup, here it is. I'll have them bring it out for you. Step to the side to wait."

Noa obliged. As she waited for the new MacBook Pro, she felt a pang. Her old computer had been in her messenger bag when she was taken. Losing it hurt almost as much as the loss of the jade bracelet. It was the nicest thing she'd ever owned. She'd just bought a similar model, slightly smaller and more portable, the 13-inch rather than the 15-inch. Chances were, she'd be carrying it everywhere for the indefinite future, so better to travel light.

A guy came out of the stockroom holding the new computer in a box. He was a slight variation on the door greeter, just as pimply but with darker hair. He grinned at her. "Nora?"

"Yup." She held out her hands for the box.

He held on to it. "This is a great computer; I've got the same one at home."

"Yeah, I know," Noa said impatiently.

"We're about to close, but if you want help setting it up, there's a Starbucks right down the—"

"No thanks." Noa reached for it again.

He looked wounded, but handed it over. "All right, then. Enjoy."

Noa didn't bother answering. She grabbed the box, tucked it under her arm, and headed out the door.

Even though her fingers were itching to tear open the box, she forced herself to wait until she was five blocks away. This time of night, downtown was quiet and desolate. She found the open Starbucks near Back Bay Station and made her way to a corner table, ignoring the pointed look of the girl behind the register who was waiting to take orders. Noa was oddly still not hungry, but the smell of brewing coffee was making her long for a mocha.

She remained freezing, though, like her insides were a solid block of ice. Noa rubbed her hands together, attempting to warm up.

She opened the box, got out the laptop, and powered it up. First thing she had to do was access some cash. These days, you needed at least a debit card to get through the day.

Noa logged on to her bank account, then checked the credit card companies. None of them could get her cash or a card replacement outside of a twenty-four-hour window, which meant she'd be stuck on the street until then. Not the worst thing in the world, but more than anything right now she wanted to be alone. The girl behind the register was still eyeing her, and Noa met her gaze, glaring her down. When the girl looked away, suddenly extremely interested in the muffin selection, Noa allowed herself a small smile and turned back to the screen.

Her eyes fell on the clock at the upper right-hand corner, and she frowned. That couldn't be right.

A well-thumbed copy of the *Boston Globe* was splayed across the next table. Noa reached over and grabbed it to double-check the date.

"Oh my God," she mumbled aloud. October twenty-fifth. The last day she remembered was October third. She'd lost three weeks.

Noa leaned back against the wall, stunned. Her hand reflexively went to her chest again, where the incision throbbed dully. She really needed a quiet place to try to figure out what had happened. Which meant that she might have to suck it up and do her least favorite thing in the whole world: Ask someone for help.

She logged into her email account and scanned through. A few messages from Rocket Science about potential jobs, the tone becoming increasingly annoyed as "Ted" didn't respond. Some spam, and a couple of online billers.

Nothing personal. She'd been gone three weeks, and no one had missed her. Noa knew it should make her feel sad, but it was oddly gratifying. It meant she was leaving a tiny footprint, which was exactly what her goal had been.

Lacking those personal connections was inconvenient now, though. She'd had a foster family a few years ago that had been okay, or at least less awful than the others. She wondered how the Wilsons would react to her showing up on their doorstep. . . .

As she was debating it, an email popped into her account. She recognized the handle, Vallas, but frowned at the message. Had this been sent accidentally? She hadn't graced a school in over a year, ever since she figured out how to game the system. Yet the email mentioned a term paper.

Curious, she responded with, *Sure. See you there.*

She closed out her email and logged on to The Quad, an online forum populated entirely by hackers. Tough to find if you didn't know where to look for it, since it was shielded from all the search engines. You had to be invited to participate, and it was a fairly exclusive community; only the best of the best were asked. Noa had been thrilled when the offer to join came in. One of the only times in her life when she'd really felt like she belonged.

Online, Noa went by the handle Rain. She'd become curious about her name a few years earlier and nosed around into the origins of it. It turned out to be a relatively common Scandinavian name. One site claimed it derived from Odin; in Denmark "Noa-skeppet" and "Oden-Skeppet" were used interchangeably to describe a type of cloud formation that meant rain was coming.

She'd always liked rain anyway, not being much of a sun person. So it suited her.

She waited until Vallas appeared as a user, then invited him into a private chat and typed, *What's up?*

Need help researching AMRF, Vallas wrote.

That was strange. She mainly knew Vallas from a hacktivist group she frequented, /ALLIANCE/. She generally shied away from that sort of thing, not being much of a joiner. Most were focused on pulling off juvenile pranks anyway, or were downright criminal, and she had no interest in drawing the attention of law enforcement. But /ALLIANCE/ seemed different. Some of what they did struck near and dear to her heart, like when they went after perverts and bullies. So she'd participated in a few of their raids over the past few months.

Still, with everything she had going on right now, she wasn't about to get involved with someone else's vendetta. She was busy enough with her own.

Sorry, no time.

A pause, then Vallas typed, *It's important. I can pay you.*

Noa was about to respond that she didn't need money, then hesitated. Actually, that's exactly what she needed. But she needed it now. Western Union would ask for some sort of ID before handing over cash; otherwise she'd initiate a transfer from her own account. But based on some of Vallas's posts, she knew he was a local kid—a couple of times he'd referenced things only a Bostonian would know about. Still, that didn't necessarily mean she could trust him. Dare she risk it?

It has to be cash, she typed. *Tonight.*

A longer pause before he wrote back, *How much?*

A thousand to start.

I can get you $500.

Noa smiled—that would be more than she'd need to get her through the next day. And barring any bank screwups, she'd be able to access her own money again by tomorrow or the day after at the latest.

Fine, she wrote. *Where should we meet?*

Peter signed off and closed the phone. He'd logged on to The Quad with his cell since he figured it would be more secure than using Bob's computer. At least in theory it would be harder for anyone to access the information, especially since he was on a forum created by some of the best tech minds in the world. The Quad was the online equivalent of a medieval fortress.

Still, he was nervous about meeting Rain in person. He wasn't even sure how old Rain was, or if he should expect a male or female. He kind of assumed it would be a guy, based on the /ALLIANCE/ demographic, but these days you never knew. They'd agreed to meet in Back Bay Station by the burrito cart. This late it would probably be deserted.

He grabbed his ATM card and headed out. It took forty-five minutes to get there, mainly because he had to stop to withdraw the maximum daily amount to pay Rain. Five hundred dollars was a lot to ask for, but Rain was easily one of the best hackers frequenting /ALLIANCE/. Maybe even better than him, he was forced to admit. Plus Peter had the cash. Bob and Priscilla were kind of clueless about money, so his allowance was way more than what most of his friends got.

Peter was more concerned about how Bob would react if he wasn't back home by the time they returned, so he drove into town rather than take the T.

He parked in a lot nearby and sat there for a second. This all felt very cloak-and-dagger, meeting a stranger late at night in a train station for a payoff. A small part of him was thrilled by it all. It had definitely turned out to be a more interesting night than he'd expected.

He checked his watch; they'd agreed to meet at ten thirty, and it was a little before that. Peter got out of the car and crossed the street to Back Bay Station.

A few homeless people were huddled near the entrance under makeshift shelters crafted from shopping carts and ragged, smelly blankets. Peter gave them a wide berth and tried to walk with a confident swagger. He wished he'd worn something other than his fleece and jeans; he felt hopelessly conspicuous and out of place. Where he lived was technically part of the city, but in reality it was more of a sheltered suburb. He'd been spending more time in Boston proper since Amanda started school at Tufts, but even then they mainly hung out on campus. This felt different, and Peter was suddenly hyperconscious of the wad of hundreds in his wallet.

He shook it off, drawing himself up straight. This was Back Bay Station, not some dark alley. There had to be cops around; he just wasn't seeing any.

Peter walked in the front doors and stopped. It was cavernous inside, much bigger than he remembered. He had no idea how to find the burrito cart where they were supposed to meet.

The tiled floor echoed under his feet as he wandered around. He went to a few of the platforms, but only saw a handful of exhausted-looking people, most staring at the ground, each clearly in their own world. No one who seemed to be waiting for someone.

Back upstairs, he walked the length of the building, then took out his phone to double-check the time. Nearly eleven. He was frustrated, ready to give up.

"Vallas?"

Peter turned. He hadn't known exactly what to expect, but it wasn't this. Facing him was a girl with raven hair and enormous blue-green eyes. She looked like she was his age, or maybe a little younger. Pale skin, to the point where in this light she almost glowed. She had a MacBook Pro box tucked under her arm.

Despite the crazy outfit she was wearing, she was gorgeous. He swallowed hard to fight the sudden dryness in his mouth.

"Rain?" he managed.

"Would anyone else call you Vallas?" she asked, blatantly

examining him. Peter got the distinct feeling that he wasn't what she'd expected, either, and not in a good way. "What's a Vallas, anyway?"

"It's the name of my avatar in WoW."

She gave him a blank look. "W-O-W? Like, wow?"

"No, not wow." Peter felt slightly silly as he explained, "World of Warcraft."

"The video game?" Her eyebrows arched.

"It's an online multiplayer role-playing game," Peter said defensively. Lots of the chat threads on wikis and image-boards were devoted to WoW discussions; he'd deliberately chosen the name /ALLIANCE/ for the site because he knew people would recognize the reference and rally to it. Pretty much every hacker he knew spent hours every day enmeshed in the ongoing battle between the Alliance and their evil counterparts, the Horde. Every hacker but one, Peter realized with consternation, judging by her reaction. "I'm a Night Elf," he finished lamely.

"Interesting," Rain said, looking bored. "You brought the money, right?"

"Yeah, it's here." He glanced around before pulling out his wallet. The few people there didn't seem to be paying any attention to them. He quickly handed her the cash, and she tucked it in the front pouch of her sweatshirt. "Brought you this, too," he said, handing her a flash drive. "In case you didn't have an extra one."

"Thanks." She tucked it in the same pouch, then abruptly turned and started walking away.

"I'm not some huge WoW geek," he explained, falling in step beside her. "It just seemed to fit."

"Uh-huh," she said. "So what's AMRF?"

"I'm not sure. But I hacked into their database tonight,

and a half hour later a bunch of guys broke into my house."

That stopped her. She turned and examined him curiously. "Were they dressed like security guards?"

"Nope. All in black, like commandos or something."

"Oh." She abruptly lost interest. "Anything else?"

"Yeah, I've got a link. They're working on something called Project Persephone. If you want, I can text it to you."

"I don't have a phone," she said.

"Seriously?" Peter was flabbergasted. He didn't know anyone their age who didn't have a cell phone.

"I prefer email."

"Okay. Well, I'll email it to you, then."

"Whatever," Rain said.

They were standing in front of the station now, facing the parking lot. Peter couldn't shake the feeling that she was trying to get rid of him as quickly as possible, and he suddenly got nervous. How could he be sure she wouldn't screw him over, just take the cash and go? Suddenly, he felt like an idiot for giving it all up front.

"You're really going to do this for me, right?" he asked.

Rain's eyes narrowed. "Why?"

"Well, five hundred dollars is a lot of money, and I don't even know you."

"If I say I'm going to do something, I do it," she said. "That's all you need to know."

She started walking away.

"Hey, wait. I'm sorry, I didn't mean . . . can I give you a ride somewhere?" Peter called after her.

Rain didn't answer; she just kept going without looking back.

Peter watched until she turned the corner and disappeared. He walked back to his Prius feeling annoyed. There were other /ALLIANCE/ members he could have gotten to do this—probably for free, too. He'd gotten too swept up in the moment, and should have stopped to reconsider the minute she asked for money. Now he just had to hope that she came through and didn't cheat him.

He didn't know why she'd gotten him so flustered, either. He had a girlfriend, and Amanda was arguably even better looking. Peter glanced at his watch—he'd have to hurry to get home before Bob and Priscilla. He shoved the strange girl out of his mind and broke into a jog as he headed back toward his car.

CHAPTER FOUR

Noa closed the door behind her and fell back against it with a sigh. She was in a dumpy hotel room ten blocks from Back Bay Station. It was a total dive, but it was cheap, they took cash, and didn't ask for ID. At the moment, that was all she needed. And considering what she'd been through over the past several hours, it looked as good as a penthouse suite.

Still, she had to admit it was pretty grim. The bedspread was mottled with stains, there were bars over the windows, and the chair's wicker seat was unraveling. Noa was almost afraid to see the state of the bathroom. But for forty bucks and no questions asked, it was probably the best she could expect.

At least there was a table set up beside a functioning outlet. Noa took a pillow from the bed and covered the hole in the chair with it, then carefully sat down. Her laptop needed more charging—she got it set up. All the nearby wireless networks were password-protected, but that was child's play. Within a few minutes she'd accessed the one with the strongest signal and was off and running.

She started by zeroing in on the warehouse complex where she'd been held. Hacking into the city records department was more complicated than getting on a wireless router, but only slightly. It was laughable how easy it was to dig around most government sites. Corporations tended to be trickier, since they went to the trouble of hiring people like her to test their networks. Most local and state governments simply didn't have the cash flow to protect themselves.

The boatyard and warehouses were registered to the same corporation: ANG Import/Export. Which sounded innocuous enough. Noa started to dig through corporate records, trying to find out more about the company.

Unfortunately, it turned out that ANG Import/Export was owned by another company based in the Bahamas, which in turn was owned by another company that didn't seem to exist outside of filing for S-Corp status. . . .

Twelve companies later, Noa sat back, frustrated. So far none of them seemed to exist as anything but a hiding place for more companies. It was like one of those Russian nesting dolls, where you pulled the two halves apart only to find another smaller doll inside, then another inside that one . . . only she was starting to get the sense that these dolls might go on forever. The clock at the top of her monitor read one a.m. Noa rubbed her eyes. She felt physically exhausted, but oddly not tired. The thin curtains over the windows were barely going to block the morning light, so she'd probably awaken at dawn, anyway. She might as well try to get some rest.

Noa wished she'd grabbed some toiletries at a drugstore. She had a terrible taste in her mouth, metallic and strange, and she'd love to wash the grime off her face. Luckily she still didn't feel hungry, because this definitely wasn't the type of hotel that boasted a vending machine. She'd be lucky to find a half-used bar of soap in the bathroom.

She used two fingers to peel the bedspread off the bed—even though she was freezing, it didn't seem like something she'd want any part of her body to come in contact with. Noa scooted between the sheets and stared up at the ceiling. She finally allowed herself to stop and process what had happened to her— *Or what might have been done,* she thought with a shudder.

Hesitantly, Noa reached under her sweatshirt and grabbed a corner of the bandage, carefully peeling it away. She ran her fingers over the incision on her chest contemplatively. It was a diagonal slice that started in the center of her rib cage and ran right at a slight downward angle for three inches. The skin surrounding it felt colder than the rest, the scab itself just a narrow line. The weird thing was that it barely hurt anymore. Earlier it had felt like her ribs were cracked and broken, the cut itself sharp and painful. But now the wound barely throbbed. And her foot already felt better, too. She unpeeled the gauze and checked; the cut must not have been as deep as she thought; it was barely even visible. Strange.

And even though she felt exhausted, Noa couldn't sleep. It was almost as if she'd forgotten how. Not that that was unusual. She'd suffered bouts of insomnia her entire life—especially at The Center, where sleep made you vulnerable. But after Noa got her own apartment, that had changed. For the first time in her life, she'd slept eight, nine, sometimes even ten hours a night. It was amazing what a difference feeling safe made.

Now, apparently, that was gone again. Noa lay there

examining the various water stains covering the ceiling, and other, darker marks that looked suspiciously like blood spatter. Her mind drifted over to Vallas, and she frowned. Meeting him in person kind of changed her whole view of /ALLIANCE/. It wasn't that he was just a kid, like her; most people her age were useless, but she'd met enough exceptions to know better than to underestimate them.

It was more that Vallas was clearly a rich kid. That bugged her. Plus he'd practically accused Noa of stealing from him, which really ticked her off. Here she was trying to figure out who had kidnapped her, and she had to waste time researching something that was probably ridiculous. *It's important,* he'd claimed. She could just imagine what a kid like that thought was important: whether or not he'd gotten early acceptance to Harvard, probably, or if they were testing shampoo on bunnies in a lab.

Not that she supported that sort of thing, but Noa hadn't gotten involved with /ALLIANCE/ because of their animal-cruelty efforts. They'd drawn her attention with other raids, against the type of people that she'd once fallen prey to.

And World of Warcraft? Really?

The whole thing irked her. As soon as she got access to her money again, she'd send Vallas a check. The last thing she wanted was to feel indebted to a punk who probably lived in some Brookline mansion.

But then, her own research seemed to have hit a dead end.

Even though it was late, Noa sensed she wasn't going to be able to fall asleep yet. Sighing, she went back to her laptop and tapped a key, bringing it out of sleep mode. A Google search for Project Persephone spit out a bunch of links to Greek mythology sites and books, but nothing that seemed to be an actual "project." She went into her email and found a new message from Vallas. He'd sent the link, along with a single word: *Thanks*.

"Yeah, whatever," Noa muttered to herself. She wondered what was up with that story about a bunch of commandos breaking into his house. It seemed ridiculously implausible, but she decided to take some precautions just in case. There were entire international proxy servers devoted to helping you cover your tracks. Set up mainly to protect financial schemers and pornography-sharing creeps, they also functioned as a sort of superhighway for hackers. Noa covered her tracks by hopping from a server in Colorado to one in Virginia, then to the UK, Russia, China, India, Texas, Brazil, Mexico, Japan . . . leaping from one to the next until she could be relatively certain that her true location would be untraceable. It was like creating a vast and complicated spiderweb. By the time she finished, even if investigators managed to follow half the threads, they'd never make it back to the beginning before she'd finished the hack, signing off and leaving behind a dead end. Because if Vallas hadn't just been lying to impress her, the last thing she needed to deal with tonight was more armed men. By the end, Noa had gone through a few dozen servers, ending with one based in Hungary, a country with few Internet laws. Then she finally accessed the corporate mainframe.

She was immediately confronted by a firewall. No surprise there; any company worth their salt had a decent one in place these days. Legend had it that the only one hackers had never managed to infiltrate was Coca-Cola; supposedly that corporation spent a fortune keeping their secret formula secret.

Noa started with the standard protocols. She compared it to trying to stick a pin into a balloon without popping it—you had to probe carefully so that it didn't just blow up in your face; a lot of sites went into automatic lockdown if they detected an infiltrator. She should know—her work for Rocket Science mainly consisted of setting up those sorts of protections. Or if the walls had already been breached, it was her job to try and mitigate the damage, and ensure that it didn't happen again.

The trick was to act as if you were someone who belonged, but were stumbling around, like a drunk guy having trouble fitting a key into his front door. At every company there were plenty of employees with legitimate access to the server who had trouble remembering passwords and entered the wrong one a few times. The truly great hackers breached the wall that way, waiting for the server to spit out hints.

This one was sophisticated, though—clearly established by people who knew what they were doing. Noa found herself intrigued in spite of her doubts about Vallas. Whatever they were hiding, it probably wasn't college admissions information.

She kept at it. Hours passed. The sun came up and daylight seeped through the thin curtains, but Noa was so absorbed she didn't even notice. It was well after eight a.m. when she finally had a breakthrough and her screen suddenly flooded with information. Noa sat back as stacks of folders populated her screen: way too many to fit on a flash drive, she immediately realized. There were thousands related to Project Persephone, amid other projects with similarly obtuse names.

Noa felt a surge of annoyance. Vallas should have been more specific about what he was looking for; she couldn't send him this much data. She decided to assemble a sampling—hopefully that would suffice. After all, it wasn't like he'd actually be paying for this. She didn't mind helping out fellow hackers for free on occasion, even when they turned out to be spoiled rich kids. And he had done a lot of good via /ALLIANCE/.

She started clicking on folders at random, moving them onto the flash drive. Twenty seemed like a good number. And if what he was looking for wasn't among them, that was just too bad. She needed to get her own house in order.

Twelve folders in, she froze on one titled, "TEST SUBJECTS: BOSTON."

That wasn't what had caught her eye, though. The third file down was named "Noa Torson."

Peter's heel beat a steady rhythm against the floor. It wasn't something he could help, just a nervous habit he'd developed as a kid. Still, he could tell it was getting on Bob's nerves.

For once, his father didn't lay into him about it. "Tell me again *exactly* what Mason said." Bob was leaning forward in the chair, elbows on his knees, hands clasped.

"I told you," Peter said impatiently. "He said to give you and Mom his best, and then he said someone would come by to fix the door, and that you should call him."

"Call him right away?" Bob pressed.

"At your earliest convenience." Peter slouched in his chair, but his leg kept moving. "That's *exactly* what he said."

His parents exchanged a glance. They'd pulled into the driveway minutes after him, a little after eleven, and immediately hustled him into his father's office.

Peter's focus kept drifting to the imprint of a large bootheel on the carpet by the armchair. The front door had already been repaired by the time he got home, so this mark was the only real proof that he hadn't imagined the whole thing.

Not that he'd had any trouble convincing his parents. And yet they were treating Peter as if he'd done something wrong.

His mother nervously fingered a string of pearls as she leaned against his father's desk. Priscilla was wearing her official "casual" outfit, a thousand-dollar Gucci sweat suit. Her makeup had gathered in the creases around her eyes and mouth, and her hair was mussed, like she'd been running her hands through it.

Peter hadn't seen either of them this anxious in a long time. Stressed, sure, but it had been years since they'd looked this tense and fearful. Like something very bad was happening and they were helpless to prevent it. It was unnerving.

"And he didn't say why they broke in?" Bob asked, eyes narrowing.

"Nope." Peter's eyes shifted away to the fireplace.

"What were you doing, Peter?" his mother asked worriedly.

"Nothing. Just hanging out."

"You must have been doing something," his dad said, a disapproving note in his voice.

"I wasn't. Man, I can't believe some jerks broke into our house, and you're trying to blame me for it."

"We're not blaming you, Peter," his mother said soothingly. "It's just—" Another glance at his father. "Well, Mr. Mason doesn't do things without a reason."

"*Mr.* Mason? Who the hell is this guy? How do you know him?"

"That's not important," Bob said.

"Well, it seems pretty important based on how you're giving me the third degree."

They fell silent.

"I'm going upstairs to crash," Peter announced, getting to his feet. "Getting beat up really took it out of me."

"We're not done talking yet, young—"

"Let him go, Bob," his mother said. "It's past midnight."

His father looked peeved, but pointed a stubby index finger at Peter and said, "We'll talk in the morning."

"Great," Peter grumbled. "I can't wait."

"Good night, sweetheart," his mother said, but her focus remained on Bob. They were doing that thing he hated, where it was like they were communicating telepathically, leaving him out of the conversation. *Typical,* he thought, stalking out of the office. They never really told him anything, still treating him like he was eight years old.

Peter trotted up the flight of stairs and down the hall to his bedroom, which overlooked the pool behind their house. Inside his room, he automatically headed over to his desk, then remembered that his laptop had been stolen. He made an exasperated noise and flopped down on his bed, digging out his cell phone to text Amanda.

Still up?

He waited a few minutes, but she didn't respond. Which meant she was either already asleep, or still working on her paper and didn't want to be bothered. That seemed to be happening more and more lately. The fact that she was already living away from home made him keenly aware of their age difference. Funny how it hadn't seemed like a big deal when she was a senior in high school and he was a junior. Now it was like she'd leaped ahead of him and joined the league of adults, and he was left behind at the kids' table.

He opened the picture he'd taken of Amanda the weekend before, when they'd met for lunch at a diner near campus. Peter had caught her unawares when she was looking out the window. *Just wondering how long it'll rain,* she'd claimed when he asked. But she had that familiar look in her eye. Amanda was a private person—it was one of the things he liked about her; she wasn't one of those girls who talked your ear off about silly, inconsequential things. It was what had first attracted him to her, the fact that she was so serious about everything. And when she gave you her undivided attention, focusing all that intense energy on you, there was nothing better.

In the photo, though, she was clearly a million miles away. Worse yet, her expression indicated she'd rather be somewhere else. Peter hadn't noticed it at the time, but now whenever he looked, that was all he saw.

He turned off the phone and sighed. He'd already applied to Harvard for early acceptance, figuring that way he and Amanda could still see a lot of each other. And he was pretty much guaranteed to get in. He was a third-generation legacy, and Bob had given the university a ridiculous amount of money over the years to make up for Peter's mediocre grades.

Now he wondered if he might not be better off applying somewhere else instead. Stanford, maybe. After all, Silicon Valley was the tech capital of the world, and he'd be working in that field when he graduated. Sunny California, far, far away from here.

It was sounding better and better, Peter thought as he rolled over and shut off the light.

CHAPTER FIVE

Noa stared at the screen, the mouse hovering over the file labeled with her name. Even though it was Sunday, there was a chance that shortly the server would be flooded with users. Which greatly increased the likelihood that her presence would be discovered. She flashed back on what Vallas had said, about the guys breaking into his house. Maybe he wasn't being melodramatic.

She clicked open the file and skimmed a few of the documents. There were slides, diagrams, pages and pages of medical notes. Noa couldn't decipher most of them; they were a muddle of unintelligible scientific jargon. All she could tell for certain was that they involved some sort of experiment.

Her hand unconsciously went to her chest again. Was that what they'd done? Treated her like a guinea pig, maybe even removed an organ or something? If so, it didn't seem to be anything she could live without—all things considered, she felt all right. Still, the thought of some stranger undressing her, cutting her open, and poking around inside her . . . it made her blood run cold. Noa forced it from her mind. With effort she dissociated, trying to treat this like it was just an assignment, a problem to solve that had nothing to do with her.

Okay, then, Noa thought, running a hand through her hair and forcing herself to draw a deep breath. It was obvious that whoever had access to these files was supposed to know the backstory; these were just test results.

She stopped dead on one photo: a shot taken of her lying on the metal table. The camera was positioned above and slightly to the right. The IV was there, and the other trays were wheeled closer, hovering around the table like casual observers. There were no other people visible. She was even paler than usual, almost blue. It looked like one of those morgue shots they showed on TV cop shows.

Noa shuddered and closed the file, then double-checked to make sure it wasn't on the flash drive she was giving Vallas. She hesitated, then sent a copy to her personal email file, along with everything else in that folder.

She signed off the server and went back to the bed to lie down. Part of her felt like she'd never been so tired in her life, yet at the same time Noa was certain she wouldn't be able to sleep. It was almost nine a.m.; she'd have to be out of the hotel room in two hours, anyway. She'd considered paying for two nights up front, but figured it was smarter to keep moving. Maybe she could find something moderately better, or at least cleaner.

And she needed to get a phone, too. She debated whether

or not to contact Vallas right away. Knowing now that the project was linked to what had happened to her, she wasn't gung ho to hand the flash drive over. Who knew what he planned on doing with the information? Was this going to be another of /ALLIANCE/'s exposés? Were they planning on pranking the people who had cut her open?

For her at least, that wouldn't suffice. Noa decided to put him off for a day. She'd just tell him she hadn't gotten around to it.

She logged on to her account. The email backup of the files was there, along with another email from Vallas. He sounded impatient, asking if she'd found anything yet.

She was about to compose a reply when another email popped into her inbox. She didn't recognize the sender, A6M0, but it was rare for spam to make it through her filter. And the subject heading read: *Warehouse Fire.*

She hesitated, then opened it. There was a jpeg photo in the body of the email. Based on the angle, it was taken from the security gate as she passed by on top of the fire truck. So one of the cameras had been positioned high enough.

Against the solid mass of the truck Noa appeared tiny, her body stretched in a taut *X* against the side rails, terror in her eyes. Seeing that, the ball of panic she'd managed to hold at bay since waking up on that table seemed to explode. Her heart hammered, reminding her of the incision in her chest. She tried breathing deeply to calm herself, but that just made her aware of how dry her mouth was. Shakily, she sat back in the chair, fighting the tears that were welling up. Why were they still after her?

And how the hell did they know her email address? It was bad enough being snatched off the street, but the virtual world was where she usually felt safe and protected. She'd deliberately structured everything, including this particular email account, to be relatively inaccessible. Still, she knew what she was capable of when she set her mind to it. Most other hackers weren't in her league, but those who were could probably track her down if they had a mind to.

She was so distracted by the image that it took a second to realize there was a link pasted below it. Fighting past a growing sense of dread, Noa opened it. And frowned.

It was a website for shampoo.

She double-checked the link, then tried it again.

Same result.

Noa sat back, stumped. What on earth was going on?

She didn't intend to sit around and wait to see if they could trace her to this hotel room. Noa quickly bundled up the laptop, pulled the hood over her hair, and left the room.

"That doesn't make any sense," Amanda said.

"I know, right?" Peter had ducked out of the house early. He hadn't slept well anyway, and wasn't in the mood for another "talk" with Bob and Priscilla. So he met Amanda at a diner just off the Tufts campus, the same place they'd had brunch last week.

Peter watched Amanda push oatmeal around her bowl. His was also practically untouched, but for different reasons. Once again, he'd ordered oatmeal to appease her, when what he really wanted was a giant plate of runny eggs. Dating a vegan wasn't always easy. Amanda never pressured him about it, but then she didn't have to. The expression on her face when he chewed on a piece of steak said it all.

"So what are you going to do about it?" Amanda demanded.

"I asked a friend to help me find out more about that

company," Peter said. "Someone from /ALLIANCE/."

"Right, /ALLIANCE/." She rolled her eyes.

"What?" he demanded. "You liked them enough when they helped with that animal lab-testing thing."

"Sure," she acknowledged. "But that doesn't mean I have to like the name."

Peter shrugged. He hated when she adopted this superior attitude. Amanda had been with him when he came up with the idea for the group, and the name. She hadn't seemed to think it was stupid back then. Of course, that was before she became a "worldly college student." "When you start a hacktivist group, you can call it whatever you want."

"Don't be like that," she said, pointing the spoon at him.

"Like what?"

"You know, angry. I'm sorry; it's a good name. I'm just stressed. I was up most of the night working on this paper."

So she hadn't taken his call, Peter noted, even though she'd still been awake. "What's it for?"

"Feminist Lit and Theory," she said. "It's an amazing class. It's making me think I might want to major in Women's Studies."

"Instead of sociology? I thought you wanted to become a social worker."

"I could minor in that. Beside, you can major in pretty much anything," she said dismissively. "I could get an art degree and work on Wall Street. Isn't that crazy?"

"Crazy," Peter agreed. Funny how they'd already veered back to talking about her. "Anyway, I'm hoping she'll find something."

"She'll?" Amanda raised an eyebrow. "There are girls on /ALLIANCE/?"

"Yeah, of course."

"But I thought the whole thing is that it's anonymous," Amanda said. "How do you know it's a girl?"

"I met her last night."

"What?"

Peter was pleased by the note of jealousy in her voice. "I paid her to help."

"Oh, you didn't. Peter, what were you thinking? How much?"

"Not much," he said defensively. "Besides, there's a kind of honor code with hackers. She won't screw me."

"Sure she won't." Amanda shook her head. "Honestly, Peter. I work with people every day who take advantage of other people."

"You're comparing a bunch of homeless junkies to hackers?" he scoffed.

Amanda stiffened and her eyes flashed. Peter immediately wished he could take it back. This was her trigger point: Her brother, Marcus, had run away from home when he was fifteen, and was found dead of an overdose under an icy park bench less than a year later. As soon as she was old enough, Amanda started volunteering at a shelter downtown that specialized in trying to get runaway teens off the streets. Of all her many causes, that one she held dearest. And he'd just mocked it.

Amanda started pulling on a pair of fingerless gloves, tucking the ends into her long wool coat.

"Wait, I didn't mean—"

"It's okay, Peter. Listen, we're both tired." She unbuttoned her purse and took out a twenty, then tossed it on the table. "We should probably just go home and get some sleep."

That sounded an awful lot like they wouldn't be going back to her dorm room to hang out, Peter thought. The cold look on her face confirmed it. "I got this," he said, digging out his own wallet.

"It's my turn. You paid last weekend," she insisted.

"Yeah, but—"

Amanda held up a hand, stopping him. "I know you've got more money than me. But we're equal, so we pay equal."

"Fine." Peter ran a hand through his hair. "I'll get the next one, then?"

"Yeah. The next one." Amanda called back. She was already halfway to the door of the diner.

Peter watched through the plateglass windows as she turned right. The wind grabbed her dark blond hair, sending it flying out behind her. She wrapped a scarf more tightly around her neck and leaned into it. Amanda disappeared into a crowd of other students before reaching the corner. *Not so long ago she would have looked back, maybe even blown a kiss,* Peter thought as he sat back down.

The waitress came over to take the check. He put his hand over it and said, "Actually, can I get an order of eggs and sausage? Over easy, please."

"Sure you don't want to try any of this stuff on?" the store clerk asked dubiously.

"Why? I know my sizes," Noa said.

"Wow." The girl shook her head, sending chandelier earrings jingling. "That's amazing. You just walked in, like, two minutes ago. I never buy anything without trying it on first."

Noa didn't respond. She didn't have a lot of patience with small talk, and had never been good at it regardless. Besides, she already owned carbon copies of pretty much everything here: black socks, a bra, and panties; three T-shirts; one wool sweater; two pairs of jeans; a messenger bag; a fake-leather hooded bomber jacket, because the real ones were too expensive; and a pair of tall black leather boots that were on sale. "I'm paying with cash."

"Okay." Looking a little put out, the clerk rang up the stack of things Noa had dumped on the counter. She'd methodically gone through the store grabbing enough to hold her for at least three days. Although when it came down to it, this was about all she ever had. Her apartment was right across the street from a laundromat, so she didn't own much, anyway. Force of habit, since for most of her life she'd been limited to one drawer at The Center.

The Center was a sort of holding tank where foster kids stayed in between families. All told Noa had spent half her life either there, with a random assortment of foster families, or in juvie. And those drawers didn't come with locks. When your stuff was constantly getting stolen, you learned quickly not to develop attachments to it.

The only exception she'd ever made was for the jade bracelet. Not that it had been fancy or expensive or anything; it was just a narrow sliver of jade, plain and undecorated, a child's bracelet that now barely fit around her wrist. But it was the sole thing left over from her previous life, the last remaining tie to her parents.

Noa realized she was rubbing her wrist, feeling the slight indentation that remained. She forced herself to stop. *It's just another thing,* she reminded herself. And in the end, things weren't worth worrying about. Her parents had abandoned her, anyway. It was silly of her to hold on to any piece of them.

"That'll be two hundred and eighty dollars and fifty-six cents," the clerk announced.

Noa handed over three crisp hundred-dollar bills with a

pang of regret. She probably should have gone to a second-hand store instead, but she'd spent nearly her whole life wearing other people's used clothing. She knew it was silly, but she was loath to do it again, even under these circumstances.

Besides, she had a small fortune stashed in a savings account. She just had to get to it somehow. On the way to the store, Noa had stopped at a branch of her bank. The soonest they could get her a new debit card was tomorrow or the day after, and an emergency replacement required ID. She claimed to have left her wallet at home and fled before the questions got too pointed. As it was, she could see the bank teller trying to make sense of this teenager with a healthy bank balance and fancy laptop who smelled like a fishmonger.

Noa was a little nervous about picking up the replacement card. She didn't have her PO Box key, and depending on who was working the desk, they might ask for ID before handing over the contents. But the cash from Vallas wouldn't last much longer. The PO Box was a risk she'd have to take. Although it probably wasn't a bad idea to start setting up a new identity for herself. The guy she'd used to establish the Lathams' social-security info was serving a three-year sentence in Concord prison. She'd have to put out feelers in The Quad for a new connection.

Which meant getting through another couple of days on less than two hundred dollars. Not impossible under other circumstances, but she really wanted to hole up somewhere that didn't rent rooms by the hour.

"All set," the clerk said.

"Thanks. I'm going to change into some of these now, okay?"

The girl shrugged and pointed. "Fitting rooms are in the back."

Noa went to the one in the far corner, pulled the curtain shut, and swiftly shed her clothes. After getting dressed, she examined herself in the mirror: black sweater, black jeans, black boots and jacket, and a white-and-black-checked scarf. It was startling to suddenly recognize herself. She'd been wearing a nearly identical outfit the day all this started. Her skin was paler from being inside more than usual, but otherwise she appeared completely unchanged.

She tucked the laptop and extra clothing into the messenger bag and left the Apple box on the floor with the stuff she'd been wearing. At the last moment, she grabbed the knit cap. It smelled, but she still kind of liked it. And in Boston, a hat always came in handy.

She walked out of the store without a backward glance and found a café down the block with a FREE WIRELESS ACCESS! sign posted in the window. She ordered a coffee, tall and black, then looked over the food menu. She hadn't eaten since . . . well, since waking up on that table. And who knew how long it had been before that. Noa was always skinny, but her clothes were hanging more loosely than she remembered.

She ordered a turkey sandwich and chips to go with the coffee. While she waited for the food, she rubbed the spot on the back of her hand where the IV needle had been. There was no sign of it anymore, not even a scab. And when she thought about it, her chest and foot didn't hurt, either.

But then, she'd always healed pretty quickly. Noa got her order and took it to a table in the corner near an outlet. She plugged in, logged in, and debated her next step. She had to find a place to stay that wouldn't ask for a credit card or ID, preferably one she could book and pay for online.

Less than a minute later she found a website that offered short-term rentals by owners. Better still, the money could be transferred directly from her bank account, along with a security deposit.

It would leave a paper trail, which was a risk. Noa sat back and debated. On-screen was a place that looked perfect: a studio apartment in Cambridge that was available for just five hundred dollars a week. Noa could hunker down there while she figured out who was after her, and why.

But whether or not she'd really be safe depended on how much they knew about her. Had she just randomly been snatched off the street, or had they been tracking her for a while? They knew her name, but did they know about the fake family she'd set up, and where she lived? Could they get into her apartment? Did they know about the PO Box? They might just be hanging around there, knowing she'd have to get to it sooner or later.

She really didn't want to look at the file on herself again, but all the information they had on her was probably in there. Fighting past the fear of discovering something terrible, Noa gritted her teeth and dove in.

Again, it proved nearly unintelligible, a mix of scientific and medical jargon. Noa wished she'd paid more attention during the three months she spent in biology class before dropping out. After sifting through more than twenty documents, she found one that contained personal information. Her heart sank at the sight of her address: not going home had been the right decision. Also listed were her height and weight, age, and other stats, the sort of thing they recorded at The Center when you had a physical.

No sign of her bank account and PO Box, though. But

those could always be on another page. There were more than three hundred documents in this file, and she'd only skimmed a fraction of them.

While she weighed the pros and cons of renting a place short-term, Noa took a bite of sandwich. At the taste, her nose wrinkled and she nearly gagged. The sandwich wasn't terrible—the turkey was a little dry and the lettuce was wilted, but that wasn't it. She popped open the potato chips to clear the taste from her mouth and had the same reaction. It was like her body went into instant revolt. And these chips were salt-and-pepper flavored, pretty much her favorite thing in the world to eat.

It was definitely weird.

Noa tentatively sipped the coffee. No reaction there. She drank another big gulp and waited: nothing.

Oh well, Noa thought. She'd been through a lot; maybe it was just some sort of delayed stress reaction.

Back to finding a place to stay. Her gut was telling her to chance it. Even if they were monitoring her bank account, any transactions would take a day or so to process. She finally committed to one night in the Cambridge apartment, adding a special request for the keys to be left with the doorman.

While Noa waited for confirmation, she checked her email. Another message from Vallas, who sounded increasingly annoyed. She responded with a single sentence: *Working on it.*

No new missives from her mysterious pen pal, A6M0.

She clicked on the email and went back to the link. It was for a shampoo—not one she used, but she recognized it. A teenage pop star who sang exactly the sort of crap Noa hated grinned out from the page, her hair long and black and glossy. Noa snorted and clicked through links. It appeared to be a standard promo site.

She scanned through it looking for unusual source code; sometimes hackers sent one another messages hidden inside HTML formatting. But there was nothing. Why the hell had someone sent her this? If they'd seen her escaping from the warehouse complex, why hadn't they tried to stop her? Was this from the same people who took her, or someone else?

Noa sipped more coffee as she pondered, wrapping both hands around the cup to warm them. She still felt unusually cold, like with every exhale she should be seeing tiny puffs of air. Maybe she was in some sort of shock.

She glanced through the picture window. There was a guy leaning against the building across the street. Around her age, wearing jeans and a hooded sweatshirt. The hood was up, so it was hard to see his face clearly. But he seemed to be staring right at her.

They gazed at each other for a minute. Then a bus stopped right in front of him. Noa craned her head, but it didn't look like he'd gotten on.

The bus pulled away from the curb and back into traffic. The guy was gone.

Suddenly wary and eager to get off the streets, Noa wrapped up the sandwich and chips and stuck them in her bag in case she got hungry later. She tucked away her laptop, slung the strap over her shoulder, and pushed back out into the cold.

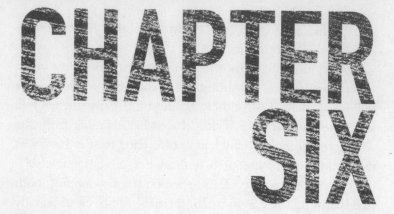

CHAPTER SIX

Peter sat in front of a terminal at the main library. His foot was tapping again, this time out of impatience. The connection here was about ten times slower than what he was used to. But he figured the men who crashed into his house last night wouldn't dare do the same here.

Still, it was frustrating. He was sitting in the computer room at the Boston Public Library. The fluorescent lighting was dim, barely aided by late autumn light filtering through the large windows. The computer was at least a decade old, some no-name model they probably sold at Radio Shack. The rest of his row was occupied by elderly people who all leaned in, peering anxiously at their screens. Occasionally they'd warily tap a button, as if hitting the wrong command might make the computer come alive and launch off the counter to bite them.

Although last night had taught him that maybe it could, Peter thought ruefully as his own hands danced over the keys.

He was being more careful to cover his tracks this time. Between that and the slow connection, it was taking twice as long for him to get to the initial firewall.

Earlier, Peter had finished his breakfast and wandered through the Tufts campus. Clusters of students hurried past him. The boys wore parkas and jeans, the girls variations on Amanda's standard uniform of a colorful knit sweater, long skirts over bright tights, boots and hats and gloves. Most had backpacks filled with books. They all looked older and sure of themselves. Which only served to make him feel lamer and more alone. So he hopped the T downtown and went to the library. Amanda's words had stung, but she might be right about Rain—she hadn't seemed like the type to screw him, but you never knew. It was stupid for him to rely on another hacker to get information, anyway. Calling in outside help had seemed like a better idea last night.

Peter's phone buzzed. He pulled it out of his pocket: Bob again, the third call today. He pressed the button sending it to voice mail. A minute later, a text appeared.

Get home now.

He ignored it. Amanda still hadn't responded to his text, which said only: *Sorry.* Maybe he should have written more, about how he hadn't meant it. Or maybe he should have waited, letting her cool down more before writing anything. He hated this part of dating, constantly trying to figure out what the hell the other person was thinking.

Before Amanda he'd never really had a girlfriend. Not because he couldn't; from sixth grade on, girls had always liked him. Even though he'd been good with computers, he also played on the soccer and tennis teams, which seemed to balance out the geek factor. He'd started dating when he was twelve, just having fun, hanging out, making out. No big deal. Then he met Amanda, and right away it was different. For the first time, he kind of got what they were talking about in all those cheesy songs. For the first time, he was the one waiting by the phone.

Usually when he sent a text, Amanda got back to him within the hour, and it had been two. Peter ran a hand through his hair. Couldn't let it stress him out. He had other things to deal with.

Peter kept at it. This time he was accessing the AMRF files via a Virtual Private Network. VPNs were mainly used by companies to give employees secured access to corporate networks. But they also allowed individuals to surf the Web anonymously, because the services employed private proxy servers that encrypted data.

Peter usually preferred to cover his tracks on his own, but this was an easy way for him to log on, and the connection would only show that he'd used the VPN server, not AMRF's. The drawback to VPNs was that they were painfully slow.

Peter checked email on his phone while he waited. Aside from the terse message she'd sent this morning, there was nothing new from Rain. /ALLIANCE/ was still abnormally quiet, too. He logged on to the site's main page to see what was going on, and was met by a 404 error that read: *Page not found.*

Peter frowned. He clicked through again, refreshing the page, and got the same result.

Someone had taken his site down.

Not only that, there was a message attached that the domain was available. Which was impossible, since he'd purchased rights to the /ALLIANCE/ URL for the next decade.

He felt a flare of rage. There was a backup wiki in place

for just those types of incidents. He went there to post a message about what was going on, and to mobilize members to retaliate . . . only to discover that the wiki was down, too.

Peter collapsed back in his chair. He was angrier now than he'd been in a long time, angrier even than last night. They'd broken into the home he lived in, sure, but destroying the online home he'd created was so much worse.

And stupid. Because there were dozens of forums and imageboards where he'd be able to get the message out to members. And once they found out what was going on, they'd ruthlessly go after the perpetrators. In the past, /ALLIANCE/ had accomplished some impressive acts of hacktivism. When Amanda found out about a trendy organic shampoo company that was secretly experimenting on stray dogs and cats, Peter organized a mission where late one night /ALLIANCE/ members hacked into the company's database and destroyed the production line, turning an entire factory into a giant bubble bath.

He'd come up with an even better revenge scenario for these bastards. Of course, first he had to figure out who they were.

The loading symbol stopped rotating on the library computer. Peter tapped a few more keys, looking for a way through the firewall. It was immediately apparent that this was going to be trickier than he thought. Cracking a system was painstaking, kind of like playing chess. There were a thousand variations, and each attempt could produce a different outcome.

Peter quickly became engaged. You could tell a lot about a company by their firewall. This one had been designed by a pro. As he probed it, he experienced a wave of admiration.

There were even a couple of safeguards he'd never encountered before, which was rare.

The hours flew past. The elderly users of the other terminals shuffled off after noisily gathering up bags and umbrellas and scarves, replaced by teens working on term papers. Peter barely noticed the shift.

When his phone beeped again, he jumped. It had made the sound for a text; probably Amanda finally getting back to him. He dug it out of his pocket and looked at the screen. The display read: *Blocked.*

Peter slid his finger across to unlock it. The text was just two words: *Get up.*

Spam, maybe? He'd been getting more of those lately; he'd have to work on blocking them when he had time to sift through his phone's code. Which wasn't today, that was for sure.

Peter was in the middle of trying another tactic to mount the firewall when his phone beeped again. This time, the text read: *Get up, or I'll make you get up.*

Peter looked around the room. There were a few middle-aged people hunched over books, teens whispering and giggling in low voices, a residual elderly man. Nobody seemed to be paying any attention to him. And nobody seemed like they'd be able to make him do anything.

Peter hesitated, then typed *F U* and hit send. He turned back to the keyboard, brow furrowed.

A few seconds later, a hand clamped down on his shoulder.

Noa stretched out on the couch with the laptop balanced on her belly. The Cambridge apartment had turned out to be even nicer than she'd expected, with brand-new furniture, a widescreen TV, and an insanely comfortable bed. Small, but cozy and not cluttered with a lot of junk. Better even than her own place, although for one hundred fifty dollars a night, it should be.

The doorman hadn't even blinked when she showed up to collect the keys, just handed them over and pointed to the elevator.

Noa entered the apartment and stashed her leftover sandwich in the fridge, cranked the heat to eighty, and kicked off her boots. She pulled one of the extra blankets off the bed and wrapped it around her shoulders. Then she plopped down on the couch and started going back through the files.

She had to fight to maintain focus; all the dense scientific jargon made her eyes glaze over. Most of them turned out to be basic charts and graphs, anyway: blood-pressure readings, heart rate, body temperature, something called "pulse/ox." The dates at the tops of the charts ranged over three weeks.

She could read computer code for hours, intuitively grasping it, but a lot of this stuff was beyond her. From what she could tell, many of the files were handwritten doctors' logs that had been scanned in. Aside from the date at the top, the writing on those was unintelligible. She'd spent ten minutes squinting at a single word without being able to decipher it.

The typed documents were almost as bad; she didn't even have a clue what half the symbols meant, and internet searches for them turned up hundreds of different potential results.

After a few hours Noa gave up. Her eyes were swimming, and she felt a migraine coming on. At least she was finally warm again. She shut the laptop and shuffled back to the fridge, keeping the blanket wrapped around her shoulders. She sniffed the sandwich again, but still wasn't hungry. So instead, she poured a glass of water and drank it standing at the window.

The studio apartment was a few blocks from Harvard Square, on the fifth floor of an old brick building. The rest of the street was primarily single-family homes, a mix of architecture that ranged from colonial to Greek revival. Trowbridge was a one-way street that ran north, black pavement confined by redbrick sidewalks set slightly above it like riverbanks.

It already looked like winter outside. Everything had a sterile white cast, like it been bleached and hung out to dry. Noa felt a pang of sadness—it was as if she'd missed fall entirely, which was disorienting. Especially since during that time span, her birthday had passed. Not that it was something she'd ever really celebrated, at least not for a long time. On the first of every month, The Center used to serve a mealy, store-bought cake after dinner for everyone who'd recently had a birthday. That was all she'd usually gotten. One foster family had made an effort, throwing a party for her in their basement. But she'd only lived with them for a few weeks, and she didn't have any friends to invite, anyway. In the end, that turned out to be even more depressing than the ones at The Center. The foster mom had grinned broadly over the candles and asked if she felt any different. Noa replied, "Yeah, fourteen sucks even worse."

And now she was sixteen.

Funny. This year, she did feel different.

Down below, a guy strolled past with a dog on a leash. No other people in sight. After leaving the café, Noa had taken a seriously indirect route to get here. She switched from the T to a series of buses, doubling back on herself to make sure she wasn't followed.

But maybe she was just being paranoid. Tomorrow would be the true test, when she tried to get into her PO Box. She planned on arriving early, well before they opened. There was a café a half block from the MailPlus where she had rented a box. Noa was pretty sure that from there she'd have a view of the front door, and would be able to tell if anyone was hanging around who shouldn't be.

Noa finished the water and stepped away from the window. Dusk was falling outside, and she was finally feeling tired. She drew the shades shut and went to bed.

Peter twisted around. The guy in the suit from the night before, Mason, was standing there. Again, he appeared more mildly annoyed than angry. His eyes were the oddest shade of gray, almost as pale as the whites surrounding them.

"Come on," he said, keeping his fingers tight on Peter's shoulder.

"I'm not done here." Peter tried to keep his voice casual as he gestured toward the computer. "Term paper."

Mason's eyes flicked toward the screen. When he saw what was there, they narrowed. "You're not a good listener, are you?"

"And you're kind of a jerk. Now get your hands off me." Peter shook loose of his grip.

Mason let go, but bent double so that his mouth was level with Peter's ear. "I left some friends at home with Bob and Priscilla. They're waiting for us."

Peter froze, his hands braced over the keyboard. There was a clear note of menace in Mason's voice. How the hell had they found him here? His pulse kicked up. He wasn't exactly close to Bob and Priscilla, but they were his parents. He didn't want anything to happen to them, especially not because of something he did.

But would it be better to try to get help from here? Once they were all stuck in the house, they'd be isolated. Peter glanced around the room—he'd been so absorbed, he hadn't noticed it had emptied. Just a few kids at the end of the row, completely fixated on their computer screens. An old man dozed in an easy chair by the stacks, a forgotten newspaper rising and falling on his chest. Peter dimly remembered passing a security guard on the way in, but was pretty sure he hadn't been armed or anything.

"There's only one right move here," Mason said softly, as if reading his mind. "You make a scene, and it'll be too late for them."

Peter remembered the fear in his parents' eyes last night, his mother saying, *Mr. Mason doesn't do anything without a reason.* What the hell had they gotten mixed up in?

"I need to get my stuff," he said.

Mason nodded and stepped back, hands hanging loose but tense by his sides. Like if Peter made a sudden move, he was braced to anticipate and block it. He watched Peter shove stuff into a backpack.

"And that." Mason nodded toward the monitor.

Peter hit a few keys, backing out of the firewall and closing down all the other open windows. He logged off, sending the terminal to the home screen, then slung the pack over his shoulder and stood. Funny, even though he had seemed enormous last night, Mason was only an inch or so taller than him, five-eleven or maybe six feet. Maybe he was just less imposing in the daytime. Still, it gave Peter a measure of confidence.

"I have to get my car."

"We've already brought it to your house," Mason said.

"What? How'd you know where it was?" Peter had left his car parked back by the diner.

Mason just continued to give him that smug smile. He held out a hand and said, "Cell phone, please." When Peter hesitated, he raised an eyebrow. "If you give it to me now, I won't have to break it."

Peter dug his iPhone out of his pocket and handed it over.

Mason kept a hand on Peter's elbow, steering him out of the room and down the stairs to the exit. Peter's mind raced, backtracking through his day, trying to remember anything out of the ordinary. Had they been following him this whole time? Or maybe planted a bug on him somehow? He could kick himself—he'd been so careful to cover his virtual tracks, yet something as obvious as a tail hadn't even occurred to him.

Mason picked up the pace as they descended the stone staircase that led to the street. An SUV was parked in the loading zone out front, engine idling. The rear door opened. Mason shoved Peter in, slammed the door shut, then got into the front passenger seat. The doors locked.

One of the big guys was in the backseat with him, taking up most of it. Peter couldn't say for sure if he'd been at the house last night, or if they all just looked alike. He was wearing the same outfit as the others, a black long-sleeved shirt and pants with a sidearm tucked in a hip holster. He glared down at Peter as if daring him to try something.

"A black Ford Explorer?" Peter managed. "Don't you think that's a little cliché?"

In the front seat, Mason barked a short, sharp laugh. It wasn't a comforting sound. Without turning around, Mason said, "The real shame here, Peter, is that you're a very likable young man."

Peter fell silent. He decided that he'd rather not know why that was a shame, at least not yet.

The guy next to him finally shifted his gaze out the window, apparently deciding that Peter wasn't going to make trouble. Peter watched the familiar scenery pass by as they snaked through downtown, headed toward the on-ramp that led back to his house.

Bob and Priscilla were sitting in the living room when they arrived forty minutes later. Two armed guys were posted in opposite corners by the doors to the room. When Mason led Peter in, his mother started to get off the couch. Bob grabbed her elbow, stopping her. Priscilla hesitated, then sat back down. There was something in her eyes that Peter couldn't quite identify—apology? Sadness?

She gave him a weak smile and said, "Peter, honey, are you okay?"

"Okay? Fuck no."

"Language," she said automatically.

"What the hell were you thinking?" Bob's voice was full of bluster, although there was a tremor behind it. "You really let us down."

Neither of them had directly acknowledged the strangers in the room. They were acting as if this were just an ordinary family meeting. After propelling Peter inside, Mason stepped back against the wall. He stood there silently watching, like they were putting on a play for his amusement.

"I let you down?" Peter said, seriously pissed off. "This is the second time in two days I've had to deal with these assholes."

"Peter," his mother said warningly.

"I told you we'd talk about it this morning. You never goddamn listen." Bob was off the couch now. He ran a hand through what was left of his hair, sending strands jabbing out in conflicting directions. "I ask one simple thing, that while you live in my house you give us the common courtesy of doing what we ask you to—"

"Calm down, Bob," his mother said, grabbing at his arm.

"I will not calm down. This kid"—he pointed at Peter—"we give him everything he wants, computers, cars, you name it. He wants to stay out all night? Fine. He forgets your birthday? Sure, no problem. But we ask him to do just one goddamn thing for a change, and he craps all over us." He turned back to Peter's mother and spat, "It's your fault for spoiling him."

"I spoiled him?" Priscilla was off the couch now, the strength back in her voice.

Peter fidgeted. It was almost as if they'd forgotten about him now, too.

"It sure as hell wasn't me!" Bob's face was florid, bright red scalp visible through his hair plugs. "I said we needed to try to keep things as normal as possible, but no, you wanted to make sure he had everything. As if that would ever make up for Jeremy and—"

Priscilla drew in a sharp breath and his father's voice faltered, breaking off whatever he'd been about to say. She dropped back to the couch, her voice a whisper as she said, "I can't believe—"

"I'm sorry, sweetheart. I'm so sorry, I didn't mean . . ." Bob said softly. He sat and tried to draw her into him, but her whole body had gone rigid. She resisted his efforts to embrace her, hands shielding her face as he stroked her hair. Peter watched, transfixed. It was like all the air had suddenly been sucked from the room. There was one tacit, unspoken agreement in their family: They *never* talked about what had happened to his brother. This was the closest they'd ever come.

"If I may," Mason said softly.

At the sound of his voice, Peter's parents jumped. They straightened, recovering themselves. Priscilla brushed some imaginary lint off her lap and edged a few inches farther down the couch.

"Sorry," Bob said gruffly, "it's just—"

"My main concern today is to make sure that we all reach an understanding," Mason said smoothly, as if the previous exchange had never occurred. "I'm afraid that we haven't been clear enough with Peter. Perhaps if he fully grasps the . . . consequences of his actions, he'll be more amenable to changing his behavior."

"What kind of consequences?" Peter asked. He jerked his head toward the guy blocking the closest door. "Is he going to shoot us?"

"Peter!" his mother said sharply.

Mason smiled thinly again. "I believe I'll allow your parents to explain." He inclined his head slightly. "I hope this will be the last time we meet, Peter."

And with that, he left the room. The guards stayed, though.

There was a long moment of silence. Finally, Priscilla said, "There are things going on, Peter. Things that you probably wouldn't understand."

"What, I'm an idiot now?" Peter said.

"Will you please sit?" she asked.

"No." Peter crossed his arms over his chest. Part of him felt like a peevish kid, but the fact that they were acting all normal, like this always happened on a Sunday evening, bothered the hell out of him.

"All right." His parents exchanged a glance. Bob looked like he was afraid to open his mouth again and let the wrong thing slip out. His mother cleared her throat, then said, "Mr.

Mason said they caught you going through your father's files last night."

"He's lying," Peter said. "I was on my laptop. That's what they took, remember?"

Priscilla's eyes narrowed. She slipped into what he always referred to as her "lawyer voice." "As you said, Peter, you're not an idiot. And neither are we. You were snooping in your father's drawer, and saw something you shouldn't have. It made you curious, so you decided to check it out on your own laptop. Can we at least agree on those basic details, and not insult each other's intelligence?"

After a beat, Peter reluctantly shrugged. "Yeah, okay."

"All right, then. Apparently, today, Mr. Mason found you doing something similar at the library."

"And how the hell did he know that?" Peter demanded. "Who are these people? What are they, following me?"

"Probably," Bob chimed in. "They're probably watching all of us."

"And that doesn't bother you?" Peter said, incredulous. He looked back and forth between them.

His parents appeared chastened. "You have to understand, there's a good reason for it," his mother said in a low voice. "We wouldn't have put us all at risk unless . . ."

She trailed off. When she didn't continue, Peter said, "Unless what? Why would you agree to let a bunch of guys follow us around?"

"Bottom line is this, Peter." Bob spoke up. "If you keep digging around the way you do, with, you know, computers—" Bob made a circular motion with his hand; technology had never been his strong suit. "Very bad things will happen. And not just to us, but to other people, too."

"You said we weren't insulting each other's intelligence

anymore, right?" Peter asked, looking back and forth between them. "So just tell me what's going on. I'm almost eighteen; I'm going to college next year. Don't treat me like a kid."

"We can't tell you," his mother said, a note of pleading in her voice. "Believe me, Peter, we'd love to. But we simply can't."

"Why not? If I'm already in danger, don't I deserve to know why?" They didn't answer, and he pressed, "What's Project Persephone?"

His mother blanched, but Bob's jaw set back into a familiar line. The authority in his voice returned as he said, "You are not to go digging around anymore. Period." After a beat, he tacked on, "And you're grounded. No car, no computer, no phone."

"Crap," Peter said, suddenly realizing that jackass Mason had taken his iPhone with him. The creep was probably reading his texts from Amanda right now.

"And if we find out you've been disobeying us," his father continued, "that's it. You're out."

"Bob—"

"Out?" Peter was floored. "Like, out of the house?"

"That's right," Bob said. "I'm done with this. You want to be a pain in the ass, go do it under someone else's roof. Here, you do what we tell you to do."

His mother tried to interject. "He doesn't mean—"

"Damn right I do." Bob jutted his chin up an inch. "Your choice, Peter. You want to be treated like a grown-up? Fine. It's your life."

"But, Dad—"

"You know what?" Bob continued, his voice suddenly cold. "Your brother would never have done anything like this."

"Bob!" his mother exclaimed with horror. "Stop it!"

He whirled on her. "It's true, and you know it. We lost the wrong son."

His mother turned toward him, mouth slightly agape, eyes wide. "Peter," she said, chagrined, "your father didn't . . . he doesn't really—"

"The hell I don't," Bob barked. He spun back to Peter, his face flaming. "You know what? Just get out. I can't stand the sight of you."

Peter felt like his insides had turned to liquid, and if he took a step they'd wobble and flow right out of him. Tears bubbled in his eyes, casting his parents in a watery shimmer. He stared back at Bob, who had gone completely stony and expressionless. They'd fought before, but never like this. Peter barely recognized him; it was like facing off against a total stranger.

His mother stood slightly behind him, looking stricken, her hands opening and closing as they dangled by her sides. She appeared to be fighting back tears, too. But she didn't say another word.

Peter turned to leave the room. The guy by the door eyed him but didn't make a move to block it. Pushing past him, Peter stormed down the hall. He heard his mother make a strangled sound, and the two of them started arguing again. He didn't care anymore.

Once he got to his room, Peter slammed the door. A wave of sound in his head like a train roaring through, chasing away the capacity for clear thought. He went back to the door and slammed a fist against it, as hard as he could. The pain brought him back.

He shook out his hand, then collapsed on the bed. But he was too agitated to remain still. He jumped back up and started pacing. The worst part had been the guilty expression in his mother's eyes. Seeing it, he knew—this was something his parents had discussed, something they secretly agreed upon. Peter could picture them sitting across from each other over breakfast, lamenting the fact that the wrong son had died.

Peter grabbed a bag from the back of his closet. He started packing it without thinking, just cramming stuff in until the duffel was full. Peter got the bag zipped halfway shut; then it strained and refused to close all the way. He yanked out a few handfuls of clothing and tossed them on the floor, then tugged it closed and pulled it over his shoulder.

He was still wearing his jacket and shoes, since he'd been hustled into the house and hadn't had a chance to take them off. His backpack was downstairs, but it wasn't like he'd need the textbooks; he wasn't planning on going to school tomorrow. Peter patted his pocket, checking for his wallet. Then he swallowed hard and popped open his bedroom window. Even though it was on the second floor of the house, there was a trellis leading down to the backyard. When he was younger and theoretically still had a curfew, he'd used it to sneak out a few times.

This time, he was using it to leave for good. Peter took one final look at his room. Then he eased out onto the ledge and pulled the window shut behind him.

CHAPTER SEVEN

Noa rarely dreamed, but when she did, it was always the same. Smoke and flames. Screaming. Leaves flickering red and orange and the smell of terrible things burning.

She'd been asleep during the accident. The most important thing that had happened in her entire life, and Noa had only regained consciousness halfway through it. Back then she'd been an extraordinarily heavy sleeper. Her father used to tease her about it, called her his little bear because she went into hibernation every night.

They'd been driving home late from vacation. A dark road in Vermont, windy and steep. The last thing she remembered was her mother singing along to the radio, some sappy ballad that had been popular at the time. Noa was snugged into a booster seat in the back, her head drifting back and forth as the car swayed around corners. The whole car danced along the road in time to the rhythm of her mother's voice. Her father chimed in on the chorus, off-key. Her mother sang louder along with him, a laugh in her voice, her hand lightly brushing his shirtsleeve.

It was winter, New Year's Day. Noa had a dim memory of staying up late the night before. A slew of older kids running around, leaving her feeling slightly awestruck. She'd been too young to be included in their games, and too old to play with the babies. That was okay, though. As an only child, she was used to spending a lot of time alone.

She'd overheard puzzling snippets of adult conversation, someone's dad getting a little too loud before being gently ushered from the room. People counting down and cheering and kissing one another. A constant din of conversation rising and swelling around her. Noa sat there for hours, wide-eyed, tired but too exhausted to sleep, until someone noticed and her father lifted her in strong arms to carry her to bed. She let her head fall limp against his shoulder, felt her mother's soft lips brush against her cheek as her eyes drifted shut. That final night she'd slept on a sagging air mattress in a room full of other kids, their breathing soft and irregular around her, the air uncommonly musty, the smell of stale alcohol and dog hair drifting up from the carpet.

Brunch the next day, the adults' voices set on mute, the roar diminished to a grumble. Kids yawned and whined and teased until someone snapped at them to quiet down. They ended up staying late, even though her mother wanted to get on the road. Her father said it was only a few hours' drive, they'd be home in plenty of time, and besides, this way Noa would sleep in the car.

The radio, the song. The sleep. Then the fire.

In the dream, Noa's eyes were fixed on the trees webbed through the shattered moonroof. They throbbed and pulsed, hot and red, in time to her heartbeat. There was a monster in the car, a loud angry one that roared as it devoured. She could hear her mother scream, fighting it. Her father never said a word; he'd already been overcome. Noa couldn't see the monster; her head refused to move. But she listened as it consumed her parents, then came for her. She felt its hot fingers stroking her legs, reaching for her hair, trying to wrap her in a tight embrace. It was like that giant snake that coiled around its victims, then swallowed them whole. The minute she felt that heat reaching for her, she pictured scales and dryness and a massive mouth opening wide . . .

At the last possible moment, Noa was torn from the monster's grasp. She was suddenly thrust out into a sharp cold that was almost as bad as the heat. More shouting and then other hands were on her, frigid ones this time, and she still couldn't see; her eyes were running too wet for her to focus.

Sometimes she made it all the way through the dream, but more often she woke up as the monster loomed above her. Every time, Noa wished she could change it, make it so that she, too, had been consumed. It would have been better for a lot of reasons.

Tonight, though, she woke up as soon as her body landed in the snow. She bolted upright, confused by the strange surroundings and the fact that she was fully dressed. Then she remembered: the operating table, the apartment she'd rented.

She still shivered, despite the fact that she had three wool blankets and a down comforter piled on the bed, and the heat remained on eighty. She got up, keeping one of the blankets wrapped around her shoulders as she turned the dial on the thermostat up even higher. Noa padded to the fridge, but the sandwich looked even less appealing than it had earlier.

The clock on the stove read three a.m. Noa stretched an arm above her head. She'd been asleep for about five hours, but felt as if she'd slept for days. She picked up her laptop and stretched out on the couch. Idly she wondered how Linux was doing. He was a ratty feral cat that had started hanging out on the window ledge outside her apartment shortly after she moved in. Noa figured that the previous tenant must have fed him, because he'd sit there for hours, giving her a reproving look. So she caved and started setting out a bowl of dry food every day. He refused to actually enter the apartment, but would nap there on nice afternoons, paws tucked beneath him. Once he even let her pet him.

Linux was a survivor like her, she reasoned. Despite his scraggly appearance, he probably had a half dozen people in the neighborhood leaving out food for him. She couldn't worry about him right now.

Noa checked her email. Nothing new from Vallas, so he'd either given up or was angry about her slow response. She chewed her lip, debating whether or not to send him an email. She could just give him the other files. But she was worried about what he planned to have /ALLIANCE/ do with them. She needed to find out more first. She'd have to finish going through the folder branded with her name.

Noa opened another document and started skimming it. To keep track, she'd categorized them into subfolders as she identified them—that way she wouldn't end up going through the same material twice. One was labeled "Stats," another "BS" (for the unintelligible doctor's notes), and a third, "Possible." This third category was the most promising. Even so, 99 percent of the contents was scientific jargon that went over her head. But Noa was convinced that if she could decipher enough of it, she'd be able to figure out what was going on. Three documents in, Noa stumbled across a typed summary of some sort of experiment. She couldn't understand everything—it was a quagmire of words like *histopathology*, *encephalopathy*, and *hemizygous and homozygous cervidized*—but the gist was that some sort of operation had been performed. It made reference to other charts and documents, and on the final line, which read, "Results," someone had typed: "Pos/Neg: see note."

Unfortunately the note was apparently in another document. Noa cursed under her breath. She'd copied backups from the AMRF's main server, and they were in a jumble, with no overriding order or organization. The original files and folders were probably arranged in a way that made sense on a separate network.

Noa was skimming a study on "transgenic mice," whatever those were, when an email alert popped up on her sidebar.

She went back to her inbox and frowned: another message from the mysterious A6M0. This time the subject was *GET OUT NOW.*

Noa sat up straight and opened the email, a feeling of dread growing in the pit of her stomach. The single line read: *You're not safe there. Leave now.*

She chewed her lip. Who was sending these? And why were they messing with her like this?

Noa quickly went to the window and pulled aside the curtain, looking down at the street below. It was poorly lit, just a few streetlamps spaced far apart. She couldn't see much in the shadows, but it didn't look like there was anyone out there. She stood there uncertainly, debating. She'd left the messenger bag by the door the night before, packed with everything but her laptop, jacket, shoes, and the clothes she was wearing. Paranoid, but she wanted to be able to leave quickly if necessary. Should she go? It was freezing outside, and she was already cold. This was probably just someone trying to spook her, or even flush her out, forcing her back out on the streets where they had a better shot at finding her.

She decided to ignore the warning and went back to her laptop. But another email had already popped up from the same sender. The subject line was the address for the apartment.

Noa's hands started shaking so hard she could barely center the mouse to click it open. She froze. The body of the message was a jpg of a building at night. In the single lit window, she caught a glimpse of her profile peeking out from behind the curtain.

Someone had taken the photo minutes before when she'd checked the street. Which meant they were right outside.

Noa slammed the laptop shut and skidded across the room, jamming it into the messenger bag. She struggled to pull on her boots—thank God she hadn't gotten the kind that laced up. Tugged on her jacket and did one last check of the room.

As she closed the front door behind her, the elevator bell chimed.

Noa raced for the emergency stairwell at the end of the hall. She heard a shout, and glanced back over her shoulder. No security guards this time, just a bunch of big men dressed in black. She pushed open the door and launched herself down the stairs. She could hear them tearing down the hall after her.

* * *

Peter rang the dorm buzzer again. He'd tried texting and calling Amanda, but she wasn't picking up, even though it wasn't that late. Which made him a little worried—could she still be pissed off about what he'd said earlier?

Peter checked his watch: a little past midnight. It had taken forever to get here without a car. He'd left his Prius at the house, with Bob's speech about how spoiled he was ringing in his ears. *Screw them,* he'd thought—he didn't need any of it. So he'd hiked a few miles to the nearest T station and waited what seemed like forever for a train to arrive. He'd just gotten to the point where he was worried that he'd missed the last train when one pulled into the station. He'd had to change trains twice to get here, each time forced to wait at least a half hour. Now he was exhausted, starving, physically and emotionally drained. It was freezing outside, too. Ice had formed a solid layer over the pavement and wind gusted over it, sending scattered leaves racing across the surface like speed skaters.

Laughter sounded out behind him. Peter turned to see two figures making their way down the path that led to the dorm: a girl and boy, walking together. The walk was slippery, but not so treacherous that the girl needed to clutch the guy's arm the way she was. His head was bent toward her, and he said something. The girl tilted her chin up, laughing in response, and Peter's heart clenched.

It was Amanda.

When they were ten feet away, she saw him. The guy with her looked up, too, then asked, "What is it?"

Amanda murmured something. They paused, then kept walking toward him.

Peter tucked his hands in his pockets. His stomach wound in on itself in a tight gyre as Amanda stopped in front of him.

"Peter," she said. "What are you doing here?"

"I tried calling, but your phone must be off."

"I had study group." Abruptly she took her hand off the guy's arm, as if she'd just noticed it was there.

Peter examined him: six feet tall, black hair, blue eyes, square jaw. Wearing jeans and a toggled wool coat. Standard prom king, the kind of guy who quarterbacked the football team, edited the school paper, and became valedictorian. The exact type Peter had always detested. Reflexively, Peter looked down: leather shoes. How could Amanda like a guy who wore leather shoes? "I'm Peter," he said, jutting out his hand. "Amanda's boyfriend."

"Drew." The guy shook, his smile tight. "I didn't know Amanda had a boyfriend."

They both looked at her. A small part of Peter was happy to see Amanda shift uncomfortably.

"Well, Peter and I are . . ."

"We're what?" Peter demanded when she didn't finish.

"What's in the bag?" she asked, brow furrowing. "Are you going somewhere?"

"It's cold," Drew said. "I should probably get going."

"Good idea," Peter said. "See ya."

Amanda hesitated, then waved her key card over the door. It clicked open, and Peter pulled it wide, holding it open for her. Before walking off, Drew called back over his shoulder, "See you in class, Amanda."

"Sure," she said. "Bye."

She ducked inside and waited for Peter, but wouldn't meet his eyes. In silence, he followed her up a flight of stairs to her dorm room.

Amanda lived in a single suite, which meant that she technically had her own room, but had to go through an outside bedroom to get to it. Mercifully, her roommate, Diem, wasn't there.

"She's been gone all week," Amanda said, passing by the unmade bed. "New boyfriend, I think."

Peter didn't say anything. She walked into her room and flicked on a lamp that was draped with a scarf to mute the light. She sank down on the bed and pulled off her knit Ugg boots. She still hadn't met Peter's eyes.

He dropped the duffel to the floor, but remained standing. It was a small room, rendered smaller by all the decorating she'd done. Amanda had pinned enormous swaths of fabric across the ceiling to hide the ugly tiles, and covered the floor with overlapping woven rugs. The walls were decorated with signs from the various rallies she'd attended over the years: PETA, NOW, Teens in Trouble, GLAAD. Oversized throw pillows dotted the floor, and an orange IKEA butterfly chair sat in a corner. Above her bed hung the standard print of Che Guevara that Peter figured they must hand out to everyone on registration day. The first time he'd visited, he'd jokingly nicknamed it the "über-radical opium den."

Now, instead of feeling colorful and exotic and inviting, the room struck him as claustrophobic. Amanda still hadn't spoken. Finally, he asked, "Are you seeing that guy?"

She shook her head. "We're just friends."

"Yeah? Because it looked like—"

"I said, we're just friends." Amanda pushed off the bed and crossed the room. On top of the built-in vanity she had an electric teakettle. She shook it to see if it was full, then pressed the on button. Without turning around she asked, "Why are you here, Peter?"

"My parents kicked me out."

"What?" She swiveled, her face scrunching up with concern. "Why?"

"I don't know. They got pissed because I was trying to find out more about that thing. You know, what I told you about at brunch today."

Her face had gone blank, and Peter wondered if she'd even been listening that morning. "They kicked you out because someone stole your laptop?"

"He didn't steal it, he just . . . that's not the point."

"What is the point?" She crossed her arms over her chest. "Let me guess: You want to stay here."

"Yeah, I do." His turn to shift. "Why? Isn't that okay?"

"It's just that—" Amanda ran a hand through her wavy hair. "I mean, I've got class early tomorrow."

"So we'll just sleep," Peter said, remembering her expression when she looked up at Drew. *Drew.* He even hated the guy's name.

Amanda stretched her hands up and dropped her head back. "It's fine, whatever," she said. "I'm going to brush my teeth. If you want some tea, help yourself."

She gathered up her shower kit and slipped on a pair of Moroccan slippers, then left the room.

Peter sank down on the bed. Tea was the last thing he wanted. He wasn't sure he could sleep anymore, either, even though he felt completely wiped out. Truth be told, all he wanted was to lie down and start crying, and he hadn't shed a tear in years.

Peter lay back against the pillows and crossed his hands behind his head, staring up at the paisley pattern that billowed slightly in the wind from the heating vent. The whole room smelled vaguely of lavender and patchouli, a scent Peter always associated with Amanda. There was a framed photo on her bedside table. She was a kid in the picture, around twelve years old. An older boy with braces, her brother, Marcus, had an arm wrapped around her shoulders. They both looked healthy and happy. She'd told him once that it was the last good photo she had of her brother. Soon after that Marcus started using, and in later photos you could see him literally wasting away. Then he'd run off and vanished from the family photo albums entirely.

It was a common bond they'd discovered, that they both knew the pain of losing a sibling. Peter wondered if Drew had any idea what that was like. Probably not—he looked like the type of guy whose entire life had been too easy, who'd never lost anything important.

Peter turned on his side to face the wall. When Amanda came back in, he pretended to have already fallen asleep.

Noa raced down the stairs, taking them two at a time. The messenger bag bounced against her side painfully, and there was a throb of protest in her chest—apparently it hadn't healed enough for her to be sprinting. She ignored the pain, panic driving her onward. The stairwell door was thrown open above her, followed by the sound of heavy boots clomping downstairs. No yelling this time, which somehow made her pursuers even more frightening.

The studio apartment was on the fifth floor. Noa had no idea where the emergency stairwell let out, if she'd end up in the lobby or on the street. Or if there'd be anyone else waiting for her down there. It sounded like the men chasing her were gaining. She pushed every thought out of her mind, focusing solely on moving faster. At the bottom of the stairs was a plain wooden door with a paddle handle. She hit it at a dead run and shoved through it . . .

. . . straight into another guy dressed in black. He'd half-turned toward the door as it opened. Right before she crashed into him, his eyes went wide with recognition. Her momentum sent them flying backward through the building lobby. Noa landed hard on top of him, knocking her head against his collarbone.

She fought to disentangle herself during the valuable few seconds before he recovered from the surprise. The guy was looking stupidly at her, wheezing—there'd been a crack; maybe he'd broken a rib when he hit the ground. She leaped to her feet and started running again. The stairwell door slammed open behind her and someone yelled, "Hey!"

She pushed through the front door. The temperature had dropped, and the cold air hit her like a slap. She skidded on a patch of black ice right in front of the building and almost went flying, but her bootheel caught the edge of a sidewalk brick at the last second, stabilizing her.

Noa headed right, toward the nearest corner. She figured her best shot at losing them was in the shadowed side streets. She kept checking for a gap in the buildings, a way to duck into a backyard, but everything was fenced off.

She didn't know this section of Boston well, which was the main reason she'd chosen it, figuring they wouldn't be looking for her here. Cambridge was dominated by the Harvard campus. The small dwellings lining the street mainly housed faculty and students. All the windows were dark and shaded, the streets empty.

Noa cut right up the next street. She could still hear them behind her. She wasn't a fast runner, even when she was in shape. She wouldn't be able to keep up this pace for more than another minute or two. Her lungs felt raw and chafed and the cold air made it worse, like every inhale was a piece of glass slashing at them.

At the next corner, Noa turned right again and came face-to-face with a solid wall of massive brick buildings bridged by a wrought-iron gate: the main entrance to Harvard Yard. It stood open.

She bolted across the street and through the gate. Inside, a concrete path veered left through manicured lawns. More brick buildings loomed out of the darkness. Noa could still hear them chasing her. She tore for the nearest gap between buildings.

It opened out on an enormous grassy quad. Quiet, but there were still lights on in a few of the windows high above. Other paths crossed and intersected the one she was on. She darted across the grass. It was hard beneath her feet, the ground frozen solid. Noa headed for the nearest door. Gave it a tug, but it was locked.

She chanced a glance over her shoulder. Six men were entering the quad. As soon as they spotted her, they started to fan out.

Noa fought back a wave of despair and gritted her teeth. *She was not going to end up back on that table.* She raced along the side of the building.

At the end of it, she broke left. The space between the buildings narrowed. She prayed that she wouldn't end up at a dead end.

Voices up ahead. Noa ran toward them. Emerging in another quad, she saw two people trotting down a long flight of stairs spanning an imposing neoclassical building—the library. Light spilled out of the enormous glass windows lining its facade. Noa made for it. She vaulted up the steps and yanked open the door.

Inside, her boots echoed on marble. She was in a huge lobby, a dome shot up three stories overhead. Slowing, she approached a small round booth with a security guard tucked inside. He was old, white-haired, half-asleep. At the sight of his uniform she initially froze, remembering the guards back at the warehouse complex. But his was dark black, with maroon patches on the upper sleeves. It looked more like a police uniform than anything else. Not that Noa had ever had much luck with cops, either. *But the devil you know . . . ,* she thought to herself.

Beside him was a security gate with a metal detector. He watched blearily as she approached.

"Gotta show your ID," he muttered.

Noa looked back over her shoulder. Through the glass panes in the copper doors, a cluster of faces peered in at her. She turned back to the guard and swallowed hard, trying to get her breath back. "I forgot it."

"Can't let you in without ID," he said decisively, turning back to a small TV. Tinny voices blared from it, the sound of scattered clapping and cheers.

"Please," Noa said, desperation in her voice. "It's important."

"Midterms," he grumbled. "You'd think it was life and death. Why you kids can't just study in your rooms—"

"I think someone's following me," she blurted out.

That piqued his interest. The guard looked up again and said, "Yeah? Like a boyfriend or something?"

"Something," Noa said. She heard the door open behind her and looked back. One of the guys was walking in. Despite his best efforts to look casual, he clearly didn't belong on a college campus.

The security guard followed her gaze, then slowly got to

his feet. "You bothering this girl?"

"No, sir." The guy held up both hands placatingly. His voice was calm and steady, authoritative. He wasn't much taller than her but looked muscular, like a bodybuilder. Hair shorn in a crew cut, a scar that seamed his face along the right side. He appeared unarmed, but there was a clear note of menace in his voice as he shifted his gaze to her and held out a hand. "Noa, you need to come with me."

"You have to let me in," she pleaded, turning back to the guard. "Please."

"What's going on here?" the guard asked, eyes narrowing.

The guy was examining the perimeter of the room—checking for cameras, Noa realized.

That settled it. She dashed past the guard, through the metal detector. It blared in her wake.

"Hey!" the guard called after her.

She ignored him. The alarm faded as Noa turned the corner and found herself facing row after row of books.

She'd never been in a library like this. Before she'd managed to buy her first laptop, she'd used the terminals at the small library a few blocks away from The Center. But that was a tiny facility, just an open room with a few terminals tucked in the corner.

In comparison, this library was overwhelming. She froze momentarily. It wasn't what she'd expected. The shelves were metal, almost clinical looking. Each row stretched a hundred feet into the distance, and there were at least a dozen of them lined up like dominoes. She trotted down a few rows. Halfway down the aisle, she spotted a small metal staircase that ascended to the next floor.

Noa heard footsteps behind her—more than one person from the sound of it. She darted toward the staircase. Her boots made a hollow clanging sound as she bolted up the stairs, but there was no helping it. They'd probably seen where she was headed, anyway.

The staircase opened onto another long series of stacks. Behind her, another staircase led up, identical to the one she'd just climbed. Without stopping to think about it, she mounted that one, too. She went up two more floors, each time encountering another set of stacks, another staircase. Noa wondered how many floors there were. She couldn't keep going up forever; at some point she'd have to find a place to hide.

Abruptly, the alarm downstairs fell silent.

Noa stopped on the next floor and made her way through the aisles of books, emerging in a corridor. Dimly lit, carpeted. Dark oil paintings of old white men glowered down at her. At hip level, standing glass display cases held ancient-looking books.

A few doors led off the hall, but they were all dark. Noa tried the handle of the nearest one: locked. She moved along, trying each door. She couldn't hear anyone behind her, but that didn't mean anything. Maybe the guard had managed to stop them. Or they figured she was trapped, and were waiting outside for her.

They might be right. She had no idea if there was another way out of the building.

Her messenger bag felt heavy, but she didn't dare drop it. She wouldn't survive if she only had the clothes on her back to work with. She needed the laptop.

The knob on the tenth door she tried was unlocked.

Noa opened it and ducked inside. Another long hallway lined with doors. The lighting was brighter, the doors narrower and less official looking. She made her way down the row. All of these were locked, too. The hallway hooked right, revealing another short corridor, more doors. Then it ended. Noa went all the way down to check, but that was it. She'd hit a dead end.

She slumped against the wall. Her breathing was still ragged, and everything hurt. She should have bought sneakers; these boots were killing her feet and she could feel the beginnings of blisters on her heels. Not that any of that would matter if she was captured again.

A familiar sound. Noa tilted her head to the side: Someone close by was tapping away at a keyboard. Halfway down the row, a slit of light crept from beneath the doorframe.

Noa hesitated, but decided she had nothing to lose. She walked over and raised her hand, then lightly rapped on the door.

The typing stopped, then a male voice said, "Tonight's my night, Caleb. What time is it, anyway . . ."

"It's not Caleb," Noa said, her voice barely above a whisper.

She stepped back as the door snapped open. Standing there was a college kid, tall and thin with longish blond hair, green eyes, and glasses. A scraggly goatee clung to his chin. He wore a T-shirt, jeans, and white socks without shoes. At the sight of her, he looked puzzled. "Uh, hi," he finally said. "Are you locked out of your carrel?"

"No," Noa said. "Can I come in?"

"I'm kind of . . . working in here." He gestured weakly behind himself. It was a tiny room, roughly the size of a large storage closet. A small wooden desk was built into one side; the opposite wall held a bookcase. There were open books and papers scattered everywhere, including the floor.

Noa quickly stepped forward, backing him into the

room. She spoke in a low, urgent voice, saying, "I just need one minute."

"One minute for what?" He appeared even more confused as she shut the door. "Did Caleb put you—"

"Shh!" Noa said. She'd heard another door opening at the far end of the hall—the one she came in through. She made sure the lock on the study carrel door was pushed in, then reached up and flicked off the light.

"Hey! This is really—"

"Please be quiet!" Noa begged. She found his arm in the dark and squeezed it. He made a small noise, but didn't say anything else.

Footsteps down the hall. A heavy tread, moving slowly. At the sound of a click, Noa caught her breath: He was doing the same thing she had, trying all the doors. A pause, another click. Then another.

It was a tiny space; they were inches apart. The college guy's breath reeked of pizza. He seemed to sense the danger, or at least he'd decided to trust her enough to stop talking. They stood in silence as the footsteps came closer.

Noa couldn't help it; she jumped when their doorknob clicked. She squeezed her eyes shut, praying that the lock worked, that he couldn't hear them breathing. An eternity seemed to pass before the footsteps moved on to the next door down. Five more, and they stopped entirely.

Noa felt the guy shift beside her. Heard an intake of breath, like he was getting ready to speak. She reached up and found his mouth through the gloom, then clasped her hand over it. His lips felt dry and warm.

The footsteps started up again, the stride more purposeful this time. They passed the door. After they turned the corner, the sound started to fade. The main door squeaked open again, then closed with a bang.

Noa realized she'd been holding her breath. She released it and dropped her hand.

The light flicked on, and the guy glared down at her. "Who the hell are you?"

"Thank you," Noa managed, suddenly completely spent. She dropped into the chair in front of the desk.

"Are you okay?" he asked, sounding concerned.

"Fine." Noa was suddenly extraordinarily thirsty. "You don't have any water in here, do you?"

"Um, yeah." A backpack hung from a hook mounted on the back of the door. He unzipped it and dug around, producing a small water bottle. "It's new," he said, handing it to her.

Gratefully, Noa opened it, chugging the entire bottle as he watched. "Thanks."

"Wow, you were thirsty." He tucked his hands in his pockets and leaned back against the door. "So who was that out there?"

"I don't know," Noa admitted. "Some guy."

"Yeah? You should report him; campus security is pretty good about stuff like that. You a freshman?"

Noa nodded.

"Which dorm? Because, I mean . . ." His gaze shifted to the floor. "I was just about done here, anyway. I could walk you back."

Noa pictured the slew of armed men waiting for her outside the building. "Is there another way out? I mean, aside from the main entrance?"

"Haven't spent much time in Widener, huh?" He chuckled. "Yeah, I didn't make it to the library much my first year, either. I don't mind walking you out, though. I mean, he probably won't bother—"

"He will," Noa said, cutting him off. "Trust me."

"Okay. If you're that worried about it, we can call campus security and arrange for an escort."

Noa didn't hold out much hope that an elderly security guard like the one downstairs would have a shot against the guys after her, either. "That's okay," she said. "I have to get some work done first, and . . . my roommate is trying to sleep," she finished weakly.

"I hear you," he nodded. "Midterms are brutal. Well . . ." He surveyed the piles of paper everywhere dubiously. "You could stay here, if you want. Just make sure the door is locked when you're done. And try not to mess with anything. I know it looks chaotic, but there's a crazy order to it, I swear." He grinned sheepishly at her. "What's your name, anyway?"

"Nora." She held out a hand.

He shook it and said, "Hi, Nora. I'm Otis. Always happy to help a damsel in distress."

Noa flushed. She'd definitely never been called a damsel before. "Thanks again."

"No problem." Otis rubbed the back of his neck with one hand. "I'm so beat I can hardly see straight. So I'm not, like, imagining all this, am I?"

"Hard to say," Noa said. "Maybe."

"Funny." He laughed again. "All right, then, damsel figment. Have a good night."

"You too." Noa watched as he pulled on a North Face parka and lifted the backpack off the hook. Before the door closed behind him, she said, "Thanks so much again, Otis. Really."

"Sure." He gave a little wave and left.

Noa sighed and slumped down in the chair. She wished she had another bottle of water; she was still dying of thirst.

There were probably water fountains somewhere on this floor, but she didn't dare leave the room.

She weighed her options. The guys chasing her were annoyingly persistent, and they seemed to know what they were doing. Noa had the feeling they wouldn't just give up after a few hours. For whatever reason, they appeared determined to capture her again.

She wondered what the scar-faced guy had told the guard downstairs. Fortunately this was a mammoth building; they probably wouldn't be able to search all of it. She could wait until morning, then try to sneak out when there were lots of students around. But what was to stop them from following her, then grabbing her at the first opportunity?

She needed a better plan.

Noa dug out her laptop. Breaking into Harvard's main server turned out to be child's play— *They really should work on that,* she thought. She went back to her email. The message from A6M0 was still at the top. She glanced at the clock: It was hard to believe that only forty-five minutes had passed since she read it.

Pensively, Noa examined the photo of herself at the window. Whoever sent the message didn't seem to be working with the guys chasing her; otherwise why would he have warned her? If she'd still been in the apartment when they showed up, there was no way she would have escaped. So either two different groups were after her, or this was something else.

She hesitated. Her pursuers already knew she was in the building. Even if they managed to track her computer again, aside from actually going room to room, they wouldn't be able to narrow her location down any further than a block radius—that was how IP geolocation worked.

In which case, she didn't have anything to lose.

Noa sent a chat request to A6M0.

After a minute, a box popped open.

Glad you got away.

Who is this?

A friend.

Noa stared at the screen. She didn't really have any friends. There had never been a reason to form bonds with people who would shortly get shipped off to another foster home. When she was younger, and had first plummeted into the system, she'd made an effort a few times. But Noa had learned quickly that it was a pointless exercise. Most of her so-called "friends" ended up betraying her, anyway.

Noa typed:

What do you want from me?

Just to help.

Prove it.

How?

Get me out of here.

A few minutes passed. Noa waited, impatient. Finally, a message appeared.

Hold tight. Working on it.

She tapped a finger against the desk while she waited. The fatigue had passed and she felt wired again, like she'd just had a double shot of espresso.

Shortly before four a.m., Noa heard sirens outside. She froze. Had she unwittingly called on the wrong person for help?

A message popped up:

Leave in two minutes. Down the hall on the left, there's a staircase. Take it two floors down. There's a bridge to the library next door. Go there and take the stairs to the roof.

There was a link to a .pdf file. Noa clicked on it and a floor plan materialized. Bold print at the top read: WIDENER LIBRARY. A shaky path dotted with periodic arrows was traced on it, basically following the same directions she'd just been given.

Noa chewed her lip uncertainly. Maybe she should just crash here tonight. No one could pinpoint exactly where in the building she was, and it would give her a few hours to figure out how to escape undetected. Contacting A6M0 might have been a mistake. For all she knew, she was being led straight into another trap.

Trust me.

Why should I? Noa typed in response.

A longer pause, then the words *Tanto Barf* appeared.

Noa started. It was an oblique reference, one that only kids who'd been exposed to what The Center charitably called "dinner" would know. Tanto Barf was traditionally the worst meal on the menu every month, a disgusting mass of glutinous turkey and lumpy potatoes smothered with a sauce that tasted like paste. Years ago, some kid had nicknamed it "Tanto Barf," and the moniker stuck.

So her new pen pal had done a stint in The Center. In and of itself that wasn't reason enough to believe him. But at the moment, she was low on people to trust. And from the sound of it, there were cops outside. Had A6M0 called them out, or was that thanks to campus security?

What's up with the sirens?

Cops—I figured they'd clear the building and give you a chance to get away. The guys chasing you pulled back, but they're still watching the exits. You need to go wait on the roof.

Then what? Noa typed. Being stranded on the roof when it was freezing outside didn't seem like much of a plan.

You'll see, it said. *Now go!*

Noa took a deep breath. She didn't have a lot of options, and her gut insisted that staying here would be a mistake. She had no idea if Otis had even made it out of the building—they might be questioning everyone who tried to leave. And who knew what sort of story they'd spun about her. There could be a cadre of armed men headed toward her right now.

Deciding, Noa shoved the laptop back in her bag and slung it over her shoulder. She carefully eased open the door and peeked down the corridor—no one in sight. She made her way down the hall, moving as quietly as possible.

The main hall appeared clear, although she could hear voices on the floors below and the sound of tramping feet. Quickly, she hurried down the hall toward the stairwell indicated on the floor plan. Noa ran down two flights and found herself facing a long, narrow causeway. It was all windows and rounded on top, like something in an aquarium.

No one in sight on the other side, but while running along it, she would be horribly exposed. Anyone outside would be able to see her.

She crossed as quickly as possible. It ended in another corridor. *Apparently college was just one big oak-paneled, carpeted maze,* she thought, trotting past yet another series of paintings featuring grim old men.

She found the utility access stairwell indicated on the map and climbed up one flight. The door at the top opened directly onto the roof. Noa stepped out into the cold and immediately started shivering. If anything, the interior of the libraries had been too warm, the heating system pumped into overdrive.

In contrast to the brick facade, the rooftop appeared

jarringly modern, covered in an industrial light gray sheath that shimmered in the dark. Mechanical ventilators and fans poked out of it like bizarre metal flowers. On the far side, a solar panel array tilted up at a jaunty angle.

She couldn't see any way down.

Noa went to the edge. The library she'd just come from was several stories taller; it loomed over this one. Still, she was three stories off the ground. There was no visible fire escape running along the outside, no other stairwell. She was trapped.

She dug out her laptop and dropped into a squat. The light from the screen seemed too bright, like a spotlight illuminating her, but it couldn't be helped. She got back online and sent a message: *Now what?*

Climb down.

Noa frowned. Heights were never her thing. She tentatively went to the edge again and looked over. At the top of every window was a narrow marble ledge that looked just wide enough for her feet. But it was at least eight feet from the top of one down to the next, with little to hold on to. Spiderman couldn't make that descent.

She went back to the computer and typed, *No f'n way.*

Far side, by the solar panels.

Noa clamped her jaw to keep her teeth from chattering and pulled on her jacket hood. She went to the other end of the roof, carrying the laptop with her.

She peered over the edge. There was a single-story drop to a lower roof. Two more stories to the ground from there, but tall trees buttressed either side. Some of the branches looked like they'd be within reach once she got down there.

Noa tucked her computer back in her bag and made sure the strap was as tight as she could get it, pressed right up against her body. She slung one leg at a time over the ledge, then grasped the cold marble lip with her fingers and lowered her body down.

Her feet dangled five feet from the next roof. Noa took a deep breath and let go.

The impact shot from the soles of her feet up into her shins and she couldn't help crying out. Noa fell to the side, wincing, clutching at her right foot—it felt like the jolt might have reopened the cut on her heel. It took a second to catch her breath. She rolled her ankles: Nothing appeared broken or sprained, which, under the circumstances, was a minor miracle. Her messenger bag had hit the rooftop hard, too, she realized. Hopefully her laptop wasn't damaged.

No time to check, though. Noa got up and limped to the nearest tree branch. It appeared thick enough to hold her weight. It was hard to see in the dark, but below she could make out more branches spaced at regular intervals along the trunk.

She scanned the ground and ticked off a few minutes in her head. The tree was on the periphery of another quad. Impressive brick buildings of various heights and shapes huddled protectively around it. The campus appeared quiet, no sign of movement. The sirens were gone. Noa forced herself to focus. Waiting would only give her muscles a chance to stiffen up, which would make the descent harder.

No choice, Noa reminded herself. And whatever the doctors in those files had planned for her would invariably be worse.

She took a deep breath, grabbed hold of the branch with both hands, and wrapped her legs around it. Noa shimmied along until she reached the trunk, the bark rough and scratchy against her palms. She didn't allow herself to look down. A few of the smaller branches jutting out from the main one scratched her face, but she barely felt them. A tremor coursed through her whole body; it took everything she had not to give in to the fear.

It took ages to climb down. Noa nearly lost her grip a few times. She'd catch hold at the last moment, clutching the branch with her whole body, panting hard from exertion and fear.

The final branch was the worst. The darkness threw off her depth perception, so it was impossible to gauge how big of a drop it was to the ground. She couldn't even tell if it was cement below her, or grass. Noa hung suspended for a long moment, paralyzed by the enormous risk she ran by staying there, but terrified to let go. . . .

She landed on spongy grass. This time it didn't hurt quite as much, maybe because it was a softer surface, or she'd done a better job of tucking and rolling. She lay there for a minute, half expecting men to materialize from the darkness, swarming and carrying her away.

But nothing happened. She took a deep breath and got up. Sticking to the shadows, Noa made her way across the quad and back to the city streets.

CHAPTER EIGHT

Peter couldn't sleep. Which was rare—he'd always been able to just shut his eyes, drift off, and wake up eight hours later, pretty much to the minute.

But he'd lain awake for hours staring at Amanda's ceiling. They were crammed side by side in her twin bed. She was on the outside, facing away from him. Usually she intertwined her feet with his and pressed her back up against him. He'd wrap an arm around her and fall asleep with stray lavender-scented hairs tickling his nose. But tonight, despite the narrow mattress, there were a few inches of space separating them. If she had thicker rugs, he would have offered to sleep on the floor.

He couldn't stop picturing the expression on Amanda's face when she looked up at the prom king, aka Drew. She used to look at him like that, not so long ago.

They'd first met at a mixer. Because all of the local private schools were so small, they pooled resources for the big dances. Thank God, because Peter's graduating class was only seventy kids, and they were one of the larger preps. It would have been depressing to go to a homecoming dance with a grand total of twenty couples.

The Winter Ball was always held at a hotel downtown. The decorations were the same every year: small white lights strung around fake ficus trees, cardboard snowflakes dangling from the ceiling, a DJ spinning decades-old music in the corner. Lame, but then that's how high school dances were supposed to be: Half the fun came from mocking them. Mackenzie Sullivan was his date. They were going more as friends than anything else, although he knew she secretly liked him. Peter figured maybe they'd get drunk, head to Donny Laurelli's after-party, and make out a little.

Then he saw Amanda across the room. Almost all of the girls were wearing red, white, or black puffy satin prom gowns. But Amanda had on a light purple dress that hit just below her knee, with a scoop neck and spaghetti straps—fancy and sophisticated, but not showy. Her dark blond hair had been curled into ringlets and she was wearing black stockings and high heels. She looked bored.

In a sea of high-school girls who were all minor variations on one another, she practically glowed. For the first time in his life, Peter was dumbstruck. It took five whole minutes to get up the courage to approach her. Which was completely insane. He'd always been lucky with girls; he was commonly known as "the easiest guy to talk to."

And yet once Peter got over to her, he couldn't think of anything to say.

She finally noticed him and turned. Peter felt self-conscious. He was wearing a dark suit and black shoes. But instead of the standard shirt and tie, underneath he had on a fake tuxedo T-shirt that he'd found at a thrift store. It was meant to be ironic, but when he saw her raised eyebrow he wondered if it came across as juvenile and stupid.

"Hey," Peter finally managed.

"Hey." She took a sip of punch and looked away from him, back out to the dance floor. Everyone was bopping along halfheartedly, like they refused to commit to dancing when the song sucked. Peter wished he'd thought to grab a cup of punch; his throat was suddenly unbearably dry.

"I'm Peter."

"Amanda."

She kept scanning the room, not even looking at him, which was unnerving. Usually the situation was reversed.

"So where do you go to school?" he finally managed.

"Brookline Girls."

"Yeah? That's all girls, right?"

She threw him a glance and said slowly, "That's why they call it Brookline Girls."

"Sure, I knew that," Peter mumbled. He was suddenly hyperconscious of how his hands hung by his sides. He jammed them in his pockets and asked, "So you have to wear uniforms there?"

"Yes," she said after a minute.

"That sucks. I go to Country Day. Coed, no uniforms."

"Mm-hm." Amanda was craning her head now, actively looking for someone else to talk to.

Peter realized he was crashing and burning. It was star-tling, unprecedented. He glanced around to see if anyone he knew had taken note. Stumbling over the words, he asked,

"Are you going to any of the after-parties?"

"Probably not."

"Why not?"

She shrugged. "Not really my scene. Besides, I have to get up early tomorrow."

"Yeah? Why?"

"I volunteer."

"Oh." Peter realized he was nodding excessively, like some kind of idiot. "Well, they don't start that late. I mean, this dance sucks worst than last year, so people will probably take off soon."

"It is pretty lame," Amanda admitted, taking another sip of punch. "I missed it last year."

"The deejay was better. I mean, he still sucked, but less badly."

They stood next to each other for a minute. Peter searched desperately for something else to say. Then her face lit up, and she waved at someone across the room. "Nice talking to you," she tossed back before walking off.

Dumbfounded, Peter watched her leave. She joined a small knot of girls and launched into conversation. She was animated, using her arms to talk, throwing her head back to laugh. The complete antithesis of the girl he'd just spoken with, like someone had inserted a quarter and she came to life. Peter wondered if she was talking about him—but a minute passed, and none of the other girls so much as glanced in his direction. Somehow that made it even worse, like Amanda had forgotten all about him before getting halfway across the room.

He sulked for the rest of the night, to the point where Mackenzie got annoyed and left the after-party in a huff with one of her friends. Peter felt a little bad about that, but couldn't summon the effort to text an apology. He ended up getting hammered and crashing out on Donnie's couch.

He started frequenting common Brookline Girls' hangouts, looking for Amanda, but came up empty.

Then one day in early spring, Peter ran smack into some sort of parade as he was coming out of the Apple store. He was trying to cross the street to get to the parking lot, cursing the fact that his car would be blocked in until the crush of people dissipated.

Peter was so focused on forging his way through that he didn't even see her. He looked down when a hand grasped his elbow, braced to tell someone off. Instead, he found himself inches away from the girl from the dance. This time, she was smiling.

"Hey," Amanda said, leaning in close so he could hear her.

Peter was flustered to see her again, but quickly recovered and said, "Hey."

"Not a lot of guys come to this sort of thing. Good for you." She was carrying a placard. Printed in large letters was NOW, with NATIONAL ORGANIZATION FOR WOMEN in smaller type below it.

"Yeah, well . . . I'm a big believer in the cause," he said.

"That's great." She linked arms with him and said, "Let's hurry, I don't want to miss the first speaker."

Months later, when they were officially a couple, Peter confessed that he hadn't originally been there for the rally. Amanda laughed and teased that he got her to date him under false pretenses. It had become something of a joke between them.

It was hard to believe that was only a year and a half ago.

He listened to the sound of her breathing. He couldn't

tell if she was really sleeping, or just lying there quietly.

"Amanda?" he finally whispered.

"Mm?"

"You awake?"

"I am now." She sounded annoyed. "I have class early tomorrow, Peter."

"I know. I think we need to talk, though."

She didn't answer. He felt her go rigid beside him, her breath rising and falling less steadily.

"What's going on, Amanda?"

"I told you, we're just friends."

"It looked like more than friends."

"It's not."

"So we're still together, then?"

A long beat.

After a minute, he said, "I can't believe you're dumping me for someone like that."

"Like what?" She turned over and leaned on her elbow, her face slit by light from a gap in the venetian blinds. Reprovingly, she said, "You don't even know him."

"Sure I do. He's Mr. Perfect. Probably on student council, sings a capella, rows crew. We used to laugh at guys like that."

She didn't answer, and he knew he'd hit a mark. Peter laughed. "No way. Does he really sing?"

"He's prelaw," she said defensively. "He wants to become a community organizer, start working for change at a grass-roots level. You and he actually have a lot more in common than you'd think."

"Yeah? Like what?"

Amanda paused, like she knew that what she was about to say was wrong. She went ahead and said it anyway. "His sister died of PEMA, too."

The silence was different this time. Peter felt like he couldn't breathe, as if his rib cage had shrunk around his lungs, rolling them into a tight ball and forcing the air out of them.

"Peter . . ." she said.

Ignoring her, he got out of bed and started pulling on his pants.

"It's the middle of the night," she protested. "Where are you going?"

Angrily, Peter tugged a sweater over his T-shirt. He dug around the pile of clothes draped over the chair, trying to find his fleece by feel in the dark. He felt her eyes on him, but she didn't say anything else.

"I really loved you, Amanda," he finally said.

"I loved—"

"Don't. Just don't." Peter slipped on his sneakers without lacing them and slung his duffel over his shoulder. Without looking back, he stormed out of the room.

It was just before dawn when Noa finally reached her spot. It was a place she'd discovered years earlier, the second or third time she'd run away from The Center.

The Long Wharf Marriott was quiet this time of morning. The front doors slid apart silently. Noa kept her head down as she cruised past the yawning clerk at the desk. He eyed her, but went back to his newspaper when she made a beeline for the elevators.

That was the trick she'd discovered with hotels—if you looked presentable and acted like you belonged there, they wouldn't kick you out. The only time it hadn't worked was when she came in sporting a black eye, courtesy of her new bunkmate at The Center.

But usually, she skated past. Of course, getting into a room could be tricky, especially at this hour. The maids' carts weren't roaming the halls yet, with master keys tucked among rolls of toilet paper. Once Noa had gotten into a fancy suite that way, two enormous rooms and a mammoth bathroom all to herself until the locks were changed at eleven a.m. She'd taken a bath, stayed up late watching pay-per-view movies, gorged on everything in the minibar.

She'd tried a few other hotels, but the Marriott was her mainstay, where she consistently got lucky. Plus on a previous foray, Noa had found a place where she could hunker down and not be bothered for at least a few hours. It wouldn't be easy to sleep, but thankfully after everything that had happened she still felt wired. And she should be able to get online there. She wanted to get back in contact with A6M0. Clearly he or she knew what was going on, and Noa was getting tired of the coyness.

She got off the elevator on the top floor and went down the hall. In the alcove past the ice machine was a battered metal door. She tried the handle: It turned. Noa heaved a sigh of relief.

She'd discovered on an earlier visit that this particular room was usually unlocked. It was tiny and windowless. A linoleum floor that didn't get cleaned as often as it should, a rickety table, three chairs, and a trash can. Some sort of employee break room, either too out of the way or so relentlessly grim that it was rarely used. Noa could care less. It was quiet, warm, and safe—and no one would be looking for her here.

Noa sat down and plugged in her laptop. She generally preferred to let the battery run all the way down initially, but given the uncertain circumstances and lack of easy

access to power outlets, she figured it was better to keep the charge up.

She could have cried when the screen jumped to life—thank God it hadn't been damaged by the drop from the tree.

The chat window was still open to where she'd left it on the roof of the library. Noa had a flashback to rough bark tearing at her hands, cold air snaking through the gaps in her clothing. She shuddered.

Still, she'd gotten away. And without A6M0's help, she probably wouldn't have. So that was something.

She logged back in and sent a single word: *Thanks.*

A few minutes passed before her computer beeped. *u r welcome* popped on-screen.

Why r u helping me? Noa typed.

It's complicated. Glad u got away, tho.

Why is all this happening?

A link popped up—the same one as before, to the shampoo site.

I don't get it, Noa wrote.

U will.

And A6M0 logged off.

Noa stared at the screen. She debated trying to trace her guardian angel's steps back through the internet, but sensed it would probably be a wasted effort. Anyone who remotely found a way out of that library was probably a hacker to be reckoned with. And besides, it seemed kind of rude. He or she had saved her, after all.

Noa propped her feet on the edge of the chair, hugging her knees to her chest. She should keep digging through the files, but she really wasn't in the mood. She was too tired to sleep, and probably wouldn't be able to in such a bright

room, anyway—that was the one drawback of this space: There was no way to turn the lights off.

So there wasn't much for her to do. The MailPlus where she maintained a PO Box was in Brookline, about a half hour away on the T. They opened at eight thirty, and she planned on casing the place for at least an hour before attempting to access her PO Box. Which gave her about three hours to kill.

Noa went back to her inbox. Apparently Vallas had given up; there weren't any new emails from him. Aside from his and the ones from A6M0, everything else was work-related or spam. This time, that fact gave her a little pang. If she had died on that table, no one would probably have noticed.

Which might, she suddenly realized, *have been the point.*

As kids got older, they ended up at The Center less and less frequently. Either they landed in juvie, or ran away for good and lived on the streets. Noa had recognized a few of them, begging on the T. She knew they probably remembered her, too, but they never acknowledged one another. One of those things that was universally understood but never discussed.

Noa had found a way out of the system. And she'd been living off the grid, largely invisible, for nearly a year.

But as far as Child Services was concerned, she was a foster kid with a history of running away—not a rarity at her age.

Maybe she'd been taken because they knew no one would notice or care that she was gone.

Were runaways even noted somehow by the system? Noa had hacked into the Children's and Family Services database before, to change the paperwork when she was establishing her fake foster family. She also dutifully provided quarterly reports on successful home visits. Social workers tended to burn out quickly—since landing in the foster-care system at the age of six, Noa had been assigned to more than a dozen of them. Wards were frequently shuffled between them, and they were hopelessly overworked. Noa was fairly certain none of them had caught wind of anything strange going on with her case.

But she'd caught someone's attention. And there had been hundreds of files in the AMRF database. Maybe she hadn't been their only guinea pig.

Within a half hour, she was perusing the virtual version of her case file. There was a long procession of foster families listed on one page. All were memorable in their own way, though few of those memories were positive. Two stints in juvie: one a few weeks long, the other a few months.

But none of that was what she was looking for. Noa moved the cursor, scanning down. There it was, three forms in: a line halfway down the page, beside the address and contact information for the family she lived with for a month when she was fourteen. Across the page, scrawled in the margin, were the words *Ran away.*

Which wasn't entirely true, Noa thought. Sure, she'd run away, but only because her new "dad" had been chasing her with a lit cigarette.

She'd ended up in the Marriott break room that time, too. Then wandered the city for a bit until she'd linked up with a group of teens living under the highway overpass by a skate park. On her third night with them, one of the skater boys tried to rape her. She fought him off, ran into the street, and was almost sideswiped by a cop car. And just because she'd managed to break the kid's arm in the struggle, she landed in juvenile detention for three weeks.

At least they'd sent her back to The Center after that. Noa had figured out how to survive there by the time she was eight, right around when she stopped getting excited about visiting day for prospective families. By then, the concept of finding foster parents who were interested in more than the grand a month that came with her had been relegated to the same category as Santa Claus and the Easter Bunny.

But The Center was perpetually in need of open bunks, so they always ended up forcing Noa somewhere else. If she hadn't been so good with computers, she'd probably still be shuttling back and forth. Or worse.

Noa dropped her chin to her knees. She'd definitely been the exception to the rule. By the time most foster kids reached her age, they'd either found a family tolerable enough to stay with until they hit eighteen, or they lived on the streets permanently.

She tried to recall the names of the ones who dropped off the grid: Dulcie Patrick, who took off shortly after her fifteenth birthday. Jenny Fulton, her bunkmate for nearly a year when she was twelve. Randy Quinn, one of the kids she'd seen begging on the T. One by one Noa looked up their CFS files: In each case, "ran away" was checked off in a special box at the bottom of the page. Noa found it depressing that runaways were common enough to merit a standard box on the form.

Then, nothing. Of course, it wasn't like there were any resources to look for them.

Noa recalled the rows of warehouses she'd run past. Had other kids been laid out on tables inside? The thought was terrifying.

Vallas's flash drive still jutted out of her USB port. She'd separated out the folder with her name at the top, but there had been hundreds of others. She'd mainly been interested in finding out what had been done to her, so she'd shifted those to the side. Now Noa started perusing the rest of what she'd downloaded.

Many folders had oblique titles: more science stuff, probably. She clicked on a few that were labeled with names, but they turned out to be more scanned-in, incoherently scrawled doctors' notes.

Halfway down the page, a name jumped out at her. *Alex Herbruck.*

She remembered Alex. An Irish kid with brownish-red hair, green eyes, skin mottled by freckles and pimples in roughly equal proportions. A Southie who compensated for his small stature with an attitude of sheer ferocity. Their stints at The Center had overlapped a few times. They'd always gotten along okay. He tried to kiss her once, but when she shoved him away he didn't take it personally, just half-heartedly called her a lesbo and moved on to Dulcie Patrick.

She'd liked Alex, at least as much as she'd liked anyone there. Noa opened the folder and discovered a similar jumble of files. She clicked a few buttons, grouping them by file type so that there would be some sort of organization as she combed through them.

Right away, a series of jpegs jumped out at her. That was odd. Her file had only had one, of her lying on the table looking dead.

She clicked, and a photo filled the screen.

It was definitely Alex. And he was definitely dead. His eyes were closed but his lips hung open and loose, paleness setting his freckles in stark relief. He looked even smaller than she remembered; it seemed like the table was swallowing him.

But that wasn't the worst part. His chest had been peeled open, each side stretched out by some sort of metal clamp. The exposed interior was bright red like the rind of a fruit. On the right side the rib cage had been cut away, revealing a glimpse of charred lung. Alex had been a chain-smoker; she remembered him puffing away when they were ten or eleven years old. Once they'd caught him stealing packs out of the janitor's locker and he'd almost been sent to juvie for a few days.

Noa clicked on the tab to close the picture. Her right hand was shaking so badly she had to clasp it with her left to steady it. Even though her screen had reverted to the default version of the night sky, she could still see the image of Alex there, like it had been engraved in permanent pixels.

She scrolled down the list of folders, zeroing in on names. None of the rest sounded familiar, but she kept scrolling down . . . down . . . down, for what seemed like pages and pages.

After fifty names, Noa stopped counting and sat back in the chair. Was it possible that there had been that many of them? And were they all dead?

There was only way to find out. She steeled herself, went back to the top of the page, and opened the first folder.

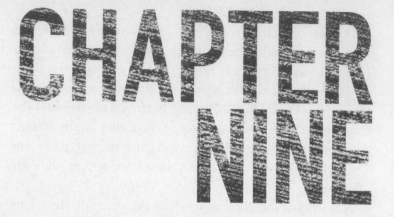

CHAPTER NINE

Peter sat before a terminal in the Tufts computer lab. Fortunately security was lax here. He'd hovered by the door for less than five minutes before another student came by and waved their ID card in front of the access panel.

He held a hand to his mouth, stifling a yawn. He'd barely slept last night. Luckily it was midterms, so the Tufts library had been open when he stumbled out of Amanda's dorm. He curled up in an oversized reading chair tucked in the corner and tried to sleep, but every half hour or so jolted awake. He had gritty eyes and a terrible taste in his mouth. He'd tried to clean up in the men's bathroom by the periodicals room, but still. Storming out of Amanda's room had probably been a mistake.

Not that he would have been able to sleep there, either, he reminded himself. Peter rolled his head from side to side, then cracked his knuckles in succession, right hand, then left, before settling back to work.

He'd learned his lesson about trying to access AMRF's files; he definitely wasn't in the mood for another visit from Mason. But that didn't mean he was going to just lie down and take it, either. /ALLIANCE/ was still down, along with the backup wiki. So he was cruising the chat forums and imageboards frequented by his minions. There were numerous new threads posted on all of them, variations on the theme, "WTF happened to /ALLIANCE/?"

He logged into the most popular one under his handle, Vallas. It took ten minutes to compose a call to arms. Part of him wished he had more information to give them, or at least a better sense of what he was getting them into. The last thing he wanted was to put any of his fellow hackers in Mason's crosshairs.

But it was unlikely that a single corporation would be able to retaliate against the sheer number of hackers he was amassing. Peter planned on posting the same message across more than a dozen boards, accessed by thousands of members of the hacker community.

Still no word from Rain when he checked his email, which worried him. She hadn't struck him as a con artist—if anything, over the past few months she'd been one of the most reliable and steadfast members of /ALLIANCE/. What he'd told Amanda about the honor code was no exaggeration: Hackers helped one another whenever they could, and a strike against one was generally taken as an affront to all.

Consequently, Peter had gone from wondering if Rain had robbed him to concern that while digging around on his behalf, she might have fallen victim to Mason and his goon squad. After a moment's thought, he shot off another email to her, just the question *u ok?* in the subject heading. Peter blew out a breath of air, thinking. He had no other way of tracking her down. He'd just have to hope that wherever Rain was, she was all right.

Feeling slightly better, Peter turned back to the post he was composing. He should have done this in the first place, he thought with a grimace, but he'd been worried about the fallout for his parents. Well, now he didn't have anything left to lose.

Peter finished typing the post and hit send, then sat back to watch the reaction. What he'd written was simple and to the point:

> *Attention /ALLIANCE/ questers: We are under attack!*
> *Someone stole our domain name and took down our site and*
> *backup wiki. They're striking at our core, trying to scatter us.*
> *But we will not be overcome! Time to strike back. Cover your*
> *tracks and stay groovy and I'll see you on the other side . . .*
> *Vallas.*

Within a minute, the thread started going nuts with people railing about how this was a typical attempt by "the man" to exert control over the internet with Orwellian big-brother tactics, others raging about free speech, still more spewing vitriol about what the bastards deserved to have done to them. The handles ticked by quickly, comments posting so fast he had to start scrolling almost immediately.

Peter skimmed the tirades. Smiling, he posted the same message on every other wiki, forum, and imageboard he could think of. Not that he needed to bother—it had probably already gone viral, shooting across cyberspace, passed along like a virtual baton. And the people he really wanted to reach wouldn't bother posting a diatribe. They would have understood the subtext of what he'd written, and were probably already gathering.

"Cover your tracks and stay groovy" was a code that any regular /ALLIANCE/ user would recognize. But Mason would probably take it at face value, assuming that a punk kid was laughably throwing around military jargon.

At least that's what Peter was hoping.

He logged into The Quad and started a thread under the heading, "CYTASG." Then he waited.

Within minutes, users began flooding the room. He waited until a few dozen were present and accounted for, then typed in, *Thanks 4 coming.*

This totally sux, man, wrote Loki.

Peter recognized that handle—Loki had helped with most of the /ALLIANCE/ operations over the past year. *I know.*

So what do we do? asked Moogie.

Peter had been thinking this over. He wanted to carpet bomb the bastards, but he also was dying to know what they were up to. *I want to go full Anon/HBGary on them.*

There was a brief pause.

Moogie typed, *Dude, seriously? Brick them?*

Grab data first, but yeah.

Silence.

Bricking, or "phlashing," was serious. The goal was to damage a system so badly that it couldn't be accessed until its hardware was replaced. And replacing hardware was insanely expensive and incredibly time-consuming. Getting information off the server first was trickier, but it had been done before.

If they succeeded, the servers involved would be rendered completely useless, effectively turned into bricks. And if there weren't backups stored elsewhere, the company could lose everything.

So any hesitation to participate in such an attack was understandable. The whole point of /ALLIANCE/ was to act within the boundaries of the law—Peter had enforced that rule from the get-go. Bricking a server was, technically, a violation of the Internet Architecture Board's proper-use policy. It was also illegal in most countries.

Not totally cool with that, typed Ariel.

I get that, Peter wrote. *Won't hold it against anyone who doesn't want in, you're all still welcome to be part of /ALLIANCE/ when it's up and running again. But trust me, these are some seriously bad guys.*

I'm in, Loki said.

Me 2, wrote Moogie.

One by one, users either signed on to the raid, or checked out of the chat room. Fewer left than Peter had been expecting; he had mixed feelings about that. Based on what little he'd told them, if he'd been on the other side of things, he probably would have been among the first to log off.

By and large, the longest-running members of his ad hoc community remained, those stalwarts who'd played critical roles in all of /ALLIANCE/'s previous missions.

Honestly, it was a little touching. Especially considering the magnitude of what he was asking.

Loki typed in, *How do u want it to go down?*

Internet vigilantism was a wonderful thing, Peter reflected as he laid out his plan.

Noa sat in a corner of the café sipping coffee. Her hair was tucked into the black cap from the boat, and she wore a pair of oversized sunglasses that she'd bought for five bucks from a street vendor. Not the best disguise, but she was at a table in the back that was partially concealed by a sickly palm tree. It afforded a good view of the MailPlus entrance and stores on either side of it, but she wasn't easily visible from the street.

She'd been here nearly an hour. Her coffee was long cold, but she still took tiny sips of it. She'd gulped down about a gallon of water already, too, repeatedly refilling her glass from the free jug on the counter until the server gave her a funny look. Noa was dying of thirst, but still not hungry. She'd tried to choke down a banana and a muffin, with little success. Which was starting to bother her. It was strange not ever feeling hungry. Stranger still was that even when she tried, she couldn't force food down her throat.

Stress, she told herself. *Just too much stress. Nothing to worry about.*

A MailPlus employee had appeared at 8:23 a.m. She was in her sixties, heavyset, hair a few shades too blond, eyeglasses dangling from a long beaded chain. She unlocked the doors, then trundled around and rebolted them behind her. No one Noa recognized, which might pose a problem.

Noa watched the woman walk around the store turning on lights and powering up copy machines. At precisely eight thirty a.m. she unlocked the front door, then went to stand behind the main counter.

A model employee, from the look of things. Also not a good sign.

Noa spent another half hour sitting there watching a steady procession of people enter MailPlus. None of them lingered, and no one looked blatantly out of place. Either they went to a machine and made a few copies, headed toward the back where the mailboxes were, or approached the counter. After a few minutes, they concluded their business and left.

Noa got up and returned to the counter. Ignoring glares from the girl working the register, she filled her water glass again and carried it back to the table.

This spot offered a good vantage point of a large swath of the street. The parked cars on either side of the block were empty, and the spaces turned over steadily; not a single vehicle had stayed more than twenty minutes. It was also seriously cold outside, so Noa had a hard time believing someone would be hanging around out there. Maybe she'd finally caught a break and the coast was clear. They might still be combing through the Harvard library for her.

Still she hesitated, last night's pursuit fresh in her mind. Whoever was after her had invested a lot of time and resources into tracking her down; that was clear. And if they'd found her in the temporary Cambridge apartment, they probably knew all about her PO Box. They'd assume that eventually she'd need access to cash, and would be forced to come here to claim it.

And they were right. She really needed to get in there. What the past few days had made alarmingly clear was that there were some things the internet couldn't provide. Noa was kicking herself for not stashing a cash reserve somewhere.

Right now, across the street in box number 460907, there should be an envelope containing a new bank card. Getting her hands on that envelope was key to getting her life back. With it, Noa could withdraw enough cash to buy a fake ID. There might even be a check waiting, from her last freelance job for Rocket Science. She could deposit it in a new account, under a new name. Find a short-term sublet on Craigslist that accepted cash, somewhere to hole up safely while she unraveled what had happened to her.

But no matter what, she had to get into that box.

The bells dangling from the café door jingled, catching Noa's attention. So far there had only been three other visitors to the café, all stroller-pushing moms who ordered lattes to go.

A guy walked in wearing a wool suit and overcoat. Hair going gray at the temples, muscular build—decent looking for an older guy. Panning down to his shoes, Noa frowned. He was wearing combat boots. Even though the dark sky promised rain, the boots definitely didn't go with the suit. And now that she looked more closely, he seemed uncomfortable in it, arms shifting like he was trying to make room in the sleeves.

The guy scanned the room, eyes glancing off Noa. Had they hesitated before continuing on to the girl behind the counter?

Maybe she was being paranoid, but it felt like a weird tense energy had overtaken the room. Like something really, really bad was about to happen.

The counter girl perked up at the sight of him. She flipped back stringy hennaed hair and smiled broadly at the guy, leaning on her elbows so that her V-neck sweater gaped open as she purred, "Can I get you something?"

Noa's instincts were blaring, and she decided to listen to them. She casually closed her laptop and unplugged it, winding the cord around before tucking it into her messenger bag. The whole time she tracked the guy out of the corner of her eye. He placed both hands on top of the counter and matched the girl's smile. His own was dazzling, teeth almost too white. "I'd love a coffee."

"What kind?" The girl bent over farther, exposing a sliver of pink bra. "I've got French roast, espresso, and our daily blend, which is, like, totally awesome."

"French roast, please. Black."

He turned away from the counter, gazing out at the street.

But Noa couldn't shake the sense that his focus was actually homed in on her.

She got up and went to the door. As she shoved it open, the counter girl said, "Hey, don't forget your coffee!"

Noa broke into a jog. Footsteps behind her. She chanced a glance back. The guy had left the café and was following her, walking briskly with a determined expression on his face. His lips were moving, and Noa noted the Bluetooth device jutting out of his ear. She scanned the street and saw another guy step out of a doorway in the building next to MailPlus. They could have been clones, both oversized guys in ill-fitting suits and combat boots. Trying to blend in and failing.

When Noa hit the corner, she broke into a run. She was annoyed with herself for not choosing a better spot to stake out the MailPlus. Annoyed, too, that she hadn't waited at least a day before going there. No helping that now, though. And she really had needed that bank card.

On the plus side, it seemed like there were only two guys chasing her. And this time she'd had the forethought to map escape routes.

She was heading for the closest one now. As opposed to Cambridge, Brookline was an area she knew well. Her longest stint with a foster family had been here—six whole months with a Harvard sociology professor and his wife. The Pratts were earnest people who'd made it clear that taking her in was their way of giving back to society. Their own kids were already in college, and as they repeatedly explained they considered it selfish to occupy such a large house alone when they could share it with someone less fortunate. Apparently they'd almost taken in foster kids earlier, but were afraid of the "negative impact" it might have on their "real" children.

The Pratts were prone to lecturing Noa about social injustice, and how the system failed kids like her. A familiar refrain was that if only more sane people adopted older kids out of foster care, a whole host of social ills would be resolved, from drug abuse to homelessness to crime.

Whenever they started to pontificate like that, Noa had to bite her tongue. Because, yeah, she was all for having normal people take in foster kids like her. The system sucked. It had definitely failed her and every other kid she'd encountered at The Center.

What was interesting, though, was that when she tried to join the discussion, sharing specific instances of terrible things that had befallen her over the years, the Pratts shut down. Noa quickly realized that they weren't really interested in her personally—more as the embodiment of an idea. They preferred to appreciate what she'd been through in the abstract; the concrete details were too frightening.

Four months in, however, the Pratts broached the possibility of adopting her. Noa was wary. They were kind of weird, but on the plus side never hit her or burned her with cigarettes or refused to feed her. Riding out a few more years with them made sense. They'd even offered to pay for college if she wanted to go.

Unfortunately, a month after they discussed adoption, Mrs. Pratt caught her husband straddling one of his teaching assistants. Their marriage exploded, and Noa was quickly swept back to The Center.

Which was a shame, because despite the fact that they were kind of snooty and full of themselves, she'd liked them. They'd also inadvertently provided a key out of the revolving door she'd become stuck in by offering unlimited access to a computer.

And Noa had gotten to know Brookline like the back of her hand. Which was one of the main reasons she'd rented a PO Box there. It was an easy T ride, located halfway between the two places where she spent the bulk of her time: her apartment in Newton Centre and the Apple store. She usually only checked her snail mail once or twice a week, anyway.

Noa raced down the block past nail salons, restaurants, and bookstores. She didn't dare look back to see how close the suits were. The line of shops became staggered the farther she got from the café, until they dissipated entirely into tiny homes.

Half a block to go. Noa left the sidewalk, cutting across a baseball field. The rain that had been lurking in heavy gray clouds all morning started to fall uncertainly, like it wasn't 100 percent ready to commit and would settle for a drizzle.

At the far end of the field, Noa locked in on her target: An enormous brick building with white stone columns that shot up four stories at the entrance and a flight of stairs that widened at the bottom like a grin.

Noa pounded across the street without checking for traffic. Heard a screech of tires, but kept going. She dashed up the flight of stairs, heart pounding, heels aching as they slapped concrete. Right outside the front doors, she paused long enough to see the guy from the café circling around a car that had stopped dead to avoid hitting her. He didn't look calm anymore; sweat poured down his face. His buddy was right behind him.

Noa raced inside. The atrium was similar to the library from last night—that's actually what gave her the idea to come here. This was one place where an adult who didn't belong would stick out like a sore thumb, and where she was familiar with every exit, entrance, and hidden corner.

Brookline High School.

She'd spent five months as a sophomore here. The Pratts had gone on about how lucky she was to be at one of the best public schools in the entire country. Noa hadn't really cared for much besides the computer lab, though. That had been impressive. The PTA had sprung for all new equipment the previous year, and for the first time in her life she had access to something besides clunky decades-old library terminals. She'd first learned Linux here, and basic programming with Python. Noa had spent hours after school exploring the internet, until one night she stumbled on a hacker site and something just clicked.

She tore past the security guard parked in a chair by the door. He looked up, but didn't seem fazed. Just another kid late for school.

She wondered how he'd handle the guys who were about to charge in behind her.

One thing had been made clear during opening assembly on her first day of school: The principal took the safety and well-being of her students very seriously. And unlike a lot of other public schools, BHS could afford a full-time security team.

Noa didn't need the guards to actually stop the guys, though—just to stall them.

A yelp behind her. The two guys must have come in.

Noa skidded into a hallway and dashed toward the nearest stairwell, her boots squeaking against linoleum polished to a high gleam. Lockers lined either side, broken up periodically by bulletin boards and classroom doors.

The hallway even smelled familiar, a mix of science-class formaldehyde, burnt dust from the woodshop, and commingled cafeteria meat all overlaid by pheromones. Noa experienced an unexpected pang of nostalgia.

She bolted up the stairs three at a time.

Unfortunately, she could still hear the guys behind her. Noa bit her lip—this had to work, she was counting on it. She yanked open the door at the top of the stairs and entered another hallway identical to the one downstairs. Class was in session; the hall was empty. Halfway down it, Noa heard the stairwell door open behind her.

What was taking so long? She felt a twinge of annoyance with the principal, and with herself for believing her. Maybe she should have followed Plan B and headed for the nearest T stop. Or her absolute fallback, Plan C—going to the nearest police station.

As she was thinking it, something hit her hard from behind.

Noa kept flying forward, but her feet were knocked out from under her. She landed hard, pinned beneath the guy from the café. Her head knocked against the floor and for a second she saw stars.

Café guy's face was bright red and he was panting. "Got you," he gasped.

His friend stood behind him, grinning. Café guy slowly got up, keeping his hand wrapped around her upper arm. He jerked Noa painfully to her feet, wrenching her arm hard and twisting it behind her back. "Make a noise," he said, "and I swear to God I'll kill you."

"Hey," the other guy said, "remember—"

"Yeah, well, they didn't have to chase this little bitch down," café guy said. "Now let's get the hell out of here."

They started down the hall. Noa felt tears welling up. She fought them back down. It was bad enough they'd caught her again; she wouldn't give them the benefit of seeing her cry, too.

And then, the alarm started to blare. Two shorts and a long, two shorts and a long. Not a standard fire drill. Noa broke into a grin.

The two guys froze, looking at each other. "C'mon," the guy holding her arm said, hurrying her toward the stairwell.

"It's a campus breach," she said calmly. "No one in or out until the cops come."

"What?" Café guy tightened his grip and Noa winced, almost crying out.

"They've gone into lockdown mode. They know you're here," she explained. "Next comes SWAT. After all the school shootings, they don't take any chances."

The other guy cursed under his breath. Noa felt eyes watching them, and turned her head. A teacher was peering through the small window in her classroom door. She held a cell phone to her ear and her lips were moving rapidly.

"We have to get out of here," café guy muttered, looking around wildly.

"Hey!" A male teacher emerged from a classroom down the hall, and Noa's heart sank. She tried to mentally will him away. "Let her go!"

The guys holding her didn't seem to know how to react. "It's okay, sir," café guy called out.

"It doesn't look okay." The teacher jabbed a finger at them, like they were misbehaving and he was about to assign detention. Noa recognized him as her former chemistry teacher, Mr. Gannon. She couldn't tell if he remembered her—it didn't seem like it; all his attention was focused on the men holding her. "Just let her go. You do that, they'll go easier on you."

Noa could sense them wavering, trying to decide what to do next. Café guy's eyes were darting around, like he suddenly realized that even though the hall was empty, there were eyes at every door, a whole slew of witnesses. They both seemed to be waiting for someone to tell them what to do.

Noa felt the grip on her arm ease slightly. "She's not a student here, sir," café guy said. "She's our responsibility."

Mr. Gannon's eyes narrowed. "Bullshit. Now let her go."

Another door opened. Apparently emboldened by Gannon's stance, a chubby man with a thick mustache who Noa recognized as the Spanish teacher stepped into the hall. Then another door opened. This time a middle-aged woman in a tweed skirt stepped out. Determinedly she held up a cell phone and said, "I'm recording this! Let her go now!"

"Just relax . . ." Café guy looked lost. He edged backward a step.

Noa wrenched away from him. Her arm twisted painfully in its socket, but slipped free. Without pausing she dashed down the hall past Mr. Gannon. Kept going until she'd almost reached the next stairwell.

"In here!" someone shouted.

Noa turned. The last door on her left was open, and a young, pretty teacher was frantically waving her in. Noa pivoted quickly and darted inside. The door slammed behind her, bolt turned. As she stood there panting, the sound of something scraping, orders being given. A hand on her shoulder.

Noa turned and found the pretty teacher looking up at her. She was blond, probably not much older than her. She looked absolutely terrified. "Are you okay? Did they hurt you?" Her voice was high-pitched, strained. Like she was trying really hard not to scream.

"I'm fine," Noa said. They'd blockaded the door with two desks set on top of each other.

The teacher followed her eyes to the ad-hoc barricade. She wrung her hands and said, "I think that will hold them. The doors are strong; they had them replaced a few years ago. And the police will be here soon, don't you think?"

There was a group of about twenty students clustered at the far end of the room away from the door. It was the health ed classroom; the walls were papered with enormous diagrams of human reproductive systems.

"Sure," Noa said. "It'll be fine."

She could feel the weight of the other kids' eyes on her, and heard them whispering.

The teacher cleared her throat, sounding slightly calmer as she said, "Why don't you go stand with the other students. I'll just call in and see if . . . well, I'll call."

Noa obediently went to the back of the room as the teacher fumbled with the phone mounted on the wall by the pencil sharpener. It took three tries for her to dial the number with trembling fingers; then she spoke in a low, urgent voice.

"I remember you."

Noa turned.

The words had been spoken by a small brunette wearing glasses with thick black rims, multicolored stockings, and a rainbow skirt. She looked vaguely familiar, but Noa couldn't place her.

"Art class sophomore year," the girl explained.

"Right," Noa said, still not remembering.

The other students remained silent.

"You kind of sucked at art," the girl said. "But you were good at computers."

"Yeah," Noa said. "I hated art."

"I thought you dropped out." The girl's eyes shifted away.

"You just, like, never came back."

"Well." Noa looked toward the door. "I'm back now."

A knock at the door. No one spoke. The teacher looked ready to dissolve in tears.

"Brookline PD!" a voice on the other side shouted. "You okay in there?"

"We're fine," the teacher called back, relief flooding her voice. "But . . . how do I know it's the police?"

"Come see for yourself, miss."

Tentatively, the teacher went to the door. She bent over, peering between the legs of the desk to see out the little window. "Oh, thank God!" She whipped around and said, "Help me move these desks so they can get in!"

Five minutes later, Noa was filing out of the building in a sea of high-school students. Everyone was extraordinarily subdued, although a wave of chatter murmured through. Rumors flew about why the alarm had sounded, and whether or not classes would be canceled for the rest of the day.

The police had established a perimeter around the school. On the other side of it, a crowd composed predominantly of terrified-looking parents had gathered. The students were herded onto the baseball field. Most immediately broke off into clusters, or started to search the crowd for their parents.

Noa stayed with them until she reached a copse of trees at the edge of the field. She scanned the scene, but no one seemed to be paying any attention to her. The girl in the glasses and tights was weeping on the shoulder of a woman wearing a voluminous dress.

Noa hurried to the sidewalk and turned left, headed toward the T green line. Every half block or so she turned, but couldn't spot anyone following her.

As she walked, Noa tried to figure out where to go next.

They'd managed to cut off access to her cash, which was a serious problem. But there was someone who might be able to help.

If he wasn't too angry with her.

To guard against another surprise visit from Mason, Peter stayed on the move. He was making a circuit of the campus computer labs scattered around town. It took some time to get from MIT to Harvard to BC, but at this hour all the buildings were open and no one blinked when he sauntered in and sat down at a terminal.

Not that Peter was actively involved in what was happening now; he'd need some serious processing strength for that, and most of these computers fell short. But he definitely didn't want to miss seeing the raid unfold.

He checked on AMRF's website a few times and was pleased to note that it was becoming progressively sluggish. By his third stop, the Boston College computer lab, the site failed entirely—there was simply nothing left.

Peter glanced at his watch—the entire dismantling of what appeared to be an airtight system had taken under three hours. He was duly impressed by the skill set of his /ALLIANCE/ minions.

Peter had taken the precaution of setting up a separate data account on an overseas network. Logging in, he saw that Loki was already uploading files. He'd volunteered to lead the assault once Peter explained that he wouldn't have the tools required at his disposal. Peter sent him an IM invite.

Everything cool? he asked.

Loki responded immediately: *Harder than I thought, but yeah. Revised HBGary model worked like a charm. Sent a list of all companies affiliated with the AMRF domain—brace yourself,*

*there's a lot of them. It'll take some time to upload data, there's
a ton of gigs here. You got enough space?*

Yeah. Thanks for this.

No worries. Let's not make a habit of it.

Gotcha. Later.

Peter watched the database fill. *Sixty gigs and counting—
holy crap,* he thought. Loki wasn't kidding; this was a massive
amount of data. What the hell could it be? Was this all related
to Project Persephone, or something else? What was AMRF
actually doing?

Peter quickly realized he might need to set up a separate
account on another server to hold all the data. He fervently
hoped that AMRF hadn't sufficiently backed up, and would
lose everything. He wished he could be there to see Mason's
face when he found out what happened. He'd kicked the
hornet's nest, that's for sure.

And the way they'd gone about it was fairly ingenious. Of
course, they were just replicating a raid that had been done
last year. Part of him couldn't believe it had actually still
worked. In the wake of the HBGary fiasco, you'd think that
every company on the planet would have taken stricter security measures.

When Peter discovered during his probes of the firewall
that the AMRF site used a third-party CMS, it gave him an
idea.

There was an international online community that
went by the name "Anonymous," a wink to comments
posted anonymously on blogs and in chat rooms. Although
it wasn't an official "group," per se; more of a loose coalition that operated almost like sleeper cells.

Anonymous members had claimed responsibility for all
sorts of hacktivist raids, from defacing the Australian prime

minister's website after he advocated internet censorship, to assaults on credit card websites after they blocked donations to WikiLeaks.

But their HBGary raid had really impressed Peter. A year earlier, the head of HBGary, a major computer security firm, threatened to reveal the identities of Anonymous members. Before he could, Anonymous members hacked into the company's servers and publicly posted in-house emails, destroyed stored data, and defaced the website.

They made it clear that they'd only assaulted HBGary because they felt backed into a corner. Peter was fascinated by what they'd done, and read up on all their other hack-tivism. A lot of it was amateur stuff, simple software programs that knocked a company's website offline.

But the HBGary security breach was something else. Hack masters used sophisticated techniques to infiltrate a company that claimed to be the leader in airtight computer security systems. Reading about it had inspired Peter to start /ALLIANCE/.

Peter had always suspected that Loki might have been a major player in Anonymous. Aside from Rain, he was clearly one of the most talented /ALLIANCE/ hackers. The fact that he'd stepped up to the plate to defend the group meant a lot. In some ways, it was the nicest thing anyone had ever done for him.

Peter was feeling pretty good. With the help of his min-ions, he'd struck back at a group of bullies who'd hassled him, taken his personal property, and systematically dis-mantled his brainchild.

But the good feeling evaporated as Peter pondered what to do next. He briefly felt a pang of sadness, thinking about his parents. But he wasn't the one who had invited armed goons into their lives. He had to figure out what AMRF was all about, and how his family was involved. And for that, he needed a safe place to comb through all this data.

The great thing about bricking AMRF's system was that with any luck, Peter had also thrown a wrench into how they'd been tracking him in the first place. Even if they managed to get everything back online, it would take at least a few hours, maybe even days. It largely depended on how proficient their IT team was.

He couldn't start digging through the files until they finished uploading, unfortunately—and that was going slowly. Peter's legs jiggled, and his stomach growled so loudly the girl sitting at the next terminal threw him a grin. He hadn't eaten yet today, he realized.

Of course, after what happened with Amanda, he wasn't very hungry. A twinge at that—he couldn't stop picturing the way she'd looked up at that guy last night, the coldness in her voice when she spoke to him. He couldn't believe that her feelings had shifted so quickly. In retrospect, though, maybe they hadn't. He couldn't honestly remember the last time she'd sounded excited when he called, or lit up when he met her for a date. Maybe he just hadn't been paying close enough attention.

Peter shoved it out of his mind. The /ALLIANCE/ assault had succeeded, and he'd struck back at the people who had been messing with his life the past two days. Right now, that was what counted. The rest he'd figure out later.

Idly, he went back to his email in-box. At the sight of Amanda's name, his heart leaped and he raced to open it. She might have forgotten that his phone got taken, and woke up feeling awful about the night before. Maybe she'd been trying to get in touch with him all day. Maybe it wasn't really over.

When he saw what she'd written, it was a gut punch. Just two sentences that read: *Your parents called and left a weird message on my voice mail. They want you to call them back right away.*

Peter sat back and read it again. He hadn't even realized that his parents had Amanda's cell number. He went from feeling hurt to pissed off. That's all she had to say? A year and a half together, and she hadn't even signed it.

Screw her, he thought, angrily closing it out. Another email suddenly appeared: He frowned when he saw the address. It was from Rain.

Similarly terse, this one read: *Need to meet and talk.*

He hesitated. Rain hadn't logged into the CYTASG chat room, which had given him another twinge of concern. No word from her for over a day now. Yet right after the raid, she rematerialized. Could he trust her? Maybe she'd been in league with Mason all along.

Peter decided that as long as he was careful, he didn't have anything to lose by meeting her in person. Hopefully Loki had managed to get everything off AMRF's servers before inducing the crash, but maybe she'd found something. If Rain had hopped the firewall, that meant she'd already had some time with the data.

Either way, he had to admit he was curious.

Sure. Where? he wrote back.

She responded almost immediately. Peter smiled at the meet spot—it was perfect.

See you there.

Amanda pushed through the doors into the waiting area of the Runaway Coalition. She nearly groaned out loud when she saw it was full. *Crap,* she thought. *Doctor day.* She'd completely forgotten about it. A local MD came once a month to provide free care to the teens who visited the center. It was the one time they were always swamped. The patients suffered a wide range of illnesses, from the common cold to drug withdrawal to PEMA. And most were filthy from living on the streets—the Coalition had a locker room with showers, but most didn't take advantage of it. Amanda always figured they didn't see any point in getting clean when they'd wind up dirty again in a few days.

Still, they came. And the Coalition provided a safe haven, even if only for a few hours each day. *Perfect,* Amanda thought. The one time she could have used a light day.

Of course, it was a volunteer position. After a sleepless night, the other community service people would have called in sick. But Amanda took these hours as seriously as a job. The thought of how much her brother could have used a resource like this steeled her. She'd grit her teeth and get through it, despite her exhaustion.

As Amanda made her way through the throng, she kept her eyes on the ground—she'd learned long ago to ignore the occasional comments and catcalls. She'd been coming here since she was just fifteen years old. The place had terrified her then, a fact that she'd admitted to no one, especially her folks. Most of the kids looked years older than their age. They were universally dark and grimy, covered with piercings and tattoos. Some were already missing teeth, their cheeks carved out by hunger and addiction. It had taken a long time for her to feel comfortable here.

Mrs. Latimar was in her usual spot behind the plateglass window that separated the waiting room from the office. She was in her midsixties—a strong, brusque woman who served as the heart and soul of the Coalition. Rumor had it that she'd lost her daughter to the streets ages ago, and formed the

Coalition to serve as a productive outlet for her grief. Amanda completely related to that—when she found out what had happened to her brother, she couldn't stop blaming all the faceless people who could have helped him, and didn't. The knowledge that they shared the same sort of loss had always made her feel close to Mrs. Latimar. Plus Amanda was the stalwart, well into her third year, while most volunteers only lasted a few months. Mrs. Latimar had even hinted that at some point, she might be able to find money in the budget to pay her. Which was nice, but not necessary. She'd come even if they charged her for the privilege.

"Morning, dear," Mrs. Latimar said, breaking into a smile at the sight of her. She smoothed her hand over her no-nonsense ponytail. The Coalition's office was tiny, two desks squeezed in between the filing cabinets. She watched Amanda unwrap the scarf from around her throat. "You look tired today. Everything all right?"

"Fine. I stayed up late studying for midterms," Amanda said, avoiding her eyes. Despite the amount of time they'd spent together, she and Mrs. Latimar hadn't ever discussed their personal lives, and she wasn't about to start now.

"Well, I wish I could say it was going to be an easy day, but . . ." Mrs. Latimar jerked her head toward the window. "We've got an even bigger turnout than usual."

"That's great," Amanda said, trying to muster some enthusiasm into her voice. "Want me to get started with them?"

"They've already gotten their numbers," Mrs. Latimar said, putting on her bifocals, which were dangling from a handwoven loop around her neck, and redirecting her attention to the stack of papers in front of her. "You can take the first one back now."

Amanda nodded and obediently went out front, calling out, "Number one?"

A scrawny kid in an oversized sweatshirt pushed off the arms of a vinyl chair and shuffled after her down the hallway. Each kid got approximately ten minutes with the doctor, more only if they were truly ill and needed to be referred out. It was her job to keep everything running smoothly so that everyone got a chance to be seen.

In the interim, Amanda filed, answered the phones, and did whatever other busywork needed doing. Fairly brainless work, thankfully, so the fact that she could barely keep her eyes open hardly mattered.

She was sitting at the desk, doodling aimlessly on a pad of paper, when a voice hissed, "Hey!"

Amanda looked up to find a young girl, probably no more than fourteen, facing her. Her head barely cleared the top of the windowsill. She was tiny, birdlike, with a sharp nose and chin and eyes set too close together. She wore a thin Windbreaker that was worn through at the elbows.

"Yes?" Amanda asked politely.

"I want to report a missing person," the girl said, keeping her voice low. Her eyes darted from side to side, as if she was terrified of being overheard.

"I'm sorry, we don't really do that here," Amanda apologized. "But we have a contact with the police—"

"No police!" the girl snapped. "And don't tell her, either."

"You mean Mrs. Latimar?" Amanda asked, puzzled. If anything, the woman would go above and beyond the call of duty to help a kid in distress. She'd left the office a minute ago to grab more medical supplies from their cabinet. "But—"

"His name is Rob Garcia, but everyone calls him Tito,"

the girl continued. "He's been gone a week."

The girl appeared genuinely concerned. Amanda bit her lower lip, wondering how to respond. Maybe the girl hadn't been on the streets long enough to know that disappearances were endemic among runaways, especially at this time of year, with the cold Boston winter coming on. A lot of them hitched a ride south, or west. Some went home to their families. Others ended up the victims of a violent crime, or succumbed to the cold or an overdose. "I'm so sorry," she finally said. "I'm just not sure there's anything I can do."

"Tito wouldn't have left without me," the girl said ferociously, as if guessing what Amanda was thinking. "They took him. I know they did."

"Who took him?"

The sound of footsteps echoed from down the hall. Amanda turned in her chair—Mrs. Latimar reappeared, blocking most of the office doorway. When Amanda turned back, the girl was gone. Amanda stood and scanned the waiting room to make sure, but there was no sign of her, and the outside door was slowly swinging closed.

"Everything all right?" Mrs. Latimar asked, sounding concerned.

"I—" Amanda started. But something made her hesitate. There had been genuine terror in the girl's eyes. And for some reason, she hadn't trusted Mrs. Latimar enough to ask about her friend while she was there.

"Everything is fine," Amanda said, forcing a smile. "I'll get the next patient."

CHAPTER TEN

Noa shuffled uneasily by the enlarged map outside American Eagle. She hated malls on principle, and rarely entered them. But when she'd fished around for a safe place to meet Vallas, the Shops at Prudential Center seemed ideal. Lots of people around, and way too many exits and entrances to cover. It was a massive building that sprawled over a few city blocks and was linked by glass passageways to another mall, hotels, and the convention center. It would be an easy place to get out of quickly.

She still had reservations. After all, Vallas had claimed that armed guys were harassing him, too. For all she knew, he'd show up with a half dozen of them, or his email wasn't well protected and they'd be waiting for both of them. Anything was possible; that had been made plain over the past few days.

But this was the guy who set up /ALLIANCE/, Noa reminded herself. He had to have enough skills to shield his email account. And at the moment, she was fresh out of options. She had less than fifty dollars left to her name, no way to access the cash in her bank account, and no one else to turn to. Things were truly grim—and she of all people should know. She was an expert on how many grim situations life had to offer.

Noa glanced around. He was late, which annoyed her. She'd gotten there early and staked out a spot a floor above where they were supposed to meet, by the escalator. The freestanding tower in front of her had a map of the entire mall on one side, and of the surrounding buildings on the other. It was a good place to hang out without looking conspicuous. Plus she could monitor the foot traffic on the lower floors.

So far, so good. No sign of goons in suits and combat boots. She wondered what had happened to the two at the high school. Hopefully they were spending the day trying to explain themselves to a bunch of cops.

Rooting for the police was an odd position to find herself in. Noa allowed herself a small smile.

"Hey."

Surprised, she spun around. Vallas was standing there grinning lopsidedly at her. He looked more disheveled than he had the other night, and there were circles under his eyes like he hadn't been sleeping. "How did you . . ."

"I came in through Copley. Just wanted to make sure . . . I don't know." He shrugged and ran a hand through his brown hair. A lock of it flopped right back in his eyes. "Anyway, I like this look better."

Vallas gestured to her outfit. In spite of herself, Noa

flushed. She'd forgotten how she must have looked when they met at Back Bay Station, wearing those baggy sweat clothes and reeking of fish guts. Not that she probably smelled any better now. She'd had a shower at the studio apartment in Cambridge, but even though that was less than twenty-four hours ago, it seemed like ages. Ever since then she'd been running around and climbing down trees, so she probably still stank. Self-consciously, she crossed her arms and clutched her elbows. "I need some help."

Vallas barked a laugh. "Join the club." He glanced around, then leaned in and said, "I think we're cool for now, but I'd feel better if we went somewhere else."

"Sure," Noa said, realizing he was right. A steady stream of people was coming up the escalator, and they were right out in the open. "This way."

He hesitated, but fell in step beside her. Silently, Noa led the way to the food court. She'd already scoped out the best position, close to the Hynes Convention Center doors and behind a pillar. Luckily, most of the tables were empty. It was only eleven thirty a.m., still early for most of the shoppers to be having lunch.

He pulled out a chair across from her and sat down. After brushing a stray fry off the shiny silver tabletop, he leaned forward on his elbows, intently locking eyes with her. "My real name's Peter, by the way."

"Noa," she responded without thinking. *Crap.* She always told strangers her name was Nora, since it was much more common. What was wrong with her?

"Noa. That's nice; I like it. Rain works, too, though."

Noa shook her head, annoyed. "We don't have time for this."

He grinned. "I know. Crazy couple of days, right?"

"Did those guys show up again?" she asked, curious.

He nodded. "Yup. Got me at the library when I was trying to blow through their firewall."

"You tried to do that on a library computer?" Noa's nose wrinkled. "Seriously?"

"I didn't have a choice," he said, raising an eyebrow. "The person I paid to do it blew me off."

Noa examined her hands. "I had a good reason."

"Yeah? I'd love to hear it. 'Cause if you weren't going to help, you shouldn't have taken my money." He looked genuinely peeved, and Noa felt a twinge of annoyance.

"You have no idea what's been going on," she said fiercely.

"Nope, that's true. But if you think you're the only one having a crappy couple of days, you're wrong." Peter sounded equally ticked off.

Noa sat back and considered him. He met her gaze levelly. When she didn't say anything for a minute, he raised both hands as if surrendering and said, "All right, I'll start. I've got some jerk after me who walks around with a team of armed guys and somehow knows my parents. And every time I sniff around that AMRF site, he shows up and threatens me."

He hesitated, like he was going to say more, but instead pointed at her. "Your turn. What do you need help with?"

"I've got guys after me, too," she said.

"Yeah? The same ones, you think?"

Noa chewed her lip, debating how much to tell him. Finally she said, "I think so."

"Huh." Peter ran a hand through his hair again. *Flop,* Noa thought as it dropped back in place. "That's not my fault, is it? Because if they're after you because of me, I'm really sorry. I didn't mean—"

"That's not why," Noa interrupted. "They were already after me."

"Oh, okay." His lips pursed. "That's kind of random, isn't it?"

"Really random."

"So what should we do?" he asked.

Noa shrugged. "I need more cash."

"More? What happened to the money I gave you?"

"It's gone," she said.

"What did you spend it on?" His eyes narrowed.

"Not drugs," she said. "I'm not a goddamn junkie."

"Jeez, I never said you were." He sat back and eyed the rest of the food court. "I don't know. I mean, I can get another five hundred dollars, but that's my daily limit. And hell, I might need cash, too. I can't go home."

"Why not?"

He shrugged. "Just can't."

Noa ran some calculations in her head, then frowned. A decent new ID would run at least five hundred. "That won't be enough."

Peter laughed again. "Man, you're demanding. How much do you want?"

"A thousand."

"Seriously?"

"I can pay you back," she insisted. "Soon."

"Sure, soon." He shook his head. "Even if I wanted to give it to you, I don't know if I could."

"Okay, then." Noa got up and started to walk away.

"Hey, wait!" Peter said, jumping up to follow her. "Where are you going?"

"I've got to figure this out," Noa said. "Thanks, anyway."

"Sure, but . . . you've barely told me anything. If the same people are after both of us, don't you want to know why? I do." Sounding smug, he said, "And I've got their files."

Noa stopped dead. "I thought they caught you before you got over their firewall."

"They did." A slow grin spread over his face. "They took down /ALLIANCE/, too."

"Really?" Noa said, her mind whirling.

"Yup. Even stole the domain name."

"Wow." Noa had never heard of such a thing. "So why are you smiling?"

"Because," Peter said, his smirk widening, "I got all their data off the server, then bricked it."

"You what?" Noa said, dumbfounded. She'd heard of that sort of thing being done, but it was rare. Only a handful of people on the planet were capable of initiating a serious phlash attack on a system.

"Yeah," he said, looking self-satisfied. "And it only took three hours."

"What? How?" It had taken her longer than that just to get through the firewall.

"Using the HBGary method. Well, with some modifications."

"Damn." Noa had to admit she was impressed. All the folks at Rocket Science had secretly taken great glee in the downfall of that particular security giant. And the way it had been done was elegant. It was the first hack she'd ever heard of that she probably wouldn't have been able to accomplish. "You did that?"

"Well, I had help," Peter admitted. "It was mainly Loki and some of the others."

"But with HBGary, they got the data and messed with the site but didn't actually brick it, right?"

"Nope. That was something we came up with. We went in through their firmware."

"Huh, that was smart." Noa was impressed. A few years earlier, she'd heard about a geek on HP's security team who developed a program that used firmware to brick a server. But that program only worked on a small scale with a digital camera. Bricking a whole server was, as far as she knew, unprecedented. And highly illegal.

Worse yet, if Peter was telling the truth, he had her AMRF folder stored in a database somewhere. "You came up with that?"

"It would help if you didn't sound so shocked," he said with a twinge of annoyance. "I did found /ALLIANCE/."

"Yeah, but you asked me to hack in."

"That's because a bunch of Special Forces guys had just bashed in my front door."

"Gee, thanks for setting me up for that," she said.

"I told you to be careful, right?" He shifted uncomfortably. "Anyway, did you ever get in?"

Noa debated lying, but if he really had gotten all their data, there was no point. "Yeah, I did."

"So why were you avoiding me?" Peter sounded annoyed again. "Wait." He grabbed her elbow, stopping her. They were standing in front of a juice bar.

"What?" She glanced back over her shoulder, prepared to bolt, but his eyes were fixed on her.

"You said they were already after you. Why?"

Noa shook off his hand and walked away, arms crossed over her chest, head down. He followed, lowering his voice as he said, "Did they do something to you?"

Noa didn't answer. She kept walking, eyes on the ground. Peter fell in stride beside her but didn't say anything else.

They passed a slew of stores. It was a weekday, and the mall was mainly filled with housewives pushing strollers and elderly men and women carrying battered-looking shopping bags. They walked through one whole wing; then Noa turned a hundred and eighty degrees and retraced her steps. She didn't look where she was going, didn't check to see if goons were lurking in the doorways of Victoria's Secret and Forever 21 and the Sunglass Hut. Suddenly, she simply didn't care. It was like all of her survival instincts abruptly switched off. She'd lost the will to run.

Peter suddenly stepped in front, stopping her. "You hungry?"

"What?"

"Hungry. You know, as in you want to grab some food?"

Noa looked up and realized they'd arrived back at the food court. It had filled up; more than half the tables were occupied now. The smell of pizza wafted over to her. Noa frowned. She was suddenly completely famished.

"I'm starving," she said.

"Great." Peter looked relieved. "You want tacos? Or something else?"

"Everything," Noa said, gazing greedily at the array of options. "I want everything."

"Man, you were hungry." Peter propped his chin on his hand as he watched her eat. He was experiencing a mix of stupefaction and admiration. She was a tiny girl, almost painfully skinny, yet he'd just watched her sock away a slice of pizza, two beef tacos, and a chow mein panda bowl. He'd never seen a girl eat like that. Hell, he'd rarely seen anyone eat like that. After tucking the final spoonful in her mouth,

Noa looked up hungrily, like maybe he was dessert.

"I want more," she said.

"Okay," he agreed uncertainly, opening his wallet and squinting into it. "I've got ten dollars left; after that we have to go to an ATM."

She snatched the bill out of his hand and made for the vendors.

"Help yourself," he grumbled, though she was already out of hearing range. "No, I'm good, thanks. Don't worry about me."

He watched her roam uncertainly from Gourmet India to Sarku Japan to Boston Chowda before settling on Ben & Jerry's. She returned to their table bearing a towering banana split, three scoops drowning in whipped cream and chocolate sauce. In spite of himself, Peter laughed.

"What?" Noa asked indignantly.

"Nothing. I'm just in awe."

"You want some?"

"Doesn't look like you really want to share," he said. "And I don't want to risk losing a finger."

"I haven't eaten in days," she said, digging in with the spoon. Chocolate sauce dribbled down as she stuck it in her mouth.

"Really?" he said, perplexed. "Why not?"

Noa shrugged. "Don't know. Just wasn't hungry."

"Yeah, I guess I haven't been very hungry, either," Peter said. He'd managed to force down a taco, but thoughts of Amanda and his parents kept intruding.

Noa abruptly set down the spoon and pushed away the ice cream, an odd expression on her face.

"Something wrong?"

"No, just . . . I feel a little sick."

"Shocking," Peter said. "Bathrooms are that way. You want me to go with you?"

She shook her head. "I'll be fine." She gathered up the various wrappers and containers and stacked them on a tray, an expression of distaste on her face. Peter watched her walk to the nearest trash can and dump everything in before coming back.

"Noa. What kind of name is that?" he asked.

"Why?"

"Just curious."

"It's Danish."

"Cool." He drew a circle on the table with his finger. "I always hated my name."

"Why?"

Peter shrugged. "It's boring. So were your folks Danish?"

She eyed him and said, "You ask a lot of personal questions."

"That's personal?"

Noa nodded. "I don't talk about my family."

"All right." Peter was having a hard time getting a read on her. Unlike most girls, she seemed impervious to his charm. In fact, he got the sense that she could barely stand him. It was discomfiting.

"We should go get the money," Noa said abruptly, standing and slinging a messenger bag back over her shoulder. "It's getting late and I still need to find a place to stay tonight."

"Yeah, me too." Peter picked up the duffel bag and slid his arms through the straps, carrying it like a backpack. He was wishing he'd brought less stuff; it had to weigh twenty pounds.

She didn't answer.

"Don't you think it makes sense for us to stick together?" he persisted.

She glanced sidelong at him. "Why?"

"You ask 'why' a lot," he noted. She didn't smile. "Anyway, if the same guys are after us, we stand a better chance if we watch each other's backs."

Noa kept walking. Her brow was furrowed, face locked in what was apparently her perpetual expression, a stony frown. But she didn't say no.

"And I'm going to need some of that money, too," Peter said. "If you want to share it, that's fine. But we stick together."

Noa huffed out a breath, then said, "Okay. We stick together. For now."

"Great."

"So where do we go?" Noa asked.

"I've been thinking about that," Peter said. They stopped in front of the ATM, and he dug out his wallet.

Noa put out a hand, stopping him. "Can you withdraw more if you go inside?"

"Yeah, maybe," Peter said. He'd never done it before, but it was worth a shot.

"Okay." She seemed to be thinking. "Get as much cash as you can. Then we need to get out of there fast. They'll be able to track the withdrawal."

"You think?" Peter was dubious. Sure, Mason had come after him when he was trying to break into their website. But could they possibly be monitoring their bank accounts, too? AMRF was probably still trying to drag itself out of the technological Stone Age /ALLIANCE/ had thrust it into.

"Yeah, definitely." She looked around. "We'll get the

cash, then take the T across town. But we need to be ready to run the minute you have that money."

"Okay," Peter said skeptically. Even given what he'd been through the past few days, her attitude struck him as excessively paranoid. "You sure we need to be that careful?"

"Yes," Noa said decisively. "And we can't stay with anyone you know."

"Huh." There went his only plan. Even though he and Amanda had broken up, she'd probably still be willing to help if he was in trouble. But his parents might provide Mason with a list of his friends. They certainly knew where Amanda's dorm was located. If they couldn't go there, he wasn't sure where to turn.

Peter suddenly realized that he hadn't been exaggerating; he really didn't have a home anymore. A panicky feeling took root in his stomach.

"What's wrong?" Noa regarded him closely.

Peter tried to shake it off. "Nothing. It's just . . . I don't know where to go."

"Join the club," she grumbled. At his expression, she managed a tight smile and said, "We'll figure it out. C'mon, let's get the cash and get out of here. Malls make me twitchy."

It turned out that Peter was able to withdraw a grand from his account, although the bank manager tried to make him take it in a cashier's check. He walked out, the cash an uncomfortable bulge in his back pocket. Noa was waiting in front of a bath store a few doors down—the pungent reek of perfumed soap added to his queasiness.

"You got it?" she asked.

Peter nodded.

"Okay, let's go." Noa walked briskly in the direction of

Copley Place. Peter followed, grateful that she was taking charge.

They were almost at the sky bridge linking the two malls when she glanced back and froze. Peter followed her eyes. There was a big guy in his twenties about forty feet behind them. He didn't look out of place: jeans, a fleece jacket, a Red Sox cap. But he was talking into a cell phone and seemed to be watching them.

They picked up the pace. The sky bridge was a vaulted glass passageway with crisscrossing white struts one story above street level. Peter checked behind them; the guy was still there.

"Do you think—"

"I don't know," Noa said urgently. "But we need to move."

She broke into a jog. Peter had to hustle to keep up with her—she had long legs and seemed to be in better shape. Or maybe she'd just had more practice at fleeing.

They shot through the bridge, barreling past people lugging shopping bags. A few grumbled in their wake, but no one tried to stop them.

Peter checked back over his shoulder and slowed. "He's gone."

Noa grabbed his arm and tugged, saying with irritation, "We have to keep moving. There might be more of them."

She hadn't slowed at all, and Peter was forced to break into a run. Startled middle-aged women watched them bolt past, and he pictured how crazy they must look. He was starting to feel silly. Maybe Noa was more than paranoid; maybe she was slightly unhinged. Sure, Mason had tracked him down before—but both of those times, he'd been trying to hack into the AMRF server. And tracing that kind of intrusion was relatively easy, especially the first time, when he hadn't even tried to hide the IP address. The library computer incident was more perplexing, since he'd used a VPN. But there were still a lot of ways to track the signal back. And he'd remained at the same terminal for hours, which in retrospect made it much easier.

But financial-institution computers were a whole different beast. How could they possibly have access to those?

Peter suddenly realized how. Since he was still a minor, Bob was the cosigner on his account. Such a large withdrawal might have triggered an automatic fraud call. But would Bob actually have shared that information with Mason?

Maybe he hadn't had a choice. And maybe Noa wasn't so paranoid after all. Peter picked up the pace.

The Pru was a nice mall, but Copley Place was more upscale, catering to wealthy Bostonians with shops like Barneys, Neiman Marcus, and Louis Vuitton. This was where Peter's mom had always done most of her shopping. In fact, a lot of the women they sped past were carbon copies of Priscilla.

Noa hesitated. They'd reached the center atrium, a landscaped section that housed two-story-tall trees. The arms of the mall branched away from them in four directions. The ceilings were painted gold, the lighting tastefully recessed. Noa appeared dumbstruck.

"What's wrong?"

"I've never been in here," she admitted.

"Follow me," Peter said. He headed for the Dartmouth Street exit. From there, it would be a straight shot across the street to the south entrance of Back Bay Station.

They slowed as they exited the mall. Peter was panting hard. His heart felt like it was trying to tear through his rib cage, and his breath wheezed in and out. The duffel bag straps dug painfully into his armpits, chafing him.

Apparently Noa wasn't in much better shape. They were both practically staggering, like a couple of old people.

"C'mon," Peter said, grabbing her hand. Dartmouth Street was four lanes separated by a slightly raised cement platform. During a break in traffic, they darted across the first two lanes, paused, then made it across the next two. Peter veered left, going past the entrance to Back Bay Station.

"What are you doing?" Noa hissed. "I thought we were catching a train!"

"Trust me." Peter pulled her into the doorway of a Japanese restaurant. He scanned behind them. The coast looked clear—just the usual downtown midday crowd. A fair amount of foot traffic despite the cold, everyone moving with purpose.

The guy in the Red Sox cap emerged from the mall. As he glanced up and down the street, they ducked farther into the shadows. An elderly woman in a moldering fur pushed past him. Red Sox cap didn't even seem to register her. Eyeing the entrance to Back Bay Station, his right hand went to his ear and his lips moved.

"We have to get out of here!" Noa said fiercely.

She was right—from this angle they were just out of view, but if the guy crossed the street and turned left, he'd be right on top of them.

"One minute," Peter said. "Relax."

Noa grumbled something under her breath, but didn't move.

Another guy suddenly appeared immediately to their left, just ten feet away. He had to have come out of Back Bay Station. Noa looked up at Peter and raised an eyebrow. He felt vindicated. He'd had a bad feeling about entering the train station—it was the obvious choice for anyone leaving the mall. The new guy crossed the street and approached Red Sox cap. They talked for a minute, then went over to the curb. A minute later, a black SUV pulled up and they both got in.

The car pulled away. Peter released his breath.

"Can I have my hand back now?" Noa asked.

"Oh, yeah. Sorry." Peter hadn't realized he was still holding it. She made a big show of shaking it out, as if he'd been clenching it.

"That was smart," she said begrudgingly. "I didn't think they'd have someone in the station already."

Peter shrugged, doing his best not to gloat. "I figured it couldn't hurt to wait and see."

"I wonder why they left," Noa said pensively. "I mean, it would have made sense for them to get more guys to help look. They know we're around here somewhere."

"Which is why we have to keep moving," Peter said firmly.

"Yeah, but where?"

"Actually"—Peter grinned—"I thought of someone who might be able to help."

CHAPTER ELEVEN

"What makes you think they won't look for us here?" Noa asked nervously, shifting from foot to foot. She'd switched the messenger bag to her opposite shoulder, trying to ease the crick in her neck from carrying it. She could still feel the phantom weight of it on her right shoulder.

"Trust me, it wouldn't even occur to my parents. They don't know we stayed in touch." Peter pressed the door buzzer again.

"Maybe he's at work?" Noa asked, rubbing her arms. It was starting to feel like she'd never get warm again. They'd left Back Bay Station and taken four different buses to get here, backtracking twice to make sure they weren't being followed. The T would have been faster, but they'd agreed it was best not to take any chances.

Peter hadn't said much about this mystery stranger who would apparently be willing to take them in, which worried her. She'd rather have chanced going it alone. But she was down to thirty dollars, not even enough for a dive hotel room. Her options were limited. Even if she managed to get Peter to pay for a fake ID, she wouldn't be able to access the cash she already had. The guys after her might have gotten in touch with Rocket Science—there was no way of knowing, so she couldn't risk hitting them up for freelance work. Which meant she might have to start over from scratch.

And she still didn't know what had happened to her on that operating table.

Right now her only option was to stick with Peter and see if they could figure something out by going through those files. That was the only way she'd have a shot at getting her life back.

They were standing in front of a duplex in Mattapan, a working-class neighborhood where the houses mirrored their occupants: They all looked worn and faded and tired, like they'd just pulled a double shift at a job they hated.

Noa was about to ask if there was somewhere warm they could wait when the door to the downstairs apartment popped open. A woman in her midtwenties with a baby on her hip eyed them suspiciously.

"Help you?" she asked in the drawl particular to South Boston. She was wearing a thick wool sweater that hung to midthigh over jeans and dark brown slippers. Her greasy-looking blond hair was shot through with pink streaks, and dots of leftover mascara peppered her under-eyes. The cloth diaper draped across her shoulder was stained blotchy yellow with what looked like curdled cheese.

"Yeah, hi." Peter cleared his throat and smiled widely at her. "We're Cody's friends."

"Oh!" She brightened immediately. "Sorry, I thought you were selling magazines or something. I swear, those bastards come by twice a day, just when I get the baby down for his nap." She nodded to the kid, who dozed against her shoulder. Despite the cold, he was only wearing a thin onesie.

"That sucks," Peter said sympathetically.

"Yeah." Absentmindedly she stroked the baby's bald head with one hand. "Pretty sure Cody's working today. You wanna come in and wait for him?"

Noa and Peter glanced at each other. "If that's okay with you," Peter said. "Sure, sounds great."

Noa followed him, thinking it was funny that people didn't hesitate to invite him into their homes. She'd rarely had the welcome mat rolled out for her.

Noa squeezed past a collapsed stroller and line of jackets hanging from pegs in the hall, following Peter into a tiny living room. A profusion of glaringly bright plastic toys in all shapes and sizes contrasted starkly with the navy sofa sagging in the far corner.

"Sorry for the mess," the woman apologized self-consciously, kicking things aside as she crossed the room.

"Great place," Peter said, sounding like he meant it.

"Thanks." The woman paused in the middle of the room and smiled broadly at him. There was a gap between her two front teeth, just a touch too large to be considered charming. "So how do you know Cody?"

"He was friends with my brother," Peter said.

Noa thought that was an odd way to phrase it. Were they not friends anymore? And if not, why was Peter still friends with the guy?

She regarded Peter closely, noting the sadness in his eyes. Suddenly, it clicked. His brother was dead.

"Cody is friends with everyone," the woman said, smiling. "He's such a sweetheart. You should see him with Ethan. Amazing." She gave the baby a nod.

"He's cute," Peter offered.

The woman looked at Noa expectantly. Clearly she was supposed to agree. Babies all looked the same to her: On closer examination, this one was even less appealing. His bald head looked freakishly large and rolls of fat spilled out the arm and leg holes of his onesie. Plus a long line of drool seeped from his mouth. "Yeah, really cute," she managed with a weak smile.

"I'm Pam, by the way. You kids want something to drink? I got water and Diet Dr Pepper."

"We're good," Peter said. "You wouldn't happen to know when Cody will be home?"

"The hours that man keeps . . ." Pam crossed the room to lower the baby into a mesh playpen. "I heard him leave when I was giving Ethan his first bottle. Kid wakes up at the crack of it," she said, chuffing the baby affectionately under the chin. "Cody doesn't have class tonight, so he should be home soon. Poor guy." She shook her head. "But I guess they get paid enough later to make up for it."

"Cody's a medical student," Peter explained to Noa. "He's working as an EMT to put himself through school."

"I swear, he'd the hardest working man I know, and that's saying something." Pam set her hands on his hips. "You mind keeping an eye on Ethan for a minute? I gotta run to the store for more formula."

"Uh, sure," Peter said.

"Great." Pam went into the hall and yanked a puffy down

jacket off a hook. "He starts crying, just shove the binky in his mouth."

"Okay," Peter said.

"Back in five." She tugged on the coat and yanked open the door, letting in a blast of cold air. It slammed shut behind her.

Noa stared at the door, openmouthed. She turned to Peter. "Did she seriously just leave her baby with us?"

"Yeah." Peter laughed. They both eyed the baby. Ethan was sitting up unsteadily, his torso rocking slightly back and forth as he gazed at them with enormous eyes. His lips gaped slightly open, like he couldn't quite believe what had just happened, either.

"That's crazy, right?" Noa asked. She didn't have much experience with good parenting, but assumed this wasn't the norm.

"Yup, totally insane. What do you think, should we take him? Probably could get some cash that way." He cocked an eyebrow at her, clearly joking.

Noa looked at the baby with distaste. "God, no."

"Not a kid person?"

"I never thought about it," Noa admitted. Few of the foster homes she'd been in had younger kids, and at The Center they were kept separate. She'd had limited exposure to anyone under the age of ten since—well, pretty much since she was that age herself. The subject made her uncomfortable. A lot of Peter's questions did that; it felt like he was probing her and she wasn't sure why he wanted to know. She decided to throw him on the defensive by asking, "So what happened to your brother?"

Peter winced, like she'd hit him. "PEMA," he said after a minute.

"Oh." Noa fell silent. She'd never actually known anyone who died of PEMA, but it was becoming increasingly common. The disease had come out of nowhere a few years ago. She remembered hearing that it had crossed over from deer or something. It mainly afflicted teenagers. PEMA was a truly awful disease—the kids who got it literally wasted away. So far it had mystified scientists—there was no common thread among the victims, at least not that they'd found yet. Initially they'd thought it had something to do with sexual activity, but that was quickly dismissed. PEMA was always fatal, and there was no cure.

Noa didn't know what to say or do. Peter seemed to have retreated into himself. She drew her feet up onto the edge of the chair and wrapped her arms around them. A clock ticked in the next room, every beat of it resonating in the stillness.

The baby started crying. Noa sprung to her feet, grateful that the silence had been broken. She dug around the playpen. The baby tilted his face up toward her. He'd rapidly gone almost purple, face contorted, tears streaming down.

"Relax," she said, finally spying the pacifier under a bear in the corner. "Here."

She jammed it in his mouth. He reflexively started sucking, and the tears immediately subsided. *Like literally putting a cork in him,* Noa thought, impressed. Shame you couldn't do that with just anyone. There were times it would come in handy.

The door opened, ushering in a blast of cold air. Pam reappeared, cheeks red and hair mussed. There was a white plastic bag over her arm. The neck of a vodka bottle peeked out the top. "God, it's freakin' cold out there!" she exclaimed. "Got you kids some chips, thought you might be hungry."

"Thanks," Peter said.

"No problem." Pam cocked her head to the side. There was a dull thud, then the sound of footsteps mounting wooden stairs. "That's Cody, then." A hint of disappointment in her voice.

Peter got to his feet. "Thanks so much for letting us hang here. It was great meeting you and Ethan."

"Yeah, great," Noa mumbled, scrambling to her feet.

"Sure, anytime." Pam appeared crestfallen. "You tell Cody if he wants dinner, it's pizza night, 'kay?"

"Absolutely. Thanks again." Peter had plastered his perpetual grin back on. Noa wondered how he managed it. If she smiled that much, her mouth would probably start spasming.

She followed him out. Peter rang the bell for the upstairs apartment. After a minute, a guy in his early twenties opened the door. He was tall, maybe six-two, broad-shouldered, dark hair trimmed close to his scalp. African-American, with pale blue eyes that drooped with dark circles. He was dressed all in navy; a round white patch on the sleeve of his shirt read EMS/CITY OF BOSTON. He looked utterly exhausted. "Peter?" he said. "What's up?"

"Can we come in?" Peter asked.

Cody looked perplexed, but said, "Yeah, sure," and stepped aside to let them pass.

Noa followed Peter up a creaking flight of wooden stairs: no runner, just a worn tread down the center of each step. Peter seemed to know his way around; at the top of the stairs he turned right along the banister. He went into a tiny living room lined with bay windows. It was identical to downstairs, except that where Pam's was packed to overflowing, this room was barren. Nothing but a thin throw rug, a futon couch with a plain white mattress, a low table, and some pillows on the floor. Stacks of textbooks balanced along a board straddling two cement blocks. It was only slightly more welcoming than a prison cell, Noa thought as she looked around.

"Sorry, I don't really have people over much," Cody said apologetically. "Take the couch, I'm fine with the floor."

Peter had already plopped down on the futon. It was tiny. Even though Noa sat at the very edge of it, their legs ended up touching. Peter didn't seem to notice.

"You going to introduce us?" Cody asked, crossing his legs as he settled on a pillow.

"Oh, yeah, sorry. This is Noa."

"Hi, Noa. Nice to meet you." Cody smiled at her before turning back to Peter. "I'm so tired I can hardly see straight. Did we have plans tonight?"

"Nope. Sorry, I would have called, but . . . well, I lost my phone," Peter said. "And it was kind of an emergency."

"Yeah? What type of emergency?" Cody said wearily. His tone implied doubt that anything Peter was involved with could achieve emergency status.

"Long story," Peter said.

Cody held up a hand, stopping him. "For that, I'm going to need a beer. You want one?"

"Yeah, sure," Peter said.

"How about you, Noa?"

Noa shook her head. She was dying of thirst, but the thought of a beer turned her stomach. She still couldn't believe she'd managed to eat so much earlier. It was weird. She hadn't been hungry for days, then suddenly she'd been ravenous for everything in reach.

As quickly as the hunger kicked in, it switched off again, and she couldn't choke down another bite. The thirst was always there, though. It didn't seem to matter how much she drank. She swallowed hard against the dryness. "Actually, could I have some water?"

"Sure." Cody got up and went back down the hall. She heard the sound of a fridge opening and closing, then a tap turning. "I shouldn't really be offering to corrupt minors, anyway. I grew up in an Irish household where you got one beer with dinner starting when you were sixteen. Hard habit to break."

"You're Irish?" Noa asked, puzzled.

In the kitchen, he laughed. "Why, don't I look it?"

She was embarrassed. Cody came back and stood in the doorway, grinning down at her. "My mom was Irish. Dad was black."

"Oh." Noa felt like an idiot. Of course he was part Irish—that explained the eyes.

Cody handed a beer to Peter, who unscrewed the cap and gratefully took a slug. Then he dropped back onto the pillow and said, "So let's hear this long story."

Noa let Peter tell it. He glossed over a lot of the tech details, mainly describing the home invasion he'd told her about and some guy named Mason grabbing him at the library. She hadn't heard the part about his parents being involved, though, and kicking him out. That got her edgy again.

Cody listened silently. He clasped his right wrist with his left hand, the beer hanging down forgotten. When Peter had finished, he took a swig, then turned to Noa and asked, "So how do you figure into all this?"

Noa debated how much to tell them. The fact that he was a med student hadn't been lost on her. It was almost too much to hope for, when what she needed more than any-thing was someone knowledgeable who could help her interpret those files. But could she trust him? Really, could she trust either of them?

Peter was watching her, too. The air of expectation was oppressive, like she was supposed to launch into some sort of song-and-dance routine. Noa flushed under the weight of their attention.

"I don't really know where to start," she finally said.

"The beginning works for me," Cody said.

Noa met his eyes. They were warm, compassionate. She realized that she liked him, and she never liked people straight off the bat. Cody just gave off a certain kind of energy, like he truly cared. It would probably make him a great doctor someday.

"All right." Noa drew a deep breath and started at the beginning. "Two days ago, I woke up on an operating table . . ."

There was a long silence when she'd finished. She'd told them pretty much everything, even the part about not being able to eat, then suddenly feeling starved. Peter's eyes had widened at that, and she wondered if he'd actually thought she ate that much all the time.

Noa tugged at her shirtsleeves, wishing they'd say something.

"Wow." Peter finally spoke. "And I thought I was having a crappy couple of days."

Cody cast him a reproving look. "Way to be supportive, Pedro."

"Sorry, I just meant . . . man." Peter shook his head. "You're pretty badass, getting away like that."

He genuinely sounded awed, which made Noa feel even more uncomfortable.

"And you're not sure what was done to you?" Cody pressed.

Noa shook her head. "No. I have a scar, but—"

"Where is it?" he asked.

Noa drew a line along the length of her shirt. His eyes followed her hand, but not in a creepy way. He nodded thoughtfully, and said, "Interesting."

Something about his tone struck her. "You don't believe me?"

"Honestly?" Cody took another sip of beer. "It's almost too crazy not to believe. And given what happened to Peter . . . well, I believe him. And your story isn't far-off from his. Plus I'm guessing that a lot of this stuff, like the Brookline High thing, I could check on. So, yeah. I guess I believe you."

"You guess?"

"Easy." Cody held up a hand. "I didn't mean it like that."

"I believe you," Peter chimed in.

He was still looking at her with a goofy expression. Noa reached for her wrist to twist her bracelet, remembering a second too late that it was gone.

"Okay." Cody gulped down the last of his beer and set the bottle on the low table. "So let's have a look at those files."

Noa got out her laptop and set it up, turning it around to face him. She went to the other side of the table and perched on a pillow beside him, then opened the folder that held what she figured were medical charts—other kids', not hers. She wasn't 100 percent ready to hear about those yet.

Cody leaned in, peering at the first file she opened. "Standard post-op stats," he said. His eyes ran down the form, and he frowned. "Huh."

"What?" Noa asked.

"The patient deteriorates. You want to see those numbers improving." He ran a finger down the screen, showing her what he meant. "And here, well . . ."

"The patient dies?" Noa filled in for him.

He nodded. "I'm guessing. Let's see more."

They went through three more files: In all of them, Cody determined that based on the steady decline in life signs, the patient probably hadn't survived.

"How many of these are there?" he asked, closing the files.

"Lots," Noa said. "And I've got these, too."

She opened the file that contained scrawled doctors' notes. Seeing the first, Cody barked a laugh.

"What?" Peter asked.

"I'm not going to be able to help with these. That's kind of the running joke: Not even a doctor can read another doctor's handwriting."

"Okay, then." Noa found the folder that held the larger reports filled with scientific jargon. "How about these?"

Cody skimmed the first, quickly becoming absorbed. He took over the cursor, scanning through another document, then another. Noa watched him read. He had a look of intense concentration on his face.

"Anything?" Peter said.

He sounded annoyed. Noa turned to find him glaring down at them from his position on the couch.

"A lot," Cody said, not appearing to notice. "Man, this is . . . where did you say you got these?"

"They're from a company called AMRF," Noa said.

"And that's the one your parents are involved with, Peter?" Cody asked, looking up.

"Yeah," Peter said. "Why?"

"Neither of you was able to find out anything more specific about this company?"

"I've got some more files on a database," Peter said with a shrug. "They're uploading now. Why? What does it say they're doing?"

Cody sat back and eyed the laptop pensively. "Experimenting," he finally said.

"What kind of experiments?" Noa asked in a small voice. Suddenly, she wasn't so sure she wanted to know.

"They're trying to find a cure for PEMA," he said. "Using human test subjects."

"Test subjects?" Peter asked.

"But I don't have PEMA," Noa said. She tried to fight the panic out of her voice as she continued, "I mean, I'd know if I did, right?" She suddenly realized she hadn't been to a doctor in years. Could she have been sick and not known it? She didn't know much about PEMA, although of course everyone had heard of it. Schools had recently started monitoring for it, but only after she'd dropped out. She tried to remember what the symptoms were. The most common was weight loss over time, but there were also weirder things. She'd heard of kids walking in circles, avoiding other people, lapsing into sleep midsentence. Had she been losing weight? She'd always been skinny, but the new jeans she'd bought barely fit her. And suddenly, she didn't have an appetite, she realized. "Did they give it to me?" she demanded in a shaky voice. "Or did I already have it?"

"I can't say yet," Cody said gently. "I need to go over these more carefully to find out. But hey, relax." He reached out an arm and encircled her, drawing her close.

Usually Noa would have jerked away from that sort of physical contact, but she let him do it. Even more surprising, she tasted salt, and realized that she was actually crying.

"Oh, man," Peter said. "My brother."

Noa peered up at him through her tears. "What?"

"That's why my folks got involved. Because of Jeremy."

"Probably," Cody said. "That would explain a lot."

Noa looked down. It was all starting to make sense.

"What's going to happen to me?" she finally asked.

"Nothing tonight," Cody said. He took hold of her chin with one hand and tilted it up so that she was forced to look in his eyes. "It's going to be okay, Noa. We're going to figure this out."

In spite of everything, he sounded so certain Noa let herself believe him.

Amanda blew hair out of her eyes and sat back on the floor. Filing was her least favorite part of volunteering at the Coalition. The nonprofit had a tiny budget, and there was only one computer in the entire facility. So the bulk of their files was kept in metal cabinets that were packed to the seams. Every few years, older files were boxed up and sent to storage, but still it took effort to squeeze a new file into the drawer every time a teen took advantage of their services.

She'd spent most of her five-hour shift cataloguing the drop-ins as the waiting room gradually emptied. Amanda tucked the last file into the drawer and slid it shut. Mrs. Latimar was in back ushering the last few teens in to see the doctor.

Amanda took a look around the office while she wiped her hands on her skirt. The filing was done, the phone wasn't ringing, and everything was as straightened as possible. She peered around the doorsill into the waiting room:

empty. Good, that gave her a few minutes. Once Mrs. Latimar came back, she'd be put back to work on something: The woman was a firm believer in keeping her volunteers occupied.

Amanda sank down in the chair behind the desk. Once Peter had left, she'd sat up in her window seat staring out at the quad for hours. She felt awful about what had happened—she hadn't handled the situation well, and she knew it. She'd never meant to hurt his feelings. All along Amanda had figured that once she went off to college, their relationship would just naturally fade away. Unfortunately, Peter hadn't felt the same way.

A flash of his look of betrayal the night before flitted through her mind. Amanda cringed at the memory.

"Excuse me."

She turned to find a man watching her, a strange smile on his face.

"Yes?" she said, automatically straightening in the chair. He was overdressed in an immaculate three-piece suit, wool overcoat, and shiny black shoes. He had short black hair and eyes so pale they were kind of spooky. Amanda forced a smile as she asked, "Can I help you?"

"I certainly hope so." He scanned the room as if looking for someone, even though there wasn't exactly space for anyone to be hiding. "Mrs. Latimar is expecting me."

"She'll be back shortly," Amanda said. His eyes darkened, and she fervently hoped that Mrs. Latimar would show up soon; she couldn't put her finger on it, but something about the guy gave her the creeps. Maybe just because he was so clearly out of his element, she told herself. Plus she was still spooked after her encounter with the girl who claimed her friend had been taken.

He cocked his head to the side, considering her. "You're one of her volunteers."

The way he said it wasn't a question. Amanda nodded. "Yeah, I am."

"Then you can help me," he said decisively, stepping into the room.

Amanda fought the urge to shy back—she was overtired, and it was making her paranoid. Still, it was a strain to maintain a smile while asking, "What can I do for you?"

"I need some files." His eyes flicked toward the cabinets. "Mrs. Latimar would have put them aside for me."

Amanda's mouth opened, then closed again. The one thing that had been drilled into every volunteer was that files were sacrosanct. Mrs. Latimar's assurances that anything they said and did would be kept confidential from the authorities, their parents, or whomever else they'd run away from was largely what kept teens coming back. She couldn't imagine Mrs. Latimar just handing over files to anyone, never mind a guy dressed like this.

"I'm on the board," he said, noting her discomfort. "It's all right, she approved it."

"Still," Amanda said, "I'd feel more comfortable if we waited for her."

He frowned and made a show of looking at his watch. "I really don't have much time."

"I'm sorry, Mr. . . ." Amanda paused, waiting for him to fill in the blanks. When he didn't, she asked straight-out, "You haven't told me your name."

"That's true, I haven't," he responded evenly. "You haven't told me yours, either."

"Amanda," she said. "Amanda Berns."

"Pleased to meet you, Amanda Berns," he said, extending

a hand. "You can call me Mr. Mason."

She shook automatically, thinking, *Mason*. The name tugged at her memory. She tried to place it, but failed. He probably was on the board; she must have seen it on the letterhead. "Mr. Mason, I—"

The sudden appearance of Mrs. Latimar in the door behind him stopped her. Amanda caught her eye. At the sight of Mason, the woman had frozen. A strong emotion— fear? Dislike?—marred her features. By the time he'd turned to face her, Mrs. Latimar had composed her face into its normal mask of affability. Amanda was certain she'd seen it, though.

"Mrs. Latimar!" Mason cried, opening his arms wide with delight. "Just the person I was looking for."

"They're in here," Mrs. Latimar said curtly, pushing past him. She offered Amanda a thin smile, then leaned around her to open the desk drawer. She pulled out a thin sheaf of files and passed them to Mason, letting go as soon as his fingers touched them. That was odd, too, Amanda noted. Mrs. Latimar was known for her warmth—she tended to stand close to people, as if on the verge of offering a hug. Clearly not with this man, though.

"Excellent." He tucked the files under his arm and nodded at both of them. "Nice meeting you, Ms. Berns. Mrs. Latimar, I'll see you next time."

Mrs. Latimar nodded but didn't move to walk him out. When the outer door slammed shut a minute later, Amanda breathed out, relieved he was gone.

Mrs. Latimar was distractedly shuffling through the piles of papers on her desk. "Did you finish the filing?" she asked sharply.

Amanda started at her tone. For a minute, it seemed as if

the woman she'd known and worked with for three years was gone, replaced by a cold, formal stranger.

"I—yes, I did," Amanda managed. "Who was that?" she asked, recovering somewhat.

Mrs. Latimar turned to face her, scowling down with dark brown eyes. At the expression on Amanda's face, however, her features relaxed. "A board member," she said. "I'd forgotten he was stopping by."

The way she said it convinced Amanda she was lying. "But, the files . . ."

"The best thing would be . . ." Mrs. Latimar looked away for a second, as though something dark and foreboding hovered past Amanda's shoulder, where a map of the city was plastered on the wall. She sighed and gave her ponytail two fierce tugs before locking Amanda with a firm glare. "Listen to me, Amanda. This is very important. I want you to forget all about what just happened. Do you understand?"

The urgency in her voice was clear—and so was the threat underlying it. Amanda swallowed hard, wondering what the hell was going on. She'd never seen Mrs. Latimar in such a state—the woman looked as though she'd been caught doing something truly terrible. Amanda wondered what had been in those files.

"Okay," she said, forcing a smile. "Yeah, sure. No big deal. Why don't I just . . ."

"The locker room needs to be checked," Mrs. Latimar said in her normal voice. Amanda heaved a secret smile of relief—this was the woman she knew. "Would you be a dear and do that before you go?"

"Sure." Amanda practically launched from the chair, suddenly desperate to get out of the room. Even though cleaning up the locker room after doctor day was unpleasant, today she welcomed the task. Anything to get her out of that office, where the air had suddenly grown too thin to breathe.

Halfway down the hall, she chanced a glance back and saw Mrs. Latimar bent over her desk, holding her head in both hands. Her shoulders shook and her fingers trembled. She was crying, Amanda realized, startled.

She stopped dead in the hall, torn between the desire to offer comfort, and the memory of how cold Mrs. Latimar's eyes had been as she stared down at her. Shuddering, Amanda pressed resolutely forward and pushed open the door to the locker room.

Peter scowled through spoonfuls of soup. Noa and Cody were sitting across the room, engrossed in stacks of paper. Cody claimed that staring at a screen for too long made him cross-eyed, so he'd prefer to read hard copies of the files. His ancient ink-jet printer had been grinding out documents for over an hour.

Cody had asked Noa to comb through the photo files, making note of the kids' names. She had a habit of chewing her lip when she concentrated. Peter couldn't decide yet if it was charming or kind of gross.

The AMRF files were still being processed by the server he'd shuttled them to, and at the rate it was going, they wouldn't be accessible for at least another few hours. Which left Peter with nothing to do.

When he finally complained about being hungry a half hour ago, Cody said, "There's ramen in the kitchen," without even bothering to look up.

"Guess I'll help myself," he'd grumbled.

Cody laughed at that. "You always do, right?"

He didn't seem to notice Peter's irritation. And Peter

begrudgingly had to admit he was right. He visited a few times a month, whenever Cody's schedule permitted. He liked it here—it wasn't fancy, but it provided a nice counterpoint to the McMansion his parents lived in. And Cody was one of the few people who actually treated him like a grownup. Hell, like a friend.

Cody had practically been the third kid in their family until Jeremy died. He'd shown up at their school Jeremy's freshman year. He was the token scholarship student, the only son of a single mother who worked as a paralegal. Because it took him over an hour to get to school on three separate buses, sometimes he'd just crash at their place during the week. Even though he was five years older, Jeremy had always been a pretty cool older brother. He never minded when Peter tagged along. The three of them would play video games for hours after school.

Then Jeremy and Cody went off to college. They remained inseparable, even managed to talk Harvard into letting them room together. Although they still came around a fair amount to visit, it was different. The house had definitely gotten lonely. It was around then that Peter really started getting into computers, doing more than just messing around on the internet. He found some hacker sites, and it just kind of took off from there.

Then Jeremy got sick.

It was unusual for PEMA to develop in someone as old as him—he was at the upper edge of the spectrum, on the verge of turning twenty. Most of the kids who contracted the illness were in their midteens.

Peter could still remember when Cody called their house in a panic. His parents got on separate extensions, talking to him in low voices. After they hung up, Peter asked what was going on, but they refused to tell him. Priscilla said, "We have to go help Jeremy with something, dear. Don't leave the house."

The look on her face, though—Peter still had nightmares about it. He'd known something was terribly wrong.

They'd torn out of the driveway. It was the week before Christmas break. The trees outside were strung with lights, and frost covered the ground. Peter had stood in the doorway for a long time, arms wrapped tight against the cold, watching the space where their taillights had vanished.

That was the longest night of his life. Peter woke up on the couch, where he'd tried to maintain a vigil, fully dressed with a kink in his neck.

No message on the home line or on his cell, which kind of ticked him off. Had they actually forgotten about him? What was happening?

Peter had drifted around the house all morning, unsure what to do. He had no way of getting to school, and wasn't sure if he should go, anyway. His parents weren't answering their phones—that almost scared him the most. He spent the morning feeling terrified and abandoned.

Bob finally showed up around lunchtime. Peter charged down the stairs, ready to give him hell about not calling. But when he saw his father's face, he stopped dead. His dad was fanatical about his personal appearance; the family joke was that it took him longer than Priscilla to get ready.

That day, though, he looked awful. Old, haggard, hair sticking out in all directions, beard growth shadowing his cheeks.

He waved Peter into the living room with a slight motion, as if he could barely summon the strength to move his arm. They sat on the couch, and he said bluntly, "Your brother's sick."

Apparently Cody had been so busy between classes and his work-study job that he hadn't recognized the symptoms. By the time he did, it had been three weeks since Jeremy had gone to class.

That same night, he was checked into Boston Medical. When Peter saw him the next day, he'd almost turned to his parents to protest that they were wrong; this couldn't be Jeremy. He was gaunt, eyes glassy. Hair thinning and falling out, and a blank expression on his face. He didn't even seem to realize they were in the room.

The worst part was that he was strapped to the bed.

"It's so he doesn't hurt himself," Priscilla had explained. Her face was calm but preternaturally pale, and there was a waver in her voice. "They walk around sometimes, and they're worried about him accidentally pulling out the IV."

After that, Peter went to the hospital every day after school. They made him wear a mask to lower the risk of contamination, but as soon as the nurse left the room, he always pulled it off. It itched him, and besides, there was no proof that PEMA was airborne.

Peter would sit there until sundown, messing around with his laptop after finishing his homework. He played around with the local networks, testing his skills against first the hospital's firewall, then the city of Boston's. His grasp of hacking techniques grew progressively stronger. The entire time, he maintained a running patter. Sometimes he talked about all the cool stuff they'd done with Cody, some of his fondest memories. Other times he'd explain the steps he was employing to hack into something. At the beginning, he'd talk a lot about the things they'd do once Jeremy got better. Get tickets to Fenway. Maybe go to New Orleans for Mardi Gras—that was supposed to be awesome. Run away to

Mexico for spring break without telling their parents.

None of it seemed to matter. Jeremy rarely responded. Day by day the bedding consumed him, chewing off pieces until his shape beneath them dwindled down to nothing.

Three months to the day after he was admitted, Jeremy died.

It had been an unusually rapid progression of the disease, so much so that Jeremy's doctors asked for permission to study him, like he was some kind of frog in biology class. When Priscilla and Bob agreed, Peter had stormed out of the room in a rage.

Not that they'd even found anything useful. Or if they had, they hadn't shared it with Peter.

After Jeremy died, Peter went into a downward spiral. He quit sports, his grades slipped, he even stopped showering every day. The worst part was that his parents didn't even seem to notice or care.

Then, right before summer, Cody showed up at school. He was waiting by the curb when Peter slouched out. "Yo, Pedro!" he called out.

Peter was half-tempted to pretend he hadn't heard him. Cody trotted over, though, and grabbed him in a hug. Cody was like that—openly affectionate, in a way that Peter's family never had been.

"How you holding up, man?" Cody asked, probing Peter's eyes.

"Fine. What are you doing here?"

"I realized it had been a while since we hung out," Cody said breezily. "Wanted to see if we could grab a burger or something."

Peter's eyes narrowed. "Did my folks call you?"

"No," Cody said, sounding genuinely surprised. Peter

examined him—Cody had never been a good liar. His gaze was open, clear. He was telling the truth: This hadn't been Bob and Priscilla's idea. Peter couldn't decide if that made him feel better or worse.

"C'mon, Pedro. I'm buying."

Peter shrugged, then followed him down the block. Their favorite burger place was a few blocks away, a popular after-school hangout named uBurger. He hadn't been here in months—as soon as he sat down, he remembered the last time. It had been with Cody and Jeremy, during Thanksgiving break.

"uBurger with guac, right?" Cody asked.

"Not hungry," Peter said, scraping a nail across the Formica tabletop. There was something crusted on it, either ketchup or barbecue sauce.

"Sure you are." Cody got up and went to the counter. Peter watched him order, exchanging banter with the counter girl. He came back with a tray loaded down with burgers, fries, and sodas. Cody slid into the booth across from Peter, then passed over a burger and fries.

"I said I wasn't hungry," Peter said peevishly. He knew he sounded like a whiny little brat, but he didn't care. The more he thought about it, the more pissed off he got. Where the hell had Cody been the past few months? He hadn't seen or heard from him since the funeral.

"I'll eat it if you don't," Cody said, unwrapping his own and tearing off a chunk. Peter watched him chew contentedly.

It was nearly impossible to faze Cody. One time at a party, a kid from another school showed up drunk and high and made a scene while trying to drag his girlfriend out. Cody had stopped him, separating the girlfriend and getting her back in the house while he barred the way. Then he just stood there while the guy unleashed a tirade of racial epithets in his face. Cody didn't respond, and the calm, relaxed expression on his face never changed. They could have been discussing the weather.

Finally, Jeremy stepped forward and punched the guy, knocking him out.

Peter realized he'd never seen Cody angry. In fact, he'd barely even displayed emotion at Jeremy's funeral.

"Sorry I haven't been around much," Cody said, regarding him as he took a sip of soda through the straw.

"I don't care," Peter said.

"Sure you do. You're pissed as hell, I can see that." Cody smiled at him. That was the worst part: He had this way of disarming you. If he smiled enough, you almost always forgot why you were angry with him in the first place. "You've got a right to be, too," he continued, his expression turning serious. "I was avoiding you and your family."

"Why?" Peter asked, even though he kind of already knew.

"It hurt too much. Especially seeing you. You look a lot like him," Cody said, looking pensively out the window. "I thought a lot about you, though. Wondered how you were doing."

"You could have called," Peter said dully.

"I know. I'm sorry, man. Really." Cody reached out and covered Peter's hand with his own. It made Peter a little uncomfortable, the way Cody's sudden outpourings of affection always did, but he didn't pull away.

"It's okay."

"Nope, it most definitely is not okay." Cody shook his head. "Not cool at all. So here's the deal. I want us to try to hook up regular, make sure we keep track of what's going on in each other's lives. That okay by you?"

"Yeah, I guess."

"It's gonna get better, Peter."

"How do you know that?" Peter demanded. Cody didn't shrink under his glare the way he'd expected. He met Peter's gaze, eyes level and calm.

"I just do," Cody said. "Jeremy's gone, and I miss him like hell. But you and me, we're still brothers. That doesn't change."

Initially Peter figured that Cody didn't mean it; he just took him out for a burger as a token gesture. But he persisted, inviting him out to shoot hoops one Saturday, or to a movie on a Monday. Cody had an insanely busy schedule, but he made a real effort to fit Peter into it.

It had probably saved him, Peter now realized. His parents were so out of the loop they never even asked where he went or what he was doing. They never knew that he and Cody had stayed in touch. Despite the fact that he'd been Jeremy's best friend, it seemed like they'd completely forgotten about him. Hell, sometimes it seemed like they'd completely forgotten about Peter. Without Cody, he might have simply fallen through the cracks.

But slowly, he started caring about stuff again. His grades went up. He started dating, going to parties. By the time sophomore year began, he was feeling like himself. And then he'd met Amanda.

As Peter finished the soup and brought the bowl back into the kitchen, he tried to pinpoint what was bothering him. Cody was coming through, the same way he always had. He'd taken them in, no questions asked. Believed both of their crazy stories. And even though he was clearly half-dead from exhaustion, he was staying up late to comb through files to see if he could help them.

And Peter kind of wanted to punch him for it.

He paused in the doorway, watching them. Noa's hair was shoulder-length and black, the color of a raven's wing. So dark it didn't look like it could possibly be natural. Her head tipped forward as she looked at the screen, so that the drape of her hair hid her face.

Peter still couldn't get over how matter-of-fact she'd been while relaying everything that had happened. Man, if he'd woken up naked on a table in a warehouse he would have completely flipped out. But Noa held herself together and got out of there. And every time the guys came after her, she'd evaded them.

He hadn't even managed to get away from Mason at the library. Listening to her story, he'd felt pathetic.

He wondered what her life had been like before she woke up two days ago. She hadn't shared any of that, just said that she was a foster kid.

One thing he was sure of: Noa didn't look like she had PEMA. And he'd seen it enough to know. Jeremy had died in a PEMA ward. As the disease grew to epidemic proportions, since they couldn't trace how it was transmitted, as a precautionary measure they locked infected kids up in separate hospital units.

Most didn't start out as badly as Jeremy. They'd still be mobile, shuffling around in circles or pacing while clutching an IV on wheels. They'd desperately barrage the doctors with questions when they came through on their rounds, then force themselves to sound upbeat while grieving relatives sobbed.

It was almost worse for them, because they realized what

was happening. Every so often, toward the end of visiting hours, a low wail would start. It would begin with the ones who knew, a stream of pleas and cries and bartering that was quickly joined by those who had already lost the part of their mind capable of reason. Soon most of the ward would be shrieking, everyone joining in out of some primal animal empathy until it became a deafening chorus of anguish.

Peter would sit there frozen, listening. There would be a lot of opening and shutting of doors, nurses bustling around injecting tranquilizers into IVs. Slowly, one by one, the voices fell silent.

He shook off the memory. The point was, Noa didn't look sick. And no one with PEMA would have been able to eat the way she did today, either. They always ate very little, or nothing at all.

"Anything?" he finally asked.

They both looked up with surprise, as if they'd forgotten he was there.

"A lot, actually," Cody said with a smile, recovering. He blinked and rubbed his eyes with one hand. "Man, what time is it?"

"Nearly nine," Noa said without looking up.

Cody groaned. "Crap. I gotta be up at five to work a shift before rounds tomorrow. Any of that soup left, Pedro?"

"I can make more. You want some, too?" he asked.

Noa just shook her head. A slight flush rose on her cheeks, though, and he felt badly about inadvertently calling attention to her weird food thing. "All right."

"I'll get some notes together while you make it," Cody said. "I think I've got a handle on what they were trying to do."

Five minutes later they were sitting back in the living

room. Cody had spread the papers out in separate piles. The printer had finally fallen silent. Noa stuck to her pillow on the floor, so Peter was alone on the couch again. He crossed his arms over his chest, watching as Cody blew on a spoon to cool the soup.

"You put something in this?"

"Just some spices," Peter said.

"Spoiling me," Cody said with a grin. Turning to Noa he said, "You ever have this guy's oven-fried chicken?"

Noa shook her head.

"Best damn chicken I ever had."

"Anyway," Peter prodded. He was a little self-conscious about the fact that he liked to cook; it was something only a few people knew about him.

"Anyway," Cody said, taking the hint. "Pestilitas Macra Adulescens, commonly known as PEMA. First case was seen a little over seven years ago. Since then it's affected almost a hundred thousand adolescents, and that number just keeps growing."

"We know all that," Peter said impatiently.

Cody raised an eyebrow, and he fell silent. "So based on what I've seen so far, the folks at AMRF were researching PEMA."

"By experimenting on kids like me," Noa said bitterly.

"They're a little vague about that in the papers," Cody said. "They keep referring to test subjects by numbers, not names—that's the weird thing; the way they filed their data is off."

"Off how?" Peter asked.

"Off in that half the people working on Project Persephone don't seem to know that the test subjects were humans. They were collating data that was provided to them. A lot of what you've got here are just abstracts."

"Abstracts?" Noa's eyebrows knotted together.

"Like a summary of the study. It doesn't list all the details, just tells the basics: what they were trying to find out, how the study was conducted, what the results were. That sort of thing. So it's like some of the people working on this actually thought it would be publishable research someday. Which, of course, it wouldn't."

"Because they were experimenting on people," Peter said.

"Exactly." Cody pointed to the stack of papers on his right. "Anyway, the abstracts are in this pile." Shifting to the one by his left thigh, he continued, "These guys, on the other hand, seemed to know exactly what was going on. Those are your doctors' notes, all the vital-signs monitoring, that sort of thing."

"So what did they do to me?" Noa asked impatiently. Peter could hardly blame her. He didn't see why it mattered who knew what was going on; it was more important to determine what had happened to those kids.

"Here's where it gets a little complicated." Despite his fatigue, there was a definite note of excitement in Cody's voice. "It looks like they zeroed in on the endocrine system, which is hardly surprising. Most PEMA research has focused on that."

"I thought it came from deer. Like mad cow disease," Noa said.

Cody shook his head. "That theory was discredited. The symptoms are similar to Chronic Wasting Disease, which usually afflicts deer and elk. But that's caused by abnormal prion proteins. They've already determined that PEMA has nothing to do with prions."

Noa gazed at him blankly.

"Anyway," he said. "Right now their best guess is that PEMA somehow interferes with the endocrine system. Which consists of all the glands that secrete hormones into your bloodstream to regulate things."

"Those kick into overdrive when you hit puberty," Peter said. This much, at least, he knew. He'd made a point of keeping tabs on current PEMA research after Jeremy died, even though there had been frustratingly little progress. "They figure that's why it mainly affects teenagers."

"Right," Cody said, meeting Peter's eyes. Sadness flashed across his features, so fleetingly Peter didn't think Noa had noticed. "But from what I can see, even though they went so far as to run tests on humans"—at that, his voice went tight—"they still didn't find anything new."

"So why did they cut me open?" Noa asked.

"The question isn't really why," Cody said. "The question is, why did they cut you open *there*?" He drew a line across his chest, mimicking the one she'd made.

Peter and Noa exchanged a confused look.

"Here's the thing," Cody said. "Most of the research has focused on the hypothalamus, which is here." He pointed to the back of his head. "Because that seems to be what PEMA really impacts. Your hypothalamus controls your body temperature, hunger, thirst, that sort of thing."

"What about sleep?" Noa asked in a small voice.

"Sure," Cody said, warming to the subject. "In fact, some doctors think one of the reasons people develop insomnia as they age is because of changes with their hypothalamus." Suddenly noticing the stricken expression on her face, he abruptly stopped speaking.

"Are you not sleeping, either?" Peter asked.

She shrugged, her gaze locked on the floor. "Keep going," she said in a hard voice.

"You sure?" Cody sounded uncertain.

"Yes."

He still looked hesitant, but continued, "So according to these files, in the earlier experiments they tried to manipulate the hypothalamus."

"Manipulate it how?"

"That's not very clear." Cody rubbed his head. "Remember, I'm just a second-year med student. A lot of this stuff is over my head, too."

Peter very much doubted that. Cody had always been one of the smartest people he'd ever met.

"So what's in my chest?" Noa asked.

"Your thymus. Another part of the endocrine system. Kind of a weird one, actually. For a long time, no one thought it did much of anything. But in the 1960s, they discovered that it grows steadily until you hit puberty, then it stops and starts to shrivel. By the time you hit your sixties, it's smaller than it was when you were born."

"Damn," Peter said. "They really are teaching you something in med school."

"I just had a test on it last week," Cody admitted. "And I've been leaning toward specializing in endocrinology because . . . well, you know."

Peter nodded. After Jeremy died, Cody had switched from law to premed, a choice that basically forced him through an extra year of college. All so that he could devote his life to finding out what had killed his best friend.

"Okay, so they messed with my thymus, and that's why I can't eat or sleep?" Noa asked.

Cody looked apologetic. "That's the weird thing. If they'd

done something to your hypothalamus, it would make sense. But there's no incision on your scalp, right?"

Noa had gone very still. "I don't know," she said slowly. "I didn't check."

"Do you want me to check for you?" Cody asked gently.

She nodded and bent her head toward him. As he ran his fingers across her scalp, Cody said reassuringly, "They would have shaved a section of your hair off, probably." He sat back, satisfied. "Nope, all clear."

"So what would messing with my thymus do?"

Cody shrugged. "Nothing, really. You're what, seventeen?"

"Sixteen," Noa said.

"So it should already have shut off."

"Well, what do the abstracts say?" Peter asked.

Cody hesitated.

"What?" Noa demanded.

"It's just—they did a lot of different types of research. And the data is all coded, so I can't say for sure which of the tests they did on you."

"But you have a theory," Peter said. It was clear from Cody's tone of voice that he'd found something.

Cody seemed to be debating.

"Tell me," Noa said quietly. She'd raised her head and was looking at him levelly. Peter was struck again by how collected she appeared. He would have been completely freaking out.

"I don't think they messed with your thymus," Cody said. "I think they gave you another one."

CHAPTER TWELVE

"Another one?" Noa asked.

"I can't say for certain," Cody said. "The only way to know for sure would be to do an X-ray. But this paper"—he lifted a sheet off the abstract pile—"hints at a major discovery related to adding a thymus gland. Which isn't that strange, actually. Some mice are even born with an extra one. So whoever was planning on publishing the paper probably assumed that the data they were looking at came from lab rats."

"Where did the new one come from?" Noa asked.

Her voice had gone completely flat, atonal. Like they were discussing the weather.

"I can't say for certain," Cody hedged.

"But if you had to guess?" she pressed.

He lowered his voice and reluctantly said, "Some of the

kids in the files . . . well, I couldn't find correlating stats sheets for them."

"What does that mean?" She looked confused.

Peter had gone completely cold. "They took it from one of them."

"What, you mean, like . . ." Noa's hand flew to her mouth and her eyes went wide. "Oh my God."

"I'm not sure," Cody hastened to add. "It just seems like the most likely possibility."

Noa was looking green again, the same as when she'd abruptly stopped eating. "So I have a dead kid's thymus inside me?"

"I don't know," Cody admitted. "Maybe."

She got up and left the room. Peter pushed off the couch to go after her, but Cody shook his head.

"Give her a minute."

Peter hesitated, then sat back down.

"So I still don't get how you two hooked up," Cody asked after a minute.

"Noa's part of /ALLIANCE/. She's a pretty amazing hacker, so when I needed help getting into their site, I asked her. But I mean, I had no idea . . ."

"Crazy coincidence," Cody shook his head. "And Amanda?"

Peter examined his nails. "Turns out she's more into college guys."

"Oh, that's—I'm sorry, man."

Peter shrugged. He appreciated that Cody didn't say what other friends probably would've: that she was a bitch, that he was a free agent now. He understood that wasn't what Peter wanted to hear. Yeah, he was mad at Amanda, but he wasn't about to let people bad-mouth her.

"I like this one," Cody said. "She's tough."

"Yeah, she's definitely that," Peter managed a laugh.

Cody eyed him but didn't say anything else. Through the closed bathroom door Peter could hear the sink running. He wondered if she was crying.

Cody got to his feet and stretched, then rubbed his back. "I'm already starting to feel like an old man. Help me pull out the couch?"

Peter helped him set up the futon as a bed. Cody went into the other room and came back with sheets and towels. He was followed a moment later by Noa. Her face had recomposed itself into that solid mask. She eyed the futon. "Who sleeps here?"

"You do," Cody said. "Unless you two are—"

"I'll take the floor," Peter said quickly.

"So I'll dig out my sleeping bag, too. Sorry I don't have more pillows and stuff," Cody apologized.

"That's okay," Noa said. "Thanks for letting us stay."

"Of course. Pedro's a brother to me." He squeezed her shoulder as he left the room and said, "You need anything, I'm down the hall."

Noa lay on the futon, staring up at the ceiling. Her hand kept going to her chest; she couldn't stop tracing the incision under her T-shirt. The rigid line felt colder than the surrounding skin. When Cody had first given voice to his suspicions, she'd raced to the bathroom, overwhelmed by the roar in her ears. Tiny spots of light darted around her peripheral vision, as if dancing in a concerted effort to make her throw up or pass out. She'd bent over the toilet, heaving. Tasted bile, but nothing came up.

Splashing some water on her face made it better. But then

she'd met her eyes in the mirror and seen the fear in them. They were little-kid eyes again, young and scared. It had taken everything Noa had not to march into the kitchen, take a steak knife out of a drawer, and start carving into her chest.

It might not be true, she reminded herself. It was just a guess. And Cody wasn't even a real doctor yet.

Still, the minute he'd said it, something clicked. Noa could almost sense it now, a foreign presence inside her. Like the extra thymus was pulsing in time with her heartbeat. She wondered who it had belonged to, if maybe she'd known them. They might even have shared a bunk bed at The Center.

Noa rolled over on her side facing the wall. She felt cold again. The heat was turned so low her breath left thin vapor trails. Cody had apologized for that, explaining that he was trying to keep the bill down. Even though she was wearing layers under a thick comforter, Noa was still freezing. But then, even in the toasty Cambridge apartment she hadn't been able to fully warm up. She wondered if that was a byproduct of having an extra thymus. And if so, what other side effects there might be.

Noa reminded herself that wasn't all she had to worry about. They might have infected her with PEMA. Somehow, the prospect of that was much less frightening than the thymus thing. Death she could handle—she'd become familiar with it at an early age, and honestly hadn't expected to live as long as she had. When the social worker handed her a cup of cocoa at the hospital and explained that her parents had "gone up to heaven," her first thought was that bad things always happened in threes. Noa had spent her life waiting for the other shoe to drop.

This other thing, though . . . that was a heavy weight to bear.

"You awake?" Peter whispered.

Noa debated whether or not to answer. She didn't really feel like talking. Still, Peter had provided a roof over her head tonight. And it had been really nice of him to offer to sleep on the floor. She hadn't encountered a lot of guys who would do that. "Yeah," she finally said.

A pause, then Peter said, "I'm really sorry."

"You didn't do anything."

"I know I didn't. I wasn't accepting blame; I was expressing empathy. There's a difference."

"I know that," she said testily.

A moment of silence passed, then he said, "Now I'm less sorry."

In spite of herself, Noa laughed.

He continued, "Anyway, it sucks. I was just thinking this must be pretty scary for you."

"I'm not scared," she said.

"Really? Because I'd be completely freaked out." The sound of knuckles cracking—she'd noticed Peter did that whenever he was mulling something over. "Waking up on that table—I probably would have lost it."

"Not helping," she said drily.

"Sorry."

"You apologize a lot," she said.

"Only because you make me nervous."

"I do?" She rolled over to face Peter, propping her head up with one hand. There were no curtains in the windows, and light from the street below faintly illuminated him. The sleeping bag was unzipped to his waist, exposing a faded Country Day soccer T-shirt. He was gazing up at the ceiling. "Why?"

He turned toward her and smiled sheepishly. "Not sure, really. Maybe because of the way you talk."

"How do I talk?" she demanded.

"Like you're trying to start a fight. Or like we're already in one. My mom would call it confrontational."

Noa thought that over. "I don't mean to," she finally said.

"Yeah, I figured. You were different tonight, when the files distracted you."

"Oh."

He laughed again and said, "See?"

"What?"

"I never have trouble talking to people."

"Lucky you," she snorted.

"No, I didn't mean it like that. It's just something I've always been good at. But with you, I have no idea what to say, and everything that comes out of my mouth is idiotic. And I can't figure out why."

He sounded genuinely puzzled. After a minute, Noa asked, "Did your folks really kick you out?"

"Yeah." It was hard to tell in the dimness, but it looked like his face clouded over. "Plus my girlfriend broke up with me."

"So you're having a crappy couple of days, too."

"You still win." His teeth flashed in the dark.

"No question."

They were silent for a minute, then he said, "I can't believe you got away from those guys. Impressive."

"Yeah, well. It wasn't like I had a choice."

"Guess not. Still, I never would have thought of half that stuff."

His voice was filled with admiration. Noa wasn't sure how to respond. But inexplicably, she felt better. Until he said, "So what next?"

"What do you mean?" she asked.

"I figure we can stay here for a few days while we work this out, but we've got to find out for certain what they did to you, right?" Peter asked softly.

Noa nodded, then realizing he probably couldn't see her clearly said, "Yeah."

"So Cody and I were talking about how we could maybe get some tests done on you . . ."

"Tests?" Her voice climbed a register.

"Not like that," Peter said reassuringly. "A chest X-ray, and maybe a PEMA test. You want to know if they gave it to you, right?"

It was a legitimate question. Part of her really didn't want to know, but she said, "I guess."

"Great. So the PEMA test is pretty easy. Cody can draw blood and sneak it in with some other lab work during his hospital shift tomorrow. The X-ray is a little trickier. But he had an idea."

"Yeah?" Noa was liking the sound of this less and less. She'd only had an X-ray once before, when she was ten and one of her foster moms broke her wrist because she wasn't washing the dishes properly. "What kind of idea?"

"A buddy of ours from high school is a vet now. Cody says we can trust him, and that way it won't be like a regular hospital where the results go into the computer. Because there's a chance . . ."

"That they're watching for that," Noa finished for him. Cody was right: She needed to stay off the radar as much as possible. But the fact that they were going so far out of their way got her guard up. "Why are you doing this?"

"Doing what?"

"Helping me," she said.

"Why wouldn't I?" Peter sounded perplexed.

"I don't know. It's just—you don't know me and . . . I guess I'm not used to it."

"That's too bad," he said. "Honestly, for me part of this isn't even about you. It's the whole reason I set up /ALLIANCE/. When we find out that some jerks are doing something terrible, we punish them for it."

"Yeah, but you already did that by bricking AMRF's system."

"They can probably get it back online. And that doesn't even begin to make up for what they did to you." His voice grew heated as he continued, "Plus they'll probably keep doing it. They might be experimenting on other kids right now."

"I'd thought of that," Noa admitted. "There were a lot of warehouses in that complex."

"Well, they know you know where that is. So unless they're total morons, they probably cleared those out," Peter mused. "Still . . ."

When he didn't continue, Noa finally asked, "Still?"

"I was just thinking, all of their files have probably downloaded by now. I can't help with the science stuff, but there should be a way for me to dig through and find out who's running this entire thing."

"I thought it was that Mason guy."

"I don't know," Peter said. "The way he and my parents talked . . . I got the sense Mason reported to someone else. He didn't seem to be in charge of everything. The real boss probably wouldn't be running around handling stuff like me, right?"

"Probably not," Noa acquiesced. "So you find out who's really in charge. Then what?"

"Then we go after them." Peter's voice was grim as he said, "It'll make everything else we did with /ALLIANCE/ look like nothing. We'll expose them to the world."

Noa wasn't entirely certain she liked the sound of that. Exposing AMRF to the world would basically expose her to the world, too, and she'd expended a lot of time and energy digging a hole deep enough to hide in. Still, she said, "Sounds like a plan."

"Yup. Well, we should get some sleep." Peter's voice dissolved into a yawn as he said, "Night."

Noa lay there, thinking.

"Peter?"

"Yeah?"

She paused, then said, "Thanks."

"Sure."

The sound of his breathing gradually evened out. An occasional car passed by, but other than that the night was still and silent. Sleep wouldn't come for her, though. Her body felt exhausted—it had been nearly twenty-four hours since she'd slept a wink. Still, her mind wouldn't stop churning over the events of the past few days, a steady stream of people and places. And underlying it all, that constant pulsing beat in her chest.

Finally Noa got up, grabbed her laptop off the table, and went to the window. Shivering, she sat in the window seat overlooking the street. No cushioning, just bare wood, so it felt like the cold was pushing through the oversized sweatpants Cody had loaned her.

She didn't have the energy to keep working on the files—the mere thought of it made her head hurt. So instead she went to her email.

There was a new message from A6M0. Nothing in the

body of the email, but the subject header read, *You okay?*

She sent a chat request and a second later, his handle popped up in the chat window.

Was starting to worry about u, he wrote.

I'm fine.

Good.

Noa's fingers hesitated over the keyboard. It was an odd thing—her gut told her that whoever this person was, he or she had the answers she was looking for. But she had so many questions, she hardly knew where to begin. *Who r u?* she finally typed.

Not important. Re: AMRF bricking. Was that u?

A friend, Noa wrote, thinking that he was wrong. It was important for her to know, especially since he seemed to know so much about her. But pushing the issue might close that channel, and she needed answers to more pressing questions.

Did u get their files?

Noa hesitated again. She might be talking to someone from AMRF. She had no idea if she was even chatting with the same person. Finally she wrote, *Yes.*

A longer pause this time, then the words streamed on-screen. *Then you have the only copies of the Project's files. They'll keep coming after them. If you found a safe place to hide, stay there.*

I need answers, she wrote back, feeling a flash of anger. *What did they do to me?*

You can't let them get you again, he wrote. *It's critical.*

So if I give the data back, they'll leave me alone? Noa asked. Maybe some sort of exchange would get them all off the hook. If the data was so important, and she and Peter had sole access to it, this might be a way out. She could set up a fail-safe system that would kick in if something happened to either of them. Make sure that AMRF knew about it so they'd leave them alone for good. . . .

She was already planning it out in her head when his reply popped up. *They'll never leave you alone,* he wrote. *You're the key. And you can't give the data back. They'll just use it to hurt more of us.*

What does that mean? she typed, aggravated. It was like trying to have a conversation with Yoda: completely maddening. When a minute passed without a reply, she added, *Who is us?*

No response. Looking over what she'd just written, Noa couldn't help but think, *Great. Now he's got me talking like that, too.*

Then A6M0 abruptly logged out of the chat, and she had to restrain herself from flinging the laptop across the room.

She slammed the lid shut, powering off the computer. A sleepy voice asked, "What's going on?"

"Nothing," she whispered, feeling badly for waking him. "Go back to sleep."

" 'Kay. Love you, Amanda," Peter said dreamily.

Noa stiffened. It was odd to hear those words again, even if they weren't really intended for her. It had been almost a decade since anyone said they loved her. She still remembered the last time. Her mother had buckled her into the car seat, kissed her on the forehead, and whispered it into Noa's hair.

Noa tucked her chin on her knees and stared out the window. She rubbed her left wrist. Even though her bracelet was gone, the motion calmed her.

Amanda pulled the hood of her sweater over her head and tugged her scarf closer to her neck. It was freezing, far colder than the end of October should be. *Thank you, global warming,* she thought. It drove her nuts when pundits used cold weather as an excuse to bolster claims that climate change was an imaginary phenomenon created by scientists. How did people not understand that global warming didn't literally mean the planet would be hotter, just that every weather pattern would become more intense? Amanda found it horribly frustrating.

She and Drew had just been discussing that earlier over coffee at the student center. It was amazing how much they saw eye to eye on everything. She'd never felt so perfectly in sync with someone before. Peter—well, Peter was Peter, and she loved him for that. He was funny and charming, and brought out a lighter side of her. But sometimes she got frustrated by the way he laughed everything off. Life was just one big joke to him. Nothing wrong with that, she reminded herself—as her psych professor said the other day, everyone developed their own worldview. The problem was that Amanda had discovered that theirs didn't mesh so well anymore. Her attention would drift when Peter launched into a long discourse on internet freedom or hacktivism. It was all just so . . . virtual. She preferred to focus on problems that were right there in front of you. And she preferred to handle them in person, not through a network of anonymity.

Drew totally got that. And he grasped what she was saying about kids like her brother, who slipped through the social safety net. Once her brother fell off the grid, there was no one actively invested in trying to save him. Organizations like the Runaway Coalition were few and far between, and mainly designed to send teens back to the streets in slightly better condition.

Drew loved her idea to develop more intensive centers

that addressed the problem. Way stations for teens that were more than glorified halfway houses. Places where they could actually get a GED, have a safe place to sleep, and receive help overcoming everything life had burdened them with. Once Drew finished law school, he was planning on taking a job with a grassroots community organization, learning the ropes. And then maybe, he'd hinted, they could tackle the problem together.

Amanda flushed at the thought. Drew was *the one*, she was sure of it. But she felt badly about Peter. She hadn't handled it well; she really should have talked to him weeks ago. She'd called his cell all day, trying to apologize, but it kept going straight to voice mail. Which was just like him, she thought, rolling her eyes. Avoiding tough conversations. The fact that he and his parents never even mentioned his brother's name had always struck her as astonishing. It was like Jeremy had never existed, the way they'd gone about systematically eliminating every sign of him from their lives.

It was a shame. But not her problem anymore, she reminded herself.

Amanda quickened her pace. The quad was empty, most of the windows dark. It was later than she'd thought. Even though she'd been wiped out after volunteering, Drew persuaded her to meet him for coffee and they'd lost track of time. She should really have paid more attention.

She flashed back to the wounded expression on Peter's face when he stormed out, and felt a pang. She shook it off. This was for the best. And Peter would be fine. Girls loved him; he'd probably be dating again within a week.

Still, Amanda wished he'd answer his phone. If nothing else, she'd like to give him some closure.

Amanda was almost at her dorm. There was a guy there

on crutches, struggling to swipe his card across the keypad to release the latch. His backpack slipped from his shoulder, and he swore.

"Here," she said, hurrying forward. "Let me get it for you."

She drew her student ID card from her pocket and swiped it. The door clicked open. Amanda bent to pick up the backpack and handed it to him with a smile.

Which quickly faded when she saw his face. The guy was at least thirty, far too old to be living in a freshman dorm. He'd dropped the crutches and was standing on both feet now.

His eyes were hard as he stared down at her.

Amanda turned to run. But a shadow separated from the bushes at the base of the stairs to her left, and another to her right. They started to close in.

She opened her mouth to scream, but a hand clamped over it from behind, muffling the sound. There was a sharp jab in her neck. Amanda struggled for another few seconds, then her muscles suddenly refused to respond. Her whole body went limp, and she fell back into his arms.

CHAPTER THIRTEEN

Noa awoke to the smell of burning toast. Her whole body ached. Something hard was digging into her back. She blinked and straightened. She'd fallen asleep in the window seat. Someone—probably Peter—had draped a wool blanket over her. Still, her back was cold where it touched the bare wall.

She wrapped the blanket around her shoulders and made her way down the hall to the kitchen. On the other side of a narrow doorframe, Peter stood in front of a tiny two-burner range. The counter was a wreck of eggshells and dirty bowls, and smoke poured out the top of a toaster oven.

Hearing her, Peter turned and smiled weakly. He was juggling a blackened piece of toast in one hand. "Morning," he said.

The smoke alarm started to blare.

Noa moved past him to the window and struggled with

the bolts. She finally twisted the last one and wrenched it open, shivering against the blast of cold air that raced past her into the flat. She drew the blanket more firmly around her shoulders with one hand. As the smoke dissipated and the room cleared, the alarm fell still.

Noa turned back to find Peter giving her that lopsided grin. "Sorry," he said meekly. "I was cooking."

Noa eyed the toast. "I'm pretty sure that doesn't qualify as cooking. I thought you were supposed to be some sort of great chef."

He frowned. "I never said that."

"Cody did."

"Yeah, well . . . it's a crap toaster oven." He tossed the ruined slices into a trash can beneath the sink.

A voice called through the light shaft, "Everything okay up there?"

"Yes, Pam. Sorry," Peter called back.

He looked at Noa and rolled his eyes. Something about the whole situation suddenly struck her as unbearably funny—precisely what, she couldn't pinpoint, but Noa was hit by a rare and extreme case of the giggles.

"What?" Peter demanded as she doubled over with laughter. "I don't get it."

"Is something else burning?" Noa managed. She was laughing so hard it was a struggle to breathe.

"Oh, crap." Peter dashed to the stove and lifted the lid off a sauté pan. More smoke poured off a blackened omelet.

Noa's laughter redoubled and she dropped to the ground, howling.

"It's really not funny," Peter said, frowning as he grabbed the saucepan handle and headed for the window. He held it outside, waving away smoke. "I think I might have ruined the pan," he said ruefully. "And that was the last of the eggs."

"Last of the toast, too?" Noa said between giggles.

Peter nodded glumly.

Noa couldn't help it—she snorted. Maybe because she still wasn't hungry, the lack of breakfast didn't have much of an impact. And the whole situation still seemed hilarious— the expression on Peter's face as he stood there holding a pan full of ruined food . . .

She lost it again.

Peter finally cracked a grin. "All right, maybe it's a little funny," he acknowledged.

"Way to keep a low profile," she choked out. "Think the fire department is on the way?"

"Maybe," he said.

Noa suddenly flashed back to clinging on to the fire truck as it drove through the warehouse complex gates. That knocked the laughter right out of her. She looked up to find Peter examining her with a look of concern.

"You okay?" he asked.

"Yeah, I'm fine," she said, collecting herself. "Where's Cody?"

"He had to go to work. We were going to wake you up to do the blood draw, but—well, you're a hell of a sleeper," Peter replied. "Cody has a break before he has to go in for hospital rounds. He said he'd come back then."

"Okay," Noa said, even though she was already dreading the thought of a needle puncturing her skin, the pulse of blood into a vial . . . bile rose in her throat, and her hand went to her chest.

"So . . . I guess I'll see if I can salvage any of this," Peter said, looking around the kitchen dubiously. "Maybe Cody has hot sauce."

"It's okay." Noa waved a hand. "I'm not hungry."

He nodded as if that was normal, even though she hadn't eaten at all last night. "Great. More for me."

Noa hated the forced cheer in his voice, but resisted the inclination to snap at him about it. Peter was just trying to make her feel better. It wasn't his fault she was suddenly a freak of human nature.

"I'm gonna get back to work on those files," Noa muttered, standing up.

"Yeah, great." He perked up. "After breakfast, I'll check the upload status. All the files should be on the remote server by now."

As she went back toward the living room, Noa heard the hiss of water hitting a hot pan. The living room was smoky, too. Despite the cold, she cracked one of the windows to let it out, then plopped down on a floor pillow, powered up her laptop, and checked email. Nothing new from her annoyingly mysterious pen pal. Out of curiosity, she did a web search for A6M0. Like her, most hackers chose an online identity with some sort of personal connection. Maybe he had, too.

A Google search only elicited a bunch of links to the Australian stock exchange and pages composed entirely in what looked like Japanese. She dug through three pages of results and was about to give up in frustration when she stumbled across a Wikipedia link.

"Ha!" she said out loud. "Got you."

"What?"

Noa turned. Peter was standing in the doorway rubbing the pan with a dishcloth. "Nothing. I just found something."

"About Project Persephone?" he asked, stepping into the room.

"No. Something different." Noa shifted the screen slightly

so that it faced away from him. When she'd told Cody and him about the past few days, she'd neglected to mention her guardian angel. She wasn't quite sure why—it had just been an instinct.

"Oh." Peter looked confused. "I'll be in the other room using Cody's computer if you need anything."

"Okay." Noa repressed a twinge of annoyance. It had been a while since she'd spent such an intensive amount of time with other people, but she didn't remember this level of small talk being the norm. It was exhausting. Yet Peter seemed reluctant to leave the room.

"Good luck," she said finally, turning back to her computer.

"Yeah, okay," he mumbled.

Noa puffed out air, annoyed. She turned back to her laptop and dug a bit deeper to confirm the Wikipedia entry—now she had a potential name for her guardian angel. An A6M0 was a WWII Japanese fighter plane—which explained all the entries in Japanese. Allied forces nicknamed it the "Zeke." So if she was right, her guardian angel was a guy named Zeke. Or he just had a thing for old planes.

None of which got her closer to any answers, she reminded herself.

A minute later Noa heard a string of curses. A pause, then more.

"What's wrong?" she finally called out, exasperated.

"I can't use this."

"Why not?"

"Come see."

She walked into the bedroom. Peter was sitting on a plastic chair that looked like patio furniture facing an ancient computer monitor. Noa's eyebrows shot up at the sight of the enormous tower by his feet. "Is that a Gateway?" she asked. "Really?"

"Really," Peter replied, sounding pained. "It has to be at least a decade old." He turned back to it.

"RAM?" Noa asked.

"Thirty-two megs," he said.

Noa laughed. "Seriously?"

Peter said, "But wait, that's not all. It's running Windows 2000."

"No." Noa was dumbfounded. She crossed the room and bent over him, tapping a few keys to call up the system stats. "Wow. This thing belongs in a museum."

"No kidding." Peter sat back in his chair and said pensively, "I thought my folks gave Cody my brother's old laptop."

"Maybe he took that one to work?" Noa suggested.

"Maybe," Peter said. "Although it's not like EMTs have a lot of time to check email during their shifts. Anyway, I don't know if I'll be able to access anything using this. If you can spare any time on your MacBook . . ."

"You want to touch another hacker's computer?" She arched an eyebrow.

"I know, I know," he said, grinning. "We don't know each other all that well yet, so it's early to be sharing computers—"

"Way early," Noa said. "And you didn't even make me breakfast."

"Hey, I tried," he protested. "But Cody printed out a lot of the stuff you need, right?"

"Right." All joking aside, Noa was loath to let anyone else touch her computer. It was kind of a geek thing, the way chefs brought their own knives to work. No one else handled the tools of your trade. Still, Peter was right—he'd need something faster than the antique on Cody's desk. And most of what she was doing today involved matching up files to individual patients—stuff that Cody had printed out, anyway.

"Fine," she said. "But I'm not sharing passwords."

"Of course not." Peter looked horrified. "Like that was even on the table."

He smiled at her, and she grinned back. Noa was suddenly hyperattuned to how close they were—she'd leaned over his shoulder to examine the computer tower, and their thighs were touching. She was conscious of a sudden tension between them, a strange, almost electric hum. Something in Peter's eyes shifted, and he leaned closer. "Noa, I—"

"I'll get the laptop," she said abruptly, stepping back.

Peter didn't say anything, but she felt his eyes on her as she left the room.

It was strange. Her ears were burning, and her heart hammered in her chest, which felt abnormally tight again. Yet she doubted that had anything to do with the operation. No, this was something different—and she wasn't sure she liked it.

The truth was, Noa had never even kissed a boy, a secret that she guarded closely. Not that they hadn't tried. Back at The Center, and in a few of her various foster homes, she'd been forced to rebut several attempts to kiss her, and worse. The thing was, she'd never wanted to do that with anyone before. *Until now,* she realized suddenly.

Noa caught herself picturing Peter's lips. They were unusually full for a boy and looked soft, and for just a second she wondered how they'd feel, pressed against her own . . . she started and shook her head, shoving the image away. She was being ridiculous. The stress of everything that had happened, and the fact that he was being so nice to her—that's all it was.

Noa scooped up the MacBook and marched back into the bedroom, hoping that her face wasn't still flushed. Peter still sat facing the doorway, watching her intently. When she entered, he gazed back at her levelly, as if waiting for something. Unceremoniously, Noa shoved the laptop at him. "Here," she said gruffly, then whirled on her heel and darted back to the living room without meeting his eyes again.

Still feeling unsettled, she went to the piles Cody had stacked carefully in the corner last night. After a moment, Peter started tapping away at the keyboard in the next room. The sound was soothing, and her breathing slowed. With effort, Noa forced her attention back to the printouts.

Somewhere in there might be the name of the kid whose thymus was inside her, Noa thought with dread. She steeled herself. She'd just try to treat the files clinically, as if this was a work project.

It was easier than she thought, once she got past the initial queasiness. The morning passed quickly. Peter tapped away on her laptop as Noa sifted through files, trying to find commonalities that helped organize them. Cody had told her what to look for: blood type first, then certain markers that would indicate the same patient.

Whenever Noa passed the bedroom door on her way to the bathroom or kitchen, she stole a glance at Peter. His heel beat a constant tempo against the bare floor. It was oddly comforting, like the patter of rain against windowpanes. For the first time since awakening on that table, she was able to relax somewhat. It was nice to have a respite from looking over her shoulder.

"Hungry yet?"

Noa glanced up. "Huh?"

"I asked if you wanted something," Peter said, walking out of the bedroom. He stretched his arms overhead. "I'm starved."

He licked his lips, and Noa felt her cheeks flush again. She ducked her head to hide it, then turned to check the clock. It was well past noon. "No, I'm not really hungry," she mumbled.

"Okay," Peter said. "If you change your mind, Cody said to help ourselves to anything in the fridge. Not that there's much."

"What time is he coming home?" Noa asked, relieved that he hadn't seemed to notice the tension between them earlier. Or if he had, he was pretending it hadn't happened, either. Which was fine with her.

"Soon, I think. His hospital shift starts at three, so he was just going to run in and . . . well, you know."

"Yeah." *Draw my blood,* Noa thought. *Poke me with more needles.*

Peter scratched his belly through his shirt. "I'm going to take a shower, too. Unless you want to go first?"

Noa wasn't entirely comfortable taking a shower here, but it might warm her up. And she probably smelled pretty ripe. She was on the last change of clothes from Urban Outfitters, too—she should wash some stuff in the sink. "Yeah, I'll do that."

"'Kay. Cody left towels on the edge of the tub."

He shuffled off toward the kitchen. Noa went into the bathroom and cranked the water to the hottest setting. Facing away from the spray, she dropped her head and closed her eyes, letting the stream loosen the tight muscles in her shoulders.

Low voices outside the bathroom door. Cody must have come home.

Reluctantly Noa got out and toweled dry, rubbing her hair hard. She ran her fingers through it and checked the mirror. The weird thing was that she actually looked pretty good. Paler than normal, which was saying something. But the bags under her eyes had vanished despite her lack of sleep, and there was color in her cheeks.

Noa pulled on the last clean clothes from her bag and brushed her teeth with her finger. She really needed to get a toothbrush. She made a mental note to ask Cody if there was a drugstore nearby where she could grab toiletries and TracFones for her and Peter.

She entered the living room to find Peter and Cody engaged in a low, intense conversation. "What's up?"

"I found something." Peter was visibly excited. "Holy crap, though. It's kind of unreal."

"Almost too unreal," Cody said, sounding skeptical.

"I think it makes perfect sense," Peter retorted.

"Are either of you going to fill me in?" Noa asked wearily. She was starting to feel tired again, and the heat was ebbing from her body, cold edging in from her extremities.

"I zeroed in on one of the shell companies listed on the property deeds for the warehouse and boatyard," Peter said. "It wasn't easy, but I tracked it back to three others, all based with offshore holding companies. And guess who finally turned up as the parent company?"

"Who?" Noa hated when people asked questions like that. If he knew who was behind all this, why not just spit it out?

Triumphantly, Peter spun the laptop around so that the screen faced her. Noa frowned. It was the same home page her mysterious guardian angel kept sending her.

"A shampoo company?" she said dubiously.

"Not just a shampoo company," Peter corrected, pulling

down a submenu. "See? Pike and Dolan have their hands in everything. Pharmaceuticals, consumer products, medical research. They even make that fake sweetener everyone uses now."

"They're one of the largest corporations in the country," Cody said. "Charles Pike has given millions for legitimate medical research. There's a whole wing at Boston Medical named after him. I just can't imagine he'd risk that by getting mixed up in something like this."

"Maybe he had a really good reason," Peter pointed out. "I found this, too." He clicked through to a different screen that displayed an image of a lovely young girl. She was blond, wan, about their age. The photo would have looked right at home on the cover of a magazine. The headline below it read, *Elinor Pike Stricken with PEMA*. "Charles Pike's kid is sick. And look what else I found."

Peter hit a few keys, and a video filled the screen. It featured a tall, broad-shouldered white guy in his midfifties. Charles Pike's hair was gray but his eyebrows remained black. He had strong features, a slightly prominent chin, blue eyes. Pike looked confident and sure of himself: clearly a man accustomed to getting his way. He stood behind a podium, in front of a large banner that read, *The Pike Center for PEMA Research*. Peter hit another key, and Pike's voice spilled out of the speakers. ". . . a blight on our times, the potential loss of an entire generation isn't something I'll countenance. Which is why I'm asking all of you to join me in donating generously, in hopes of finding a cure for PEMA."

Peter tapped another button and the man fell silent. He waved a hand at the screen. "He goes on like this for a while."

The video kept running, and Noa stared at it. Charles

Pike looked so . . . normal. Impassioned, but ordinary. Yet he might be the one ultimately responsible for what had happened to her. At the thought, a chill ran down her spine.

"I'd heard that his daughter had PEMA. But still . . ." Cody rubbed a hand across his face. "I don't know, this whole thing just keeps getting crazier."

"You said they aren't close to finding a cure," Peter said. "And Pike's daughter has been sick for nearly a year now. She probably doesn't have much time left. He might have gotten desperate."

"The files date back more than a year," Noa said in a low voice.

"What?" Cody asked.

"I said, they've been doing this for longer than that." She couldn't take her eyes off the photo of the girl. She recognized something in her eyes, a haunted quality. "The testing started before she got sick."

"There's a lot of money to be made here," Cody acknowledged. "If a company could find a cure, or even a vaccine, well . . . it would be worth a fortune."

"That explains why Bob's involved," Peter said bitterly.

"Maybe he's trying to spare other parents the pain of what they went though," Cody said gently. "He and your mom probably don't have any idea about the experiments P and D were conducting."

"Sure. They probably thought Mason and his thugs were some sort of candy stripers," Peter retorted.

Cody shook his head. "I know it's tough, Peter. But we should give them the benefit of the doubt."

"Do what you want, but I'll keep doubting them," Peter said. "So what now?"

They all fell silent.

"You've got all the data related to Project Persephone, right?" Cody asked.

"Yup. They probably have copies, though."

"They don't," Noa said.

"How do you know that?" Peter's eyes narrowed.

Noa backpedaled, saying, "I mean, even if they do, they can't get to them right now."

"That would explain why they keep coming after you," Cody acknowledged.

"I'm the key." Noa suddenly understood what A6M0 had meant.

Cody and Peter were both looking at her oddly.

"The key?" Peter asked. "What does that mean?"

"Nothing," Noa said. "Just . . . we should probably find out for sure what they did to me, right? Since they keep coming after me, I must have something important that they need."

"Maybe," Peter said, eyeing her. "Or maybe they're just worried you'll tell someone what happened."

"Who would believe me?" Noa pointed out. "I'm a foster kid who's done time in juvie. You think anyone would listen if I said that Charles Pike hired people to kidnap and experiment on me?"

"No, I guess they wouldn't," Peter acknowledged. "So why do they care so much?"

They all fell silent for a minute. Finally, Cody cleared his throat and said, "I can take you to get that X-ray now." He glanced at his watch. "He said any time after noon would work fine."

"Great, let's go." Noa crossed the room and grabbed her jacket, then started to gather up her laptop.

"Oh, are you taking that? 'Cause I thought I'd stay here

and keep working on stuff," Peter said apologetically. "Now that I know what to look for, I thought I'd track down some of Pike and Dolan's real-estate holdings. You know, places where they might be keeping . . . others. Like you."

"I need to take it with me," Noa said.

"Seriously? I mean, it's not like—"

"It stays with me," she said sharply.

"Jeez, relax. I was just—"

"Why don't you come along, Peter?" Cody interceded. "I'm sure Jack has a wireless connection you can piggyback on."

"I thought the whole point was to keep a low profile," Peter grumbled.

Noa glared at him, and he raised both hands in surrender. "Fine. I'll get my jacket. But it'll just take longer this way."

The table was about two feet too short for her, so Noa's lower legs hung off the edge at an uncomfortable angle. The room reeked of sickly-sweet disinfectant mixed with animal piss and wet fur. A shelf on the far wall held medicine jars labeled DOGGY TREATS, KITTY TREATS, and REPTILE TREATS.

She swallowed hard. Above her, the beige camera gazed down blankly like a giant, malevolent eye. Cody's high-school buddy, Jack, finished draping a heavy lead sheet over her lower body.

"Sorry about the table length," he said. "It's really not built for people."

"That's okay." Noa forced a smile.

Cody was standing in the far corner, facing the monitor that the images would appear on. Peter was in the waiting room outside. She wondered how much Cody had told his friend Jack. The vet seemed only mildly perturbed by the fact that a person was using his X-ray equipment. This had to be an unusual occurrence for him, though.

"Ready?" he asked.

Noa nodded.

The machine clicked a few times.

"Okay." Jack stepped forward and pulled off the lead shield.

"That's it?" Noa asked.

"Yup. All digital now," the vet said cheerfully. "So we get the results instantly. You can go look, if you want." He turned to Cody. "I got a retriever coming in that was hit by a car. You okay to see yourselves out?"

"Yeah, man. Thanks again."

"No problem." Jack smiled, turning to Noa. "Nice meeting you. Come on back if you need deworming."

He left the room, chuckling at his own little joke.

Cody's smile faded the instant the door closed. He bent over, examining the screen. Noa hesitated, then slid off the table and went to stand beside him. The monitor displayed an enlarged black-and-white image. Pale white ribs stood out in sharp relief, like slender fingers. Under and around them, she could discern a bunch of lumpy-looking masses.

"So?" Noa finally asked, after a minute had passed without him saying anything.

Cody didn't meet her eyes. "We were right." He pointed. "This is your heart, here. And beside it, this smaller one is probably your original thymus. Next to that, well . . . this shouldn't be here."

Noa eyed the mass. It was almost as large as her heart. "What does the thymus do, anyway?"

"I talked to a buddy today who's specializing in endocrinology," Cody said. "Basically, your thymus gland produces and educates T lymphocytes."

Noa looked at him blankly. "Was that English?"

He laughed. "Sorry. Do you know how the immune system works?"

"Kind of." Noa shrugged. "It keeps you from getting sick, right?"

"Exactly," Cody said, warming to the topic. "And specific types of cells combat disease. But those cells don't start out knowing how to do that. When you're first born, the thymus provides kind of a boot camp for immune cells. It trains them to become T cells, which are the white blood cells that fight infection. By the time you hit puberty, all those cells know their business, so the thymus shuts down."

"So what would giving me an extra thymus do?" Noa asked.

"I did a little research today during my break, and there have been a few studies," Cody said. "Remember those mice I told you about, the ones that are born with an extra thymus?"

"Yeah?"

"Well, in their case, both thymuses shut down at the same time. So the second one was just superfluous. But one researcher theorized that if you managed to keep at least one activated, you might be able to use it to develop newer, stronger T cells. Maybe even ones that could be trained to fight specific diseases."

"Like PEMA," Noa said slowly, following his line of reasoning.

"Exactly."

"So now do we test my blood?" Noa said.

"If you want," Cody said. "I realized this morning that I hadn't asked, I just assumed you'd want to know. It's fine if you don't, though." He gazed at her with a look of concern.

"I want to know," she said decisively, holding out her arm. "Let's get it over with."

Cody pulled out a small kit. She turned her head away as he rubbed the inside of her elbow with an alcohol pad. He was good; she barely felt the needle as it pierced her skin. Watching her blood pump into the vial, Noa asked, "Do you think it'll be positive?"

"No idea," he said. "How about we cross that bridge when we come to it?" Cody's hand was warm on her arm as he pressed a piece of gauze down, then taped a Band-Aid over it. "Done."

"Thanks. When will you know?"

"By this evening. It's a quick test," he said. "I'll slip it in with another patient's blood work."

"Could you get in trouble for that?"

"I'll be careful," Cody said casually.

Noa got the sense that he was taking a far greater risk than he let on. "Why are you doing this?" she asked warily.

"I told you. Pedro's like a brother to me," he responded without meeting her eyes.

"Yeah, but still. You'll get in a lot of trouble if you get caught, right?"

Cody made a noise in his throat that wasn't quite a laugh. "Yeah, I sure will."

"So why?" Noa asked again.

He looked up, meeting her eyes. "You ever been in love?"

"What?" Noa said, taken aback. Recovering, she slowly shook her head. "No." Something dawned on her, and she said with disbelief, "You're in love with Peter?"

At that, Cody laughed openly. "No. I mean, I love the kid, just not like that. But . . ." His eyes seemed to look through her then. "I loved exactly one person my whole life," he continued in a voice so low she could barely hear him. "And then that person died. But I promised I'd take care of his brother." His eyes shifted back and focused on hers intently again.

"Oh." Noa cleared her throat and said, "I won't tell Peter."

His gaze softened and he squeezed her knee. "I know. That's why I trusted you with it."

They sat in silence for a minute. Noa couldn't repress the feeling that there was someone else in the room with them. It didn't frighten her, though. It was oddly comforting, like there really were guardian angels out there. *After all,* she thought to herself, *Peter is standing right here.*

Finally, Cody glanced at his watch and said, "We should get out of here. Can't leave Peter alone out there for too long; he's always been a sucker for puppies."

Cody tucked the vial of blood into his jacket pocket and they left the room in silence.

In the waiting room, Peter was hunched over her laptop. An overweight woman in her forties clutched a cat carrier as she stared openly at him. Noa couldn't really blame her. Peter looked nuts.

"Finally!" he exclaimed, seeing them. He fumbled the laptop back into Noa's messenger bag. "Man, you are not going to believe—"

"Let's talk about it outside," Cody said.

They pushed back out to the street. The animal hospital was located a few blocks from Boston Medical Center's main lab, where Cody planned to drop off the blood work.

"So what'd you find?" Noa asked.

"You first," Peter said. "How was the X-ray?"

Noa fixed him with a steely glare. Out of her peripheral

vision, she saw Cody give a little headshake. Peter caught it and his eyes darkened. He cleared his throat and said, "All right, I'll go first. I found a few possibilities. They're all big warehouse complexes, like the one in South Boston. Supposedly Pike and Dolan are storing products there, but I couldn't find any shipping manifests related to them."

"Shipping manifests?" Noa asked, puzzled.

"Smart, Pedro," Cody said admiringly. "If P and D was using those warehouses to store products before shipping them, there would be a steady stream of trucks and cargo containers in and out. And each of those shipments would have to be tracked."

"Exactly," Peter said. "And there was nothing like that. So I'm thinking they might be using them for more labs."

The prospect gave Noa a chill. "How many did you find?"

"So far? Three." Peter's voice turned somber as he continued, "And one is just across the state line, in Rhode Island. About an hour away. Two days ago a truckload of stuff listed as miscellaneous was shipped there. That was the first delivery they've had in a long time. So I'm thinking that might be where they moved the operation. After, well, you know . . ."

His voice trailed off. *After you got away,* Noa filled in. She thought of the other buildings she'd passed during the escape. At the time, part of her had sensed that there were other kids there, trapped inside. But she kept running. There was nothing else she could have done, she reminded herself. But now, maybe, there was. "We have to get them out."

"One thing at a time," Cody cautioned. "After my shift, we can meet back at my place to discuss options."

"Yeah, but—"

"You can't go there on your own. There were armed men at that warehouse, right?" Cody raised an eyebrow. "It was hard enough for you to get away from them before. I think it's time we bring in the cops."

"And tell them what?" Peter demanded. "There isn't enough here to get a search warrant. My mom's a lawyer, remember? She'd have a field day with something like that."

"Peter's right." Noa jutted out her chin. "We need more proof. So far we don't have anything directly linking Pike and Dolan to this. Plus, I don't like cops. They show up, I'm out of here."

Cody ran a hand over his face wearily. His eyes sagged with exhaustion. "One step at a time, okay, guys? Tell you what. I'll drop off this blood work, then tell them I'm coming down with something and need to go home. We'll hunker down at my place and try to find more links to P and D. Then we'll figure out a strategy."

"Sounds like a plan," said Peter.

"Yeah?" Cody eyed them both. "Because that sounded suspiciously like you were thinking about going off and doing something stupid."

"Nope," Peter said. "We'll be waiting for you."

Noa didn't say anything.

"You got the TracFones, right?" Cody said.

Peter held up the drugstore shopping bag. "I activated them while I was waiting."

"All right, give me the numbers for them," Cody said.

Peter handed over the bag. Cody dug out the two disposable phones, clicked them open, and punched the numbers into his mobile while they watched silently.

"I want you to call me as soon as you get in," Cody said, handing them back. "Got it?"

"Yes, Mom," Peter said.

"This is serious, Pedro." Cody's brow wrinkled. "You know, it's only another few blocks. You could come with me . . ."

"We'll be fine," Noa said firmly. "We'll meet back at your place."

"All right." Cody put both hands on Peter's shoulders and said, "Don't do anything stupid."

"I won't," Peter mumbled.

"I mean it, man. You're practically the only family I got."

With one beefy arm he wrapped Peter into a bear hug, then grabbed Noa with the other and drew her in. She was too startled too react. After a solid ten seconds, he released them both and walked off without a backward glance.

Peter and Noa stood silent for a minute, watching until Cody turned the corner.

"We're going, right?" he said, turning to face her.

"Definitely."

CHAPTER FOURTEEN

"**M**y car is still at home," Peter said. "Maybe we could borrow Amanda's."

"Too risky," Noa interjected. "They might be watching it."

"Yeah, you're right." Peter thought for a moment. "We need a car, though. No way to take the T or a bus all the way there. I looked it up and it's pretty out of the way."

"Well, obviously," Noa said. "Shame they couldn't have put the illegal labs in a more convenient location."

"Seriously," he said, feigning indignance. Adopting a British accent, he continued, "I'm planning on writing that Mason chap a strongly worded letter when this is over."

Noa couldn't restrain a smile. He grinned back. "See, you think I'm kidding. But I've already got it started in my head: 'Dear Dickwad. Thanks for taking my laptop and phone and, oh, yeah, for getting me kicked out of my house.'"

"I really appreciate being cut open," Noa chimed in. "And much gratitude for the new thymus, it's working out famously."

"A million heartfelt apologies for bricking your server and stealing your data. I assure you, it won't happen again. Most sincerely, Vallas and Rain."

Noa laughed.

"Wow," Peter said, still grinning.

"What?"

"Nothing. You just . . ." He examined the ground. "You look pretty when you smile."

Noa's face flushed. "I don't look pretty otherwise?"

"Not as pretty, no," he said seriously.

Noa felt her cheeks grow even hotter.

The light turned green. He put a hand on her lower back, guiding her across the street. When they got to the other side, a small part of her was disappointed when he let go.

"Anyway," Peter said, "we need to get a car."

They walked down the block. There was a cold snap in the air, and the sky was paneled with heavy white clouds. It was early for snow, but anything was possible. Noa again wished she'd chosen a different pair of boots, something lined that she could run in. Cold seeped through the thin soles, penetrating her socks and nibbling at her toes.

"I don't suppose . . ." Peter started tentatively, then said, "Never mind."

"What?"

"Do you know how to hot-wire one?"

Noa stopped dead in the middle of the sidewalk, pulling up short so quickly that a guy in his midthirties nearly crashed into her. He tossed them an evil look as he wove around, mumbling about punk kids.

"Why would I know that?" she demanded.

Peter shrugged helplessly. "I don't know. I just thought that maybe . . ."

When he didn't continue, she glared at him and said, "Maybe it's something they teach in foster care?"

Peter looked wildly uncomfortable. "I thought maybe you'd picked it up somewhere."

"Sure. They teach that right before lock picking and after mugging."

"Yeah? Shame they didn't throw in charm school, too," he retorted.

They stared each other down for a solid minute.

"You know what?" Noa said. "I can get there on my own."

Peter didn't answer. He had an odd look on his face, gazing at something behind her.

"Hello?" She snapped her fingers in front of his eyes. "I said, I'm taking off."

"Too bad," Peter said, a grin slowly spreading across his face. "Because I just figured out where we can get a car."

Noa stuck close to Peter's heels as he sauntered into the parking garage. "Hey," he said, nodding to the attendant in the box. "I'm on six. Should I just go get it myself?"

"If you're blocked in, come back down," the attendant said without glancing up from the paper.

"Sure thing."

They went to the elevator. Peter pressed the button, then tucked his hands in his pockets. He rocked back and forth on his heels as he gazed at the panel. The floors lit up in progression as the elevator descended.

The doors slid open. "After you," he said, waiting for Noa to get in before following.

As soon as the doors slid closed, she hissed, "This will never work."

"Sure it will," Peter said. "At least the first part."

Noa chewed her lip, arms crossed over her chest as the elevator climbed six floors to the roof. This was just the type of stunt that could get her sent back to juvie.

"Are you sure—"

"Just relax," he said. The doors slid open. "Trust me for once, okay? Have I steered you wrong yet?"

Noa didn't answer. She followed him out of the elevator.

Dusk had fallen, and the lights lining the parking garage roof had winked on. Every slot was full. Other cars were parked perpendicular to those spaces, blocking the cars in.

"Let's see," Peter said, walking down the row. "We want something fast, but not too flashy."

"It doesn't have to be fast," Noa said.

He didn't reply. Peter stopped dead in front of an Audi sedan. He bent over to peer in the driver's-side window, then lay a hand on the hood. "Perfect," he said. "Keys in the ignition, and it's still warm."

"This is insane," Noa said. Her eyes darted across the roof. She felt exposed, like a police chopper might descend at any moment to catch them in the act. "That guy will never believe this is our car."

"Maybe not your car, but I was born to drive something like this." Peter opened the driver's-side door. "He's not even going to glance up, trust me."

"How do you know?" she demanded.

"Because I spent a lot of time driving in and out of this garage," he said grimly. "My dad used to joke about the lax security. He always acted shocked when we came back and his Beemer was still there. It'll be hours before anyone even notices it's missing."

He slid inside and turned the engine over. Noa waited an instant longer, then sighed and got in, slamming the door. She clicked on her seat belt without looking at him.

"Ready?" Peter asked.

She didn't respond.

He eased out of the spot, then drove to the ramp leading down. They descended in silence through all six floors. As they got lower, Noa's pulse picked up, the rush of blood loud in her ears. A small part of her was screaming to just get out and run. After all, none of this was really her problem. Fine, she had an extra thymus now. And she might have PEMA. But nothing they were about to do would change that.

When she was five years old, Noa had begged her mother to take her on a roller coaster. She was so excited to finally be tall enough to ride it. But the moment that bar clamped over her legs, she panicked. And by then it was too late. Her mother bent over, holding her as she screamed and cried in terror. She'd never ridden one again.

This felt similar. They approached the exit.

"Just relax," Peter said. "I know it's an effort, but try to act normal."

Noa threw him a sour look. She kept her eyes fixed out the windshield as they eased up to the booth. A yellow bar blocked the exit.

"Ticket?" the attendant said. He was an older Indian man dressed in gray coveralls.

Peter fumbled around, checking under the visor, then in the side console. Noa's throat started to constrict. She could practically hear the clicking noise of a roller coaster ascending, that terrifying moment before the plummet. He reached across and yanked open the glove compartment.

"Sorry," Peter said apologetically, turning back to him. "Can't find it."

Noa debated jumping out and making a run for it. The guy was scrutinizing them now. He licked his lips, then said in a lilt, "You must pay for a full day, if you can't give me the ticket."

"Man, that's a drag." Peter was trying to sound nonchalant, but Noa detected the edge of stress underlying his voice. "How much?"

"Twenty dollars."

Peter leaned forward, digging a wallet out of his pocket. "This totally sucks," he said. "I thought I'd left it in the car."

He dug out a twenty-dollar bill and handed it over.

The attendant took it but didn't move, looking past him. "Your friend. She is okay?"

"She's fine," Peter said. "Why?"

"She looks ill."

"It's a hospital, right?" Peter said. "We're going to get her prescription filled now."

Another hesitation, then the attendant punched a few keys. The register door opened with a ping. The yellow bar inched up.

"Thanks," Peter said with a wave.

"Next time keep your ticket." The attendant turned back to his newspaper, and Peter put the car in drive.

They turned left out of the garage. Noa released her breath.

"See?" Peter said. "No big deal."

"How long until we get to Rhode Island?" Noa asked.

"An hour or so, depending on traffic." He glanced over at

her. "You do look kind of sick. You okay?"

"I'm fine," she snapped.

"Sheesh, just asking." He followed the signs leading to 93 South. Traffic closed in around them, a steady line of cars inching up the ramp. Noa squeezed her eyes shut. The owner would probably be coming back for his car soon. He'd call it in as stolen. At this rate, they wouldn't even make it a few miles before getting pulled over.

And Peter was right; she did feel ill. Noa tried to pinpoint how much of that was simply due to the stress of the situation, but it felt like more. Her blood was still pulsing hard; she could practically feel it streaming through her veins. She wished she'd asked Cody more about what having an extra thymus might mean. The thing on the monitor had been enormous. Maybe it was putting too much of a strain on her body. And weren't people who received transplants supposed to take some sort of special medication? Maybe the new thymus was dying inside her. Maybe just having it would kill her.

Bile rose in her throat again. "I think I'm going to throw up."

"You want me to pull over?" he asked, sounding concerned.

Noa shook her head. "No."

"You sure? I could stop and try to find a place that sells water or something . . . or we don't even have to do this. We can go back to Cody's and wait for him."

Noa hesitated. It was tempting. She could even just ask him to drop her off at a T station. Get on a train and get the hell out of here. Head west, somewhere no one would find her. Start over.

But if she was sick, then there would be no one to help her. Noa flashed back on Alex Herbruck, how small he'd looked lying on that table. How there might be other kids just like him trapped in different facilities. And no one else even knew or cared that they were gone. They'd been written off, just like her.

Noa swallowed hard. "No. Let's go. Just . . . talk to me."

"Talk to you?" Peter glanced over quizzically. "About what?"

"Anything. Just distract me."

Noa leaned her head against the car window. It felt cool against her cheek, and she realized that she felt uncommonly warm. Especially considering how cold she'd been lately.

"All right." Peter's eyes darted around. They'd finally reached the top of the on-ramp and he hit the blinker, slowly shifting over to the left lane. The cars around them crawled forward, taillights glowing red. "You know what I was wondering last night?"

"What?"

"How'd you first hear about /ALLIANCE/?"

Noa closed her eyes, but that made the nausea worse so she opened them again. They were passing the water tower painted with a rainbow. "It was when you nailed that social worker in Carmel who had stacks of kiddie porn."

"Oh, right. That was a bad one," Peter said.

"How'd you find out about him, anyway?" Noa asked. She'd always been curious.

"Anonymous tip, the way most of them come in." Peter glanced at her. "I always figured someone had hacked into his hard drive for another reason and stumbled across the pictures. Why'd you latch on to that one?"

"I've known a lot of crappy social workers," Noa said.

"Oh, man. Did . . . never mind."

"No," Noa said after a minute. "That never happened to

me. At least not with a social worker."

They drove in silence for a few minutes. Noa was gradually feeling better; the wave of nausea ebbed. The heat under her skin dissipated, and she could sense her heart rate slowing. Maybe it had just been nerves, some sort of panic attack or something.

"He's in jail now," Peter noted. "Five years, I think."

"Should be more."

"Definitely." Peter nodded. "We did a good job on that one, though. At least now people will be aware."

Noa didn't answer. She'd been truly impressed by the way /ALLIANCE/ had dragged that pervert into the light. They'd gotten cops sent to his house in response to an alleged suicide call. Then while the cops were inside, as the jerk tried to convince them he was fine, every TV in his house clicked on. /ALLIANCE/ had hacked into his home entertainment system, and the cops were treated to a slideshow presentation of all the smut tucked away on his hard drive.

Noa had stumbled across news of it on a forum. She researched /ALLIANCE/ further, and the work they were doing struck a chord with her. She liked the idea of helping people and animals that couldn't protect themselves. The timing had been kind of perfect, too. It was about a month after she'd moved into her own place, after finally circumnavigating the system. What she hadn't anticipated was that after years of being forced into tight living quarters with other people, being alone could get lonely. Plus she finally had her own computer, and twenty-four-hour access to the internet.

When she'd read about what /ALLIANCE/ had accomplished, it occurred to Noa that up until then, she'd always been struggling to keep her own head above water. And now that she was floating, she could use her newfound spare time to help others like her.

Which is kind of what she was doing now.

The silence in the car felt awkward. Peter was probably struggling to figure out the right thing to say. To change the subject, she said, "You know, I did steal a car once."

"No way." He mugged an overly shocked face.

"Yeah. I was fourteen."

He flashed that grin. "So they do teach hot-wiring in foster care."

"I boosted the keys from a foster mom," Noa confessed. "Ended up crashing it, though. I didn't really know how to drive."

"They usually recommend learning before you get behind the wheel," Peter noted wryly. "Why'd you take it?"

"I had somewhere to go."

"Obviously," Peter said. "So are you going to tell me where? Because trust me, you don't want me to start guessing."

She didn't answer.

"All right, you asked for it," he said. "Disney World. No, wait—you were fourteen. A concert? Was Miley Cyrus playing the Garden?"

"I wanted to visit my parents' graves," Noa said. "No one would take me, so I decided to try and go by myself."

"Oh, man. Sorry." He winced. "Now I feel like a jerk."

"It's okay," Noa said, rubbing her wrist. "You didn't know." She'd barely gotten five miles before accidentally hitting the accelerator instead of the brakes. She'd badly dented the car's front grill and taken out a mailbox. The end result was her longest stint in juvie, six months.

"Still. I'm really sorry." Peter shifted his gaze from the road long enough to make eye contact. He had nice eyes, large and brown with long eyelashes for a boy. It was funny that she hadn't noticed that before.

Traffic was easing as they approached the turnoff to 24 South. "Probably about another hour," he said. "You want to try to sleep? You look tired."

"I'm fine," Noa said, but he was right; her eyes ached.

"We should call Cody," he said. "Tell him we made a stop before going back to his place so he doesn't worry."

"I'll do it," Noa said. "I've got to send an email, anyway."

"Yeah? To who?"

Noa wrestled with what to tell him. She felt obligated to let A6M0 know about what was going on, just in case something happened to them. But Peter still didn't know he existed, and she wasn't sure how he would handle that knowledge now. She finally said weakly, "It's part of the plan."

"Glad someone has a plan," Peter said. "So what are you thinking? Go in guns blazing?"

"We don't have guns."

"Right, that's a problem. We might not even be able to get in," he said soberly.

"We'll find a way in," she said. "And after that, you'll just have to trust me."

"Hey! Get up!"

"What?" Amanda tried to focus. Her eyes felt glued shut.

"You can't crash here. Gotta keep moving."

Slowly, she managed to force her eyes open. A kid was facing her. He looked familiar, but she couldn't place him. Safety pins ran in a jagged line down both ears and there was a stud stuck in his chin. He was dressed all in black and carried a skateboard. He looked filthy, but that might just be from the goth makeup.

He looked both ways, then tapped her foot again. "Seriously. That's how they take you."

"How who takes . . . what?" Her head felt funny, tongue thick. It was hard to speak. Amanda eased up to sitting. She was on a bench in the middle of a park. A dead leaf skittered past behind the kid, who was gazing down at her with something approaching concern.

"Shake it off," he said. "You need to ride the high out, do it somewhere safer."

He dropped the skateboard to the ground and kicked the back so the nose jabbed up, then hopped on and rolled away. She watched until he turned the corner where the path swooped around a bush.

Amanda pulled her jacket tightly around her. There were people walking through the park, but no one looked at her; in fact, everyone who passed was making an effort to avoid eye contact.

She rubbed her forehead with one hand. What the hell had happened? The last thing she remembered was being in the Campus Center with Drew. Walking home in the dark, the stars overhead . . .

But that didn't make sense; there were still fading fingers of pink traced along the sky above the trees. Had she been here all day?

Her teeth started chattering. What the hell was going on?

Amanda tried to get to her feet, but was too wobbly. Which was completely bizarre. She didn't drink or do drugs. Would never even consider it, after seeing what addiction had done to her brother. Had she been drugged by someone?

Had Drew done this to her?

He couldn't have, Amanda thought. Yet no matter how hard she strained to remember, the last thing she could recall was walking across the quad toward her dorm.

Should she go to the cops? What would she tell them? Amanda didn't even know if anything had happened to her. All her clothes were on. Her backpack was beside her on the bench. She unzipped it and checked: Her wallet was still inside, with the forty dollars she'd withdrawn from the campus ATM. Maybe she'd had some sort of weird seizure; she'd heard of that happening.

Amanda experienced a sudden and overpowering urge to start crying, but choked it back and stiffened her jaw. There had to be a good explanation. She'd get back to her dorm room, then figure it out.

She got up gingerly, testing her balance. Carefully lifted her backpack and slung it over one shoulder. Turned around to get her bearings.

As soon as she saw what was behind her, she froze. Amanda knew exactly where she was. Knew this park, this strip of sidewalk, this park bench.

It was the same one where her brother, Marcus, had been found dead five years ago.

CHAPTER FIFTEEN

"We're almost there." Peter glanced over. Despite her protests, Noa had nodded off soon after they crossed the Massachusetts/Rhode Island border. It was amazing how different she looked when she was asleep. He kept sneaking peeks at her: the sharp angles of her face, that choppy jet-black hair. She was unbelievably gorgeous when she wasn't glowering.

Noa blinked and yawned, then stretched her arms up above her head. "I can't believe I fell asleep," she muttered.

She sounded a little worried about it. Peter couldn't blame her; it was weird and unnerving how quickly she'd lost consciousness. Like driving with a corpse in the passenger seat. A few times, he'd been tempted to reach over and check for a pulse.

Meanwhile, every one of Peter's nerve endings was tingling. Stealing the car, then driving south to confront

God knew what . . . he was climbing out of his skin. His throat was dry, and he definitely needed to find a bathroom soon; his insides were churning uncomfortably.

Noa had a plan, he reminded himself. Peter hoped it was a good one, because the closer they got, the more he realized how completely nuts this all was. Three days ago, his biggest concern had been fighting boredom on a Saturday night. Now he was a car thief on the verge of breaking into a top-secret research facility that was probably filled with highly trained armed adversaries. He couldn't go home, and he was partnered with a girl he barely knew. Could he really trust Noa to watch his back in there? He wasn't even sure she liked him.

Noa rubbed her eyes blearily and yawned, then sat up in the seat. They were approaching a desolate peninsula at the tip of southeastern Rhode Island. According to what he'd seen on the internet, it was a naval base that had been abandoned during budget cuts in the midseventies. This part of the state was heavily forested. Towering trees draped over the road; their sagging branches blotted out the sky.

They hadn't passed another car for miles. From the turnoff a mile back, it rapidly became apparent that there was one road in, one road out, which made him anxious.

"Pull in there," Noa said, pointing.

Obediently, Peter turned left down a narrow lane. It had once been paved, but years of harsh winters had caused the concrete to buck and heave until it was more a collection of potholes than a road. The car kicked into all-wheel drive as it grated against the larger chunks jutting up from the soil.

A few hundred yards in, the road became impassable. He slowed, then drew to a stop and turned off the lights.

"This is good," Noa said approvingly.

"Yeah?" Peter couldn't hide the shakiness in his voice. Noa still seemed preternaturally calm, as if they were on their way to grab a burger. The farther they'd driven from Boston, the more the insanity of this had gripped him. More than once he'd been tempted to turn the car around.

But he'd kept right on driving. And now they were here.

"The cops might not come," Noa said, apparently guessing his thoughts. "They'd need a warrant, anyway, and there's not enough for them to get one. Even if they believe us, which is unlikely, by the time they show up, all the evidence might be gone."

"Yeah," Peter said. "You're probably right." Still, he was harboring serious second thoughts. "So what's this genius plan you've got?"

"You bricked their main server, right?" Noa asked.

Peter nodded.

"So I'm guessing they're probably stalled out for a few days until everything is up and running again. They'll have security here, but probably not on the same level as the place where I . . . well, you know."

That seemed like wishful thinking to Peter. Uncertainly he said, "Okay . . ."

"We'll scope out the security system and sneak in. Make sure that they're doing experiments here. Then we get the cops to come before they can hide anything."

"How are we going to get the cops here?" he asked, puzzled. "Like you said, they'd need a search warrant."

"Not under certain special circumstances," Noa said.

"Circumstances like what?" Peter said, brow furrowing. "I don't get it."

"Just trust me," she said impatiently. "C'mon, let's go."

★ ★ ★

Amanda hung her head forward, letting scalding hot water course down her back. Usually she was strict about showers: five minutes in and out so as not to waste a drop of water. She found it appalling when people left the tap running while they brushed their teeth—didn't anyone realize that sometime soon the potable water would run out?

Today, though, she allowed herself an extra five minutes. She needed it. Everything ached after spending the night on a park bench. At least Amanda assumed that was where she'd spent the night. She'd been experiencing odd flashbacks of bright lights, hands on her. She filed them away as bad dreams. She'd already booked an appointment at the campus medical clinic for tomorrow morning after class. If they suspected anything was seriously wrong, they'd send her to Boston Medical. And if that happened, she'd decided, then and only then would she tell her parents. After Marcus ran away, they'd become overprotective to the point of nearly smothering her. The last thing Amanda wanted was to give them something else to worry about.

Besides, she was hoping it would turn out to be nothing, a minor blip. After getting back to her dorm room, she'd done some research online. It turned out that seizures were actually startlingly common among teenagers. A doctor could test whether or not that was what had happened to her. And if so, it was treatable, which was a relief.

Plus, amnesia was almost always a factor. People lost track of the minutes and sometimes hours leading up to the seizure. So it was normal that she couldn't recall anything after crossing the quad the night before.

How she'd ended up clear across town on a park bench— that park bench in particular—was another issue. But obviously it was buried in her psyche. And really, who else would have known about it? Somehow, in a confused state, she must have wandered there on her own.

Amanda turned off the shower and toweled dry. The more research she'd done, the calmer she'd become. Now she felt silly for even considering calling the cops. And she was really glad she hadn't gone home, which had been her first instinct. She'd like to talk to Peter about it, actually— he'd always been good at cheering her up. He'd probably joke about how she'd lost her mind without him, or say something equally stupid that would make her laugh.

Oddly, it hadn't occurred to her to call Drew. Amanda knew it wasn't fair, but in her mind he was inextricably linked with what had happened to her, even though the two things were obviously completely unrelated. It was silly, she told herself. Anyway, tomorrow she'd know more. Until then she planned on laying low.

She leaned over the sink as she brushed her teeth, the towel wrapped around her.

Another girl from her hall padded in wearing fuzzy slippers and a pair of Victoria's Secret flannel pajamas. She nodded to Amanda; they knew each other by sight, but weren't really friendly. The girl was a future sorority sister, the type who'd spend half an hour blow-drying her hair before class. Amanda had no patience for that sort of thing.

The girl went into a bathroom stall. A flush, then she came over to wash her hands in the next sink.

"Who's Peter?" she asked as Amanda bent over to rinse out her mouth.

"What?" Amanda was startled. Whenever Peter stayed over they hung out in her room, and he used the guys' bathroom on the floor downstairs. He'd had very little contact with her hallmates.

There was a hint of mockery in the girl's voice as she said, "Peter. Is he your boyfriend?"

"Why?" Amanda said sharply, not liking her tone.

"'Cause it looks like he branded you, girlfriend." The girl shook her hands to dry them and winked, then pushed back out into the hallway.

Amanda slowly turned so that she could see her back in the mirror. Her eyes widened at the bold black marks on her skin. She dropped the towel. A sentence was scrawled across the widest part of her back. Dark ink strokes stretched the entire span, arcing over her shoulder blades. The words read backward in the mirror, so it took a minute to decipher them:

TELL PETER HE WAS WARNED.

Amanda spun and made a dash for the closest toilet stall. Dropping to her knees, she started heaving.

It took them a half hour to reach the perimeter fence. They hadn't parked far away, but Noa kept them inside the tree line, circling the compound until she settled on a spot well back from the main road.

Peter was clearly still having doubts. He'd paused a few times and started to say something, but she shushed him before he could continue. They'd come this far, and she was resolved to see it through. The thought that they were slicing up kids like her in there, treating them like lab rats, or worse, just a pile of spare parts, was seriously pissing her off. And Noa knew how the legal system really worked. Most of the time it didn't matter whether or not you were right. Laws contained a labyrinth of loopholes designed to help people like Charles Pike and to oppress people like her.

Noa peered at the row of Quonset huts hunched inside

the perimeter fence. They were particular to naval bases, small prefab buildings with rounded roofs that functioned as warehouses, barracks, and commissaries. Something about the way they huddled together, old and battered and forgotten, reminded her of a lost herd.

Still, he was right about one thing. It didn't look promising. Not a single car had driven down the road. Torn plastic bags dotted the fence, stuck where they'd been blown by an earlier strong wind. Most of the lights were extinguished, either burned out or shattered. No guard visible in the outpost by the main entry gate, and no cars in the enormous lots surrounding the buildings. The fifty-acre complex dead-ended on the waterfront.

The entire facility sat dark and still. Clouds hung heavy above, braced to drop a deluge. It seemed utterly desolate and abandoned.

But if they were right, that was exactly the impression the company wanted to convey.

Noa had sussed out the best spot to infiltrate. The razor wire capping the ten-foot chain-link fence had split here, leaving a six-inch-wide gap for them to climb through. Tricky, but manageable if they were careful. Once inside the fence, she and Peter would have to clear about eighty feet of wide-open space before reaching the first building.

"Ready?" she whispered.

"Wait!" Peter said. "What's the plan?"

"Just stay close," Noa hissed.

Without waiting for a response, she latched her fingers through the cold steel and started to climb. Below her, Peter swore in a low voice. She ignored it.

Noa scrambled up quickly; compared to the tree the other night, this fence was a piece of cake. At the top, she hung back, slowly easing her right leg through the gap. She awkwardly shifted sideways, sliding her narrow frame through the split in the razor wire. She held her breath as her torso edged through: So far, so good. She carefully drew her other leg over, then clambered down and jumped the final few feet.

Noa kept low, huddled against the fence. It clanged slightly as Peter swung over it.

"Shh!" she said when he issued a small cry.

He dropped down beside her. She could barely make out his features in the dark, but he appeared to be wincing. "I sliced my arm," he said in a strained whisper. "Crap. I can't remember the last time I had a tetanus shot."

"How bad?" she asked.

He tugged up his sleeve and held out his arm. Noa tilted it, squinting to see in the ambient light. There was a scrape, long but not too deep. "Press down on it," she said. "You'll be fine."

She was wishing that Cody had come instead. Peter was obviously more comfortable performing subversive acts from the comfort of his home. *Sheltered life,* she reminded herself. But he was here, after all.

He didn't say anything, just pulled his fleece back over the cut and gripped the injured arm with his opposite hand.

"Okay, let's go," she said.

Bent double, Noa trotted quickly to the closest building. Her messenger bag hung heavily to her right side, nearly knocking her off balance a few times. It took a couple minutes to reach the shadows of the Quonset hut. The whole time her chest was tight, breath coming in small gasps. She kept expecting a spotlight to suddenly flare to life, trapping her in its beam.

Peter was fast—she'd give him that. He'd matched her pace, reaching the western corner of the building at the same time she did. No visible doors or windows on this side. The hut stretched fifteen feet skyward before arcing over. There were vents at the top, but they were too high off the ground to be accessible.

Noa waved for him to follow. She slipped along the length of the building. Her footsteps sounded unnaturally loud, boots scuffling against concrete. She reached the corner. Peter was breathing hard behind her.

"How do we get in?" he asked in a low voice.

Noa leaned forward to peer around the edge of the building. There was a door carved into the metal shell about halfway down.

This was the first in a long line of Quonset huts. Mirroring them was an identical row. Their doors all faced in toward the main road, like soldiers standing in military formation. Twelve on each side, marching toward the water. The road ended in a wide concrete pier.

And there was a boat tied to the pier. Small, new, and definitely not naval.

So maybe this place wasn't abandoned after all.

She pressed up against the building so that he could see past her, and pointed. Peter nodded—he'd spotted it, too.

"What do you want to do?" he asked.

Noa debated. She was a little surprised they hadn't seen any signs of life yet; she'd been expecting swarms of guards, like the place where she'd awoken. Yet she hadn't been able to detect any security measures—not even mounted cameras or motion-sensing lights, at least not that they'd encountered so far. "Let's try to get inside."

"What if there are people in there?" Peter sounded worried.

"Then we run like hell for the fence."

"That's the plan?" he asked incredulously.

"I didn't say it was perfect," Noa grumbled.

She was betting there wouldn't be anyone inside, though—she got that sense, even though she couldn't pinpoint precisely why. These buildings were much smaller than the warehouses at the other complex. Each was maybe thirty feet long and fifteen feet wide, probably just one big room.

She eased around the front of the building, Peter sticking close to her heels. Noa tried the door: The knob twisted easily under her hand—someone had oiled it recently. Noa drew a deep breath and opened it just wide enough to slip inside.

The interior was pitch-black. A nudge against her back as Peter entered, then the door shut behind him.

"Looks empty," Peter whispered.

A thin beam of light pierced the darkness. Noa turned in surprise—he was holding a small flashlight. "Grabbed it from the glove compartment," Peter explained. "Audi owners—prepared for anything."

He stepped forward and Noa followed. The beam illuminated a concrete floor streaked with dirt and dust. He panned the light slowly around the room. The rounded interior walls were rusty and tarnished. There was a sharp tang to the air, like it hung heavy with absorbed metal filings.

Peter stopped dead. Noa halted beside him and her heart leaped into her throat.

In the center of the room was another glass box, similar to the one she'd woken up in, but smaller. The same steel table, light strung from the ceiling above, scattered trays and machines. Everything was silent and still. The table was empty.

"Looks like we're in the right place," he said in a low voice.

Noa couldn't answer. Her throat had suddenly constricted, panic squeezing the air from her lungs and sending her heart back into overdrive. She could practically feel the IV in her arm, the cold steel against her exposed flesh. Her scar was throbbing as if the scalpel had just sliced into her.

"You okay?"

Noa forced a nod, although even that small motion was difficult. All her muscles had gone rigid.

Peter's hand slipped into hers. His palm felt warm, solid. The grasp steadied her, bringing her back into herself. She wasn't on that table. She'd gotten away. And maybe whoever else had been here had gotten away, too.

They stood like that for a minute. For the first time in recent memory, Noa was glad she wasn't alone. Peter's presence beside her was comforting. Even though he didn't say a word, she sensed he was struck by the horror of what she'd survived. Somehow that made it more tolerable.

Peter panned the rest of the room with the light. Aside from the chamber, there was nothing there.

"Next building?" he asked. "Or should we call the cops now?"

The voice in her head geared toward survival was screaming at her to tear through that door, make for the fence, and keep running until there were miles between her and this awful place. But Noa forced herself to say, "We need to find a computer. Let's keep looking."

He gave her hand a final squeeze, then released it. Together they crept back to the door. Peter clicked off the flashlight before opening it. This time he took the lead, cracking it and peering out, then slipping back into the night.

Compared to the impenetrable darkness inside, the night seemed brighter, the clouds less oppressive. Noa sucked in gulps of fresh air, thankful to be out of that place. They stuck to the shadows, trying to clear the gaps between buildings as quickly and silently as possible.

They got lucky. All the doors were unlocked. The second building was completely empty, lacking even a glass chamber. But in the third they found some sort of command center. Two neat rows of terminals on adjoining tables, standard office swivel chairs in front of each. All the towers were shut off, the screens blank.

"So I'm guessing this is where the plan part comes in," Peter said.

"We're geeks, right?" Noa said, feeling more like herself as she slid in front of a terminal. "This is how we fight." She closed her eyes and offered a quick prayer for electricity. Hopefully these terminals were still linked to a generator.

She hit the power button and the tower hummed to life. In stark contrast to the dilapidated surroundings, it was a state-of-the-art HP. Noa turned on the screen, relieved to see an updated version of Windows. The desktop was clotted with folders. She clicked on one to open it and saw the same type of stats sheets. Maybe her guardian angel was wrong, and they hadn't gotten all the data. Or this was different information that hadn't been funneled into the main servers.

Either way, there would be something here for the cops to find. These computers were about to become the centerpiece of an extremely extensive and thorough investigation.

She clicked on another folder and found a jpg. Noa steeled herself before opening it: A waifish girl with cropped blond hair lay on the table. Her chest had been peeled open, just like Alex's.

"She's just a kid," Peter said softly.

That was all she needed to see. Noa closed it again and started typing a series of commands.

"Can I help?" Peter asked. "Although it would probably be easier if I knew what you were doing."

"I'm hacking into the NSA," Noa explained, rapidly clicking through keys.

"Seriously? The National Security Agency?"

"You heard me," she grumbled. "Keep an eye on the door."

"I can help with their firewall," Peter said. "If you want. I mean, I've gotten through it before."

"Please. Who hasn't?" Noa resisted an eye roll. "But you were careful to make sure they'd never know, right?"

"Well, yeah," Peter said. "It wasn't like I'd want them to—" He laughed softly, realizing what she was getting at. "That's genius. They'll come running."

"If I screw it up badly enough that they can track the IP address then, yeah, they should." The National Security Agency was in charge of all of the sensitive and classified data in the country. Their firewall was notoriously impenetrable, so that the information wouldn't fall into the wrong hands. Every day, the NSA batted back thousands of attempts to hack into their servers. They were the modern-day equivalent of a castle under siege, constantly hurling flaming oil down at every idiot trying to scale the ramparts.

Noa's goal was to hurdle enough obstacles to seriously spook them.

"They won't need a search warrant for a threat to national security. They'll send in a SWAT team, and they'll find all this." Peter's voice was filled with admiration. "Damn, that is a good plan."

"Just watch the door," Noa said. "This shouldn't take long."

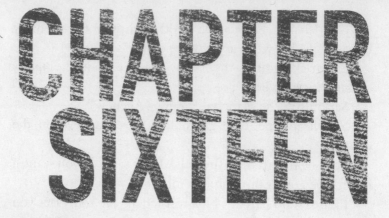

CHAPTER SIXTEEN

Fifteen minutes later, Noa hesitated outside the building. They'd shut off the screen but left the terminal humming with the malware program she'd installed. Hopefully if anyone came by they wouldn't notice, although the tiny green light cast an unearthly glow in the room. Chances were that by the time anyone went in there, it would be too late. The IP address would already have been traced, and the cavalry would be en route.

She only hoped that the NSA was as capable as everyone claimed.

"What's wrong?" Peter asked.

"I think we should check the boat," Noa said.

"Yeah?" Peter sounded dubious. "You sure? The cops'll be coming soon."

"It'll only take a minute." Noa couldn't explain why she was suddenly fixated on the boat. Peter was right to be nervous; every minute they remained here put them in more danger. And the boat's presence meant that someone might be in one of the buildings they hadn't checked yet.

Still, she had an almost overwhelming desire to investigate it.

Despite clearly having reservations, Peter said, "All right, but then we book it out of here."

"Agreed," Noa said.

It took them five minutes to reach the hut closest to the pier. Raindrops had started falling, heavy and thick, advance emissaries of a nasty fall storm. Noa tugged the cap down low over her ears. Peter pulled up the collar of his black fleece.

The boat bobbed in the waves. An approaching squall had kicked up whitecaps that splashed against the hull, cresting it at times. It was tied at the bow and stern with ropes wrapped around cleats.

One of Noa's foster dads had been a crab fisherman. He and his wife took in kids for the government checks that enabled them to make ends meet during the off-season. They kept "the good ones," as they referred to them, for crab season, too. Unfortunately they hadn't counted Noa among them.

This boat reminded her of his, battered by years of hard use. It was a twenty-footer with low gunwales and a small open shed protecting the captain's chair. It was stacked high with pots, even though crab season had ended months ago.

Peter whispered, "What do you think—"

The Quonset hut door ten feet away suddenly slammed open, cutting him off. They both ducked back into the shadows along the side of the building. Noa held her breath and braced to run.

Footsteps crunched on the sandy gravel outside the building. They paused. Noa turned her head and saw Peter's eyes gazing back at her, wide and scared, mirroring the terror she felt.

"Christ, is this the last load?"

"One more," a man's voice said.

"Damn, my back can't handle much more of this," the first guy grumbled. He sounded older; a smoker's wheeze rumbled through his words.

"Storm's coming up, might have to wait."

"No freakin' way I'm hauling them back off the boat," the smoker complained. "I say we take our chances."

"Yeah?" The other guy sounded dubious. Noa couldn't blame him. The rain was coming down harder now. A small boat like that would be tossed mercilessly by the waves.

"We only gotta go out and drop, what, ten pots? Take us an hour."

"If you say so," the guy said. "Don't want to run into the coast guard out there, though."

The smoker grunted. "Yeah, all right. Kick back for a bit? I got a sixer of Sam Adams."

"Cole said he'd be back soon," the other guy said nervously.

"Hell, he don't want this boat tipping over, either. Least not until it's supposed to." Laughter that ended in a cough. "Come on. I'm getting soaked out here."

"You want to just leave them?"

"It's not like they're going anywhere."

The door slammed shut. Footsteps echoed against concrete inside, and there was the sound of a chair scraping the floor.

She and Peter were both hunkered down, and her knees were aching. She slowly got to her feet. Peter hesitated, then straightened. He leaned over, lips brushing her ear as he said urgently, "We gotta go!"

Noa held up a finger, gesturing for him to wait. Without giving herself a chance to reconsider, she ducked around the side of the building.

A few feet in front of the door sat an oversized cooler, the kind fishermen used to store bait. The bottom of the container was blue, and its white top was smeared with red streaks.

The metal tinkle of a bottle cap hitting the floor sounded from inside the Quonset hut, then another. Noa kept her ear attuned to the building, straining to hear the low conversation, any indication that one of them might be coming back out.

Her fingers were trembling. She fought to still them as she unclasped the cooler's latch.

Inside, something was swaddled in plastic. Noa reached out a shaky hand and gingerly drew back the top layer with two fingers.

Her hand brushed against something cold and hard. She drew a deep breath and squinted, trying to see in the darkness, wishing she'd thought to grab the flashlight from Peter.

Finally, she reached down and drew it out.

She'd been braced for fish guts, maybe squid. But when she held it up to the light, she realized it was a human foot. Small, female. Chipped black paint on the toenails. The big toe was curled slightly upward.

Noa couldn't help herself; she dropped it. It made a small thud when it hit the ground.

"What was that?" came from inside the hut.

Noa scrambled for the foot, overcoming a wave of nausea

as she grabbed it and chucked it back in the cooler. She closed the lid. Footsteps approaching the door again. She hurriedly redid the clasp and rushed back to where Peter waited.

The door opened again. Silence. Noa's cheeks ran wet with rain and tears that came so thick it was hard to see. She wanted to wipe them away, but couldn't stand the thought of touching anything with that hand. She could still feel the cold flesh against her palm. She repressed a shudder.

"Anything?" the smoker called out from inside.

"The wind, I guess." But the guy sounded uncertain. "Maybe I should do a quick check."

"Be my guest," the smoker said. "I'll keep a seat warm for you."

Another long pause, then the door slammed again. Muffled this time, the guy said, "Probably nothing."

"Damn straight. We're in the middle of hell and gone." The smoker barked a laugh. "Night like this, who'd be out there?"

Noa winced as Peter grabbed her hand, *that* hand. She shook him off, ignoring the puzzled look he threw her. She motioned for him to follow, then turned and ran for the next building.

It seemed to take an eternity to reach the fence. Noa kept listening for a pursuit, expecting someone around the bend of every building. She couldn't get up and over the fence fast enough. The barbed wire snagged the leg of her pants, but she yanked it free. She heard a rip and felt a sharp pain in her calf. She ignored it and dropped down, stumbling a little before regaining her footing. Noa kept her arms clasped to her chest as she ran for the safety of the woods.

Finally she dropped against a tree trunk, gasping for air.

Her soaking wet clothes clung to her, making her shiver even harder.

Peter dropped into a squat in front of her. "Are you okay? What the hell happened back there?"

Noa shook her head. She couldn't bring herself to say the words, even though she now realized that as soon as she'd seen the crab pots, she'd known. The tables weren't empty because the kids had escaped. They were empty because the kids were dead. All of them.

"Crab pots," she finally managed.

"Yeah?" Peter prodded when she didn't continue. "What about them? That's what was on the boat, right?"

"I thought you grew up in Boston."

"I did." His brow wrinkled. "So?"

"So you don't know about crabs?"

"Just that they're delicious. Why?"

"Bottom-feeders," Noa said. Bile was rising up her throat. She desperately wanted to throw up, get rid of everything inside her. But that would only weaken her at a time when she needed all her strength. So she choked it back and said, "I lived with a crabber once. He used to joke that you should never piss off a guy who owned a boat and a crab pot."

"Why not?"

"Because if you put a body in one, there won't be anything left," Noa said harshly. "Crabs are like pigs; they eat all of it. Bones, eyes, everything. There would be nothing left to find."

"But . . ." Peter's voice trailed off as he realized what she was saying. He shook his head as if to clear it, then stood and extended an arm down to her. "Come on." His voice sounded stronger, more adult. Like he'd suddenly aged a decade. "We have to go. The cops will be here soon."

Noa let him lead her back to the car. It was a cold, wet walk through the woods. A few times she stumbled on roots that jutted up out of the soil, or felt the scrape of a branch against her cheek. Each time Peter caught her and kept her from falling. By the time they got back to the Audi, he was practically carrying her. She leaned her head against his shoulder. Her calf throbbed where the wire had gouged it—hopefully the wound wasn't too deep.

Peter opened the passenger-side door and helped her in. The NSA program was up and running, she reminded herself. They'd done all they could.

Now they had to get out of here before the storm troopers showed up. How ironic that she was relying on antihacking government agents to save the day.

She just hoped that her assault had caught their attention, and quickly.

Peter pulled on his seat belt and reached for the ignition. He frowned.

"What?" Noa asked.

"I left them in here," he said, half to himself. "I could swear I did."

"You left the keys in the ignition?"

"Yeah, just in case . . . well, I figured one of us might not make it back." He examined the steering wheel. "That way you could still get out of here, even if I got caught."

"Oh," Noa said. That wouldn't even have occurred to her. Of course, she'd just assumed that if they got caught, it would be over for both of them. "Sure they're not in your pocket?"

"I'm sure." He glanced nervously into the backseat. "You don't think—"

Peter was interrupted by a rap at the window. Noa went

cold. The guy who'd chased her into the college library was leaning over, squinting in. He leered at them, dangling a set of car keys from his hand.

Swiftly, the guy opened the door and slid into the backseat.

Peter didn't recognize him, but then all the guys who stormed his house had basically looked the same. He was dressed in what was apparently their standard uniform: black pants, a heavy jacket, a black knit cap. A nasty scar ran the length of his face—you'd think he would remember seeing that before.

"You're Cole," Noa said bluntly.

The guy tossed the keys into the front seat and said, "Drive."

Peter hesitated. Something cold pressed against the side of his head. He turned and found himself staring down the barrel of a gun. Peter picked up the keys with shaky hands and fumbled to get them in the ignition.

"Back to the road," Cole ordered.

Peter obediently threw the car in reverse. The tires dug into mud for a second, then lurched free with a jolt.

"Where are we going?" he asked, slowly backing up. The car bumped and jolted over ruts in the road. Peter prayed for the tires to get mired. If that happened, he might be able to distract Cole, and at least Noa would have a shot at getting away.

"Back to the base. I'll give you the full tour this time." Cole's voice was low and deep and filled with menace.

He tapped Noa on the shoulder with the barrel of the gun. "Can't believe I got so lucky. I should buy a lottery ticket. How'd you crazy kids end up together?"

Peter glanced over at Noa. She sat rigid, staring straight

ahead through the windshield. She didn't answer.

"Doesn't matter," Cole said dismissively. "Makes my life easier. Mason is gonna love this."

They reached the main road. Peter checked the mirrors, then backed across so he was blocking it. There were air bags on his and Noa's sides, he suddenly realized. He could gun the engine, ram the car into a tree. Cole would go right through the windshield.

He glanced into the rearview mirror. Cole was eyeing him. "Don't get cute, kid," he said. "Trust me, I can put a hole in both your heads before we get five feet. Now turn right."

Peter gritted his teeth but complied. The headlights illuminated the swath of road leading back to the abandoned naval base, windshield wipers working hard against the solid wash of rain. Some of it collected at the bottom in icy pellets.

The gate stood open. Beside it was a guy dressed identically to Cole: probably one of the men from the boat. He looked miserable. Cole muttered something under his breath about incompetence. "Stop here," he said, and they pulled up next to the guy.

The guy leaned in. Peter guessed he was the one with the gruffer voice. Close-up he looked like a fisherman, graying scruff on his cheeks, oily strands of hair pasted to the sides of his face below a watch cap. He had on a black Carhartt jacket and thick rubber boots. He leaned in as Cole unrolled the window.

"I told you, we didn't—"

A sharp *crack!* and the guy staggered back a few feet, a shocked expression on his face. A red hole had appeared in the center of his forehead. He dropped to the ground.

Cole rolled the window up. "Keep driving," he ordered. "All the way to the end."

Beside him, Noa gasped. Peter would have made a noise, too, but found that his voice box had stopped working. He was frozen with fear, utterly paralyzed by it. His ears throbbed from the concussion. He'd never heard a gun go off before. It was loud, much louder than on TV. His eyes were locked on the guy's still form. A steady line of red seeped out the back of his head, joining a muddy rivulet created by the rain.

"Pull it together, kid," Cole said, sounding bored. "Drive, or I do the same to you and take the wheel."

Peter looked at Noa. She was staring at the empty space where the man had stood, mouth agape with shock, eyes abnormally wide. Her gaze shifted to him, and they shared a look of horror.

"You'd better do what he says," she finally said in a hoarse voice.

Peter forced himself to turn back to the road in front of him. The windshield swam as though the car had slipped underwater. Mechanically, he flicked the wipers to the highest setting and eased his foot off the brake. The car edged forward.

The line of buildings hunched like lonely sentinels as they passed. They seemed to have assumed a life of their own, bloodthirsty creatures awaiting the order to pounce.

"Stop," Cole ordered, and they pulled up alongside the final building. The door was ajar. Inside Peter could make out a shadowy figure: the other guy who had been loading coolers onto the boat.

"What's going to happen to us?" Noa's voice was oddly bereft of emotion, like she'd already given up.

"Not sure yet. I gotta call it in." Cole smiled, his teeth startlingly white. "Don't worry, sweetheart, you're the golden goose. Your buddy here, though . . . he might have a date with a crab pot."

Noa drew her breath in sharply. Peter wanted to reach out and take her hand again, let her know that it was okay. Maybe his parents would be able to convince Mason to let him live. He pictured the rage on his father's face the night he left and his heart sank. Probably not. Bob and Priscilla might already be remodeling his bedroom. Jeremy's was a guest room now. He hadn't been dead a month when the decorators came in.

He'd never forgiven them for that. They'd sent Peter on a ski trip, ostensibly to "get away from it all." And he'd returned home to find that all of his brother's possessions had been packed up and sent away. He hadn't even had a chance to grab a small token, like Jeremy's lacrosse stick or science-fair medal.

Bob and Priscilla had probably already decided that the death of their sole remaining child was for the best, all things considered. They were practical that way, and as they constantly pointed out, he caused them a lot of trouble.

"Out," Cole barked, interrupting Peter's thoughts.

Noa and Peter exchanged a glance. Peter hated feeling like he was voluntarily marching to his death. If he made a break for it, though, there was no guarantee Noa would get away. Maybe they wouldn't kill her, but they sure as hell planned on strapping her to a table again. And he felt responsible for her now. She put up a good front, but underneath all that was something vulnerable; he could sense it. Deep down, he suspected they were more alike than she'd ever admit.

He just had to hold Cole off long enough for the NSA cavalry to show up. Peter prayed that their program was still running, and that it had attracted enough attention to elicit a response. That Cole hadn't discovered it and shut it down before it got flagged.

Noa's face was locked in the same mask as always, but she met his eyes and he could tell she was thinking the same thing. *Stall them. Stay alive.*

He drew a deep breath, forcibly tamping down the fear. They were smart. They'd get out of this. They had to.

"I said, out!" Cole smacked his head with the barrel of the gun. Peter winced—the hard metal felt like it had made a dent. Reluctantly, he got out of the car.

The rain had turned to sleet; hard, icy stones pelted him. Peter huddled deeper into his collar and tucked his hands in his pockets. He should have thought to grab something, he chided himself—even a knife, or some pepper spray. Not that either would have been much help against an armed man.

"Where's Fred?" the guy called from the door of the Quonset hut. He was small, wiry. Midtwenties, with a smoker's pallor. A scrubby-looking soul patch marred his chin.

Cole didn't answer. He gestured for Noa and Peter to go inside—apparently he wasn't enjoying the rain, either.

The wiry guy moved aside as they approached. This Quonset hut was different from the others. The overhead lights were on, an entire block of them. It was glaringly bright in contrast to the other buildings, everything set in stark relief. It looked like a cafeteria. There were long tables set in rows with metal chairs tucked beneath them. A coffee station sat at the far end of the room, beside the same stainless-steel-and-glass serving setup they had at Peter's school. A stack of red trays perched on the metal railing in front of it.

It was the kind of thing you'd find in a real hospital, albeit on a smaller scale. Peter tried to imagine what type of person would be able to sit here and eat after experimenting on a bunch of helpless kids.

Right behind the serving area was a freestanding, enormous walk-in freezer. The door stood ajar. Inside, Peter could make out empty gurneys. The counter had been shifted back to make room for a long table. It was the kind contractors used, with a built-in saw on one end. The table was spattered red, and there were . . . he forced himself to look away.

Another blue cooler stood open beside it.

He glanced at Noa. She'd noticed the cooler, too. He was getting better at reading her expressions. Outwardly she projected the usual blankness, but he could see rage and horror in her eyes.

"You should be done by now," Cole said flatly.

"Hey, man." The wiry guy looked scared. He held his palms up. "We were trying. But the weather turned to hell, and we figured there was no way to take the boat out without the coast guard coming by."

Cole grunted at that, looking back toward the door.

"So are these . . ." The guy glanced at them, then looked away. "I mean, I thought we were done here, right?"

"Done doing what?" Cole demanded, stepping close to him.

The guy shrank away. "Nothing. I didn't mean—"

"We don't do anything here, and we never have," Cole spat. He turned away, muttering, "Goddamn incompetents."

Cole yanked out a satellite phone with a long antenna. He punched a few buttons and stepped away, speaking in a low voice. He kept his eyes locked on them the entire time, like he was daring them to try to escape. The other guy had retreated to the depths of the room. Like a rat, he paced a few feet back and forth, tugging incessantly at the growth on his chin.

Peter looked at Noa again. For the first time, she appeared truly frightened. Meeting his eyes, she managed a small smile and slipped her hand in his. Her fingers felt icy.

"It'll be okay," he said, trying to sound reassuring. "They'll be here soon."

Noa gave his palm a squeeze and whispered, "I won't let him hurt you."

"That's good, because I really hate being hurt."

Noa made a strangled noise that sounded like a laugh. Cole's head jerked toward them and he frowned.

Peter drew a deep breath and said in a low voice, "I won't let them take you," he said. "No matter what."

Noa didn't say anything, but she squeezed his hand again. Releasing it, she stepped forward and said in a loud voice, "Tell him we'll make a trade."

Cole stopped talking. His eyes narrowed and he came back toward them. "What did you say?"

"A trade." Her voice was calm, steady. "I'll stay, and we give you back all the data. But you have to let Peter go."

"Wait, no—" Peter protested.

Cole laughed. "You're misunderstanding the situation here, sweetheart. You stay no matter what. And I guarantee that after ten minutes alone in a room with me, Peter will cough up more than I need to know."

"He can't," Noa said. "I changed the cipher."

"What the hell's a cipher?" Cole demanded, looking at her blankly.

Noa rolled her eyes. "They didn't hire you for your brains, huh?"

He snarled and stepped toward her. Peter quickly inserted himself between them. Cole stopped just shy of his toes and glared down at him, as if deciding which body part to dismember first.

"A cipher is a cryptographic algorithm," Noa piped up. "It's like a dead bolt on the files. And I have the only key."

"So we'll get it from you," he said dismissively.

"You could kill me, and I still wouldn't tell you," she said sharply. "And it doesn't sound like you can do that, anyway. Golden goose, right? You only get the cipher if you let Peter go. Explain that to Mason."

Cole hesitated. Something shifted in his gaze as he examined her. Clearly he was debating whether or not to believe her.

Peter held his breath, praying they would fall for the bluff. There was no way she could have changed the cipher he used to access the server. He'd set that key up himself. It would have taken a team of computers years of calculations to come up with it. Or Cole about ten minutes to work it out of him, probably. But maybe he didn't know that.

"Go ahead," Noa said calmly. "Ask Mason."

Cole's brow darkened, but he turned back to the phone and said something in a low voice. Apparently he didn't like the response, because his glower deepened as his gaze slid over to Peter.

They were going to let him go, Peter realized. The elation was immediately supplanted by guilt. He couldn't just abandon Noa. They'd already made it clear that they were planning on doing more terrible things to her. They'd whisk her away and bury her so deep he'd never be able to find her.

Their hands were still intertwined. Under his breath, he said, "I can't let you do this."

"One of us has to get away," Noa said. "Someone has to keep trying to stop them."

"Then it should be you."

"They won't let me go," she said impatiently. She was looking past him, toward where the door remained ajar. Suddenly, she frowned.

"What?" Peter asked.

"Nothing. I just thought—"

Cole clicked the phone shut and came back over to them. "It's your lucky day, kid," he said, cuffing Peter on the side of the head. "Mason said to cut you loose. As long as your girlfriend gives up the cipher."

"As soon as he's gone," Noa said firmly.

"Nope, that's not how it's gonna work," he said.

"Can I go now?" a whiny voice called from the rear of the hut. Cole frowned and raised his gun again. "Almost forgot about you, Monte. You wanted to know about Fred, right?"

A whimper. "Please, Cole. I wanted to keep going, I swear. Fred stopped me."

"Yeah?" Cole pointed toward the freezer. "So get the rest of the coolers on the boat."

"Alone?" Monte said dubiously. At Cole's glare, he blanched and muttered, "Yeah, okay. I got this. No problem, man, I got it."

He moved past them and ducked out the door. The sound of a cooler being dragged against concrete, punctuated by Monte's strained grunts.

Cole shook his head. "Morons. This was always my least-favorite site."

"So there are more of them?" Peter asked.

"You really think that's a good idea?" Cole raised an

eyebrow. "Asking that sort of thing? I just said you can go. So get out of here."

"Just like that?" Peter said.

"Just like that. But, kid—" Cole stepped close enough for Peter to smell his breath. It was oddly metallic, like he'd been chewing on nails. "Drive straight home. You make any detours, to the cops, whatever . . . your whole family dies tonight. Understand?"

Peter managed a small nod. He looked past Cole's shoulder at Noa. She was standing still, her eyes cast in shadow. She lifted a hand slightly, as if saying good-bye.

That slayed him. Peter turned, cheeks hot, feeling like the world's biggest coward. Everything inside him protested, making the simple act of placing one foot in front of the other seem impossible. He couldn't sacrifice her like this. Noa was . . . well, maybe not his friend, exactly, but right now probably the person he was closest to in the whole world. And he was just walking out on her, the same way his parents and Amanda had abandoned him.

Peter's mind churned. He could spin around, rush Cole, surprise him, and grab his gun. Scream at her to run for the door. He might die, but at least then he'd be the hero.

He stopped and turned. Cole was still watching him warily.

"I can't," Peter said, hating the shakiness in his voice. "Not without her."

"Your choice," Cole shrugged, raising the gun and aiming.

"Go, Peter!" Noa's voice was hard. "I don't want you here."

"But—"

"I mean it!" she said fiercely. "You're useless, anyway."

That stung. Worse yet was the look in her eyes, the same one she'd had the night they met. The one that said she'd taken his measure and found him lacking.

A wave of desolation swept over him. Rigidly, he turned back around and kept walking.

Behind him, Cole sneered, "Just you and me now, sweetheart."

Peter paused in the doorway. The NSA wouldn't get here in time. They might not even be coming. Cole and Noa would be long gone by then.

Screw it, he decided. He'd get in the car and drive to the nearest police station. Tell them the whole story, and convince them to stop Cole. His parents could fend for themselves.

Resolved, Peter stepped across the threshold. The sleet had slowed to a trickle, easing visibility. He looked left. The blue cooler was halfway to the pier, but Monte was nowhere in sight. The boat still bobbed on the waves, rubber bumpers squeaking against the pilings. Maybe Monte got smart and took off. Peter had the feeling Cole was planning on stuffing him in a pot as soon as he finished loading the boat.

He trotted toward the car. He'd only gone ten feet when there was a loud *pop* from inside the building, followed by another, then another. Peter froze. Gunshots? *Noa,* he thought, heart clenching.

Peter raced back toward the Quonset hut.

CHAPTER SEVENTEEN

It was pitch-black inside. Noa had started moving as soon as the first light blew overhead, sending shattered fragments of glass cascading down. She hadn't known what to expect when she saw the shadow flit past the door. Hadn't even been sure it was him, that he'd gotten her message in time.

But then the enormous fluorescent bulbs that dangled above started to burst, flames dancing around a few of them. Cole's eyes jerked up to the ceiling. Noa took full advantage. She dropped to a crouch and made for the exit. As the lights blew she heard a yell, then a shot, louder than the bulbs popping. The air filled with the smell of gunpowder and something chemical and sinister. Within seconds, all the light had been extinguished. It took her eyes a moment to adjust. A faint gleam emanated from the door Peter had left open. Hopefully he was already back at the car.

Noa could hear Cole crunching toward her on the glass. The door was only a few feet away. She'd be exposed while dashing through, but if she stayed low hopefully Cole wouldn't have time to aim.

She didn't let herself think it over.

As she was about to plunge toward it, the entrance was suddenly blocked by a tall figure.

"Noa!" Peter yelled.

Noa swore under her breath. A roar sounded from behind her—Cole, getting ready to fire.

Peter abruptly shunted sideways, knocked straight off his feet. He vanished from sight. Noa darted for the door, focused on the dim light outside, filtered white by the rain.

Just as she was about to bolt through, a flaming bottle rolled past her.

Peter landed hard and grunted. His arm had twisted beneath him at a funny angle, pinning his shoulder back. Reflexively he struggled against the weight on top of him.

"Go to the boat!" a voice hissed in his ear.

"What? Screw you, I'm getting—"

"I got her. Now go!"

Peter stumbled to his feet just in time to see his attacker light the fuse on a Molotov cocktail. The guy looked past him over the flame. He was young, maybe eighteen or nineteen, with dark hair that hung below his ears. Lean and grungy-looking, like the runaways at the shelter where Amanda volunteered. He glared at Peter through the rain. "Move!" he ordered, then tossed the bomb into the building.

Peter fought through the confusion. Who the hell was this guy? Where had he come from? He seemed to be helping them, but no one else knew they were here, not even Cody.

Obstinately he stayed put. He'd already abandoned Noa once. If she was in there, he was going after her.

Smoke poured through the open door. Shouts inside, the sound of someone running.

Suddenly Noa emerged, breaking free of the black smoke. The guy grabbed her elbow and dragged her toward the pier.

It took Peter a second to react—just enough time for Cole to clear the door. He was coughing hard, an arm wrapped around his mouth. The gun dangled from his hand.

Quickly Peter checked back over his shoulder. The guy and Noa were only halfway to the boat. They'd never make it.

He bent double and charged, crashing his head squarely into Cole's gut. He heard the sound of metal on concrete. Somewhere his brain processed that he'd managed to knock the gun free, and at least for the moment Cole was unarmed. Peter felt a surge of hope. He lashed out with every ounce of pent-up rage from the past few days. The way his parents had turned their backs on him. Amanda's betrayal. All the horrible things that had been done to Noa. Aside from some occasional wrestling matches with his brother, Peter hadn't been in a real fight since the second grade. He pummeled Cole as hard as he could, driving his knuckles into what felt like a solid rock wall.

The hope faded quickly. Suddenly he was on the ground with Cole straddling him. "Who taught you to fight, kid?" he asked, wiping a stream of blood from his lip with the back of his hand. "Not your buddy. He put up more of a fight."

"My buddy?" Peter was startled. What the hell was Cole talking about? "Who are you—"

Cole had drawn his fist back. Peter didn't even have time to flinch before it connected with his jaw. He realized why they compared it to getting hit with a hammer, because that's exactly what it felt like. Cole punched him again, and again. Each time, a different piece of Peter was jarred loose. A tooth. Part of his eye socket. Systematically, like it was a job he'd clocked in for, Cole kept beating him. Peter felt himself fading. The air seemed to be growing lighter around them. He wondered if this was what it was like to die.

"Hands in the air!" a woman's voice screamed.

The words echoed strangely. Peter was groggy, unable to focus. His head felt like it was swelling up like a balloon.

One last blow to his chin, so hard his teeth clacked together. The voice again, yelling, "Federal agents! Hands in the air now!"

The sound of people running. Peter squinted, trying to see. The weight on his chest suddenly released. He heard Cole protesting. Another voice, authoritative, ordering, "Get to that boat!"

Rough hands dragged him to his feet. Peter's head lolled forward. No matter how hard he tried, he couldn't lift it.

"Take this one inside," the same voice said. Peter let them carry him, his toes bumping over the doorsill as he was dragged into the building.

"We need light in here!"

A slew of orders being barked, the sound of general chaos. Peter let himself drift off for a bit. He wasn't dead, which was a start. He wondered if Noa had gotten away. He hoped so. Peter realized that her plan had worked. At the thought, he choked out something approaching a laugh. The cavalry had come after all. A little late, but they were here.

"What's so funny?" a female voice demanded.

"Nothing." Peter raised his head and strained to see through the slits narrowing his vision. They'd brought in some sort of special lantern that cast long, triangular-shaped shadows everywhere. In its light, he could make out an older woman in jeans, a turtleneck, and a navy Windbreaker. She was frowning at him. "It's all going to be okay now."

"Love the confidence," the woman said drily. "Especially under the—"

"Ruiz, you need to see what we found over here."

The woman turned abruptly and followed another guy across the room. They had on matching Windbreakers, navy blue with *FBI* emblazoned in bright yellow letters across the back. They stopped in front of the walk-in freezer to examine the contents of the cooler. Even though their voices were low, he could detect a shift in the atmosphere of the room.

"There's a chopped-up kid in there," Peter called out. The words slurred together. He tried to enunciate as he continued, "More outside, in the other cooler. And on the boat."

"What happened here?" The woman was back. Odd, Peter hadn't even seen her cross the room. There were two of her now, too.

He smiled through throbbing lips, trying to set her at ease. "I'll tell you everything. But first, I need to lie down. Just for a second."

The room shifted, sliding away from him. This time, Peter let it.

Noa huddled against the back of the boat, trying to stay as far from the coolers and crab pots as possible. It was hard, though. The storm had churned the sea into a nasty, roiling froth. They were cruising up six-foot-high waves, then smacking down forcefully on the other side. Everything on deck, including her, kept shooting three feet up in the air before landing hard. Noa tried to take the shock of the impact in her knees, staying crouched as if poised to jump, but it didn't help much. She was exhausted. And worse yet, really, really cold again.

Zeke kept glancing back to check on her. Her own personal guardian angel, though he certainly didn't look like one. He was tall, maybe six-two or six-three, her age or a bit older. Skinny, as if he never got enough to eat. Dark hair, skin, and eyes—maybe Latino, but it was hard to say for sure.

Zeke was good at the helm, though; he must have had some experience driving boats. He was underdressed for the weather in jeans, a dark flannel shirt, and black sneakers, yet the cold didn't seem to bother him.

She, on the other hand, couldn't stop shivering. Her teeth were chattering so hard it made her jaw ache. Freezing salt spray pelted her cheeks until it felt like she was being encased in ice.

"Not much farther!" he called back, the wind snatching the tail end of the sentence.

Noa tried to nod but couldn't. She kept her shoulders hunched and let herself be shot up and released by the boat, shot up and released.

They'd very nearly gotten caught. She'd tried to go back for Peter, knowing as soon as he tackled Cole that it wouldn't end well. But Zeke wouldn't let her. He dragged her to the boat, yelling that the feds were right behind him; they had to *go go go* . . .

He was right. As they pulled away from the dock, the whole place was swarmed by people in dark Windbreakers yelling orders. Noa watched them overtake Peter and Cole, then head for the pier. Zeke gunned the boat's engine and they leaped out into the waves so sharply she nearly hurtled overboard.

By the time the agents reached the edge of the dock, the

boat was fifty feet out into the water. The large waves nearly upset it, but Zeke managed to keep the hull pointed forward, righting it each time.

"Where are we going?" she called out, but Zeke didn't answer.

Noa was worried. In a storm like this, the coast guard would be busy, but probably willing to make a boat carrying potential NSA infiltrators a priority.

It was impossible to see the shoreline through the dark wash of waves penning them in.

"Hang on!" Zeke yelled.

Noa clutched the nearest rope, her stomach lurching as the boat swept right. A wave caught the side of it, and she started to slide across deck. Black water climbed the gunwale below her, opening up to receive her like a giant mouth.

Another shift, and the boat leveled.

And just like that, the waves abated. Zeke throttled down the engine. Noa saw a flash of something big and green on their left: a buoy. As if on cue, the rain diminished in intensity. She could make out the faint lights of houses on either side. They were cruising down a narrow channel between strips of land.

"The Kickemuit River," Zeke explained. "There's a nature sanctuary here. We can ditch the boat and make it to the road."

How the hell does he know that? Noa wondered. She was relieved that Zeke had gotten her message about the facility, but she hadn't expected him to actually turn up there. Although if he hadn't, she might not have survived the encounter with Cole.

He turned the boat into an even narrower canal. Long wet grass brushed the sides of the boat as they approached a small wooden bridge. The boat ran aground and Zeke cut the engine.

"We'll have to wade a little, but it's not deep," he said, coming back to her. "You okay to walk? I wasn't sure if you got hurt back there."

"I'm fine," she said, before adding, "Zeke."

His eyes met hers and he smiled. "How'd you figure out my name, anyway?"

"Please," she said. "A6M0? It took five minutes to find out that's what the Allies called Japanese fighter planes in World War II."

"Guess I'll have to come up with a new handle," Zeke said reflectively. "'Course, you probably will, too."

"Probably," Noa said. Which was a shame. She'd liked being Rain. It suited her.

"Laptop in there?" he asked, pointing to her bag.

"Yeah, but the saltwater probably ruined it," she said ruefully.

"Then leave it; we'll need to travel light. Any and all cell phones, too, especially the one you used to email me." Noticing her reluctance, he said gently, "It's easy enough to get more, right?"

Noa hesitated, then dug out the devices. He was right. She popped out the flash drive that held the Project Persephone files and tucked it in her pocket. With a pang of regret, she released the MacBook into the water, followed by the cell phone. She watched them vanish below the surface.

Zeke glanced up. It was late, but a few houses across the way were still lit.

"Where are we going?" Noa asked. "What about Peter?"

"The guy we left behind?"

Noa flinched and nodded.

Zeke shrugged. "Nothing we can do for him right now, especially if we get caught. Let's get out of here."

"Then you'll tell me everything?" she demanded.

"Everything I know, yeah." A shadow crossed Zeke's face. "But you probably know the worst of it already."

They both looked at the coolers lining the back of the boat. Five of them, strapped together and lashed to the crab pots. Noa shuddered, wondering how many kids were inside. One per cooler? Or had they managed to squeeze in more?

"Let's go," Zeke said, more gently this time.

Noa followed him, sloshing through the shallows toward shore.

CHAPTER EIGHTEEN

Peter slowly opened his eyes. He had to be dreaming. He was lying in his bed at home. The curtains were pulled back, and soft wintry light dappled the floor. Everything was just as he'd left it: closet door open, empty hangers dangling, drawers spilling their contents.

He tried to sit up and immediately collapsed back against the pillows, panting. Everything hurt and his head swam. *What the hell happened?* he wondered. *How'd I end up here?*

Soft footsteps down the hall. His bedroom door cracked, then was thrown open. His mother rushed in, eagerness lighting up her face. Priscilla slowed as she approached the bed, clearly uncertain of her reception. "You're finally awake!" Relief flooded her voice. "Oh, Peter, you had us so worried."

"What happened?" he asked, slowly managing to get up on his elbows.

"Here, let me." She reached behind him and fluffed the pillows. He fell gratefully back against them. "We're not sure, exactly. We were hoping you could tell us."

"How did I get here?" Peter asked. It all came back in a rush: Cole beating him. Noa running for the boat. That guy who came out of nowhere and threw a bomb. The feds storming in. "Did the FBI bring me?"

"The FBI?" His mother looked perplexed. "No, honey. The police found you and brought you to a hospital in Rhode Island. Although what possessed you to go down there . . . your father and I just assumed you were with Amanda, then we got this terrible phone call." Her brow furrowed with concern. "Anyway, the doctors didn't want to move you, but you should have seen that hospital. No way we were leaving you under their care. They said it was only a concussion, anyway."

"So they didn't arrest me?" he asked.

"Well . . ." His mother plucked at the comforter. "The police figured that all things considered, you'd probably learned your lesson. And trespassing is only a misdemeanor. Those poor other children—you were so lucky, Peter," she said fiercely, leaning in and planting a kiss on his forehead. "You were the only one to survive the fire."

"Fire? What fire?" Peter's brain felt sluggish, dulled. It took a minute to process each of her sentences; the words seemed disjointed, part of a different story. He wondered if that was due to the concussion. "What about Noa?"

"Who?" Light dawned in his mother's eyes. "Was she one of the other kids that was . . . staying there with you?"

Peter dropped back against the pillows and closed his eyes. It was easier to focus that way, and his mother's rare outpouring of emotion was starting to irk him in light of how they'd left things. "Just tell me what they told you."

"Well, apparently, a group of kids—you among them—were camping out at an old naval base in Rhode Island," she said slowly. "And there was a fire. Something about an illegal generator. Most of the kids were overcome by smoke, or fumes, or something . . . they're not quite sure. But you're the only one they found alive. And we're so happy you're okay, Peter," she said, voice softening. "I'm sorry you ended up there. You should never have been placed in that position."

"But wait, what about . . ." His voice trailed off. It didn't seem possible. The FBI had been there. They'd seen the dead kids, the tables. The computers filled with all that incriminating information. "So there wasn't anything else? They didn't say anything about experiments?"

"Experiments?" his mother asked in a guarded tone. "What kind of experiments?"

"Those kids weren't squatters; they were being experimented on there," he said impatiently. "Project Persephone. The one Mason—"

"I think you should get more rest," his mother said, abruptly standing and cutting him off. She glanced at the door, her voice climbing a few decibels as she firmly added, "They were just a bunch of squatters who died in a fire, Peter. Mr. Mason had nothing to do with it. Now, I'd stay with you if I could, but I really need to get going."

"Going where?" he asked, noticing for the first time that she was all dressed up in a black dress and pearls.

A strain shone at the corners of her eyes as she tugged at her necklace. "I really hate to have to tell you, after everything you've been through, but . . . I don't suppose you remember Cody Ellis? Your brother's friend?"

Peter bolted upright, ignoring the pain. "What happened to Cody?"

"Another fire, I'm afraid." His mother made a rueful face. "Apparently a space heater shorted out in some slum he was renting. Your father and I thought we should make an appearance at the service, since he and Jeremy were so close."

Peter sank back down, stunned. "Cody's dead?" Disbelief filled his voice.

"Try not to think about it right now," his mother said, patting his leg. "Just focus on getting better." She pecked his forehead again with dry lips. "I love you, sweetheart. And you're okay. That's all that matters."

"We should be safe here for now," Zeke said.

Noa nodded. She was feeling dazed by the events of the past few days. Her messenger bag was slung across her shoulder even though she was sitting down. She was having a hard time taking it off; it still felt like at any moment they'd have to start running again and she'd be left with nothing.

They were in an abandoned house in Warren, Rhode Island. Apparently Zeke had a whole system for finding places like this, foreclosures set deep in the woods. It was a sad little house, tucked into a dense thicket of trees at the end of a long gravel driveway. Its white exterior paint was peeling away in strips to reveal an earlier shade of brown. They'd walked all night to reach it. There was no furniture, just a few abandoned odds and ends left in cupboards: an old can of pumpkin-pie mix, a jar of white rice, a rusty can opener, an empty tampons box. The power was shut off, but Zeke had found an emergency generator in the garage. Not that she needed power anyway, without her laptop.

Her bag felt light without it. Even though she'd only had it for a few days, Noa missed it.

Zeke had picked the lock to let them in—quickly enough that she was impressed. Peter would have been, too, she thought with a pang. Noa felt awful about leaving him back there. She couldn't stop picturing the way he'd lunged at Cole. Peter had saved them. Hopefully the FBI had intervened before Cole had seriously injured or killed him. She desperately wanted to get online and see what the fallout had been, if they'd actually succeeded in shining a light on Pike & Dolan's illegal experiments. And, she admitted, to see if Peter was okay. It was killing her not knowing.

When they'd finally reached the house, they were both too tired and drained to talk. Using her bag as a pillow, Noa had fallen asleep minutes after they got inside. Thanks to the cold, she slept fitfully. She'd pulled more clothes out of her bag and layered them, but still constantly woke up shivering. Her feet were still icy from wading through the salt marsh to shore, even though she'd put on both dry pairs of socks.

Without asking, Zeke had curled up behind her, back-to-back. Noa fought the urge to move away. Despite the fact that he'd been her guardian angel, she still barely knew him. But the warmth felt too good to pass up.

He was hunkered down across from her now, arms wrapped around his knees as he watched her from under hooded eyes. Zeke wasn't quite what she'd expected. Dirty, like it had been weeks since he'd showered. Longish dark hair, dark eyes. Strikingly good-looking, to the point where it made her self-conscious. Noa ran a hand through her hair. It felt greasy, snarled.

"If you want to shower, I can get the generator up and

running," he said, noticing. "The neighbors are too far away to hear. No towels, though."

Noa had so many questions, but felt oddly shy, as if speaking would break some sort of spell and bring the weight of reality crashing back down upon them. Not that this wasn't real enough, she thought with a shudder as a gust of cold air brushed her neck.

Noa cleared her throat. "So you said you'd answer my questions."

"Yeah, right." He smiled slightly. "Those."

She fished around, debating how to start. For whatever reason, the phrase *Tanto Barf* popped up, reminding her of why she'd first trusted him. "You were at The Center, too?"

He nodded once. "Yes."

"For how long?" she pressed when he didn't continue.

He shrugged. "On and off for years. You know how it is."

Yes, she knew. Noa recognized the haunted eyes and tensed shoulders, combined with the constant expectation of impending abuse. She couldn't help thinking that Peter would never understand the level of desolation instilled by growing up like that.

"I don't recognize you, though," Noa noted.

"No?" Zeke cocked his head to the side. "I remember you. You were about thirteen, I think. You came in right before I took off for good."

"Yeah?" Noa searched her memory banks. When she was thirteen, she'd spent about three months at The Center in between families. But he still didn't look familiar.

"Guess I'm not as memorable," he said with a wry grin.

She wasn't sure how to respond to that, so asked, "When did you leave?"

"Around three years ago, when I was fifteen." He drew a

finger across a floorboard. "Just got sick of it, you know?"

Noa nodded. "I kind of ran away, too."

"You did it the smart way, though," he said ruefully. "Wish I'd thought of it. Setting up a fake family was genius."

Noa flushed slightly at the compliment. "So what did you do?" she asked, curious.

"Same as everyone. I lived on the streets for a while, with a couple other kids who'd run away." His brow darkened. "Then they took me."

"Who?" she asked, although she already suspected the answer.

Zeke met her eyes. His own were almost black. "You know who. The assholes from the Project."

"But, you're . . . I mean, how did you . . ."

He looked away again, concentrating intently on the floor as he said, "I don't like to talk about it."

"Did they . . . were you cut?" Noa ventured after a few minutes of weighted silence.

"No." To prove it, he raised his shirt. Zeke wasn't as gaunt as he appeared; his stomach was a solid washboard. Noa forced her eyes up—no scar.

"And they didn't give me PEMA, either," he continued, letting the shirt fall back into place. "I thought they might've, but it's been almost two years. It would have showed up by now, so I must've gotten away before they could. Well, I guess I was rescued, really."

"Rescued by who?"

"There's a whole network of us." He dropped the shirt and settled into a squat facing her. "Kind of an underground railroad. We've managed to get a few kids out—you were at one of the really tight facilities. There are others that used to be easier. They've all stepped up security, though," he said ruefully. "It's gotten a lot harder than it used to be. How'd you get the FBI there yesterday?"

"Hacked into the NSA through their server," Noa said.

Zeke didn't seem impressed. "Risky move. You should have steered clear like I told you."

"I thought there might be more kids there," she retorted. "How'd you get the lights to blow out?"

"Juiced the generator," he said. "Since they were the only lights on, they couldn't handle the overload."

"That was smart," Noa said begrudgingly. Everything he'd said was sinking in, though. She frowned. "If there's this whole network, why didn't you just tell me about it in the first place? Why'd you leave me all alone out there?"

A look of regret crossed his face. "I wanted to. But the thing is—you're a big risk. No one else wanted to touch it."

"Why not?" Noa demanded. "You just said you've been rescuing others. Why not me? Especially after I got away?"

"Because you're the one they really want," he explained, looking at her intensely. "Don't you get it? You're the cure."

"The cure for what?"

"PEMA, definitely. Maybe everything. We just don't know." He shrugged.

Noa took a minute to absorb that. "So the others didn't survive the surgery?"

Zeke shook his head. "And some of the ones we saved had already been infected. They didn't . . ." He looked away, toward where a narrow window provided a glimpse of the surrounding forest. "Anyway, it's been tough. There aren't many of us, and the company was after you in a big way. The others thought it would attract too much attention if we helped."

Noa digested that for a minute. It was reassuring to

discover that she and Peter weren't the only ones who knew about the experiments, that in fact there was a whole network of people trying to stop them. But they hadn't done anything to save her, or the kids at the base, she thought with a rush of fury. Well, at least most of them hadn't. "You helped me," she pointed out.

"Yeah, but I wasn't supposed to." Zeke managed a small grin. "They're not happy with me right now." Seeing her expression, he hurriedly continued, "They'll get over it, though. They know we need to help you now. And I've helped them plenty," he finished, sounding more sure of himself.

"Helped them do what?"

"With the rescue raids. And I've been warning runaways, telling them what to watch out for."

"In Boston?"

"Everywhere," he said proudly. "Plus I'm good with computers. Not as good as you," he amended, "but decent. So I've helped with that side of it. You could do more than I can, though," he said thoughtfully. "They've already realized that, based on how you took down the AMRF site."

"That wasn't me," Noa said. "Peter did that." She had a sudden flash of how proud he'd looked when he told her about it. Tears flooded her eyes and she ducked her head.

"He's okay," Zeke said gently, as Noa wiped her eyes with the backs of her hands. "They won't hurt him."

Noa wanted to ask how he could be so sure, but she wanted to believe it so badly she let it go. "What next?" Noa finally asked. "I mean, we can't exactly stay here, right?" She gestured with one hand at the empty house.

"Well, like I said, they're going to get us IDs. We've got a guy who mocks up licenses so good they'd get you on a plane."

"We're not going on a plane, though, right?" Noa asked.

"Hell no. But they'll be good to have. There's a cash-flow problem right now, though," he said thoughtfully, scratching the shaggy growth of beard on his chin.

"I've got cash." She still had the money Peter had given her.

"Yeah? How much?"

"A few hundred dollars."

"That won't get us far."

"I might be able to get more," Noa said slowly, thinking of her PO Box. It would be risky, but if someone could access it, her new bank cards should still be in there. She had over ten grand in her account. Zeke could pose as Ted Latham, and they could potentially get all of it. Draining the account would send up warning flags, but Pike & Dolan already knew she'd gotten away. They probably wouldn't expect her to do something as stupid as going after the box now, not after everything that had happened. "Do you have someone who's good at breaking into things?"

"Yeah," Zeke said with a slow grin. "Me."

"It's dangerous," she warned.

"I figured." He laughed. "Trust me, Noa. There's no way for us to be completely safe anymore."

CHAPTER NINETEEN

There was a light knock on his door, but Peter ignored it. He was lying on his side in bed. Technically he was supposed to be "up and about." At least that's what his mother kept saying. Priscilla had let him lounge around for a few days, ostensibly to "aid the healing process." But a week had passed, and apparently enough was enough. She'd enter his room briskly every morning, whisk open the curtains, clap her hands together, and announce that it was time for breakfast. When that didn't get a response, she sent in Bob. His father shuffled awkwardly from foot to foot, directing a rambling discourse on the importance of a good education at the rug as he avoided Peter's eyes.

After that failed, there were a lot of urgent whispered conversations just outside his door. Next came the threats, but his parents were quickly forced to acknowledge that those were ineffective since Peter showed no interest in any of the things they could take away. He didn't want to go out, so grounding wouldn't work. He hadn't even switched on the TV, or the computer. He barely ate. They couldn't exactly punish him for refusing to get out of bed.

Most of the time, he lay in bed staring up at the ceiling, thinking about what a royally screwed-up place the world was. And how he no longer had the energy to try and fix it. What was the point? In retrospect, everything he'd accomplished with /ALLIANCE/ seemed pathetic and laughable, like a gnat buzzing around a water buffalo. The gnat might occasionally succeed at being an annoyance, but the buffalo would still go ahead and do whatever the hell it wanted.

Peter didn't care anymore. He didn't plan on going back to school. Hell, he didn't plan on doing anything. He just wanted to lie there and think about how he'd not only destroyed his life, but got the one person left in the world he could trust absolutely killed.

And it had all been for nothing. Pike & Dolan might have established a dozen more labs by now. He'd logged into his email once, but there had been nothing from Rain, so maybe Noa had been recaptured. She was probably strapped to a table somewhere right now. And there was nothing he could do about it.

His bedroom door creaked open.

"Go away," he said, unable to summon the energy to sound angry at the intrusion. Peter closed his eyes.

"The maid let me in."

Peter flipped over in bed, a quick motion that still induced a wince. Amanda was standing there. She was wearing her usual patchwork outfit: a colorful bulky sweater over a dark gray skirt and striped tights, fingerless gloves, a scarf that shouldn't really have matched, but somehow did. She looked tired, though. There were dark circles under her eyes, and the hair tumbling out from her knit cap was stringy.

But then, he probably wasn't looking so hot himself. He hadn't shaved yet, and could barely remember the last time he showered. Suddenly self-conscious, he tugged the sheets up over his bare chest. Like the first time they met, Peter was at a loss for words. Finally he managed, "Hi."

"Hi." She smiled wanly at him. "I thought maybe we could talk."

"Yeah, sure." Peter sat all the way up. He wished he could get out of bed, maybe talk to her on the sofa across the room. But he was only wearing boxer shorts, and the way things were between them now, he wasn't comfortable sauntering across the room in them.

She cautiously approached the bed and perched at the foot of it. "You look terrible," she said after a minute.

"Thanks," Peter said wryly.

"Your mom told me what happened." Amanda cast her eyes down to the floor. "I feel awful about it. You could have stayed, you know."

"No, I couldn't have," he said.

She looked up at him. "I'm sorry about that, too. If it makes you feel better, I pretty much haven't seen Drew since then."

Peter mulled that over. Surprisingly, he discovered that he didn't really care. Just seeing her was like stumbling across vestiges of a past life, similar to finding a photo album of a family vacation you'd long forgotten. Almost like their relationship had happened to someone else. He didn't know what to say, so he shrugged.

Amanda's face clouded over. "I came here because . . . well . . . something happened. To me."

Peter scratched his cheek. The beard growth was starting to itch. Maybe he should shave today. "Amanda, I'm kind of wiped out. I don't really—"

"Look, I know you're angry at me, and you have every right to be. But it's just . . ." Amanda's voice cracked and tears spilled down her cheeks as she said, "Please, Peter. I don't have anyone else to tell about this."

After everything that had happened, Peter discovered that his anger at her had dissipated. Watching Amanda cry, his chest didn't contract the way it would've a week ago. But he didn't exactly feel nothing, either. Something inside him shifted, and he opened his arms. "Okay. I'm sorry, come here."

She buried her face in his shoulder and sobbed. Peter rubbed the back of Amanda's head, the wool of her cap scratchy under his fingers. He noticed that she'd brought something in with her. It sat at the foot of the bed.

"You got me a laptop?" he said before he could stop himself.

"What?" She sat up, wiping her eyes, and followed his gaze to the foot of the bed. "Oh, no. The maid found it on the doorstep this morning."

"No one had to sign for it?" Peter asked, puzzled.

Amanda shrugged, looking nonplussed by the interruption. "FedEx must have left it."

Peter reached down and pulled the box up to him. It was a brand-new, top-of-the-line MacBook Pro—the same one Mason had stolen from him. No packing slip. No FedEx or UPS stickers on it. "Weird," he said.

"Peter," Amanda said, sounding annoyed. "This is serious."

"I know, sorry." He set the box back down. "Tell me."

Peter sat in the window seat that overlooked their pool and brooded. Amanda had left an hour earlier. He'd asked her to stay, said she could crash in a guest room if she wanted—after all, they had three. But after spilling the story of what had happened, she'd started acting strange. Like maybe she shouldn't have told him after all.

Sure, he'd been angry. It was bad enough that creep Mason had messed with his life, and probably killed Cody. But now he'd gone after his girlfriend—or whatever she was now. Had they actually done something to her? Or was it just another cruel joke, a way to demonstrate the power they had over him and everyone in his life?

At the thought of them stripping off her clothes and marking up her skin, Peter's fists clenched. If he ever saw Mason again, he'd strangle him. Didn't matter how many thugs were there; they'd have to kill him before he'd stop.

His eyes fell on the laptop again. Was that from Mason, too? Probably came preloaded with spyware or something. Well, he wasn't about to let a Trojan horse into his life.

Peter got to his feet and crossed the room in three steps, grabbing it off his bed. He'd throw it in the trash, maybe knock it around with a hammer first to release some of his rage.

Then he saw the note. It was so tiny he almost missed it. Black print scrawled within the photo of the laptop in the center of the box. He drew it close to his face, squinting at it. Two words, written along the seam where the laptop closed. They read: *burnt toast.*

Noa.

He sliced his finger on a slip of cardboard while wrenching the box open. Slid out the laptop: There didn't seem to be anything unusual about it. All the standard Mac slips of paper were there: the warranty, crap about getting started. Frustrated, Peter laid them out and examined them: nothing. He started going through everything else in the box: the plug and USB cables, lots of accessories sealed in plastic. Nothing.

Peter plugged in the computer and turned it on, waiting for it to power up. After what seemed like forever, the welcome screen popped up, the standard Apple display of a night sky shot through with stars. He sifted quickly through the applications menu: It contained the usual preloaded software. He dug deeper into the registry, looking for anything out of the ordinary. . . .

Fifteen minutes later, he spotted it tucked away in a cache file: /Library/Caches/QuadNekro. The kind of thing you'd only find if you were looking for it, a useless bit of code that wouldn't have any effect on a computer's performance. A message left more or less in plain sight.

He fell back against the pillows. Noa was okay. She'd gotten away. Peter felt a rush of relief and elation. Maybe there was hope after all.

But he had to go somewhere else to get online; it wasn't safe here. Quickly he threw on some clothes and grabbed the laptop, wrapping the power cable around it. That gave him a little pang—he pictured Noa doing the same when they'd left Cody's place.

He forced the thought away. Grabbed an old backpack from his closet and put the laptop inside, then tucked his wallet in his back pocket. Raced downstairs and found his car keys hanging where they always were, on the metal strip in the kitchen.

His mother was opening the door as he crossed the hallway. Seeing him she startled, almost dropping a stack of mail.

"Peter! You're—"

"Bye, Mom. I'll be back later." He dashed outside without waiting for a response.

He tore down the driveway in his car. No way to know if Mason's goons were still following him. There was a Walgreens a mile away. Peter needed a new cell phone anyway, and there was no way he'd go back to one that could be monitored. He'd buy another TracFone, and use that to get on the 3G network. It wouldn't be as fast as a wireless connection, but it should work.

Twenty minutes later he was in the parking lot of a supermarket down the street from Walgreens. He'd parked far from the entrance, keeping a solid twenty feet between him and the nearest car. He'd been checking his rearview mirror the entire drive, but couldn't tell if anyone was behind him. Not that it mattered. The NSA wouldn't be able to access what he was doing if they were parked right beside him.

Part of him hoped they were watching, wondering what he was up to. Peter felt like daring them to mess with him again.

It took an excruciatingly long time to get the TracFone hooked up to the laptop so that he could sign in to the Quad. He immediately scrolled down the page, scanning the chat threads, praying it would be there.

It was. Nekro was listed as invitation-only and required a password.

He typed in, *burnt toast*.

And just like that, he was in. There was only one other user, listed by the handle PER5EF0NE.

Peter smiled. Noa must've appropriated the project name for her new handle, which was kind of a cool way to thumb her nose at the bastards who'd experimented on her. To confirm it, he typed, *Why'd you steal that car?*

A few moments passed. His heart thudded against his rib cage as he waited. Finally, PER5EF0NE wrote, *To visit my parents. What was the baby's name?*

Smart—she was just as paranoid about making sure it was him. The baby? She must mean Cody's neighbor's kid, the one they babysat for ten minutes. Crap, what was its name . . .

Ethan! he typed triumphantly.

A beat, then she wrote, *Sorry about Cody.*

Peter fought back a tear. He hadn't cried yet, oddly hadn't been able to. But seeing those three words on-screen nearly unleashed the flood. He wiped his eyes with the back of his hand and typed, *Yeah, me too. U okay?*

4 now.

U need to get out of Boston, he wrote, thinking about the risk she'd taken delivering the laptop to his doorstep. *Like, yesterday.*

Already gone.

Good. Don't let them get u again.

They won't.

I still can't believe they covered it up. Peter pounded at the keyboard, fuming. *I mean, the goddamn NSA and FBI? Why did they go along with it?*

Bigger than we thought. I told you not to trust cops. We're going to stop them, though.

Peter wrestled with his emotions. He wanted to believe her, but they were still just kids; those were just words. They'd already taken their best shot at stopping all this and had utterly failed. Still, he typed, *How?*

Just get /ALLIANCE/ up and running again, we'll need it. Check in here every day. Don't worry, we've got a plan.

Sounded like she was still with that guy, the one he'd dubbed "Molotov cocktail man." The thought bothered Peter more than he'd like to admit. But at least Noa wasn't alone, he told himself. It was good that someone was watching her back. Even if for the moment, it wasn't him. Peter typed, *Better than the last plan, I hope.*

Definitely. This time we'll be the cavalry.

And she signed off.

Peter spent a long moment staring at the screen, then logged off and powered down the phone and laptop. He tapped his finger on the steering wheel, thinking. Did he really want to get involved in all this again? Risk his parents, and Amanda?

Yeah, he thought, remembering Cody. *Hell yeah.* He'd do whatever they needed him to.

If you've found this, then you're already one of us. This won't be an easy thread to follow. Because of the people we're up against, you'll have to work for it. We'll always leave bread crumbs, but they might get swept away, or be too hard to track. But we're trusting that even if you only find this entry, you'll pass it along. Because the one thing we have going for us is numbers. There are more of us. And if we work together, we can stop them.

I don't like talking about myself, but I don't have a choice anymore. I was taken by them. Experimented on. And I'm not the only one. They're preying on everyone outside the system, the kids no one cares about.

Well, I care. And I'm going to fight them. We're building an army, both here and in the real world. We're going to beat them at their own game. Even if you think you're safe, even if you're one of those people with parents and a social security number and a warm place to sleep, you need to listen. Today they're coming for us. Tomorrow, it might be you. So I'm asking for your help. I'm asking you to open your eyes, your ears. See what's happening in every major city across the country. Kids are vanishing. Kids are dying. And the cops and the government are part of it.

Follow me and we can save them. We'll lead them back into the light.

My name used to be Noa. But you can call me PER5EF0NE.

Posted by PER5EF0NE on November 7th
/ALLIANCE/ /NEKRO/ /#PERSEF_ARMY/
<<<<>>>>

Acknowledgments

Books are always a group effort, and this one was no exception. My wonderful friend Lisa Brown provided an introduction to Daniel Ehrenhaft, who in turn gave me the opportunity to run with these characters and see where the story took them. I was fortunate enough to have Barbara Lalicki and Karen Chaplin expertly shepherd the project from there. My agent, Stephanie Kip Rostan, and her colleagues at the Levine/Greenberg Literary Agency are the best team a writer could ever hope to have in her corner. Without all of their efforts, there wouldn't be a book in your hands right now.

A heartfelt thanks to my panel of experts: Dr. Kjersti Kirkeby, who told me more about the hypothalamus than I ever wanted to know, and Jonathan Hayes, a formidable writer and forensic pathologist who cheerfully answered any and all postmortem inquiries. Kelli Stanley, auteur and classicist, helped me come up with a plausible Latin name for an imaginary disease. Bruce Davis, certified computer genius, taught me how to hack into the NSA (not really, but he patiently responded to all the tech questions this luddite lobbed at him). I also want to thank the Bostonians who sent photos of their fair city to provide backgrounds for specific scenes, including Krista Clark, Andrew Hirsch, and Annie Fuller.

My beta readers bravely waded through the rough terrain of my first draft, and they improved the manuscript tremendously with their feedback and suggestions. This time around I'm indebted to Noah Wang, Trish Collins, Dana Kawano, Jason Starr, and Chynna Starr.

My sister, Kate, always serves as my first reader and editor. She's a fantastic sounding board and a constant source of lovingly constructive criticism (with regard to both my writing and my wardrobe). The rest of my family (especially my parents) have supported me through a wide variety of zany careers, including this one. Much love to you all.

Kirk Rudell threw me a rope whenever the plot led to a dead end, and was always there for me when I needed him. Thanks for that.

Ironically, my laptop suffered a terminal meltdown during the editing phase and I lost a few years' worth of emails (if only I possessed even a fraction of Noa's skills!). Consequently, there might be some people that I'm unintentionally forgetting—if you're one of them, please accept my abject apologies and know that I'll thank you twice in the next book and will send you a muffin basket. At least one of those things will definitely come true.

On a serious note, while PEMA is an imaginary illness, the plight of children in the foster-care system is very real. As a society we are largely failing these kids, but there are organizations that advocate for them, including Court Appointed Special Advocates for Children (www.casaforchildren.org) and the Children's Defense Fund (www.childrensdefense.org). And you don't have to be an adult to help—the American Academy of Pediatrics has a list of suggestions for teens, including starting a backpack program so that children in foster care have items for school. More information is available at www.aap.org/fostercare/advocacy.html.

Turn the page for a sneak peek at the second
thrilling book about Noa and Peter.

ON THE RUN.
OUT OF TIME.

DON'T
LOOK
NOW

MICHELLE GAGNON

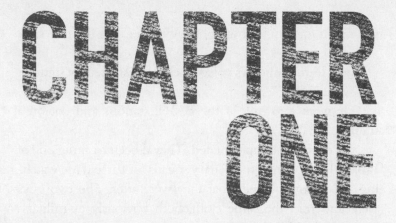

CHAPTER ONE

"I thought California was supposed to be warm," Zeke grumbled, rubbing his arms.

Noa stayed focused on the tiny radio in her hand. It was new equipment they were trying out, top-of-the-line military-grade communicators. They hadn't been cheap, but hopefully they'd be worth it—during their last raid the radios had died, with nearly disastrous consequences.

Noa pursed her lips. The rest of her team was supposed to call in five minutes ago, and they were rarely late. "It's February," she said without lifting her gaze. "Everywhere is cold in February."

"For once, I wish they'd set up a lab in Hawaii," Zeke mumbled. "We could be having fruity drinks, instead of—"

The radio suddenly crackled to life in Noa's hands, and

she waved for him to shut up. Drawing it to her lips, she said, "Report."

"Lost him." Janiqua's voice crackled, distorted by static.

"What? How?"

"He went into one of the BART stations and got on a train."

Noa chewed her lip, irritated. They'd been tracking one of Project Persephone's mercenary squads for three days, watching and waiting to see what they were after. The two guys were cut from the same cloth, both obviously ex-military. Her team had been following them ever since they landed at SFO. But this morning the duo had unexpectedly split up, heading in opposite directions after leaving their hotel. She and Zeke were keeping an eye on one of the men, who was currently sitting in front of a café enjoying a cup of coffee. The news that the other team had lost track of their target was unsettling.

"What do you want us to do?" Janiqua asked.

Zeke was watching Noa expectantly. Sometimes serving as the de facto leader of a group of kids still threw her; they always assumed that she had all the answers. And right now, she felt as clueless as the rest of them. "Get on the next train and try to find him," she finally said. "We'll stay on his partner."

"Got it."

As the radio fell silent, Noa repressed a shiver. They'd been standing out in the cold for over an hour, hunkered against the side of a building. They couldn't stay in this position much longer—the owner of the bodega across the street kept throwing suspicious glances their way.

As if on cue, Zeke said, "Looks like he's going for the phone again. Time to put on another show."

Noa sighed and rolled her eyes. "I swear this is your favorite part."

"Definitely." Zeke smiled as he backed her against the wall, then lowered his face down to hers. They held the pose, just inches apart. His breath tickled her eyelashes, and with every inhale her nostrils filled with his distinctive scent: soap and shaving cream mixed with a sweet underlying musk. Past his shoulder, Noa saw the bodega owner watching them. After a moment's hesitation, he set the phone back down.

"We're good," she murmured.

"Maybe we should give it another minute, just to be sure," Zeke responded, resting his forehead against hers.

This was supposed to be for show, but his lips hovered a fraction of an inch away from hers. Noa could see the gold flecks that dotted his brown eyes, like spokes of pure sunlight. She felt a shudder down her spine that had nothing to do with the cold. Trying to regain her composure, she noted wryly, "Try not to get us arrested for public indecency."

"I'm willing to risk it," Zeke murmured, leaning in so that his whole body pressed against her.

Noa was suddenly finding it hard to breathe. He was just messing with her, right? They were friends, partners. So why was her whole body careening into overdrive? She gently nudged his shoulder, easing him away as she sternly said, "Focus. We're supposed to be keeping an eye on our target, remember?"

"You really know how to suck all the fun out of a stakeout," Zeke smirked, stepping away.

Noa didn't answer. This wasn't the first time they'd pretended to be a teen couple making out; the last thing they needed was a beat cop nosing around, asking why they'd been standing on the same street corner for more than an hour. But this had felt different; like maybe it hadn't all been for show. She surreptitiously studied Zeke, who was peering around the corner toward the café. After all these months together, his face was almost as familiar as her own—slim and angular, sharp cheekbones, tan despite the climate. The first time Noa met him, she'd been flustered by how attractive he was; but since then he'd become more like a brother. Although she was pretty sure that what she'd just felt wasn't sisterly love.

Noa frowned—*now who was distracted?* She forced herself back to the task at hand, asking, "He's still there, right?"

"Yup. Still just reading the paper."

"Maybe we're wrong about this," Noa said. "Maybe they're not here on a job at all."

"Sure." Zeke nodded. "I hear that San Francisco is where all the bad guys come on vacation. They just can't get enough of the chowder bowls and trolley rides."

Noa ignored him, leaning forward to catch a glimpse of the café. Their target was sitting at an outside table despite the cold, sipping from a large mug as he scanned a newspaper. He was a bulky guy with close-cropped hair, dressed in dark jeans, a peacoat, and combat boots. If she didn't know better, she'd think he was just a soldier on leave, enjoying some down time.

But she did know better.

"Be ready to move," she warned Zeke, stretching her legs to get the kinks out.

He snorted. "I'm always ready."

"Sure you are." She grinned. "Like in San Diego, when you almost got left in the lab after the radios crashed."

"Hey, that wasn't my fault," Zeke protested, lightly

punching her shoulder. "I figured the kids might be in the other part of the building."

They both fell silent at the memory. The raid had gone smoothly—except that by the time they got inside, there wasn't anyone left to save. Zeke cleared his throat, then said more soberly, "So you think these two are here to scout another lab?"

"I don't know," Noa admitted. "But something is going down." The two commandos hadn't gone anywhere near the warehouse district, though, which was unusual. She was having a hard time getting a handle on what they were after; they'd spent the entirety of the past two days walking through the Mission District.

"He's on the move," Zeke announced.

Noa's head snapped up—the guy was halfway down the block, headed toward Valencia Street. "Remember to stay half a block behind me," she said in a low voice. "If I have to pass him, you take over."

"Got it," Zeke said.

Noa pulled her watch cap lower, ducked her head, and trotted across the street in pursuit.

Teo Castillo was tired and hungry. He'd spent the day panhandling on BART, shuffling from one subway car to the next, begging spare change from commuters who studiously avoided eye contact.

He was halfway back to the encampment where he'd been living the past few months when he realized someone was following him. A lanky, rough-looking street kid. No one he recognized, though, and by now he knew all the homeless teens on this side of town. Teo had first noticed him studying the subway map near the turnstile at the Twenty-Fourth Street BART station. And now here he was again, walking down Mission Street fifty feet behind him.

Teo stopped abruptly and bent to retie his filthy Vans. Covertly, he glanced back. The kid was standing in front of a dollar store, examining their inventory with the same intense interest he'd given the subway map. He was tall and gangly, with knobby elbows jutting out of an oversized white T-shirt and jeans belted halfway down his thighs.

Teo tried to brush aside his paranoia. The kid was probably just headed in the same direction as him.

Five blocks later, he was seriously doubting it. The hair on the back of his neck prickled; he'd been jumped before, and wasn't eager to go through it again. Last time he'd suffered three broken ribs and a concussion.

Plus, over the past year he'd heard plenty of horror stories; some kids even claimed that a group was snatching runaways off the streets to experiment on. Teo wasn't sure he believed that; it sounded too far-fetched. But he knew bad things happened to kids like him if they were out here long enough.

And he had no intention of becoming a cautionary tale. He'd make a break for the underpass where he'd been crashing; hopefully some of the others would already be there. As he turned the corner onto Cesar Chavez Street, Teo broke into a trot. Within seconds, his lungs throbbed and he felt sick. He'd barely eaten all day, so even slight physical exertion made him dizzy. Pathetic. Not so long ago, he'd been the star sprinter at his high school. Might even have had a shot at a college scholarship if everything hadn't gone sideways.

After seven blocks, he hazarded a glance back over his shoulder. The kid was not only still there, he'd been joined by two others—a black girl and guy. They weren't even pretending not to follow him anymore, they were flat out chasing him.

Crap, Teo thought. Three against one—he'd end up in the ER again for sure. He tried to run faster, but his legs were shaking too hard to maintain the pace.

To throw them off course, he abruptly darted left down Hampshire Street, then took a sharp right through the empty soccer field at the rec center. Dodging left again, he lurched onto a footpath that led through overgrown bushes. It was hard to spot unless you were right on top of it; with any luck, they hadn't seen him make the turn.

Seconds later he emerged in the camp, a bare patch of earth beneath a busy section of highway. It was hemmed in on all sides by soundproofing walls, a chain-link fence, and large bushy hedges. The clearing was cluttered with makeshift shelters: big boxes with tarps for roofs, a couple of muddy tents. The ground was dotted with soiled food wrappers, empty bottles, and syringes.

Teo's heart sank: there was no one else there. He was on his own.

Suddenly, a hand grabbed his arm. He winced reflexively, bracing for a blow. . . .

It never came. Teo opened his eyes and did a double take when he saw not the ragged trio of teens, but a good-looking guy in his thirties, well-dressed in jeans and a dark jacket. He was huge, easily six inches taller than Teo, and built like a tank.

"Teo Castillo, right?" the guy said with a smile.

Teo jerked his arm free and took a shaky step back. "Who are you?" His chest was still heaving, and his legs felt rubbery.

The guy held up both hands. "Hey, man, take it easy. Just wanted to make sure you were okay."

The guy looked normal, but something felt off. Teo eased back a few more inches. "How do you know my name?"

The guy squinted and cocked his head to the side. "You don't remember me?"

Teo shook his head slowly. The guy didn't look familiar, but the way he was acting . . . maybe one of his former social workers? Or a teacher? But what was he doing here?

"That's okay, it was a long time ago." The guy was still grinning, although the smile hadn't made it all the way to his eyes. "I'm here to help you, Teo."

"I don't need any help," Teo said quickly. "Thanks anyway, though."

"Oh, I think you do. What about those kids back there?" The guy jerked his head toward the bushes. "Looked like you were in trouble." He stepped forward. "And living in this dump? Not good."

"I'm fine," Teo snapped. He was sick of adults thinking they knew what was best for him. He turned and marched deliberately toward the other side of camp, where another narrow path led out to Potrero Avenue.

Before he reached it, though, another big guy emerged from the bushes, blocking his way. He was dressed in jeans and a fleece jacket, with a ball cap pulled down over his ears. Teo halted, confused.

"We're here to take you somewhere safe," the first guy said from behind him. "Trust me."

Teo's mind raced. The two guys were blocking the exits: the only other option was the chain-link fence on his left. If he could get over it, there were cars a block away—plenty of witnesses.

He bolted toward the nearest section of fence. Panic sent adrenaline coursing through his veins, spurring him faster than he'd ever run before.

He was halfway over the fence when a hand clamped down on his leg. Teo yelped in pain as he was yanked back and slammed to the ground. Both guys loomed over him; one of them was holding a syringe.

"Hey, listen . . . I don't do drugs," Teo said, panicked. "Seriously, I'll do whatever you want. Just don't stick me with that thing."

"Got a clean one here, Jimmy, you hear that?" the first guy said.

Ball Cap nodded. "That's why they want him. Nice, clean subject."

"A clean . . . what?" Those experiments he'd heard about, Teo realized suddenly. *They were real. . . .*

The guy with the needle leaned over and tugged at his jacket collar. Teo struggled, but the other guy pinned his arms and pulled his head to the side, exposing his neck.

Teo squeezed his eyes shut and prayed it would be over soon. He waited for the needle to pierce his skin.

And waited.

Suddenly, there was a strange chattering noise close by. Teo opened his eyes: The guy with the needle was standing bolt upright, his whole body twitching uncontrollably. His mouth gaped open, exposing gleaming rows of white teeth.

Simultaneously, Ball Cap's legs buckled. He landed on the ground looking perplexed, and oddly frozen.

Teo lurched to his feet, grasping the fence for balance. His first thought was, *What the hell just happened?* Followed immediately by, *Who cares—get out of here, now!*

As he turned to run, Teo nearly crashed into a girl who'd

materialized right behind him. He'd never seen her before: She was stunning, with close-cropped dark hair and bright-green eyes. She was dressed all in black like the other guys, and held something that looked like an oversized TV remote.

"Relax," the girl said without taking her eyes off the guys on the ground. "We got this."

A group of teenagers swarmed out from behind her. They were all dressed differently: a few Goths, some skate rats, a couple of stoner types. All straggly and unkempt-looking, like most street kids. But Teo had never seen any of them before.

He'd heard of them, though. This had to be the other thing everyone murmured about, late at night as they huddled in the dark. The group that was trying to protect street kids: Persefone's Army. He hadn't believed in them, either—a bunch of teenagers acting like some modern-day version of Robin Hood? He'd assumed it was just another urban myth.

But here they were. His eyes swept around the group—the three kids who'd been chasing him were standing guard over the guys on the ground. And the girl with them, who was clearly the leader . . .

"You're Persefone," Teo said, his voice filled with awe.

The girl gave him a funny look. "Actually, my name's Noa. You all right?"

"Yeah, sure." Teo scrambled to his feet.

The kid who had been following him earlier came up and sneered, "You were lucky. Why the hell did you run?"

"I thought—"

"He thought you were chasing him, Turk," Noa snapped. "You were supposed to stay on your target. What happened?"

Turk hunched his shoulders and mumbled, "Janiqua lost him."

"Oh, yeah, it's my fault." The black girl rolled her eyes. "*You* were supposed to keep up with the target on the train. The hell'd you go, anyway?"

"I didn't see him get off." Turk kept his eyes glued to the ground. "'Sides, I knew that dickwad was after the kid, he couldn't stop staring at him. Even followed him through a few cars."

"So you lost the guy, but not the kid?" Janiqua snorted. "That doesn't make sense."

"That's what happened," Turk snarled back, jutting his chin out as he stepped menacingly toward her. Janiqua didn't give an inch, though—she closed the space between them while reaching into her pocket for something—

Noa quickly intervened, stepping between them. "Enough. We'll sort it out later. Now get moving, these guys'll be coming around soon."

After another long, hard stare, the two of them separated, heading to opposite ends of the camp. Janiqua pulled a long plastic cord out of her pocket as she bent over one of the guys, then used it to tie his wrists behind his back. Two other kids helped her.

Teo's head was spinning—this was all too surreal. There were eight kids total, and they each moved with purpose. On the concrete buttress next to where he kept his sleeping bag, a scrawny black kid was spray painting a logo in red: the letters *P* and *A*, intertwined. The rest of the group hunkered down around the two guys who'd assaulted him, securing their ankles and wrists with impressive alacrity.

Teo suddenly saw the encampment through their eyes— small, cramped, dingy—and felt a twinge of embarrassment.

"Sure you're all right?" Noa asked, examining him. "You look a little shaky."

"I'm fine," he said, fighting to keep the squeak from his voice.

"What's your name, anyway?"

"T-Teo," he stammered. "Teo Castillo."

"Nice to meet you, Teo," Noa said distractedly, her eyes scanning the clearing. She raised her voice and announced, "We'll take the blonde."

Teo realized she was talking about the guy who had first spoken to him. He watched a girl in a black pleather mini-skirt and torn fishnet stockings matter-of-factly place a strip of duct tape over the blonde's mouth. "What did you do to them, anyway?"

"Taser," Noa explained, holding the remote up. "We don't like guns."

"Okay." He wasn't a big fan of guns, either. "So are these the guys who have been experimenting on kids?"

She scrutinized him. "You heard about that?"

Teo shrugged. "Yeah. Everyone has."

"Well, it's true. Don't go anywhere alone from here on out. They might still be after you."

A cold ball of fear formed in Teo's gut. He glanced back over his shoulder, half expecting to see more huge guys huddled in the bushes. He wondered where everyone else was—had the other kids known, somehow, that these guys were lurking around? And if so, why hadn't anyone warned him? Suddenly, he felt more alone than ever. "Where are you taking him?"

"Better if you don't know." More loudly, Noa added, "Don't forget the tarp."

Obediently, a few of them wrapped the first guy up like a burrito in a large blue plastic tarp. Once they had him inside, they lifted him off the ground, spreading his weight between them. Teo watched them march toward the bushes. They were like an army, he realized. Organized, following commands . . . despite their ragged appearance, he was impressed.

A minute later, he found himself alone with Turk, Noa, and the girl in fishnets. She was cute, despite her wild shock of blue hair. She caught him looking at her and raised an eyebrow. Teo flushed and shifted his gaze, examining the ground at his feet.

"The usual with the other one?" Turk asked.

Noa eyed the guy in the ball cap. "Yeah."

"You want to mess him up first?" Turk asked solicitously, directing the question to Teo.

"What? Uh, no. I'm good." Teo stared at the man on the ground; Jimmy, the other guy had called him. Jimmy was coming around; his eyes darted frantically from side to side.

"We'll leave him for your friends, then. I'll bet they'll have some fun with you, huh, jerk-off?"

The guy flinched as Turk dealt him a hard kick to the ribs.

"Turk," Noa warned sharply.

Turk threw her a sneer, then seemed to catch himself. He knelt down to tighten the zip ties another notch. The guy on the ground winced as the narrow bands dug into his wrists. "Just wait," Turk muttered in a cold, flat voice, "World of hurt coming for you, buddy."

Teo watched Turk haul Jimmy to his feet and frog-march him to the nearest pillar. Turk held him in place while fishnets wound duct tape around him, pinning him to the concrete support beam like a trapped moth.

"All right, let's get out of here." Noa lifted a small radio to her mouth and said, "Back at the van in five."

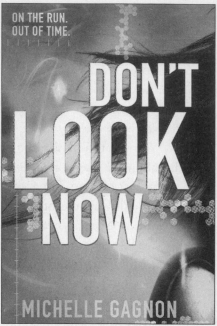